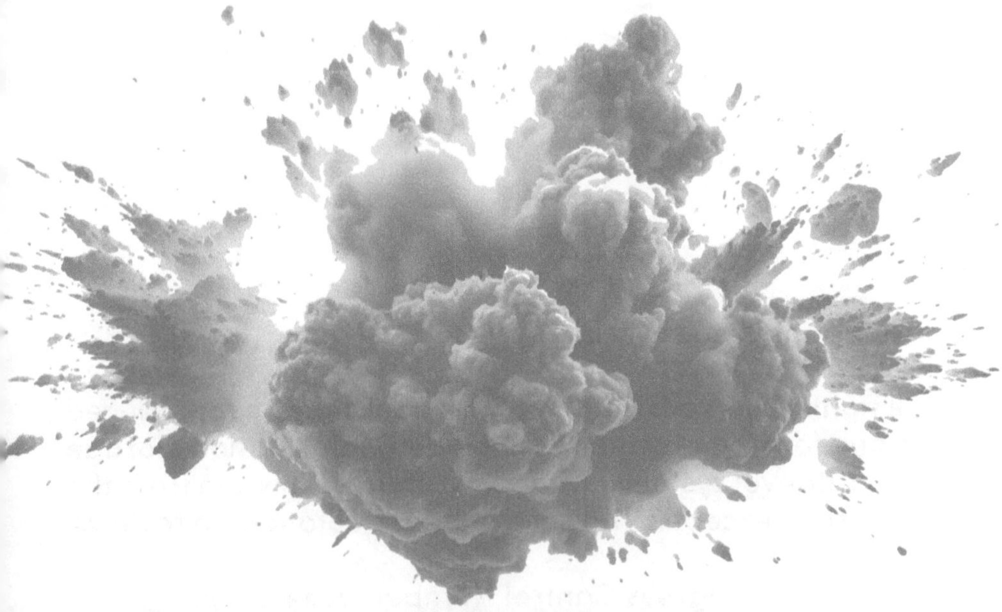

FLOOD

VAST COLLECTIVE BOOK XI

Nicole Hayes

Library of Congress Control Number: 2023901193

ISBN (Hardcover Edition) 979-8-9868220-4-4
ISBN (Softcover Edition) 979-8-9908310-5-6
ISBN (Ebook Edition) 979-8-9868220-6-8

Printed in the USA

Iona Print
nicolehayesauthor@gmail.com
https://nicolehayeswriter.com/

THE VAST COLLECTIVE SERIES

Last of Daylight
By the Pale Moonlight
Asylum in Firelight
Nox's Verse
Glass Chains
Pyrite Prison
Restraining Silver
Korac's Verse
Thirst
Levee
Flood
Xelan's Verse
Cascading Light

Loyalty is the strongest conviction and the only one with any virtue.
Never let go.

CONTENTS

ACKNOWLEDGMENTS

As always, I'll start with Batman. Thank you for reading eleven books. Thank you for taking me for coffee walks where we discussed what you liked and what you'd like to see next. And thank you for tolerating my constant reminders to read every time you alluded to a restroom break.

Firefly, I love how you started as a critique partner and over the course of the series became a fan and my number one supporter. Every second with Korac is especially thanks to you. And a few Andrew and Lucas scenes, too. Thanks for inspiring so many great adventures, jokes, and maybe one or two smut scenes.

Jasmine, the outcome of Tameka's character arc is the direct result of our conversations together. I hope you love it as much as I do.

ONE

DRINK DEEP OF THE AIR BEFORE THE CURRENT PULLS YOU UNDER

{ENKI | NEW CINDER}

"THANKS, KID."

On all fours in his own consciousness, Chris focused sharply on the manifestation of Celindria, who glared at him with no small amount of alarm inside his mind.

The words. Came from his mouth. His actual mouth, currently under her volition control, but somehow—some fucking how—Chris had managed to speak.

This was it.

The volition exchanged hands by forfeiture from his own lips.

"I give up."

That didn't work.

"I give my will back."

Still nothing, but now Chris was so desperate to see this through that he refused to look at the Shadow watching him from their cell. Their hopeful gazes would put too much pressure on this delicate operation.

Already, Chris sensed Bones and Para crowding the cell's bars. Jack's eager hopefulness and Ross' undeserved kindness both emanated optimistic radiation. Devis and Andrius gasped, crowding the unconscious Seamswalker, T.A.O., and the love of Chris' life, Karter. Both women would receive medical help once Chris got his shit together, returned his volition, and they all escaped.

Likewise, he couldn't look at Celindria inside his mind. She would figure out a way to subdue him any minute. Chris only knew this because, out of his periphery, her eyes were doing something truly terrifying.

Spark.

Dull.

Live wire.

Lights out.

Think! What had Karter said when Remorse relinquished control of Karter only two hours ago? Celindria was hurting the Valkyrie leader, hurting the Tritan inside her by default, and Primary Rem had screamed—

"I relent!"

The words came out of Chris' mouth on a bellow, and everything changed.

Ears popped. Eyes strained. Every muscle contracted. Tendons tightened—

Pulled.

Chris was being pulled inside-out. Would he fall unconscious like Karter? Why was he awake and aware but blind and deaf at the same time—

Sound hit him all at once.

"Chris! Chris, it's Jack. Can you hear me?!"

Para's sweet voice cracked. "Chris! Please tell me you're all right?!"

Everyone came loud and clear, but he still couldn't see—

Oh.

Chris' eyes were closed. He opened them and found himself on all fours, staring at a rug on the cave floor. Blood dripped onto it—His blood from his mouth. With a lick of his lips, Chris knew he'd bit his tongue in the process.

All the while, the others shouted.

Alone.

Chris was alone in his body, in his consciousness. The space he'd shared with Celindria was gone. "I'm me." His voice sounded rough.

A metallic shriek ripped through the mad woman's laboratory as bars were wrenched apart. Pandemonium ensued. All at once, Jack knelt beside Chris, talking while Para ordered the others to retreat back to Cinder's Shrine.

Jack asked, "Are you okay, man?"

Para said, "Fury completed the mission. We need to leave."

Devis and Andrius weighed in. "Yes. We must go before Celindria returns." "Collect Pax before we escape."

Bones carried Karter in his arms and nodded at Ross. "Can you get him for us?"

Wait.

Tameka had said something important before Celindria took her away. *"Don't forget Chris. Leave Pax to me."*

There was a reason why she'd said it that way—

Chris momentarily forgot what thinking was and why he even had a brain when Jack threw Chris' arm over his shoulder to lift him.

The older man groaned in agony, and the young King Regent muttered, "I got ya, buddy."

Meanwhile, Ross marched right up to the door to Celindria's bedroom, opened it, and screamed. While she backed away from the door, Celindria stepped through it. A breeze from nowhere flowed through her skirts and lifted her braids and locs back from her face.

"Fuck." Bones said it all.

Para shouted, "Get Pax and get out!" She speared the First Progeny into the nearest wall, and the air currents of Celindria's power formed a tunnel centered on their fight.

Bones handed Karter over to Andrius. He and T.A.O. Seamswalked Karter to safety, much to Chris' relief. Free of his charge, Bones jumped into the fray with Celindria.

Para, the smallest Valkyrie, moved so fast Chris couldn't track her, but Celindria didn't seem concerned. She took two hits to the face and three blows to ribs. Chris heard the bones break from across the lab—

Para shrieked in agony and crumpled to the floor at Celindria's feet. Chris didn't even see the other woman land a punch, so why—

Blood spurted from Para's mouth.

Para's lover, Bones, heaved Celindria back and smashed her face into the cave wall. He grated her skull along the rough basalt rock—

Without so much as a hand on him, Bones went flying across the lab.

Celindria faced the room and—what a face! Skin and muscle hung off, yet no blood welled or dripped. It was just ground meat with bits of rock in it. With her beautiful skin ruined, Celindria crossed the room to Jack and Chris in easy strides. No one could stand in her way—

Devis stepped between them. He held out his hand with something small pinched between his fingers. "Take it, Celindria. Take it and end all this."

It was a tiny capsule. Chris thought he'd remembered Sagan describing something like this technology from Razor's Emporium of Exotic Experiences.

Devis opened it, and it contained a small pin. "It's a memory. One of my own. I believe it's what you need."

Celindria tilted her head to the side, with a comprehending light in her alien eyes.

Bones crawled to Para to check on her. Ross crouched in a corner, terrified to move, but still inched toward the bedroom door. T.A.O. was due back any second.

Celindria reached out to Devis, and the ground shook. At first, Chris thought the earthquake which had sent glass shattering from shelves and left them all hanging on for shelter, was Celindria's doing, but she peered around as confused as the rest of them. With the first quake, she retreated from Devis' offer and a look of dismay and panic crossed Devis' face.

Chris would never forget it. There was something between those two.

When Celindria backed into the darkest corner, the rock split open, and something enormous reached in and snatched her from the room. Something Chris hadn't seen since the Volcano Day battle. On that day, Tumu had broken some galactic rule and decompressed to his full sixty-five feet of height.

The hand which had taken Celindria belonged to a Gargantuan Tritan.

Remorse had returned for some payback in time to save their lives.

{ENKI | GAIT}

"*Armageddon.*"

Matt was sure this was it.

Puk's physical and mental stress strained his voice over the earpiece. "Fan-fucking-tastic timing, bro. Truly, this is the proudest moment of my life and all sixteen seconds left of it." Sarcasm dripped from every word.

With no one around to see, Matt preened. He'd finally guessed the movie relevant to their current mission: destroy a planet-sized asteroid heading for the hull of Enki. Specifically, into one of several oceans on the surface of the Dyson's Sphere. Any minute now, the Tritans would blow the charges which Matt, Puk, and the other members of the demolition crew had peppered across the rock. The Tritans had hoped it would protect Enki's hull.

Until then, the artificial gravity had kicked the bucket. Primary Rem, a.k.a. Remorse, had left the demo team for dead, clinging to the rock.

So now, Matt was preening in an abandoned space scraper, letting its walls keep him tethered to the half of Gait careening toward their doom.

Matt wished Lucy were here, and couldn't wait for the moment when she saved them, and he could thank her properly.

"She'll make it in time, right, Ginger?"

This was about the third time Puk had asked the same question. Given their circumstance, Matt couldn't blame the Monarch 3 drone. They were seriously about to die, but Matt had placed all his faith in his woman. "She'll make it in time. Trust me. Trust her."

Puk sounded more confident. "You know I do."

Yeah. He did.

Hang on.

Don't die.

Wait for Lucy.

Even as Matt gripped rebar hanging upside down with all his strength while the inertia threatened to fling him from the planet, he knew they would make it.

In the meantime… "It *was* a pretty stellar soundtrack."

"Fuck. Off."

{Enki | Medical Bay}

Triss was about to break Lynn's hand.

Again.

The woman's labor was excruciating. Lynn didn't need the readout from the pain instruments to tell her that. Sweat, blood, and tears poured from the villainous Lyrik, Triss, giving birth to the future adopted daughter of two people Lynn cared for very much, Sagan and Korac. So, the Chief Weapons Engineer to the Shadow would grit her teeth and bear the secondhand pain of this delivery.

If only Lynn had a third hand.

"Ignore what's happening out there and focus on me, Triss. I won't let anything happen to you. Remember? We had a deal?"

Lynn's husband, Dr. Pablo Suarez, was referring to his promise that Triss would see her baby's daddy one last time before they let her succumb to her injuries. She'd passed the point of no return about an hour ago. Lynn was holding a dead woman's hand.

It was warm, and it *wanted* this baby to live.

Which may or may not be complicated by the sudden emergence of Imminent soldiers at the medical bay's doors. Lynn shouted, "Give me an update, Caedes."

The gruff Icarus snarled, ripping out some Reipon Lamia's throat with his teeth. "No nacres. No memory to overwhelm. Isn't that the case, Bethany?"

Lynn spared a glance at Kyle and Ross' younger sister. The recovering girl nodded, still unable to speak because of her own terrible memories.

Okay. No nacres. Think. Think... "How are the hand guns working out?" Each of the Shadow carried one traditional Earth gun to fight nacre-less opponents.

Twenty-One held up his forty-five with a slight pout on his face. "Out of ammo."

Miy sighed and tossed him a clip. "That's my last one."

Triss screamed, and Pablo spared a glance at the Tritan doctor, who assisted him with her delivery. Pablo asked, "Do you know if more soldiers will come?"

Qas shook his head with regret in his eyes. "I don't know. I don't even recognize those people or their gear. That's not Enki-issued."

"Imminent," Caedes snarled again.

With all the lilac blood dripping down the bald Icarus' his face, Lynn kinda saw the appeal for Pehton—

The box which had formed inside Triss' uterus stretched against her swollen belly and wiggled its fingers. All the while, the former Lyriki leader bowed her spine and screamed. Two of Lynn's fingers were toast.

All around, more conversation carried on between the Shadow and the Tritan guards, but Lynn focused and put her face near Triss'. "Look at me, you narcissistic bitch. Look at me!"

Triss opened those yellow eyes, hard like citrines, and glared at the human daring to insult her. Her teeth gnashed together, and foam sprayed from her mouth. Triss' spit was tinged orange with Lyriki blood from where she'd bit her tongue despite the guard in her mouth.

Lynn gripped the woman's tiny pitch-black hand. "You are *not* dying until you see Razor again, remember? Or were you ever really as much his acolyte as you made yourself out to be? Maybe you weren't actually woman enough to serve a god like him. Because if you die now, what chance is there for his daughter to survive?!"

Triss fumed. No, literally. Kerosene filled the air with little wavy lines off her skin. Around the bit in her teeth, she vowed, "I will not fail him."

While patting her sweat-drenched forehead with a cloth, Lynn soothed the crazy bitch. "You're damn right you won't."

Qas read off the projected readings. "Another contraction inbound."

Pablo sat at the end of the alien medical bed and met Triss' eyes. "Get ready."

Triss stared at Lynn, and on the younger woman's nod, she bit down and pushed.

Three bones broke this time.

{ENKI | CINDER'S SHRINE}

Torrentus, the terraforming machine, swirled its malfunctioning anguish over one massive continent in a perpetual storm. This was Kyle's second time seeing it. His first was when he and the other modern-day Progeny came to Enki years ago for their nacres. In all those instances, the storm was a beautiful gray whirl.

Now it raged in flames, a hurricane of fire no one could survive.

"Ta—Tameka..."

Xelan, the Traitor Prince of Cinder who'd gathered the armies of the Vast Collective here to watch for Tameka's signal, did *not* sound as if the storm's transition was the signal he'd expected.

With his eyes four-times their size, Kyle stared at their leader. "Xelan. Xelan, what does that mean?"

Korac, General of the Icarean army on Xelan's right, let his typical icy facade slip, and when Kyle saw the fear in that man's white eyes, he knew this wasn't part of the plan.

Tameka was gone.

Kyle stepped around a bewildered Pehton and ignored the concern on Iuo's Lamian face to see confirmation of his assumption from Xelan. The sight made him take a step back.

In Atramentous, Xelan's normally black eyes were swallowed by their midnight blue ring with a white slit for his pupil. Tears spilled from them, and some of them were blue, the color of Icarean blood. He was staring without seeing at the blazing storm, mouthing something.

Kyle took a step closer and then another until he made out the words. "Please don't be dead. Please don't be dead." Repeatedly.

Beside Korac, Sagan cupped a hand to her mouth, and Andrew placed a hand on her back.

Meanwhile, around them, Tumu, Pehton, Lamassau, and Iuo checked their earpieces. Something was happening with the other Shadow. Kyle wouldn't know since he'd elected to switch his to Rayne's channel only. If they ever found her—

Queen F8 left her army of drones and Monarch 3 queens to approach the broken Icarean Prince. She smiled for Kyle before addressing the General, "This wasn't intended, no? The other leaders aren't aware of this. They're still awaiting Fury's signal."

Tameka, codenamed Fury, and the galactic ambassador was killed in action, and now someone needed to tell these people that the woman they had looked to as their leader had met her end down there in that storm—

"To the Pantheon!" Korac ordered with his axe raised.

What.

The.

Fuck?!

Kyle's eye twitched as the Icarean General continued, "Onward to 'the tomorrow where your future begins!'"

Some armies cheered, some armies grunted, but all of them turned and looked at a distraught Sagan. Predicting this, Korac had leaned over and whispered in her ear, rubbing circles on her back. She nodded. Eyes in violet Atramentous, Sagan opened several conduits for the armies, leading into a white field. The Pantheon.

They marched while Kyle overheard Andrew and Pehton discussing their radio feed. " . . . Is Chris free? Is he conscious?"

Tumu muttered to them. "There it is. He's free."

Why was Korac continuing this campaign with Tameka dead and Xelan out of his mind? Why was Sagan helping him? And what the hell was happening in Celindria's lab?

All this commotion swirled around Kyle like those flames swirled around Tameka and threatened to blow him away. It was too much. Kyle was one final straw from losing his mind—

"Ross, are you all right?" Korac whisper-shouted into his earpiece after stepping aside. "Stay away from Celindria. Get them out of there."

After meeting Andrew's eyes, Kyle rushed over to him for confirmation of his sister's status.

Andrew calmed his fears immediately. "Ross is fine. They're getting—"

A conduit opened, and T.A.O. stepped through, with Andrius holding Karter.

The entire time, Xelan stared at Torrentus in his personal breakdown, while the Vast Collective armies filed toward Enki and Imminent's end.

{Enki | Pantheon}

Korac stared at Andrius. Not at the glistening nacre fibers in his dark skin. Nor at the stress-carved lines of his face.

No.

The half-Aegis Atheneum and Icarean General stared at the tall woman in Andrius' arms. He swallowed before holstering his axe and holding his hands out. "I'll take Karter."

Grateful, Andrius poured the unconscious Valkyrie into Korac's care. Learning his mother's face anew, Korac nearly ignored Andrius' warning. "Celindria's fighting the remaining Shadow."

Beside Korac, Kyle's muttering held an edge of anger. "What're you doing sending the armies to the Pantheon after we all watched Tameka—"

"Don't say it." Andrew put a finger in Kyle's face. "We need to maintain the crusade and send reinforcements to the Shadow in Celindria's lab." He was right, of course.

But Korac wanted to ignore all of them. All of it. He wanted to take his mother to the medical bay and remove the fail safes Celindria had installed in her motor cortex. He wanted to sit and talk to her about how funny their lives had worked out—

What about Xelan?

Beyond all the confused, hurt, and angry faces, the Prince of Cinder stared at the fire hurricane, which may have consumed the mother of his child, and hugged himself. One great motion heaved his shoulders—A sob. Soundless in the vacuum of angry mutters and milling boots.

He was alone—

Reality returned with a pop in Korac's ears. Ignoring the immediate rabble, he walked over to T.A.O., who also seemed to have retreated into her head. At Korac's proximity, she shook herself, lifted those violet Atramentous eyes up at him, and smiled.

Korac asked, "Do you know who she is to me, T.A.O.?" Even before Razor exposed the first Seamswalker to Cascading Light, she *knew* things.

T.A.O. held her hands behind her back and swayed sweetly when she nodded.

To the others, Korac ordered, "Stay still. We're taking Karter to the medical bay, and then I'll return to straighten this shit out."

Korac glimpsed Sagan's understanding eyes before he and T.A.O. stepped through the conduit and into… a bunch of bodies everywhere.

Caedes, Twenty-One, Miy, and some Tritans blinked at him.

Korac nodded at Miy first before addressing the rest. "What the fuck happened here—"

A scream pierced the confusion. It came from the tier above where Triss was in fucking labor.

Chief Lynn shouted along with her, and Dr. Suarez encouraged her, "You're doing great." The Tritan beside Dr. Suarez nodded for Bethany to empty another bag of Aegis blood into some tank. She did so with a wave at Korac.

Concerned, Korac took a step toward the next level. "Is she all right?"

Caedes stepped up with his arms out. "I'll take Karter to the next bay."

"Wow, that's *the* Karter?" Miy's voice sounded impressed to see the legendary Valkyrie in person, and Korac's cheeks burned from the swell of pride in his chest. "She's so cool." Miy looked up at Korac and narrowed her eyes. "Are you sure she's *your* mother?"

Twenty-One took her hand and kissed the back of it. "You're getting rude again."

To Korac's surprise, the Lyrik spared the massive Icarean warrior a seductive glance, saying, "Maybe I need another fix."

"Okay." This was enough for Korac. "I don't care what's happened here anymore. Caedes, thank you, but if you could just show me to the next bay. We have little time."

Lynn called between Triss' cries. "How are things going?"

Not good, but thanks to Sagan's influence, Korac found himself wanting to hope once more. He hoped Tameka yet lived, and hoped the mess in Celindria's lab could afford the time for this errand. So, with all the hope in his chest, Korac ignored her question and asked, "Dr. Suarez, when you get a minute . . ."

"I'll see to Karter, General. You get back to the Shadow."

T.A.O. opened the conduit, and they stepped back into the shrine.

Again, Kyle asked with a hint of indignation, "What are you doing, Korac?"

And again, Korac ignored him. Instead, he took Sagan's hand and kissed it. Their child was on the way into this world, and Karter was in their care.

These were gifts.

Sagan took a deep galvanizing breath, but she eventually squeezed Korac's hand.

With that, he released her hand and turned around to Xelan, ordering, "Tumu, with me."

Tumu walked up to Xelan with Korac. Beyond the Prince, through the glass, Torrentus blazed on, and the broken man wept. Korac glanced at Tumu. They nodded together. Ready.

The Icarean General went first. "You must be fucking insane if you believe for one second Tameka would lose to a firestorm. You make for a pitiful 'most dangerous warrior in the galaxy.'"

Tumu gaped at Korac, startled by his harsh words, but at least Xelan responded.

The Prince of Cinder opened his wings and looked over his shoulder at his General. It was *not* a friendly look.

More gently, Tumu played good cop. "Xelan, whatever Peaches is facing, she'd want you to maintain the mission."

It was coaxing and reassuring, but Tumu basically said the same thing Korac said, only nicer.

Over their earpieces, Devis tried to reason with a madly pissed off Celindria. *"It's a memory. One of my own. I believe it's what you need."*

Some exceptional thunderous crash followed, and everyone in Celindria's lab screamed.

Korac turned and ordered, "Pehton, Kyle, Lamassau, and Andrew—Go with T.A.O. to rescue the others!" He raised his voice loud enough to add emphasis without advertising their dilemma to the hordes of soldiers marching through Sagan's conduits.

Of course, that's why Korac didn't ask her to go. The strain around his girl's eyes said this was hard enough for

Sagan. She squeezed Kyle's shoulder, bumped Lamassau's gauntleted fist, hugged Pehton, and kissed Andrew's cheek. "Be careful."

Pehton saluted Korac before they stepped through the conduit. He managed to smirk for her, but the moment she disappeared, it fell.

Sagan blew him a kiss and returned to orientating Andrius to the here and now.

They needed their leader. They needed Xelan.

Korac went around to Xelan's front and took in the full impact of his grief.

A train wreck.

That's what Xelan looked like.

Korac glanced from Tumu's concerned voids to Xelan's solid blue eyes. The old Tritan was more audience than Korac wanted for this, but dammit, they were out of options. On a leap of faith, he stepped into Xelan's personal space without touching him and whispered in his ear. "Tameka would never leave you—*No one* would ever leave you."

Xelan reacted by tilting his head, listening.

"But sometimes you fool yourself into thinking relationships—friendships, lovers, family—are already over without fighting for them..." Korac pounded a fist to his own chest. "And *I'm* not letting you do it this time. My Prince, get out of your head and fight for Fury and your son before you really do lose them to this war."

Xelan turned with his face inches from Korac, who pressed, "Not until you see the body. Do you understand me? Don't mourn until you *know* for certain, and even then, you pick yourself up and rip her killers apart. Agreed?" He held up his hand between their faces, waiting for the Prince to clasp it.

Tumu stood behind Xelan and met Korac's eyes over his shoulder. "Not until we see Peaches' body."

Another bloody tear rolled down Xelan's cheek, and Korac prayed to Elden for the first time since Sagan was trapped in the Seam for this to work.

If the last three years had proven anything, it's that the Shadow couldn't win this war without their Wingmaster.

Please, Elden, let this work.

{ENKI | TORRENTUS}

Thank Elden, Tameka was still alive to kill Celindria and save Pax. All thanks to the strange person with a hidden bunker conveniently located at the continent's conduit entrance.

When Tameka first arrived, she'd tried to drain the Aegis-made storm of its power. It responded unexpectedly by screaming and throwing a rain of fire at her. Before the first gale of flames took her out, this stranger grabbed Tameka's ankle and dragged her below ground.

And into a cave carved of diorite, polished white rock with a scattering of black chunky mineral throughout. It formed a tunnel which stretched North and South. Various supplies and rations occupied the shelves. Everything was slightly damp. Probably because Torrentus never stopped storming overhead.

There was still no reception in Tameka's earpiece to give the Shadow her signal, so she'd make do until she found a way to destroy Torrentus, escape the lost continent, and rescue her son. But first... "Thanks for saving my life. I'm Tameka."

She held out her nacre-cuffed hand to the stranger, hidden under layers of leathery materials.

They stared at it through goggles before tentatively reaching out, unlocking the cuffs, and accepting it. With their hands wrapped in more of the material, Tameka couldn't make out any physical attributes beneath the layers except that their grip was firm.

Tameka said, "It's nice to meet you."

Favoring their left leg, they stepped back and gave a sharp nod before waving for her to follow. They turned and headed South.

Uncertain what else to do, Tameka followed and straightened her clothes. Black soft leather shorts and a top which matched the woven leather bracers on her forearms, and it was all accented by gauzy blue material fixed here and there for a flowy effect—

What the fuck?

The small bloodstain on Tameka's shoulder from Celindria opening the conduit to Torrentus. It was originally red like any other human or Progeny, and now it was blue. Icarean blood. Why was Celindria's blood changing color?

Tameka shivered and muttered to herself, "Weird bitch."

Her savior paid no mind, and they traveled further into the underground of Torrentus' continent.

What *was* that storm? It had shrieked at Tameka. Wait—

Was Torrentus somehow... alive? Did Tameka try to drain a living creature unintentionally?!

She called out, "Hey!"

The stranger stopped and turned to her.

Tameka hugged herself, bothered by her train of thought. "That storm. Do you know anything about it?"

They shook their head and waved for Tameka to follow once more. Unwilling to arm wrestle them for information, she did so and the gauze had dried enough to billow around her legs like pants with every step. Eventually, the tunnel ran into a junction where they headed West. Voices carried from further down.

Tameka wasn't nervous about meeting strangers on a supposedly uninhabitable continent. She could drain or fight her way out of anything. No, Tameka was nervous about how long the others had went without her signal, and that maybe she'd accidentally harmed a living being—

The voices grew louder and more voluminous. The tunnel spilled into a massive station with an army's worth of people loitering throughout. Tameka's appearance didn't shock them into stopping or peering. They went about their business as if her arrival were normal. All of them were wearing the leather material in layers.

"Welcome."

A woman with russet-colored skin, green curly hair, and soft blue eyes approached them. She was the only person not covered in the layered material. Instead, she wore a pale shift, so thin Tameka could see through it. Oh, and her joints bent in the wrong direction. In a melodic voice, she introduced herself, "I'm Aya. I know you're disoriented, but you're safe here. We'll see to it you're taken care of." When she reached them, Aya gently touched the wrapped stranger, and Tameka's savior left to join the others.

Tameka wet her lips before asking, "I'm sorry if I'm being rude, but are you from Lacceirus Capra?"

Aya smiled sweetly. "Yes, I was born there, but it's been so long. I was raised on—" She swallowed some emotion and straightened her shoulders to recollect her self-esteem. "I was raised on Gait. In the prison."

Gait.

How did someone from Gait end up here? Wait... wait... What was it Tumu said?

"Anyone that goes into that conduit will never come back. None of the prisoners have, anyway."

Andrew asked, "Prisoners? I thought they went to Gait."

Tumu explained, "Not the bodies of research. Remorse wouldn't let them out of the Dyson's Sphere."

But surely none of those prisoners had survived? Tameka asked, "How long have you been here?"

Aya choked on the question, like it hurt her to think of the answer. "I don't know. Inanis took us hundreds of thousands of years ago."

Inanis.

Tameka's heart pounded. "You're... Aya, you're the children of Gait. You've been here this entire time? That was two and a half million years ago."

The color drained from her russet complexion, and Aya shook herself as if regaining her grip on reality. Breathless, she asked, "That long? How do you know of us, then?"

Gently, Tameka steadied Aya as she said, "The boy with the white hair—"

"Korac?!"

"—He's a... uh... friend of mine. We live together with the rest of my crew. He told us all about his time on Gait, including a Caprent girl who was nice to him. Are you that girl?"

Aya bit her lip, but tears rolled down her cheeks, anyway. "He remembered me?"

"He never forgot you, Aya. Your kindness saved his life." Now Tameka was getting a little teary.

Kindness bred kindness, and paying it forward eventually came back when the originator needed it most.

Swallowing this unexpected emotion, Tameka asked, "Were you an experiment?"

Aya shuddered, but eventually nodded.

So Remorse had told the truth. Imminent *did* put the children of Gait through hell on Enki. Did Celindria know no decency? Already certain of the answer, Tameka asked, "Did Celindria push you in here, too?"

With a confused frown, Aya shook her head. "No. Although Celindria pushed some people here through the conduit, it was an Icarus who 'disposed' of the children stolen from Gait. Xelan was his name."

TWO

WORLDS OF VIOLENCE BREED CHILDREN OF VIOLENCE

{ENKI | NEW CINDER}

BONES NEEDED TO THINK AND QUICKLY. A fully decompressed Gargantuan Tritan, presumably Primary Rem, had snatched Celindria out of her lab like a doll from her house. The cave's integrity was compromised with all the subterranean activity, and the Shadow crew needed to get Pax and evacuate immediately. He shouted, "Cave in! We need to move. Now!"

Halfway between the cage and the door to Celindria's bedroom, Ross cried out, "What about Pax?!"

Chris said his first words since relenting his volition. "Tameka said to leave him to her." And his words made sense.

Jack patted Chris' shoulder.

Bones looked at Ross. "Are you good with leaving him for Tameka—"

T.A.O. returned, and thank Elden, the little angel brought backup.

He and Ross spoke simultaneously. "Man, am I glad to see you." "You're a sight for sore eyes!"

The Seamswalker seemed aware but unaffected by the state of the crumbling lab as she said, "Korac waits. All the tin soldiers migrate toward the final winter."

Lamassau stopped blinking at the gaping rock hole long enough to turn that blinking stare at the cryptic woman.

Kyle pushed by him. "Ross!"

She was in the middle of helping Jack scoop Chris onto their shoulders and smiled at her brother. "Let's get out of here—"

The ground shook and rock erupted from the breach in the wall, and it never. Stopped. Falling. Two boulders collapsed from above and divided the lab, cutting them off from each other. Pehton cried out, stumbled, and fell into Andrew, who was nearest to the cell. Bones and Lamassau crouched and covered their heads near the lab's exit. Closest to Celindria's bedroom, Devis held Para, and Ross and Jack held Chris. T.A.O. and Kyle were with them, and, through a rain of gravel, he suggested, "We'll come back for you!"

Bones waved them off. "Hurry and—"

An avian screech pierced the sound of thundering rock. Loud enough that they covered their ears and ducked as if expecting a giant bird to attack. Following the sound, the smell of jasmines perfumed the air.

Were Remorse and Celindria fighting or fucking?

Andrew shouted "Go!"

T.A.O. Seamswalked them presumably back to Cinder's Shrine. Although, with The Afflicted One leading the way, it wouldn't surprise Bones if they ended up at Six Flags.

Another boulder crashed into Celindria's workbench, and Bones declared this his limit. "Let's go up top!" He shouted loud enough for Andrew and Pehton to hear. Lamassau nodded and together, the four lifted the rock separating them and crowded the entry together, ready to head out until Pehton touched Bones' arm.

"One second."

She concentrated for a moment before the smell of kerosene nearly overpowered the jasmine. Fumes became flames.

Pehton surrounded their quartet in a ball of fire. Remnants of the rock shower torched on impact and disintegrated into ash before reaching them. She said, "It'll help with the smaller stuff, but not the big rocks—"

The ceiling collapsed behind them, and Bones shouted, "PAX!"

Someone else joined him until they formed a chorus of shouts. A shape moved through the dust where Celindria's room once stood. In the darkness, two midnight orbs glowed in Atramentous, but standing at a third of the height of an adult.

It was Pax.

He opened his tiny wings and flew out through the hole in the ceiling with no regard for them.

Bones felt relief and fear in equal measure. What the fuck was really happening here?

Lamassau shouted over the rhythmic, deafening pounding in their wake, "Do you know how to get out of here?!"

Andrew answered before Bones could. "In ninety-eight percent of the Probabilities where we survive, it's because Celindria built a secret stairwell as an emergency exit strategy."

Pehton sounded as nervous as Bones felt when she asked, "And what about the ones where we don't survive?"

Andrew's normally tan skin turned green as he said, "Sometimes it's the Tritan lift rendered useless by the cave-in. There! That corner."

Collectively, they rounded the next junction, and everyone sighed in relief.

Stairs.

And they were clear of debris.

Bones suggested, "Celindria must have reinforced this build."

"So did she know she might one day face a decompressed Primary?" Incredulity lightened the terror in Lamassau's voice.

Pehton laughed, and it was haughty. "Are you kidding me? She builds all of her fail safes for the day I come knocking. Pay back's a bitch, and her name is Pehton. Now, let's get out of here."

No one wanted to talk about Pax.

Ross came over the earpiece. "Hey, team, we're trying to come back for you, but T.A.O. says it isn't possible. Are you okay?"

Lamassau answered her. "We escaped before the ceiling caved in. Pax escaped, too, but... He's not with us. We're on our way to the surface of wherever these caves come out. Over."

Iuo interrupted the frequency. "Be careful out there."

As they rounded the final spiral to this never ending staircase, Bones mused, "Don't worry, Porn Baron. We've got more poker to play so I can win Lamassau's stash of watermelon Jolly Ranchers from you. Over."

Bones had never been flipped off by a Pil platinum middle finger before, but Lam made it look natural with his gauntlet—

They spilled onto a mountain of black rock, and not just any mountain. This was Li mountain, same as on Cinder now, but covered in cranberry vegetation and black-barked trees with bright orange leaves, like Pehton's feathers.

"Is this Cinder?" Her voice held so much wonder.

Lamassau reminded her. "New Cinder on Enki, but yes. This was before Li's devastation—"

An earthquake unsteadied them—

Nope, not an earthquake.

Half a mile away from them, they could see the hole in the mountain from the collapse in Celindria's lab. Through that, Bones made out the Gargantuan Tritan's blue body, shifting in a cavern of his making. He'd hollowed out Li Mountain for a battleground, and somehow Celindria was alive and still fighting. It was harder to make her out, but occasionally, Bones glimpsed her dark violet complexion and the white gown she wore, frayed but not covered in blood. She wasn't flying so much as flitting around, moving too fast for Bones to see.

Pehton ran a hand over her orange feathers, gaping. "I… I can't believe what I'm seeing. Why are they fighting—No." She held up a hand. "No, I know why. It's Celindria. She pisses everyone off."

Andrew pointed and whispered, "There's Pax."

He was right. Bones had almost missed the tiny Progeny, gazing down into the wreckage. He asked, "What's he doing?"

Lamassau's tone was more serious than normal. "He's waiting for her to tag him in."

They all turned and stared at the green Tritan, expecting him to elaborate.

"Think about it. Pax is the child of half a Gargantuan Tritan, half a descendant of Elden, and his mother is one of the most powerful beings in the galaxy. If Remorse proves too much for Celindria to handle, Pax is more than a match for his grandfather."

They were faced with two options. Get off this mountain before it collapsed under the pressure of Celindria and Remorse's battle. Or stand and watch. Lamassau was the only one without wings, and Bones would snatch him if they needed a speedy escape.

With all that in mind, Bones decided. "Is it callous to ask for popcorn?"

Lamassau handed him a bag of Cheetos. As Bones gaped at him, the Tritan said, "You're welcome."

But now, Bones gaped at something beyond his truest of friends. Beyond the cliff's edge. Out where the Ignis Desert should be with its basalt lava fields, bodies littered the ground.

Pehton, sounding concerned, asked, "Bones, are you—Oh. My. Elden. What am I looking at?" She'd obviously looked across the plane as well.

"What is it—" Lamassau turned and stopped talking. He stopped breathing beside Bones.

Andrew took a step closer to the edge, looking not at all surprised and sounding not at all concerned to Bones. No, when he spoke, Andrew sounded final.

"This is it. This is why."

{Enki | Cinder's Shrine}

Xelan stared at the lifeline Korac was offering him.

"My Prince, get out of your head and fight for Fury and your son before you really do lose them to this war."

Yes.

The Prince clasped his General's hand. "Agreed." Before the other man could pull away, Xelan grabbed Korac and pulled him in for a hug. Muffled, Xelan muttered, "She's not dead."

After a second of stiffness, Korac relaxed into the embrace and assured, "There's not a chance in the Wrong Side of Eternity she'd leave you—"

"I want to let you keep having this moment." Tumu spoke from beside Xelan. "But the others are in danger. They need us."

The Shadow still needed Xelan, and so did his son, Rayne, and even Celindria.

Xelan pulled away to nod at Tumu. Sagan stood within a respectful distance, with concern lining her face. Korac went to stand beside her. Opening his wings to their full span, Xelan said, "Let's get to the others—"

T.A.O. Seamswalked into the shrine toting Ross, Kyle, Jack, and Devis carrying Para. Between Ross and Jack was Chris, conscious.

Tumu knelt to check on the guard and murmured an exchange with Jack and Ross.

Kyle ran closer to keep from alarming the soldiers parading into the Pantheon. In the quietest voice, while also conveying extreme alarm, he said, "Remorse is attacking Celindria, and the lab is collapsing."

Sharply, Tumu met Xelan's gaze.

No. A Primary was too much for her—

"We need to save Pax—What is it, T.A.O.?" Korac looked down at the small woman's hand on his arm.

She shook her head. "Can't. Gone."

Ross got to her earpiece first. "Hey, team, we're trying to come back for you, but T.A.O. says it isn't possible. Are you okay?"

Lamassau answered her from wherever they ended up. "We escaped before the ceiling caved in. Pax escaped, too, but… He's not with us. We're evacuating through the caves as we speak. Over."

Iuo, marching his army into the Pantheon, interrupted the frequency. "Be careful out there."

Bones sounded in decent spirits as he said, "Don't worry, Porn Baron. We've got more poker to play so I can win Lamassau's stash of watermelon Jolly Ranchers from you. Over."

While everyone relaxed from the relieving news, Xelan waited for the back and forth to finish before checking with Iuo on the earpiece. "Iuo, we're retrieving the rescue team. How is the migration to the Pantheon?"

"Beautiful." The Lamian Prince sounded optimistic. "They're funneling into formation and eliminating the Overseers as planned. Good luck rescuing our team."

"Thanks. Over and Out." Xelan said before he changed frequency. "Rescue team in need of a rescue. This is Wingmaster. We're coming to get you. What's your location? Over." With a smile at Sagan, he lowered his wings beneath his coat. Easier to travel by conduit without them retracted.

She took his hand and squeezed it. "We got this."

The strain around her eyes made him reach out and cup her cheek. "You're damned right we do."

Tumu stepped away from Ross, Jack, and Chris to say, "We need to mobilize for the others while Celindria and Remorse are distracted—"

"Wingmaster." It was Bones, and he sounded bewildered. "I'm having trouble believing my eyes right now. To my left, Remorse—decompressed—is battling with Celindria *inside* of Li mountain, while Pax waits his turn. And to my right… Well, it's an infinite sea of bodies. Over."

Ross and Jack exchanged a confused frown, steadying Chris between them. Kyle took Para from Devis.

Tumu's lidless voids widened.

Pehton came on the line next. "The bodies—They're all copies of Nox and Rayne. And there are millions of them scattered around—GET DOWN!"

"We're going." Sagan opened a conduit. "Li Mountain, New Cinder."

Devis ran over and held out something for Xelan. A capsule. "If you somehow get close enough, give this to Celindria. I *know* it will help her."

Korac ran a hand through his hair in a frustrated gesture only Xelan and maybe Sagan would recognize as Korac asked Devis, "What will *you* do?"

Andrius, Devis, and T.A.O. came together with Torrentus behind them.

Xelan's First Wave Progeny.

Overwhelmed, his voice shook when he said, "I'm . . ." So happy, but there wasn't time to bask in this reunion. Instead, he asked, "Can you three take Chris and Para to the Medical Bay? Korac, go check on your mother and Triss. Then return here to oversee the migration with Tumu."

Tumu gave a salute. "Bring my boyfriend back."

Korac stood at attention. "Yes, your highness." The best soldier.

Devis reached once more for Para's unconscious body.

Kyle muttered, "Be careful with her."

The other man nodded. "And you take care on the battlefield."

"Sagan, with me." Xelan stepped through the conduit, knowing she'd follow despite the strain. If someone had made copies of Rayne and then murdered them, Sagan would surely want to see it for herself.

They stepped onto Li mountain in a paradise Xelan only saw in his mother's stories. He wished Tumu had told him about this place a long time ago. It just seemed cruel of Enki to keep it from the Icari, and now the rogue half of Gait would destroy it if all things went well. Anything to prevent the Probability Matrix's predictions of Rayne's death from becoming reality—

The mountain roared, followed by the shriek of a great bird.

"Over here!" Pehton called from a peak north of their current position.

Sagan climbed the path ahead and spared a glance back at Xelan. With one of her kind smiles, the Seamswalker said, "Tameka's alive, and Pax will be fine."

Xelan stared, stunned. His heart ached in loss while he tried to convince his brain everything was salvageable, but sometimes all it took was hearing the mantra from the right person for it to sink into his thick skull.

Tameka was alive.

Pax would be fine.

"Thanks, Aegis-Slayer."

With Devis' capsule in hand, Xelan opened his wings and flew alongside Sagan to the peak and—

Dodged.

An entire tree flew by them like an evergreen, but orange dart.

They were close enough to hear Lamassau shout, "They're fighting in the canyon!"

The team pointed to the crevice split along the mountain range that never ran alongside the real Cinder's Li Mountain. The planet's ashy water couldn't erode rock to this degree when in such short supply.

Xelan and Sagan alighted on the peak, lush with orange-leaved trees and cranberry grasses.

Pehton immediately pointed toward the canyon. "Pax."

On the precipice, Xelan's son, even bigger than when Xelan had last seen him, stood watching the fight below. And his people were right. Pax *did* look as though he were waiting his turn.

All the violence these worlds asked of his children. Xelan wanted peace for them. For *all* of them. He swallowed before saying, "Sagan, get them out. I'm saving my son."

Someone touched Xelan's arm. He turned to meet Andrew's sad eyes. Exhausted and anxious, Xelan asked, "There's more?"

Andrew waved for him to follow and walked toward the edge of the cliff. He pointed out at the horizon. There, bodies carpeted the ground.

All of them were a clone of the cursed King of Cinder and the brave young woman who'd killed him.

Finally, Xelan's past had caught up with him.

Without another word, he opened his wings and flew into the canyon. In doing so, maybe Xelan could make up for at least one wrong this day.

{Enki | New Cinder}

Nox back flipped to avoid the next blow. Out of his periphery, he saw Rayne mirror him before they both speared their opponents into a throng.

Rayne and Nox copies.

Weapons filled with yellow Aegis blood and bones of nacre. They weren't without surprises.

The Rayne Weapon in his face opened its mouth and released a projectile disc, which Nox barely caught before it struck him between the eyes. Bladed, it cut into his fingers. Nearby, true Rayne reacted to his hand injury with a curse, experiencing the pain. He crammed the disc down fake Rayne's throat without a sound of protest.

These were not Rayne. Their eyes were lifeless, hair more brown than black, and Imminent had dressed them in a replica of her Volcano Day gear.

True Rayne glowed like a beacon. From the light emanating within her skin to the bright sun burning in her eyes, she was radiant. Dressed in a form-fitting, cobalt fighting suit, she held it together with matte black chains. The battle barely affected her pitch-black hair. All the braids and the ponytail were holding fast, proving Rayne possessed Korac's style in battle.

In shadow form, Nox's hair moved fluidly with him and remained out of his way, like receding smoke. Dressed in the same black jeans and black tee he'd worn in her conscience, it was bemusing how the shirt irritated his skin even as a weightless shade. When another fake Nox clutched him from behind, it reminded the real Nox why he hated anything covering his shoulders, ribs, and stomach.

He head-butted the fake Nox hard enough to dent its face into its nacre-glass skull.

Calibrated.

Optimized.

Stabilizing...

Unable to stabilize.

Warning: Sixty-five hours and eleven minutes until maximum destabilization.

That afforded them another thirty minutes.

With her real translucent wings, Rayne flew overhead, only to dive with Night Killer, her staff, impaling a Nox. These fakes couldn't seem to fly or weren't programmed with that in mind for combat. It made it less challenging, but no less satisfying to kill them. Rayne wrenched Night Killer from one Nox and impaled a fake Rayne on the staff's opposite side, twirling the blade out of its chest and lending to a shower of yellow gore all around.

Thunder disturbed the surrounding ground, despite the clear sky. Their trail of battle-scarred land had brought them to an orchard of black trees with red and orange leaves. Bodies trampled tall grasses in shades of cranberry, and a stream raced by in crimson water—

This was familiar.

Nox ripped the nacre from a fake Rayne's chest, crushed it in his fist, and threw its body into the next wave of opponents. All to afford him a moment to gaze at the scenery.

His mother's stories. Uncle Vinco's Verse.

"Cinder."

This was Nox's homeworld before the expansion of Li had swallowed them in ash.

Magnesium light consumed the orchard, melting their opponents and blinding them. Nox's stability wavered a bit, the smoke compromised, separating temporarily until the light receded into Rayne once more. While the counterfeits stumbled, unseeing, she crossed the battlefield to him in an instant.

"Did I hear you say, 'Cinder?'"

Her eagerness touched Nox. He'd said one word, and Rayne had leveled the field to check on him. In his lifetime, Nox knew only two other people with this much consideration, and he'd foolishly pushed both of them away.

To Rayne.

Calibrated.

Optimized.

Stabilizing . . .

Unable to stabilize.

Warning: Fifty-nine hours and fifty-nine minutes until maximum destabilization.

Damn.

They were struggling to maintain their separate bodies against the Weapon's diminishing fuse, and there Nox was staring at Rayne searching for meaning in her kindness when it simply *was* kind. He answered, "The map led us here, to this replica continent of Cinder before Li exploded."

Rayne's eyes widened as she looked way up at him, even in her high-heeled combat boots. With her drenched in yellow Aegis blood, the entire effect was endearing. Astonished, she asked, "They designed a Cinder on Enki?"

Nox nodded. "I recognize it from the Verses." He gestured at the mountain not half a kilometer away. "That's Li Mountain, but not as I know it. The vegetation, the waterfalls, and the canyon—"

Thunder roared louder than before, and the ground quaked.

"That's the second time," Rayne echoed Nox's thoughts aloud. "What do you suppose is happening?"

Before he could answer, a fist burst through Nox's smoky stomach and blood exploded out of Rayne's abdomen.

Crimson gushed from her mouth, and she fell to her knees when the hand retracted from him.

Calibrated.

Optimized.

Stabilizing...

Unable to stabilize.

Warning: Sixty-five hours and twenty-two minutes until maximum destabilization.

With a growl, Nox turned and tornado kicked the fake Rayne's head hard enough to bend its neck completely sideways with an audible shatter of glass bones. Without hesitation, Nox knelt to check on the real Rayne.

Already healed, she met his eyes with a groan. "Ugh... that sucked. Let's not do it again."

At the slight widening of her eyes, Nox turned to find a replica Nox behind him and ripped out its nacre. Out of the millions they'd killed on this continent, only a few remained. Without the adrenaline from the initial rushing army, the last remnants proved tedious, but no less dangerous. Insects to exterminate.

Rayne stood and checked the results of her accelerated healing efforts. No hard or soft tissue repair system worked as fast as hers.

And thank Elden for that.

Nox more than paled a little at the bright red blood mingling with the yellow on her armor. Shaking himself, he scanned their surroundings for more. "We should near the end of them soon. We devastated the East. Do you think we should head West—"

A screech rocked the valley.

Rayne's laughter was half-wonder, half-excitement. "Oh, I call dibs on whatever that is."

Nox fought the impulse to sulk and folded his arms.

With a spin of Night Killer, she glanced up at him and huffed. "What? It's only fair since you killed Squilly." Her eyes sparkled. "Maybe we can keep it as a pet. Like Many Feet. Come on, Nox. The sound came from the canyon. Let's go get it—"

The cliff face erupted and a blue giant stumbled out, menaced by a flitting, white bird.

"I believe we've found it."

{ENKI | NEW CINDER}

Razor, Gait, and the Aegis?

Gone.

L. Capra mine?

Buried.

Monarch 3 gas farm?

Lost.

Para and Karter?

Released.

Rayne?

Freed.

All casualties Imminent had suffered in the past few months while Celindria failed to make further advancements with the volition, memory, and Seamswalking research. Per usual, there was hardly any reaction from her at all. Three Two Four—Razor—was the most brilliant mind in the galaxy, and she possessed so little emotion in her body to spare concern for the genius upcycled into their enemy's hands.

He could give them the key to Ishkur.

Fortunately, Remorse knew Three Two Four well enough to trust his good sense. Any attempt by the Atheneum to gain intelligence through upcycling would result in subterfuge and further chaos for the Probability Matrix.

Imminent loved chaos.

Unless it disrupted their otherwise harmonious existence. Like now.

In the tremendous canyon separating Li Mountain from a column of jutting plateaus, Celindria flitted about the black rock with remarkable agility, dodging Remorse's powerful strikes, which laid waste to the mountainside. Sometimes she appeared low. Sometimes she appeared above his sixty-five foot advantage. Each evasion was faster than he could see.

How was she moving like this?

Remorse was testing her, of course. Celindria had never formed wings. Clearly, she'd held out on him either in her advancements of the Seamswalking technology or in her own personal abilities.

Even more confounding, Celindria's eyes remained the usual vibrant blue without shifting into Atramentous, despite her Icarean heritage.

Rage ignited Remorse's black blood. He reached for her, knowing she'd evade below, and stomped exactly where she flitted to.

The murderous angel in her flowing white gown disappeared beneath his boot with a satisfying crunch. Her cry was an avian howl, which pierced through the canyon like the sweetest birdsong in Remorse's ear holes—

Something shifted.

No.

Impossible.

Remorse gave all his strength to that boot, and still it lifted. Higher and higher until it revealed the woman beneath. Ribs, an arm, and a shin bone protruded where he'd crushed her. No blood flowed from the injuries. Truthfully, he focused on the tediums to avoid her eyes.

When Primary Rem finally met Celindria's stare, he stepped back.

Nothing.

There was nothing there.

No rage or concern. Not even pride.

Remorse may as well have been fighting a statue. Her clothes were tattered and had peeled away from her, leaving Celindria almost exposed. She could care less.

Truly soulless.

There was no stifling the Primary's shudder, revolted to his core. All the while, Celindria stared him down, the injuries healing before his eyes.

Somewhere in the recesses of his conscience, Remorse heard Vi's laughter. He'd underestimated another woman.

"Go home, Rem." Celindria's voice was as empty as her heart. "I still have use of you, unless you wish to perish." At the last, her eyes flicked upward toward the cliff.

Remorse followed her gaze and spotted Pax with his wings spread wide, ready. The sight broke Rem's heart. That was his grandson, and the child was more attached to this bloodless abomination than his own blood.

So much.

In his long life, the Primary had lost so much. His wife and half their race to the unforgivable atrocity committed by the Aegis. Savis. Xelan. Three Two Four, who he came to see as a surrogate son. All the security and stability he'd established over the long years was dissolved in only a few months. And soon… Enki.

But not Pax.

That boy was Remorse's chance to start again. With him, Primary Rem and Primary Bol could revitalize their research, hidden on a planet like Lukemore or Reipon. One with sympathizers of their depleting race. They'd take all the bulls with them and isolate those genes in Pax to recreate another Project Surra. One unable to speak or think for itself.

Then they could breed enough to re-conquer the Vast Collective.

Remorse turned his back on the empty person and reached out to his grandson. "Pax, I know how to retrieve your mother. Would you like that? Come with me, and we can help her together."

Pax frowned and looked at Celindria for guidance.

Which turned the Primary's stomach. He said, "C'mon, son. Uncle Nock is alive—"

Celindria showed the first sign of emotion in a decade when she gasped from behind.

"—He's with Rayne."

Despite the boy's physical appearance of Earth-age seven or so, he still spoke like a four or five-year-old. "Auntie Rayne? In da box with her?"

Remorse smiled and held out his hand for Pax to jump into his palm. "She's no longer in the Martyr Complex, and Nox is her shadow. Isn't that fun?"

A beautiful grin blossomed on the boy's face. "Silly. He not her shadow. He too big."

Adorable. "Too true." The brute was a massive beast. "But I saw it with my own eyes. If you come down, I'll take you to see them." For however long they still lived. Hopefully Abresson had finished evacuating the depositories by now—

Darkness loomed over Remorse, and he glanced up, expecting to find a cloud. Instead, he found the shade of the canyon stretching and casting over him.

How in Eternity was this happening—

Remorse spun around to the most disturbing sight he'd recalled since the Tritan females' ship disintegrated before his eyes.

Celindria was gone. Only her eyes remained, held level in the shadows. They were bright in contrast to the shaded surroundings. All the rock was hidden beneath the gloom.

Tired of the spectacle, the Primary stomped on Celindria's eyes. He expected a satisfying pop, like squishing two grapes, but nothing happened. When he lifted his foot, there was nothing there.

Celindria's voice came to his ear in a whisper. "You should have informed me. Do you have any comprehension of what this new development means for the Probability Matrix?"

Remorse turned to the source of the words, but nothing was there.

It continued, undisturbed. "I was inclined to let you live, but you've proved as incompetent as Abresson. Good night, Remorse—"

He reached out to her previous location and squeezed into the shadow. There, the shade gathered in a tuft. From inside his fist came strangled noises.

Pax ran to the edge, eyes in Atramentous, ready to fly. "Sissy, no!"

"Shh, shh, Pax." Remorse stared at his fist, feeling everything rectified within. "This isn't Celindria in my hand. It's a rodent to crush. No need to interfere. It'll soon die."

"Not today she won't, *father.*"

Primary Rem's heart dropped into his stomach as he whirled to face the only man fit to be his judge, jury, and executioner.

"Son."

{Enki | New Cinder}

Pehton held her breath, and so did the others. Although Sagan had arrived to Seamswalk them to the Pantheon for the ultimate battle, no one wanted to move an inch, lest they disturb the most epic confrontation in the Vast Collective's history.

Xelan was facing off with Primary Rem. The former stood on the cliff, wings open, body tense. Ready. His eyes were drowned in midnight Atramentous. The latter gaped in the canyon below, staring up at his son with a mixture of horror and, strangely, relief. As if Remorse had waited a long time for this moment.

Well, Pehton had a few choice words for the Tritan who'd fathered her children. Gently brushing by Bones, squeezing Lamassau's arm, stepping around Andrew, and nodding at Sagan, Pehton crossed the peak and took up beside their leader. Xelan knew she was there because his feathers rustled, but aside from that, he made no other indication she'd interrupted their tête-à-tête.

The muffled screams in the Tritan's fists unnerved her, even though she despised Celindria more with each passing day.

When Pehton straightened her shoulders and held up her chin, Primary Rem's voids flicked to her in acknowledgment. Arms crossed, she asked, "Remember me?"

Pax glanced up at her with a grin, making her curious about how much the boy was registering the mortal peril surrounding him.

Remorse wet his not-lips before answering, "The Lyriki egg donor. Your contributions guaranteed Enki's continued prosperity. So greatly, in fact, that I'll overlook your participation in Gait's destruction and remove your bounty if you convince my son to join us."

Again, Xelan's feathers rustled, especially as black blood welled in the Tritan's closed fingers. Celindria was clawing her way out.

Unbidden, shame and heartache twisted like a knife in Pehton's heart. Impressed by the steadiness of her own voice, she reminded Remorse, "What about *our* son? And our daughter? The ones you tortured? You expect me to help you subject Pax and Xelan to more of your underhanded tyranny after what you confessed to—"

No. Pehton could see she wasn't getting anywhere by the dullness of Remorse's voids. Her gliders flared as she said, "Never mind. I'm just here to kill you, Remorse, hoping I spare another young woman your idea of breeding."

Pax snickered with a pink blush on his cheeks.

Xelan took a step toward the cliff's edge. "Let her go." His voice came in three pitches, booming through the canyon.

Remorse didn't dignify Pehton's words with a response and addressed the mighty Icarus beside her. "I *need* this. Celindria has spurred every horrible event in your life. Don't you see—"

"Pax. Now!" Xelan called with such ferocity that Pehton startled beside him.

The mini-Xameka? Telan? Opened his wings wide, and the midnight blue in his solid irises swirled.

Remorse snarled and crashed to one knee, lessened by the boy's efforts.

Xelan flew up and shouted down to Pehton, "Keep up!"

Oh, as best she could. The fastest fighter she'd ever seen, outside of a video of Rayne, zipped at Remorse and disappeared from Pehton's vision. Even the Tritan lost sight of Xelan in his anguish, ducking his voids in exhaustion.

Pehton ignited the Siren's Gale and followed, dipping down to Remorse's face in a flaming sphere of her making.

The Tritan was still grimacing as he succumbed to Pax's drain, and she was happy to further his misery.

Fire concentrated at the core of Pehton's Siren's Gale and released on a blazoned flare between the Primary's eyes.

Bingo.

The Gargantuan Tritan growled in the recoil and stumbled onto all fours. His collapse reverberated throughout the canyon, releasing a massive plume of dust.

Midair, Pehton placed her hands on her hips. "For our children."

But where was Xelan? What about Celindria? Remorse's fist was still closed—

Pehton shrieked as her vision blurred—No. Not blurred. All around her, the world shifted in a cascade of existing instances. Hundreds of thousands of this moment occurred all at once. This continuance felt right, but what felt wrong was that Pehton could witness it.

On the cliffs above, Lamassau shouted over the raucous chorus of existing worlds, "How were we exposed to Cascading Light?!"

Sagan asked, "Why does it feel like the time I let Kyle talk me into drinking his uncle's moonshine?"

"This is fucking awful," Bones sounded worse than hungover.

Andrew was unaffected. "This is what I see when Kyle and I haven't checked in for a while."

But why were they seeing it now?

Pax suggested the obvious. "Close your eyes, Uncle Bones."

Sure. When experiencing sensory overloaded, deprive the senses—

Whoa.

The Probabilities pulsed.

Pehton's head rolled on her shoulders. So dizzy. So... heavy...

Falling.

Air whooshed around Pehton in a thousand lifetimes. Deafening. As definitive as the ground, ready to catch her when she landed. Not long now. The fall wasn't high enough to kill her. She'd be fine. No more broken on the outside than on the inside.

What had Pehton's hundreds of thousands of existences amounted to?

Her children. She couldn't even remember their names. What they looked like. Everything surrounding her children's existence was so negative, but... Pehton would never forget the love she felt when she held their hands. Embraced them.

Korac was a 'good' in her contributions column. Pehton had helped him many times throughout his life.

Caedes' rare smirk came to mind. French toast. A kiss that never was.

Razor accumulated the worst of Pehton's deeds. Yes. When Pehton reached Eternity, judgment for her complicity in so much of his evil would taint the otherwise positive account of her life.

But all this would come once Pehton landed and healed all the broken bones in her battered body. Assuming Remorse didn't recover and take advantage of her prone state—

Powerful arms caught her under the knees and shoulders.

Pehton was still too dizzy to open her eyes and see, but her savior was warm like an Icarus. "Xel—Xelan?"

"I got you."

For the love of Elden. The Icarus's cheesy catch phrase cleared the haze enough for Pehton to hear the others shouting.

Bones sounded better off than her. "You all right?"

Sagan offered, "I can get us out of here anytime!"

Lamassau's voice was honed with urgency. "Remorse is recovering! Everybody get in the ring."

Pehton opened her eyes, muttering, "Xelan, why am I so dizzy? My nacre..."

"We're closer to Celindria than the others."

That ambiguity made her frown. "What?"

Pehton felt them hovering backward, turning her stomach. Near them came a barrage of rocks shifting and the ground trembling.

Remorse was standing up.

Weakly, she swallowed back vomit and gripped Xelan's shirt. Insistently, she asked, "What's happening?"

Emotion had thickened his voice, and Pehton swore Xelan was crying.

"Celindria's dying."

{ENKI | MEDICAL BAY}

Ross kept her eyes on Korac's back and balanced her half of Chris' significant weight on her shoulder. Along with them, Jack, Devis, Andrius, Para, and T.A.O. stepped through the Seam. Its purple Monarch Hall matched the General's robe as they walked into the Medical Bay. All the while, Ross was grateful Bethany didn't receive an earpiece. At least she hadn't witness any of the trauma Celindria had put their team through—

A stack of bodies across from their entry greeted them, sending Ross into a panic. "Bethany?! Are you—"

A primal scream tore through the bay.

From behind her, T.A.O. muttered, "Lyriks with feathers the color of fire. Not much longer now."

Jack glanced at Ross from Chris' right side. She looked upward, toward the source of the cry. Triss was in labor, and Bethany was upstairs helping Pablo and some random Tritan doctor. The flurry of activity left Ross' head spinning until she needed to shake it to see straight.

In her overstimulated distress, Jack's voice boomed as he asked, "Where do you want us, doc?"

The list of priorities included Chris hanging between Ross and Jack, Korac here to see his mother, and Devis carrying Para, who was regaining consciousness. All of it swirled in a spiral of mounting confusion.

Too much.

Especially with the extra Tritans loitering around, armed and guarding the main entry.

Pablo answered, "The doctor is busy at the moment. Nice to see you, Chris. General Korac, can you take him to the same bay you took Karter?" He pointed without looking away from Triss'… dilemma.

Chris muttered to Jack in a strangled voice, "Please."

Ross squeezed her eyes shut to stop the spinning while Jack responded, "Don't worry. We'll get you to her. Jeez, I miss Tameka's power boosts at a time like this."

Yes. That sounded amazing.

Devis sighed his exhaustion. "No kidding." Then he gestured to the main area of the room. "Andrius, this is Caedes, Miy, Twenty-One, and a squad of people I don't know."

Ross opened her eyes as Korac led their parade of casualties toward the bay Pablo had pointed out. Her head ached, and it was difficult to focus.

One foot in front of the other. Don't drop the traumatized man in tow.

Andrius gave an awkward wave.

Caedes greeted them with a curt nod.

Miy rolled her eyes and nodded toward the First Wave Progeny. "How many more people are here to witness the birth of Triss' kid?"

Devis cleared his throat and readjusted Para as she stirred in his arms. "We only came to drop off Chris and check on Andrius. We'll leave you to your…" He nodded toward the bodies. "Murder architecture shortly."

But she had already stopped listening to him, crossed the room to Twenty-One, and whispered something in his ears to make him blush.

Ross glanced back when T.A.O. whispered, presumably to herself. "The only light which matters. Yes. Let it burn brighter than Enki's star." Her words were as scrambled as Ross' brain.

Andrius tucked his Progeny sister against side, as they took a seat out of the way.

The parade led by Korac, Jack, Ross, and Chris crossed the threshold beneath Pablo. The mysterious Tritan assisting him called to another unfamiliar Tritan, saying, "Help with the others. Dr. Suarez, if our patient agrees, I think we can spare you for the Valkyrie..."

The rest of the transaction trailed off as Ross entered the next bay. She felt the shift in Chris' weight as he tried to carry himself. He kept his eyes away from her, and she hated the shame in the act.

Ross would talk to him once her heart stopped racing.

Jack gripped Chris's shoulder until the man patted his hand, and he finished walking the next two steps on his own. The medical bed held one of the most infectious and fantastic women Ross had ever met. Karter was larger than life, and it had been too long since she held any agency over her body.

Ross shuddered even in the haze of her thoughts. Volition control was awful.

Korac brushed by Jack, and Devis was in his wake, muttering to Para in his arms. This little mish-mash of a family gathered together at Karter's bed and, while Ross was moved by the thought of it, she could no longer see it.

Beyond frazzled, her brain misfired, and the hypnotic chaos brought Ross to her knees.

"I'll be the Captain, and you can be the first mate."

A younger, shorter Jack groaned from the ground below an enormous tree. "How come you always get to be the captain?"

Ross stood beside him, gazing up at the boughs. Curious, she tried to reach for the boy, and her hand went through him. Present, but not interactive.

Fourteen-year-old Rayne, at the age when Ross had first met her, grinned from a massive branch high above. Fearless, she stood with hands on her hips while the wind kited through her hair. As if explaining the answer to the oldest question in the universe, she proclaimed, "'Cause I'm the oldest—Hey!"

Jack rubbed his eyes to hide the tears. This was his memory, and Ross felt it all. He wanted to be the captain. It was the only way he wouldn't be left behind when Rayne eventually got too old to play with him.

"Hey."

Jack opened his eyes. Rayne had jumped off the massive branch and came to kneel in front of him. Her bright blue eyes softened as she reached to gently pull his hands down from his eyes.

Ross ached for the vulnerable heart exposed. Jack cried openly until his sobs caught in his throat and formed hiccups. Rayne would leave him if he couldn't grow up fast enough to keep up with her. Already, she spent more time with her friends, Sagan and Tameka, than she spent with him.

Rayne used her sleeve to wipe away his tears, and Jack calmed down. She asked, "Are you ready to tell me about it?"

After a sniffle, he confessed, "Don't leave me behind."

She laughed and ruffled his hair. "Don't worry, bro. I'm not going anywhere."

"Promise?"

Ross felt the weight in the word. This meant the world to him.

Rayne held out her pinky. "I promise to always be here for you."

Jack locked his finger with hers. "Always."

Ross blinked into adult Jack's wide eyes. When a tear rolled down his cheek, she reached out to take his hand. She had to swallow before saying, "Rayne won't ever leave you."

Pablo sighed in relief behind her. "Thank Elden. We couldn't reach you, Ross. Are you okay?"

Peering around her, Ross took in the worried faces of her friends. Devis, Chris, Korac, and Para glanced at her from Karter's bed. All of them appeared decidedly better, if a little concerned. Jack looked stripped bare of his defenses and ashamed from her intrusion. Pablo stepped around to put his warm brown eyes in her line of sight.

Still a little unsteady, Ross shooed them off. "Don't worry about me. I'm fine. Get to helping Para and Karter, doc—"

A crystalline waterfall emptied into a refreshing pool amid all the dry sand. Date palms stretched high and provided shade. Devis found an alcove among the rocks near the waterfall. This was his quiet place. He came here to relax after working hard at the forge and studying Xelan's endless scrolls of boring histories from planets they'd never get to see.

Their *father* would never let them leave the stronghold for more than these day trips. Already, Celindria begged Xelan to visit the Icarean fortress.

Their maker refused. "At least, not yet."

Devis rolled his eyes and stuffed one of said scrolls in his vest—

A flash of white among the trees startled him upright. Was that...

Ross thought he saw her at first, but even though she stood in plain sight within his memory, waving her hands, Devis looked right through her at Celindria.

Wow. The desert suited her. The woman glided into the oasis like a ghostly mirage, gorgeous and serene. Too bad all Ross could see was a monster in a beautiful dress.

Although after this enlightening memory, Ross knew Devis didn't see Celindria as a monster.

He waved. "How did you find this place?"

Celindria laughed, and it sounded genuine. "You are easy to follow."

He beamed. *She* followed *him*.

Love.

Devis loved Celindria.

Oh, Ross really didn't want to be in his head right now.

The villainous psychopath gave him a radiant smile. "I grew tired of father's lessons and thought I would see where you go when you disappear for myself." She took a measuring look at the oasis, and her voice held awe. "So spectacular."

Ross hated the swelling of pride in Devis' chest. Given the tragedy this woman had wrought on everyone, his thoughts twisted the knife in Ross' heart.

Hopeful, he said, "You can see it all from up here. Would you like to come join me?"

Celindria turned back to him with a curious raised brow, the breeze carrying her braids in her face. After his heart skipped two beats, she finally said, "I would."

While she climbed the rocks, Devis straightened the blanket and pack he used as a pillow. He wanted her comfortable—

Celindria appeared on the ledge after traversing a climb which normally took him twenty minutes in less than five.

Again, the awe in Devis' voice left Ross uncomfortable as he asked, "How did you manage that?"

With a wink, Celindria dismissed his astonishment. "With practice, you will manage it one day. Is this for me?" She pointed to the pallet, a wry smile forming on her lips.

Devis blushed and nodded, uncertain what to say. He wasn't presuming anything; he only wished to make her comfortable.

"Thank you." Celindria touched his shoulder with sincere kindness. An inclination Ross was convinced the architect of so much suffering had never experienced.

The woman Devis loved stretched out and peered up at him expectantly. Something passed behind his eyes.

Fear.

Ross wasn't sure when this took place in their lives, but Devis already feared being vulnerable with Celindria. She felt it in his gut.

Despite those instincts, Devis laid down behind her, and Celindria pulled his arm around to spoon her. They stayed that way without words until the sun went down.

It was the happiest moment of Devis' life. The most peaceful.

Ross returned to her reality with a shudder. Ignoring the concerned faces in her immediate vicinity, she found Devis' eyes. He stared at her with a tear, much like Jack, but with more horror than shame.

She accused, "That's the memory in the capsule. You want her to feel how you felt."

Devis couldn't speak, so he nodded.

Andrius answered from the threshold between the bays. "We hope to reach her through emotion. It's the one taboo she will not tolerate."

T.A.O.'S words chilled Ross. "The soulless cannot enter Eternity. She will never know peace."

Korac sounded incredulous. "So you mean to force Celindria to feel with the memory Ross witnessed?"

Devis finally answered, and his hope broke Ross' heart. "I mean to free her."

"There is no freeing evil."

Ross was surprised by her own words as much as everyone else in the room.

THREE
THE LOVE WHICH BINDS US

{ENKI | TORRENTUS}
"I'M SORRY. What?"

Tameka must have misheard the other woman because the air left the room in a vacuum.

Aya, the Caprent girl from Korac's Verse and a child stolen from Gait, explained to Fury, "We were subjects of experimental nacres. I only know because Xelan told me so. I don't think he ever saw us, and I don't think he knew we were in the crates. Primary Rem and his lackey locked us in them, but I knew Xelan pushed us through the conduit. I'd never mistake the kindness in his voice as he unknowingly condemned us to this fate."

Tameka's ears popped.

The Shadow's allies were amassing on the battlefront, Imminent wanted to corrupt her son, and Rayne was somewhere in Enki, facing a destined fate.

Xelan was the father of Tameka's child. He'd trained the Progeny and gathered all these people together to fight on the side of good and hope. No matter how murky his past continued to grow, he was the most amazing person in the galaxy.

And frankly, Tameka didn't have the energy to deal with this right now. "One thing at a time," she muttered to herself. To Aya, she asked, "Are you the leader here?"

The woman swept her green curls over her shoulders, elbow bent in reverse. Casual alien stuff. "I look after us, if that's what you mean."

Tameka smiled and gazed around, her voice filled with wonder. "You're doing one hell of a job." She returned her eyes to her newest ally. "I have so many questions about how you managed all this, but two questions take precedent."

Aya nodded for her to continue.

"Are there a pair of half-Lyriki, half-Tritan twins around here? And is Torrentus… how do I put this… Alive?"

The Caprent girl's eyes widened. In hushed surprise, Aya whispered, "How do you know of Aria and Torch?" Despite her quiet tone, everyone in the surrounding hub stopped and stared at them.

Tameka glanced around at the eavesdroppers and licked her lips. How much should she spring on these people all at once? "I know their mother and wish I didn't know their father."

Shocked glances were exchanged, and gasps erupted from the crowd of people hidden under layers of material and goggles.

Okay. So Tameka had triggered something she could only hope was a good thing. To Aya, she elaborated, "Their father, Primary Rem, had them—Aria and Torch—taken from their mother when they were young, and Pehton wasn't in a position to find them. Meanwhile, the man responsible for Inanis convinced everyone it was a permanent phenomenon which had surely killed all of you."

While Tameka explained, Aya wrapped her arms around her back, similar to a human hugging their ribs for comfort. Eventually the Caprent girl repeated from earlier, "Two and a half million years?" She choked on the last word, cleared her throat, and moved on. "We'll need permission from our gods to speak to you. They can tell you more about the beast in the sky."

Torrentus—

Wait. "Gods?"

Aya was already walking toward the central tunnel of the junction and called over her shoulder, "Follow me."

It was the same as the other tunnel, only this one opened into a luxury apartment covered in carpets of the mysterious material dyed Icarean-blood cobalt. They hung from the ceilings like drapes and lined the walls.

On a palette within, two Lyriks knelt on both knees, eyes closed in meditation. Naked. Like their mother, their skin was pitch-black, but unlike any Lyrik Tameka had ever seen, the twins' feathered manes were Tritan-skin blue. The color of a gas flame.

They opened their gemstone eyes to reveal sapphires, an identical set.

They narrowed on Tameka as she gently brushed past Aya to address them directly. "I'm so happy to find you alive. You have no idea how relieved your mother will be once I take you to her."

The girl, presumably Aria, said in a soothing voice, "Tell us what you want."

Tameka frowned. Succinct. She should try for succinct. "I want to save all of you, my son, my best friend, and my lover from Imminent's cruelty."

Torch tilted his head like a bird. "And the beast?"

Beast? Tameka asked, "Do you mean Torrentus? The storm? Is it alive like I thought?"

Aria dipped her head in the affirmative.

Why on Earth would the Aegis make a living terraforming machine? How did they lose control of it? And for Elden's sake, how was Tameka supposed to kill it knowing this?

She chafed her arms as she asked, "Is it sentient—Feeling, I mean?"

"Yes," Torch answered.

From behind, Aya elaborated, "It doesn't normally react as violently as it did with you. I've never seen it attack with fire before."

Great. What should Tameka do? She asked, "Is that why you were right beneath it? Do you use Torrentus for cover?"

The two Lyriks remained silent, so Aya answered, "If Celindria can't find us, she can't permanently 'dispose' of us. They assume we're dead because of the beast in the sky."

This made sense to Tameka. If she could spend more time with its nacre, she might find its source of power, because surely something so enormous fed from an impossibly abundant generator. With a deep breath that shook Tameka's shoulders, she committed. "I'll save Torrentus, too."

The Lyriks smiled simultaneously, and Torch said, "We will leave with you and help tame the beast."

Tameka rubbed her shoulder in an awkward gesture. "Great. Uhm. Do you think you could get dressed, too? We're in the middle of a war, so you might want some of this fabric to cover your vital areas." She gestured at the draping leather material.

Aya's gasp drew Tameka to turn and spare her a glance. Had she said something wrong?

But Aria only smiled, amused. Again, in her soothing voice, she said, "Unless you are volunteering, we have no one to spare for our garments."

No one… to spare?

Aya whispered, "It's part of our death ceremony. We wear the gone so they are not forgotten."

Tameka almost felt her brows go up in shock, but stopped them.

"You know what? I've heard weirder today. You do you and meet me outside."

{ENKI | NEW CINDER}

Every pulse of the realities around Xelan was another cry for help from Celindria. Her dying screams rippled across the multiple existences so all the worlds would know her suffering.

They'd been here before, hadn't they?

But since the last time, Xelan had learned a few things about his begotten created daughter. Celindria had manipulated him against his brother, reproduced her line from the Tritan responsible for so much of the royal Icarean family's misery, tried to steal his son, and...

Tameka...

In fact, Xelan couldn't recall one good reason to save Celindria's life, even over the millennia of him chasing her.

A gentle weight in his arms, Pehton fought the overwhelming waves of Cascading Light's side effects. Ones only Celindria could produce.

The Lyrik muttered, "I can still fight, Wingmaster. Don't count me out yet."

"No. You're done for now," Xelan informed her softly. Louder, he said to the others on the cliff, "Stay back. I'll handle this. Sagan, can you get Pehton, Pax, and everyone else to safety—"

The Seamswalker appeared beside him. "You bet— Whoa... the effect is so much worse here. Are you sure you're okay by yourself?" The concern in her violet eyes touched him.

Guilt gnawed at Xelan's stomach as he planned what she might consider a betrayal. While she scooped Pehton from his arms, he said, "I'll be fine. I need a few words with my *father*." He noticed she shivered from the iciness of his tone before nodding and Seamswalking away.

Remorse wouldn't feel the effects of Celindria's requiem as the same as those who hadn't touched Cascading Light. He was halfway to his feet, fist still closed on Xelan's estranged daughter, who'd grown silent.

The Gargantuan Tritan faced his son. "Not much longer. I can feel it. Her heartbeat has slowed to nothing. Come with me, Xelan. We can rebuild Imminent together with Pax. You can convince Tameka—"

"Celindria sent her to Torrentus, and it engulfed her in flames." Xelan shook his head and looked into the voids of his maker. "I want nothing to do with you. Let her go and leave my son alone. I'll make it quick."

Primary Rem blinked filmy membranes over voids as big as his half-Icarean son. He declared, "An impasse."

Xelan swept his coat back to reveal dual sickles on his hips. "This is no impasse, Remorse. These are your last words. Make them count."

"I loved your mother—"

Wrong. Answer.

The Primary would get no Verse.

In his practiced speed, Xelan charged for him and sliced a prominent black vein in Remorse's neck.

The Tritan villain snarled in pain and swatted with enough speed to actually strike his Icarean assailant.

Xelan crashed into the cliff face, but recovered before Remorse punched it, opening access into the existing series of tunnels, validating Nox's accounts in his Verse.

Xelan flitted to the fist containing Celindria. He sliced the knuckles, hoping Remorse would release her.

He didn't. Instead, he squeezed tighter.

Fighting a Gargantuan was proving strategically difficult—

Oh. Of course.

With a glance at Remorse's expanded belt, Xelan knew how to end this fight. He prayed to Elden he wasn't too late as he avoided the next blow and beelined straight to the compression orb—

"Daddy!" Pax's warning sliced through the canyon.

Sagan's words echoed after him. "C'mon, Pax. We have to go."

Pax's voice was accompanied with wriggling, struggling noises. "I can helps."

No!

As if Remorse had predicted Xelan's next move, he reached for Pax just as Xelan struck the compression orb with both sickles. The shock wave sent him flying back into the crevice housing Celindria's lab. Debris went everywhere, and chaos erupted above, reverberating throughout the ravine.

Bones shouted, "Pax! Pax, where are you?!"

Andrew asked, "Sagan, are you and Pehton okay?"

Lamassau kept his eye on the prize. "Did anyone see what happened to Celindria? Primary Rem? How did I lose a sixty-five foot tall Tritan?!"

Bones confirmed, "We all lost him, and he took Pax. He couldn't have gotten far. Split up and find them!"

Xelan sat up and shook his head straight. The Cascading Light effects had stopped, so either Remorse had released Celindria or—

A violent cough sounded from across the way, toward the bedroom. Xelan gripped the counter to stand in the unstable cave dwelling. White fabric streamed in the dust plumb. Blue eyes searched. They stopped when they found Xelan.

Celindria was barren of love and devoid of hate. Her initiation into Imminent had only made it worse.

"Where did I go wrong with you?"

"You cannot see the worlds as they could be. Everything I do cascades into reality. We must break events and people to find where we are meant to be."

"If you do this... you will never recover your humanity. Your sanity."

"I will be imminent."

The debris settled. Xelan holstered his sickles and took in the state of Celindria. Bones protruded from her skin, bloodless. He'd never learned why the inconsistency in her bleeding. It seemed too cruel a thing to research. Instead, he hoped one day she would tell him about her own findings.

That day never came.

This certainly wasn't it. He saw it in the rigid lock of Celindria's jaw, and the painful reconstruction of her regal carriage. The age of her eyes had always frightened him. Monoliths collapsed within them.

All Xelan could think about was how different she was from Rayne. Cold where Rayne was warm. Unyielding where Rayne was made of forgiveness. Celindria was self-centered. Rayne was self-sacrificing. On and on, their differences went.

This was his fault. A flaw in Xelan's making of her. Compared to the average person's life, Celindria only experienced emotions about ten percent of the time. And even those experiences would only equate to five percent of the expected intensity. He made her broken, and he *needed* to fix it.

Celindria said, "Well, father. This is the time to strike. I am weakened and easy enough for you to eliminate."

Celindria still didn't understand Xelan.

The disappointment broke his heart, and Xelan knew he couldn't do it. He climbed over a boulder, shuffled through smaller rocks, and ducked beneath a collapsed panel until he stood before Celindria. She showed no signs of fear. Perhaps she was feeling nothing right now, but Xelan planned to change that.

"Take this. It's from Devis." He held up the capsule.

Celindria let her eyes flick to it and looked back to his. "Are you allowing me to live?"

Xelan lifted her open hand, ignoring the broken bone still visible in her forearm. He closed the capsule in her palm. "Only if you use this here and now."

She narrowed her eyes at it, pressed the trigger to release the pin, and pricked her healing wrist with it.

Without knowing what was in it, Xelan trusted Devis to share something only absolutely vital. This would not—*could not*—fail. While she experienced the memory, he glanced around the lab for—

There it was. Xelan hopped over a boulder to retrieve Tameka's chain dart from the lab counter. Something else caught his eye. "Korac's been looking for this." The Phoenix Dragon whip—

A sniffle turned him back around to Celindria. Moisture glistened in her eyes. Xelan couldn't trust it after the countless times she'd faked it in the past. He said, "No more, Celindria. Your research into your ailment can't infringe on the happiness and health of others any longer. You're finished. Don't make me kill you."

Celindria shifted, mercurial as always, from the tears to resolute grit. "I will never stop searching for the soul you denied me."

Xelan closed his eyes, and, when he opened them, she was gone. He'd regret this, but after... After he found Remorse and ended him. After he saved his son from his father. And after he recovered Tameka from the Torrentus continent.

Following one of the cave channels Primary Rem had punched through Li Mountain, Xelan carefully emerged at the base. All around, bodies littered a field of cranberry grasses. At the otherwise beautiful sight, he let his tired head hang.

Was there no end to this fight? A future where Xelan lived a happy life with Tameka and Pax. A future where everyone he loved was safe. One where Rayne—

"Xel—Xelan?!"

Now he was imagining her voice.

Exhausted, Xelan lifted his head and stared at a mirage. Blood covered the War King. The bodies were *her* kills. A ghost. A—

Did... did that hallucination's shadow just disappear into itself? If this was Rayne, was Remorse telling the truth about Nox? No. Surely Xelan was losing his mind again—

"Xelan!"

The apparition moved like Xelan with a liquid speed, running to stand in front him. Bright blue eyes gazed up at him. Tears spilled, even with her lips spread in a radiant smile. The smell of ocean water and ice cream filled the air.

Xelan didn't care about the gore as Rayne bounced up and wrapped her arms around him in a death grip. In all their hugs during her time growing up, she'd clung to him as a lifeline.

This time, Xelan held onto Rayne for dear life.

"I'll never let you go again."

{ENKI | NEW CINDER}

"I'll never let you go again."

Rayne and Xelan said the same words at the same time. They both meant them. For the first time in years, she felt at home, at peace.

Nobody hugged like Xelan.

Rayne could hold him and wipe snotty tears on his fancy coat like this forever, and it still wouldn't be long enough—

Calibrated.

Optimized.

Stabilizing . . .

Unable to stabilize.

Warning: Twenty hours and forty-eight minutes until maximum destabilization.

"Rayne."

The gentleness of Nox's voice made her leave the moment with Xelan and stare up at the man in her consciousness. In that same tone, he reminded her, "We expended your fuse in excess on me, and now . . ."

Right.

This beautiful reunion with Xelan was draining Rayne's reserves, but couldn't she hang on a little while longer?

Xelan's knees gave out, and Rayne went down with him, not letting go as she promised. They hugged on the ground, soaking in this moment amid their evident exhaustion—

"Ow."

Well, that was an odd thing for Xelan to say.

"Ow. Ow." Chuckling, he pulled them apart and nudged what was prodding him. "What's this?"

Rayne beamed—all her smiles would beam for him from hereon. "It's my staff. I named it Night Killer."

Emotions rippled through the midnight pools of Xelan's eyes. He reached out to either side of her face and pressed his forehead to hers. Softly, he said the words Rayne had most wanted to hear. "I'm so proud of you, Rayne Echo Callahan."

Her breath left on a shaky exhale, half-choked on a sob. Nikki, her parents, John—Billions of people had died in this war. And those words from Xelan were all Rayne needed to hear to know that what she had to do next was worth it.

Calibrated.

Optimized.

Stabilizing...

Unable to stabilize.

Warning: Fifteen hours and thirty-two minutes until maximum destabilization.

To Nox's credit, while Xelan praised Rayne for killing his brother, said brother remained silent, respecting the moment. However, the latest update spurred him. "Time is running out, your majesty."

It was the 'your majesty' which brought Rayne back to the reality of things. Inside her head, she gave him a solemn nod. They had work to do. To Xelan, she asked, "How much do you know?"

Her Icarean guardian winced. Elden, after these last few years and experiencing the Verses, Rayne could read Xelan better. He always seemed so cool and confident, certain of their abilities. But now Rayne saw the strain of fear in his eyes. She wanted to hug it away.

Xelan said, "More than you'd think. More than you'd want me to know. Rayne, I have to be honest with you."

Rayne pulled away and gently pulled his hands down from her face. She needed to separate, even though it broke her heart. She stood and held her hand out to him. "So tell me."

He took the offered hand and stared at where he held it in his palm. Rayne's hand was so little compared to his, his slender fingers longer than her palms. Xelan looked ready to confess something when he met her eyes. "I designed—"

"Holy shit!"

Rayne took her eyes off Xelan and looked way up the mountain.

Andrew gaped at her from atop the cliff. She'd sworn he muttered, "So we're in this one." Louder, he called behind him, "Guys! Guys, you won't believe this!"

Rayne laughed, happier than she'd been in a while. She looked back at Xelan and frowned in confusion. He looked so grave and even lost color to his complexion.

Inside her head, Nox quietly explained, "What my brother wanted to say cannot be said in front of the others."

"Oh." That made sense. Rayne reached out and took Xelan's other hand, wincing at the twenty minutes it cost her. "There will be another chance to tell me. First, let's see them, and then I want to meet your son."

Nox warmed beside her. It was the only word for it. He hadn't spent a second in Pax's presence, but he already thought fondly of his nephew. It endeared him to Rayne.

Xelan squeezed her hands and let them go. Staring at her, but not speaking to her, he answered a question. "This is Wingmaster. Roger. I located Rayne. Over."

She giggled. "Still using that call sign? And technically, *I* found *you*."

As if suddenly remembering their setting, Xelan glanced at the field of bodies.

Inside her head, Rayne caught her breath and hugged herself. She sensed Nox assessing her response and took comfort in the lack of judgment in the gesture. He'd never make her feel wrong about the carnage, but that one look from Xelan burned her.

The Prince of Cinder shook himself from the sight and held something out in his hand. It was an earpiece. Rayne couldn't contain the smile as she plugged it into her ear.

For three years, Nox was her only company. He was reassuring in a way her friends could never be, but he wasn't family. A cacophony of cheers greeted her.

"Give my sister a hug for me—Better yet, bring Rayne here so I can do it myself."

Jack sounded more grateful where Kyle sounded partially concerned in his surprise. "Is it really Rayne? You really found her? Is she okay?"

"Tell her we'll renew our vows so she can be a bridesmaid this time." Lynn could count on it.

Para's nervous apology made Rayne snicker. "Your majesty, if you can hear this, Bones and I are real sorry if you were aware of everything that went on in the pit. We had no idea."

"Everyone quiet down." How could Rayne mistake the charisma in that order and the elegance in its cadence? Even Xelan smirked as Korac continued. "All they really want to know is whose Verse was better? Mine or Nox's."

Nox actually snorted beside Rayne, and she about dropped into a fit of giggles right there in front of both brothers. When she stopped laughing, tears fell from her lashes. Each one in joy.

Family.

The former King of Cinder patiently allowed her to absorb every second, and in this moment, Rayne loved him for it.

The channels held a collective breath and at Xelan's nod, Rayne said into the comms device, "This is War King. Enki has less than fifteen hours left. Who's ready to bring down Imminent? Over."

Wow.

Both Rayne and Xelan pulled their earpieces out to keep the cheers from busting their eardrums. Sure their nacres would heal it, but who wants to deal with that?

Above them, Sagan shouted and jumped up and down with the green Tritan, who must be Lamassau. Pehton and Andrew stared in confident resolution. Bones saluted with a fist to his chest.

Rayne couldn't stop smiling, and when she said the next aloud, she smiled at Nox in her head. "And Korac?"

"Yes, your majesty."

The way Korac said it made Rayne feel safe, and she appreciated that quality in someone intending to wed her girlfriend. Rayne continued grinning at Nox as she said into the earpiece, "Sorry, the first is always better than the sequel."

Xelan barked a hearty laugh. "Oh, that ego is fragile. Be careful with him. C'mon. Let's get you up to see the others. Then we'll need your help to rescue Tameka."

"Tameka? What happened?" Rayne opened her wings when he did.

Xelan held up both hands to stave her concern. "Celindria pushed her onto a continent plagued by a malfunctioning terraforming machine, but don't worry. I have every faith that with your help, we can save her."

Nox shifted beside Rayne and, without a word, reminded her of their mission. But how could she ever forget with the bodies surrounding them? Something must be done about the Rayne and Nox Weapons. With her diminishing countdown, Rayne was the only one with the potential to destroy Enki.

Softly, Rayne said to Nox, "What if they could think of another way?"

"By all means, try. I won't stand in the way of this reunion, Rayne." Nox manifested a three-dimensional projection of Enki and its continents. He populated them with the Weapons. "I'll calculate alternatives while you—" Say goodbye. "—galvanize your troops."

A sadness filled Rayne. She should tell Xelan about Nox. Right now. When she had first recognized the man emerging from the cave as her guardian, Nox retreated. Originally, Rayne had assumed it was out of respect and kindness to give her a moment she desperately needed. That might still be the case, but now she wondered if Nox feared Xelan's judgment, and that tightened Rayne's heart.

"I still plan to tell them about you."

Nox didn't look away from the model as he said, "Do what you will, but your way is right. Maintain your connections to those you love. It's the only way to avoid becoming like I am—was. Like I was."

Later.

Rayne would coax Nox into the big reveal when she was better equipped to make him comfortable with it. Later.

In the meantime, the channels on the earpiece were blowing up with love from her family. It saddened Rayne how much it overwhelmed her. So many voices, so many words.

Xelan's voice was more soft and grounding. "Are you ready, Callahan?"

Damn, Rayne missed him. "Do you think you can keep up?"

"Pfft. Easy." He grinned that full signature smile, and Rayne nearly cried again. "Ready?"

"Set."

"Go."

They raced up the cliff in seconds. The others wouldn't likely see them fly at all. In fact, when they alighted at the top, Rayne wasn't sure which one touched the peak first. They grinned at each other.

Sagan interrupted the moment with a cry. Rayne snapped to her as the girl cupped a hand over her mouth, tears falling from her eyes. Shaky, she breathed, "Rayne..."

Without another moment wasted, Rayne ran to her and squeezed Sagan in her arms. She couldn't give completely into the moment or risk crushing her girl. Instead, she settled for the healthy beat of Sagan's heart against Rayne's chest. Confirmation of her safety and love—

Calibrated.

Optimized.

Stabilizing...

Unable to stabilize.

Warning: Thirteen hours and fifty-three minutes until maximum destabilization.

Elden damn the Tritans!

Rayne wanted one moment without the constant reminder of the Weapon.

"Elden, I missed you." Sagan brought Rayne back to the moment. "I have so much to share with you, and you'll be here to meet my daughter."

Daughter.

Wow.

Even Nox spun around from the Enki model to stare out of the view with his brows raised. They had both learned about the oncoming adoption of Triss and Razor's kid, but wow. It was already time.

And Rayne didn't want to miss it. She squeezed tighter and made contented sounds. "I'm so happy for you two."

Sagan gave a little laugh, which shook them both. "You can't know how relieved I am to hear you say that. I never knew if you fully approved."

Rayne pulled away enough for them to face each other. "Of course. So long as Korac knows he's second to me."

Everyone—including Nox—laughed, reminding Rayne of their audience.

Andrew stood the closest, his eyes filled with admiration. "You got enough left in you for my hug?" His expression was full of knowing.

Rayne swallowed and slid a fleeting glance at Nox inside her mind.

Permission.

Rayne was seeking his permission. For someone to tell her it was okay to be selfish for the span of another hug. It would be the last one, she promised. Please…

In the corner of Rayne's eye, Nox nodded.

She had a feeling he could never tell her no.

{Enki | New Cinder}

Rayne hugs.

Elden, Andrew missed this. The family was coming together. Soon, they'd find Tameka. He'd flip his coin to see what it would take to rescue Pax from Remorse. That was a new, but not insurmountable, obstacle.

Everything was working out.

Andrew hated that Rayne's fuse was lessening even as they embraced. He couldn't miss the flinch in her eyes as she let go. All hundred thousand pairs of them.

Before the battle started, Andrew would need to touch base with Kyle. The exposure to Celindria's throes heightened Andrew's immersion in the Probability Matrix. He was seeing duplications of everything again. In one of them, Rayne glowed.

And Xelan was missing from several. Since he returned with Rayne, the Icarean Prince kept averting his gaze from Andrew. There was no mistaking it. Just now, Andrew tried to look at him directly, and Xelan ducked his eyes, swept back his fancy coat to reach his pockets, and leaned against a tree while Rayne formally introduced herself to Lamassau and Bones and reacquainted with Pehton.

Regretfully, Andrew scanned Xelan's intentions.

I must deflect Andrew's attention for now. He can't scan me while I'm overwhelmed and exhausted. It's all too raw, and he'll see.

What was there to see?

Andrew could pry, or for Elden's sake, he could trust someone again. If he was willing to keep his faith in Lucas a little while longer, then surely he could spare some confidence in their leader.

Out of kindness, Andrew stepped over to Xelan who straightened from the tree and faced him, flinching. The younger man shook his head. "At ease, man. I'll leave you alone, so you have one less thing to worry about."

The tension in Xelan's shoulders and neck visibly melted as he sighed with relief. "I—"

"No. No explanations. Let's bask, okay? Tameka will reemerge. I promise. And..." Andrew flipped his coin in the air and let it fall to the ground. "Heads." He skimmed the borders of the Probabilities, stretching some to see clearer. Shrinking others which only clogged the perception—

There.

Andrew said, "There are twelve Probabilities where Primary Rem steals Pax, and only in three of them do we fail."

Xelan looked thoughtful as he confirmed, "Three. That's a seventy-five percent success rate."

Now Andrew smirked. "We've beaten worse odds, Wingmaster, now let's get Rayne and get back to the battle."

"So you breathe fire?" Rayne asked from behind.

Lamassau sounded less than modest. "I'm the only Tritan who can."

Bones snorted. "That's because you're full of hot air."

Sagan cackled.

Andrew heard the roll of Pehton's eyes in her tone. "Ignore these two. Watch this."

A whoosh told Andrew she'd ignited the Siren's Gale, and Rayne's enthusiasm was as infectious as it was missed. "Holy cow! Woman, you are literally on fire! High-five— Douse the flames first!"

Laughter all around.

Korac came over the earpieces, "Dr. Suarez is almost finished with Karter and Chris. Then we'll return to the troops. Over."

Sagan answered him. "On our way." To the people on the mountain, she said, "This has been fun, but I need to check on the mother of my kid. Anyone want off this rock?"

Andrew and Xelan joined them as Sagan opened a conduit. The group lined up to file in. Everyone but—

"I can't go with you."

Rayne.

Andrew frowned, but he let Xelan take the lead here, as he was doing in every Probability. Xelan asked, "Why not?"

Their strongest warrior looked out over the field of dead copies. Her voice sounded so sad as she said, "There are…" She paused as if receiving her next word from an internal source. "Quadrillions of those Weapons across every continent but one in Enki."

They all shared the same wide-eyed, terrified expression as Rayne went on.

"Their bones are made of nacre ore. None of you can break nacre glass, but I can. I have an idea, and I'll need your help."

They listened. When her skin pulsed blue, Xelan took the time to explain Silence's warning about Rayne's nacre expiring. She said, "Well, that's perfect because..." She went on to elaborate how the second countdown worked for her plan.

Once Rayne finished, Andrew pointed out. "This is all contingent on Tameka's return."

Rayne ducked her head, abashed. "I was kinda eavesdropping and overheard you say she was coming back soon." She entreated Xelan. "And I can *feel* it. She's alive and strong. And probably dominating some underground empire, poised to return with reinforcements when we need it most."

Xelan laughed as if he couldn't help it. Those two had that effect on each other. "Fine, but what will keep *you* safe?"

Andrew wondered about that himself. If Rayne positioned herself to destroy Enki using the weapon, then didn't that mean it would destroy her with it?

Rayne insisted, "Well, that's the beauty of it." She paused, as if listening to something, before continuing. "Alone, I don't think I could survive, but with Tameka's ability, I can become strong enough to heal it."

Xelan asked, "How can you be sure?"

Andrew knew the answer. "Because that's what happened when we would train together, right Rayne?"

She beamed at him. "Exactly. I responded to Tameka's ability this way. Almost like it was engineered."

Bones offered, "There's always the chance Operation Gait will destroy Enki."

The King of Earth and Cinder frowned. "Operation Gait?"

Pehton explained, "Matt and Lucy are ensuring half of the broken planet collides with Enki's hull."

Lamassau held out his fist. "Once again, nice one, Seamswalker."

Sagan bumped his fist with a proud grin.

This was Andrew's family in all their continuous potential. He would die to protect them. So he tried his best not to stare at Rayne, and all the swirling Probabilities surrounding her. The light was so bright it blinded him.

Andrew would do anything to keep it from burning out.

{ENKI | NEW CINDER}

How endearing. The Shadow still hadn't learned to look up.

Silence smiled at the family reunion on the mountaintop below. She didn't need to look at Lucas to feel the warmth of his beaming grin beside her. Even Smith, piggy-backing on the Icarus, smirked broader than usual.

With a feline stretch of her blue wings, Silence admitted, "This was worth it."

"We did good," Smith agreed.

Lucas remained quiet. Silence peered at him through her periphery. Her companion's radiant expression had faded to a smile full of longing as he gazed down at one particular member of the Shadow.

When Sagan led Xelan, Pehton, Bones, and Lamassau through the conduit, Andrew lingered behind with Rayne. An intensity amplified between them the longer he stared at her in silence. Answering some wordless question, Rayne nodded, and Andrew seemed satisfied with this. He took one last look at the defeated Weapons littering the plane before turning and slipping through the conduit.

Lucas sighed, and Silence knew it was involuntary. She'd let out a few of them herself.

Smith reached out and chafed his friend's arm. "You'll see him soon, buddy."

The interaction expanded Silence's heart. She'd built this small family and never questioned how it had integrated so well into the Shadow. This was all she ever wanted—

Azure pulsed under Silence's skin at the same time as it pulsed under Rayne's. Her companions shot Silence concerned glances. Softly, she said, "It's fortunate they told her about the deadline. Look how resolute she is."

Rayne hugged herself below, so vulnerable in the midst of the destruction she'd wrought. Silence had been appalled by the Nox and Rayne depositories, given Abresson used the image of her grandson and the woman who slayed him. Even though Imminent manufactured them using Xelan's perfected concept from four thousand years earlier, their likenesses weren't configured until Nox died a few years ago. It only took a software patch of his and Rayne's DNA for the nanites to convert their appearances all across Enki. In Silence's short time among this refurbished Imminent, she noticed Celindria's veiled irritation over the veneers.

Silence understood.

"Look," Lucas called softly and nodded back at the scene.

Smith's smirk was audible beside Silence as Rayne opened her wings once more and ascended. He said, "That's our cue."

"So it is."

Silence and Lucas darted downward before the upward girl noticed them. Alighting on a separate mountain, they watched Rayne fly into the heart of Enki. Something gnawed at Silence. "Where do you get your courage, girl?"

Lucas sounded certain of the truth. "Your grandsons."

Smith gave an approving chuff from Lucas' back.

While Silence agreed some of it was their influence, she knew better. She said softly, "Stardust in her blood and electricity in her eyes. On your death, a world ends with you. Know the stars will fall still and weep for you."

"Amen," Lucas and Smith said at once.

Despite the structural damage, travel through Li Mountain's cave system proved easy enough. They made the journey in companionable silence, no pun intended. In flight, Silence found herself twiddling with the pendant containing Rayne's blood. It had become a comfort, and as they emerged through the conduit to their location, she was glad to have it.

Across the Pantheon's barren tundra, the Vast Collective positioned its armies. Primary Bol would know, and wherever Remorse fled to, they would join forces to distract their mutual enemies from what would take place in Enki's center above.

Smith smiled even as he cursed. "Do they know what they're up against?"

Lucas' laugh was bitter. "How could they?"

They were right. The Shadow were better prepared after talking with Rayne about the Weapons, but nothing could prepare them for the raw experience.

Silence couldn't take her eyes off the conduit to the continent beneath Torrentus. Any minute now...

"Silence, what would you have us do with Fury once she emerges?"

Lucas asked a good question. Tameka was the greatest threat to Silence's happiness, to her life. That and the Atheneum's potential noncompliance. Kyle understood how her life depended on finding Ishkur, but the Shadow were still unaware of what Ishkur was.

Nevertheless, Tameka was Xelan's mate and Pax's mother. Silence said, "No harm can come to Fury. No matter the risk to us."

Approvingly, Lucas said, "Understood."

Smith smiled with his nod. After another moment, he asked, "What will we do with Remorse?"

Lucas answered, "Once they access the bridge, we can use it to locate all beings possessing nacres within Enki, including him and Pax."

Silence gestured at the masses below. "He'll show for this. The Primaries and Abresson will want to witness the trial run in person."

Repositioning on Lucas' back, Smith said, "Oh yeah... Wasn't that rat supposed to evacuate the reserves?"

He was right. The last order Primary Rem had given his subordinate was to evacuate the depositories before Rayne destroyed Enki. This way, Imminent could enforce the New Galactic Order using the Weapons fashioned after her and Nox. Yet, Abresson had retreated from the authentic Rayne and her Nox shadow before successfully migrating the horde.

Lucas said, "We haven't seen a trace of him since he failed earlier."

Smith laughed. "Maybe Remorse finally killed him—"

"Yes." Silence was sure of it. "He'll face his end this day, but the Matrix offers so many Probabilities." She did *not* keep the smile from her face. "Fuck that son of a bitch."

Her companions chuckled. Smith said, "Kyle really rubbed off on you."

The name made her wince, and Lucas reached out to squeeze her bicep. He offered in consolation, "Me, too."

As if summoned, the Progeny with a penchant for memory, stepped through one of Sagan's conduits into the Pantheon. Silence stopped herself from assessing how well the combat suit fitted Kyle's form, how the green in his eyes popped with his brunette curls swept back, and the way his grin held so much hope from recent good news.

"Do you need us to leave you alone with your thoughts?" Smith's voice held too much humor for a deputy in Silence's army.

She drew out the motion of turning her head to glare at him. The wordless expression said enough.

Smith stopped smiling and stared into Silence's eyes, tracing Probabilities for a demise at her hands.

Lucas snickered and broke the tension.

They both nudged him with their elbows.

Eventually, Lucas asked, "Silence in our stars, will you join the battle or spectate from a vantage our simple allies cannot seem to discover?"

Again, a good question.

Below, Iuo and Kyle exchanged a high five, both elated by Rayne's return. It was palpable and contagious. And sad, but that sadness was inevitable.

Decided, Silence announced, "I will intervene when they enter the bridge." Azure pulsed under her skin, and she added in a sad murmur, "I must locate Ishkur."

Smith asked, "And if the Primaries should interfere?"

"I will finish what I started."

{Enki | Tritan Residences}

"So, Lucy, the guards tell me there's some confusion with your background. How about you sit here and explain the situation to me?"

Lucy liked the way Abresson patted on the sofa for her to sit beside him. She liked the white scars on his wrists, and the way they contrasted so starkly against his indigo complexion. When he looked at her, the black vein in his neck fluttered.

Abresson inhaled and muttered, "Lemonade."

Strange how people kept saying that word around Lucy.

Never mind.

This would be a moment she'd never forget. With the chilled drink in hand, Lucy practiced as much poise as possible to unfold her knees and stand, curving her back and presenting her breasts as she did. In her steps toward the couch, she kept her eyes averted and gulped shallow breaths. Nervous. Demure. Even a little terrified.

For who could stand before the powerful Eminent and not tremble?

In her peripheral, Abresson's expression took on a coaxing note as he said, "Now, now, child. Why so timid? Would I offer you a drink if I intended to bite you?"

Lucy knew it was drugged. The smell told her so, like sulfur. She sipped it.

Abresson relaxed and looked pleased. "Good girl." He leaned back with his arm stretched over the back of the sofa. "It's honestly fortunate that you're here. You're the perfect last meal." He snorted into his drink.

Interesting. "I'm s-sorry?" Lucy shivered slightly—not too much—and chafed her arms where goosebumps formed.

After swallowing, Abresson gave a satisfied sigh before elaborating. "My superior… He'll kill me when he learns I've failed him again."

Gently, Lucy tested the boundaries of this interaction. In a soft voice, she asked, "Why is that?"

Staring into his drink as he circled it to make the green liquid swirl, Abresson shrugged. "He has high expectations for me. Too high, I'd say." He gestured over his shoulder at the door. "I regret mistreating the guards. We're all under so much pressure."

Lucy bit her lip and dared to gaze at him directly, eager to hear more. "That seems unfair."

Abresson's smile in return was sad. "Too true. All of us suffered a shock, awakened to learn half our race was decimated. 'Oh, and you're an archivist? Well, here's your gun. Now go to war for our kind.'" He waved incredulously and took another drink. "Fucking Aegis."

Lucy darted her gaze away for a long moment, then looked at him from beneath her lashes. "Do you want to talk about it? I'm not going anywhere."

The chuckle Abresson gave was expectant and knowing. "You're not wrong. Drink up." She took a sip as he sighed heavily and continued. "We're the last of our kind, and we're not even allowed to exist as we wish—"

His words stumbled as Lucy gingerly took his hand.

When Abresson met her eyes next, he looked genuinely startled. She bled sincerity into her eyes, opening them wide enough to let tears start.

He allowed the contact, cleared his throat, and began again. "I worked in the organic stacks, uploading genetic memory for Rem and Quet's experiments into perfecting our race. One day, I discovered a flaw in their coding design. A glitch which prevented the separation of chromosomes. See, Tritans start as males and become females before gestation. In fact, the reverse is intentional. We wanted to ensure female production as much as possible, because eventually we tampered with it so much that we degenerated the chromosome shift."

Yito came over Lucy's earpiece. "Are you staying awake during all that?"

Lucy tried not to smile with the swell of endearment. Her new followers wouldn't let anything happen to her. Instead, she let her genuine interest show. "And I bet you confronted them. I imagine it was a heroic scene."

Abresson smirked with a delectable amount of ego. "Have another sip." She did. Satisfied, he continued. "You're right, of course, but they're Primaries. I was put in my place, dejected..." The Tritan Eminent startled Lucy as he tilted, stretched out on the couch, and laid his head in her lap. "I hope you don't mind?"

Acclimating to the task, Lucy smiled and grazed her nails down his scalp. "Go on."

Pleased, Abresson wriggled until comfortable, which included squishing Lucy's thigh. He sighed heavily again. "That feels nice, Lucy. Don't neglect your drink. Where was I?"

"Dejected."

"Thank you." He gripped her knee and muttered into the bare skin of her thighs. "I mean that. It's been so long since another comforted me. You remind me of my Lena."

Lucy tilted her head curiously to the side and gently pushed. "Lena?"

Again, that heavy sigh. She was starting to wonder if Abresson was clinically depressed. He said, "My pairing ceremony was the next day. A lot of ours were. They're done in batches, you see?"

With a kind expression, she nodded for him to go on.

"Lena was pure and sweet. A biological alchemist. Fantastic, really. She was part of the team which contained the plague responsible for the destruction of our homeworld. Brilliant. I'd wager you're brilliant, too, Lucy. You were on the Gait project, after all." Abresson kissed the top of her thigh.

Lucy kept raking her nails on his skin and noted a faint dizziness. She emphasized the weakness in her voice. "I feel funny."

He patted her leg. "Don't worry. I'll take care of you. Keep drinking."

Paired against Abresson and Razor, Justice Lee was so unambitious. This was true predation. Lucy could taste it.

Abresson carried on, the sound of his voice lulling her further to the abyss which beckoned. "Lena died without us knowing one another as physical partners."

"Virgins?" Lucy sounded loopy without trying. Desperate to maintain her grip, she hummed a tune.

He nodded, his face grazing against her skin. "An old tradition about prolonging the anticipation to further the enjoyment. You call it 'abstinence.' We call it 'the long game.'" The trademark heavy sigh. "My sweet, pure Lena gone in an instant. You can't imagine what it's like. I woke up one hundred and twenty million years after her death. The only consolation Remorse offered me? That I could join their efforts to steal the Aegis's home from within."

Lucy started singing, barely tracking the conversation as her vision blurred.

Abresson remarked, "Your voice is beautiful. Finish your drink—That's right. Bottoms up." He reached up and tilted the glass, forcing her to down it. Then he returned to drawing circles with his long fingers on the inside of her thighs. "Anyway. Primary Rem asked too much of me. Out of any of us. We never had time to grieve, and they refused to let us help brainstorm options to recover our race." The Sigh. "We'll die out before too long—Hey, is that a *Night Rayne* song. I like that one. Has anyone ever told you, you sound exactly like her? You know that crazy bitch killed a whole... bunch of... fans..."

Voids and mouth open wide, Abresson shifted and looked Lucy in the eyes. "You!"

Lucy wanted to say something cool and dramatic like, "This is for T.A.O., Oleen, and John," but she barely had enough energy in her to shove the glass in Abresson's mouth and pounded it in. Black blood geysered into it along with the sound of his screams. The Tritan's body jerked and convulsed. He flailed, grabbing her everywhere.

Cold, so very cold—

With a violent lunge, Lucy rolled Abresson onto the floor, quickly pooling with his blood. With all the strength in her, she stomped on his right elbow. A muffled shriek and gargling followed into the glass lodged in his face, and he stopped grabbing with that hand. She repeated the process on his left arm, disabling his ability. His knees, too, out of thoroughness.

Abresson rolled over in tears, blood gushing from every orifice. He twitched and flinched from the pain. Screamed and shouted incoherently for the guards.

But they listened to Lucy now, and she'd ordered them to stay outside no matter what they heard. Still, she wasn't completely devoid of compassion. She lowered her face closer to Abresson's and said, "I'm sorry about your race. I don't know why, but your story touched me, much like you did. So I'll escort you out of this life with one assurance. The Shadow is freeing the innocent Tritans. Your guards and techs are coming with us. No more war for people not meant to be soldiers. You can go now, Abresson. You're dismissed."

Abresson's spine bowed, and Lucy took it as an invitation. One fist through the chest, and she gripped his nacre. He fell flat when she ripped it out.

One less monster in the galaxy—

Lucy toppled back onto the floor. Into her earpiece, she urged, "Yito, Praw. I need help. Abresson attacked me like you said he would, but I killed him. Not before he drugged me, though—"

They'd already burst through the door. "Lucy?!"

"Here!" Despite her attempt to shout, her voice was so faint.

Praw's voids widened when he discovered Abresson. He looked from the dead Eminent to Lucy covered in Tritan blood and back again, sniffed the air, and narrowed his voids. "That's some impressive self-defense. There's not a scratch on you."

Lucy's lashes fluttered, barely holding on.

Yito checked her pulse. "It's faint. She's going under."

Praw sighed in surrender and scooped her up. "Dolton, check in with Eminent Lance."

The other Tritan stepped out of the room, muttering, "Come in, Eminent. What's your progress with those pods? Over."

It was all more commotion than Lucy could follow. "So... heavy..."

Yito brushed Lucy's hair from her eyes. "What next, Morning Star?"

"...Matt... Save... Matt..."

Yito grinned. "You got it, Lemonade."

FOUR

RELIEF ANCHORED BY HARD DECISIONS

{ENKI | MEDICAL BAY}

WOULD KARTER WANT KORAC FOR A SON?

The question scraped at the Icarean General's skull no matter how hard he tried to ignore it. His knee bounced with it as he sat, waiting for his mother to regain consciousness. Chris, too, and that was a separate consideration. Was the human equivalent to a step-father for Korac? Or was Para more qualified? How did this family thing work?

A heavy sigh left him.

"Uncertainty left you bare in new birth."

Beside Korac, T.A.O. was her own kind of helpful. Her cryptic language in madness contributed gentle insights here and there, reminding him she was fully alert in that twisted labyrinth of her mind.

He looked away from the hands steepled in his lap and gave T.A.O. his full attention. She smiled sweetly at Korac. He said, "Damn, I missed your disarming fae-ish ways."

Something caught T.A.O.'s attention behind him, her Atramentous eyes flicked to it while she said, "Not every second. Not by half."

A bustle erupted behind him, and Korac whirled to find Sagan smashing into him. She fell on him so haphazardly it sent him crashing back into the chair, holding her steady. He chuckled at the welcome distraction. "Aren't you supposed to shout 'incoming' before barreling at me like a missile—Hey, what's wrong?"

Sagan trembled with a sob, and it cracked her voice as she said, "I held her. I held her for an entire minute. How long did I cost her?"

Rayne.

Korac smoothed his hand along Sagan's back and kissed under her ear. "Shh... I know it was worth it." He opened his eyes to see Xelan step from the conduit.

Before his Prince could hide it, Korac glimpsed the graveness in Xelan's eyes. Then the martyr-Icarus plastered on a grin before Andrew, Bones, and Lamassau followed him into the Medical Bay. The Prince confirmed, "It was worth *every* second, and there will be more seconds, Sagan."

Andrew darted a wary glance at their leader. The knowledge behind the look filled Korac with further anxiety. As if he needed more.

Did Andrew know something the others didn't—

Sagan squeezed Korac, speaking into his chest. "I hope so, too, Xelan. Until then, I'm just gonna hang on to my General, if that's okay?"

The vein in Xelan's forehead pulsed faintly, but he agreed. "Do what you need to do. I'll be ready to leave once I talk to Pablo." He disappeared into the main bay.

Lamassau addressed Korac as he nodded at T.A.O. "Do you mind if we trade Seamswalkers for a bit? We need to check on Tumi and Torrentus."

T.A.O. peered up at him from where she sat, turning her head this way and that.

Could she see him in the Probability Matrix since Razor exposed her to Cascading Light? Was she sifting through a million instances of the green Tritan to discern his place in her grasp on this reality?

Korac muttered to her, "Will you go with them?"

"Toasty toes?"

Bones audibly strained to contain his laughter, but gave up in the end at the sight of Lamassau's nonplussed frown.

Andrew winked at her. "Toasty toes. And soon."

They shared some freaky Matrix connection before T.A.O. hopped to her feet. "Ready. More seconds to count. Down they go. Not much longer."

Triss screeched loud enough for the sound to careen like ricochet throughout every bay.

Korac shifted his and Sagan's axes slightly to help with their embrace, while he brushed her hair soothingly with his fingers. Mostly, he was shifting the pocket beneath her in his robes to hide the contents inside. Waiting to ask Sagan was wreaking havoc with Korac's nerves, but the right moment would come—

Xelan hurried around the corner. "Karter's awake. Para said she's asking for you."

Urgently, Korac and Sagan sat up together and rushed to the bay's entrance. Xelan waited, watching with a warm smile on his face. Before taking the corner, Korac hesitated, and the two Icari locked gazes.

For all his existence, Korac had wanted to find his people and where he'd come from. The closest he'd ever had to finding a family was on Cinder. The Princes, specifically the youngest Prince, contributed to that belonging.

But after Gait, everything had changed. Korac had a father, currently residing inside him. And a mother, waiting for him upstairs.

Xelan was there for all of it. Tears shone in the Prince of Cinder's eyes. He nodded and gripped Korac's shoulder. "She's waiting for you."

Korac swallowed, and when a tiny hand squeezed his, he turned and smiled down at Sagan's teary eyes. "Let's go and meet her properly."

T.A.O. nodded beyond Sagan.

Yes.

Taking the stairs two at a time, Korac reached the top of the bay first. Sagan followed. Xelan remained downstairs.

Para sat on the end of Karter's bed, catching the taller woman up on all the Shadow news. " . . . and Jack can fly now. He's so strong, Karter. You'd be proud. I think Ross is, if you know what I mean—Oh, hey, Korac. Sagan. C'mon over."

Karter's deep gray skin shimmered with the nacre filament implants from a previous near-death experience. It took away from the frailty of her lying in an infirmary bed. That and her substantial muscle mass paired with her height. She always was a force to be reckoned with.

Korac's mother turned and smiled a thousand-watt beam at him, half-green, half-black eyes sparkling. He didn't realize he'd squeezed Sagan's hand until she returned the gesture.

Composure.

This wasn't completely unfamiliar territory to Korac. Karter had practically raised him with Para and Savis. She was always a warm presence in his memory, but this moment felt monumental, and something shifted inside of him.

Sagan climbed all the way on her tip-toes to whisper at his jaw, not quite tall enough to reach his ear. "I'll check on Triss."

Perfect understanding.

Korac brought her fingers to his lips and kissed her knuckles, grateful. Sagan walked away, holding his hand until their arms reached for each other, breaking only when she descended the stairs.

Para looked between Karter and Korac before leaning down and kissing the former's cheek. "I'll check on Bones before he goes with Xelan. Give you two some privacy."

Karter smiled her gratitude, and her gaze lingered on Para's short-clad ass the whole way out. "I love watching that female move."

Korac barked out a laugh, completely unexpected. His mother was an addict. "Well, that's a weight off my shoulders." He moved around some pods to her bedside.

"How is that?" Her eyes watched him with a gentleness he feared.

He swallowed before answering, "You two are the longest lasting relationship I've ever known. It's a record to beat."

Her laughter was soft and warm. It ended with an affectionate tone. "You couldn't have chosen a more worthy female."

Korac shook his head. "She chose me, and every day I thank Elden for it." He flipped his hair over his shoulder to give his words a cavalier air, but there was no taking the weight from them. "I love her."

Karter beamed. "Trust me. The entire Vast Collective knows." Again, that laugh. "Will you union with her?"

Korac gave a conspiratorial look left, then right. All clear. He retrieved the nacre glass box from his pocket and held it out for Karter to see.

With a gasp, Karter reached for the ring. "An Earth custom. How touching. But isn't that...?"

With a smirk, he nodded. "Yes. Yes, it is. Of course, I wanted it to dazzle her."

"Oh, it certainly will. It took my breath away."

As the subject of his love for Sagan dissipated between them, the gravity of everything else consumed the conversation.

"I wish I'd known—"

"I think I felt it from the start—"

They both spoke at once, stared at each other in their pause, and laughed. It stretched into a long moment, rich with their memories of each other. Karter lifted her hand out to him, and he clasped it in his, gripping as warriors do.

She mused, "All those times I utterly destroyed you in our sparring matches..."

He shook his head in good humor and reminded her, "I suppose you'll take genetic credit for all the times I defeated you as well."

"You know it."

Leaning over her, Korac's hair fell into his face again. Karter reached with her free hand to brush it back. "My son..."

He prided himself on his composure, his facade, but with only Karter here...

A tear fell on her combat suit, and it was Korac's. "Mother."

Karter sat up and wrapped her arms around him.

That was it.

The Vacating, losing Nox, damned near losing Xelan forever, confronting Razor, reliving his past, Sagan's distress—

The dam unlocked, and Korac cried into his mother's caring embrace. Like earlier with Sagan, Karter smoothed her hand down his hair, soothing.

Abruptly, he pulled away from Karter and scanned her face. "Are you all right? Did they hurt you? I'll kill Remorse, myself—"

"Shh. Shh. I'm all right, son. Silence protected us."

That's right. Para and T.A.O. had told them so. It was hard to believe, Silence being the mother of Imminent and all that, but damned if Korac didn't owe her some gratitude. "Good."

They both turned and peered at the pod beside them as if its occupant had uttered a sound.

Korac nodded at Chris, still unconscious. "Is he yours?"

Karter smiled brilliantly at her human lover. "He is."

"I suppose he's a worthy mate?" Funny how finding out she was his mother suddenly made him protective of her.

The warmth in her eyes made it all better. "I wouldn't tolerate anything less. Plus, Para likes him. We'll need a big house once we win this war." With that, Karter made to stand.

Korac stepped back. "You're joining the campaign?"

Sheer confidence greeted him in her grin. "There's no way I'm missing this." She looked over at Chris. "I want to wait until he wakes, but I'm afraid he'll insist on enlisting."

With a frown, Korac asked, "Is that a problem?"

Her voice was soft as she said, "He suffered more than the rest of us. I worry about him *here*." She touched a hand over her chest.

Korac took Karter's free hand and sighed. "Stay with Chris."

She frowned. "The battle—"

"That's an order."

The Valkyrie came to attention with a disappointed frown.

Korac stared at her hand and its unnatural glint. "Don't leave him. If my mental health had suffered the way his has, I wouldn't want to wake without Sagan here. Then, after he clears with Dr. Suarez, you can both join. You should have your revenge together."

The click of her tongue brought Korac's eyes back to Karter's face. She looked so put-out, and with a roll of her eyes, she said, "Fine. But don't think you get to order your mother around more than once a century, child. I brought you into this world..."

"I'm the Atheneum, remember, mother? It'll take more than you to take me out."

"Keep pushing, son. We'll see."

"I can't wait... mom."

{ENKI | MEDICAL BAY}

Sagan stood on the stairs between the bays, letting Korac have a moment with his mother while Sagan took one for herself.

So many conduits were open, and she could feel the souls tramping through each one. Eager boots, some barefoot, and some on wings—All of them her responsibility. Sagan's bones were weary with it, her head heavy from it, and her heart was beating fainter for it. Not to mention—

"I'm starving."

The last of her food was in Korac's robes after Sagan depleted her own pocket reserves—

Someone whistled.

Below, Xelan stood at the foot of the stairs like a sentinel—One who was holding a Yun chocolate and nut nutrition ration. It was like a gourmet MRE.

Sagan might have drooled as Xelan nodded for her to come get it. "Thank you!" She was halfway down the stairs before a thought occurred to her. "Aren't you supposed to go with Lam to watch for Tameka's signal? After all, Rayne's crazy plan won't work without her."

Xelan's eyes flickered with reproach—caught.

Sagan figured it out and pointed at him. Her voice was a hoarse whisper as she accused, "You stayed to check on Korac, didn't you?"

He made a show of adjusting the collar, lapels, and sleeves of his straight-up pirate frock. "I have no idea what you're talking about." He refused to look at her.

Sagan laughed, and oh yes, it sounded like a witch's cackle. It softened when she saw how exposed he looked. Her mentor was stripped bare and left vulnerable. "Don't worry. I won't tell." She reached for the nutrition ration—

Xelan snatched it and dangled it high above her. Curse Icarean royalty and their tippy-toed tallness. He raised a brow at her. Serious, but not serious. "Promise?"

Sagan leveled her flat gaze at him. "I promise. You act like I don't already keep a Verse's worth of your secrets—Oooh!" The bag fell in her hand. "Thank you."

Xelan ruffled her hair and made to turn away.

"Xelan?" Sagan stopped him.

He paused and looked over his shoulder, really hamming up this new look of his. Before they knew it, he'd commandeer a tricorne from an Enki museum or something.

She suppressed the need to laugh, because what she wanted to know wasn't funny at all. So her voice was soft, unsure, when she asked, "Do you think Rayne can manipulate the Weapon like she described?"

Again, something flickered in Xelan's eyes, but Sagan didn't catch it this time as he said, "She told us Elden taught her the techniques needed to do so. I trust her." Those eyes narrowed, and his foundation sounded less solid when he asked, "Why? Don't you?"

That was a hard question to answer. In the years since Xelan had passed, Rayne acted more independently from the Shadow. She was with them—yes, always—but more like every move she made protected them. Even if it meant isolating herself. No—Especially so.

How does one trust a martyr?

Trust.

"I trust her to save the Vast Collective..."

Xelan searched Sagan's eyes. "But?"

Damn, he was quick, or she was that transparent.

Sagan swallowed, considering her words. How did she voice this flaw of her dearest friend and partner? "Well, it's just that Rayne—"

"Para, mother wants to see—Oh. You two are just standing down here, stalking me." Korac finished gliding down the stairs, folded his arms to lean against the threshold, and smirked.

Frustrated, Xelan threw his hands in the air. "I am *not* stalking you!" When he winked at Sagan, she laughed almost involuntarily at how unexpected it was in contrast to their previous topic. He kissed her forehead before turning to walk away. Xelan waved as he said, "I'm heading to Cinder's Shrine. Tameka will call soon."

"Damn right she will," Korac muttered under his breath, watching the other man go. He shook himself and warmed his smirk for Sagan. "How's my girl?"

"Well, Triss is in a lot of pain. She still won't let me into the delivery tier. Pablo says it's taking a while, but Echo will be here—"

A pale finger to her lips stopped Sagan from finishing the update. She peered curiously up at Korac in a way that made her eyes cross.

He chuckled and lowered his hand. "I meant *you*. How are you? Lil amos will need another nickname, so I can better distinguish between the two of you in our sprawling mountain lodge—"

Sagan gaped at him. She couldn't help it. Not since before learning Razor was his brother had Korac spoken that many words in such a lighthearted tone. Frankly, she was more than a little affected—

Korac's eyes closed, and he inhaled gently. When he opened them, his eyes had shifted into Atramentous. On a soft growl, he said, "Watermelon."

Assume the position.

As Korac surged toward Sagan, she backed against the wall, wrists up for him to pin them. She purred when the exposed skin of her back met the cold material. He lifted her leg to wrap around his ass before he leaned down for a kiss—

"I want everyone to see what it looks like at the heart of Enki."

Rayne.

"It's like being in the center of a beach ball with every stripe alternating a continent and an ocean. The shrines are completely invisible as far as I can see. Then there's the star... It's still several million miles away, but I can feel its warmth from here."

Sagan choked back a whimper. There were too many conflicting emotions. Triss was dying upstairs, but at least Echo was on the way. No one knew if Tameka was alive, but everyone talked about her as if she were on her way back to them. Remorse stole Pax, but Celindria died.

That last one felt hollow.

Sagan expected the First Progeny to die with more of a galactic-destroying bang, but Xelan assured them all the waves of Cascading Light's effects were her last breaths.

Then there was Rayne.

Korac gently set Sagan straight and kissed the top of her head. "She comes first."

"Actually, Rayne's really generous—Oh, you mean..."

His smile was the wryest of the wry, and Sagan felt all the blood rush to her cheeks—

"You gave everyone a hug but me."

Kyle's complaint over the earpiece, and the whine with it, made Korac bark out a laugh and Sagan snort into her hand.

"Watch this." With a wink, Korac said into the earpiece. "Your majesty, this is Silver General. I just want the Porn

Baron to mark for the record that I also did *not* receive a hug. Over."

Iuo responded, "Roger that, Silver General. I will also note for the record that I have yet to receive one, your majesty. Over."

A "humph" came across the line, which could only mean Caedes was left hug-less as well.

On the mic, Pehton said, "Don't worry, Master Graveller. I plan to give you one. Over."

The secondhand thrill exhilarated Sagan into punching the air. "Yes! They're official!"

Korac grinned, more with mischief than with excitement.

Sagan asked, "Are you looking forward to giving Pehton shit?"

"Oh, yes."

Sagan shoved her hands in her pockets to keep from touching him further. Playful swatting could so easily turn into inappropriately timed caressing, moving lower—

Her hand found the dossier drive from Razor buried in there, a reminder of their journey so far. She asked, "Do you think this will work on the bridge?"

Korac peered at it, his voice filled with suspicion. "What could be on it to require this much security?"

Sagan shrugged, uncertain, and shoved it back into her pocket. "Razor said all of Imminent's secrets, but for all I know, it's the recipe to Colton's cheesecake—"

"Seamswalker, come in. This is War King on your private channel."

Sagan straightened and mouthed, "Rayne," to Korac before answering, "Go ahead."

Despite flying an astronomical unit in an hour, Rayne sounded unaffected and rather serene. "Sorry for the intrusion, but I don't want to disturb the others from their work." *Martyrs gonna mart.* "I'm as close to the center of Enki without making best friends with the nameless star. As it turns out, that's right outside the shrine to Thailea. Can you locate me?" A pause followed before she added, "Oh yeah. I forgot to say 'Over.' Over."

Korac chuffed and smirked at Sagan, who looked a question at him. "Go to her."

She motioned a finger between them. "I plan to finish what we started."

"Take from me what you need."

Sagan Seamswalked into space. Proper, middle of nowhere, nothing but the edges of Enki stretched far on the horizon—Space. No Rayne either. Into her private channel, Sagan mused, "Do you have any idea how hard it'll be to find you? Can you describe a specific speck of space dust for me? Over." She poofed, attempting another location.

Rayne giggled. "I have every faith you'll—"

Sagan poofed beside her and opened her black wings.

"—manage." Rayne grinned. "Hey, gorgeous. Nice outfit. Sorry I didn't say anything earlier. You know? Mixed company. I hate making Wingmaster blush."

Unable to help herself, Sagan *did* blush. "Right back at you. Hey, where's Night Killer?"

Rayne gave a cavalier shrug. "I stored it."

With a crinkle of her nose, Sagan said, "Actually, it's kinda odd your outfit coordinates with the rest of the Shadow."

"I noticed." Rayne's grin dimmed to a sad smile. "I owe many people hugs."

Sagan stamped her foot in space. "Stop that. You know what Tameka would say about it."

Waving her off, Rayne said, "Yeah, yeah. 'Get off your cross.'" She snickered. "I *do* owe her a hug."

With a smile at her girlfriend, Sagan circled slowly to take in the scenery. "Elden, it's beautiful. Too bad you have to destroy it—Hey, how are we breathing?"

Abruptly, Rayne's eyes faded in their brilliance as she went off somewhere in her head to return with the answer. "The nanite field converts any nearby gases into oxygen. We happen to be in a nitrogen cloud. The field is also keeping us warm."

Sagan nodded along, tracking. "So once Tameka starts powering you up, your field could convert all of Enki into atmosphere."

Again, that distant look before she said, "You're right, but that's obviously not what we're up to. The Weapon will likely do the opposite and burn all the gases."

That kinda dampened the fun space talk.

Sagan changed the subject. "I found you, so now we can make sure Tameka does, too. I can also Seamswalk you out when it's time to escape." She laughed. "It'll probably be one of those close, down-to-the-wire, cinematic moments."

Rayne smiled. "Something like that." Then she buffeted her wings, bringing her closer as she asked, "I have an idea which might help, but I need to speak to Elden alone."

That tilted Sagan's head. "How...?"

"Can you open a conduit to the nacre chamber for me? I know you're overtaxed with all the others—"

Sagan opened the conduit beside them. "If it's important enough for *you* to ask me for help, I'll always give it, Rayne. Always."

Rayne swallowed hard and couldn't seem to form words. She simply nodded on her way through the conduit. Sagan lingered outside, musing about their first time in Enki. How the sight of it without a nacre left all the Progeny dizzy. Now, she was in the heart of the Dyson's Sphere and in awe of the sheer ingenuity.

Sagan couldn't wait for Tameka to return and see Rayne. Then she'd bring Kyle and Andrew up here. All of them together.

While she waited, she munched on the Yun nutrition ration. Perfect chocolate with a hint of something close to Earth espresso. Would this be enough? All those conduits tugged at Sagan's limits. Her ability had gloriously blossomed over the last few years, but she wasn't a goddess. No matter what Korac said in bed—

"Thanks for that. I think it'll do the trick." Rayne stared at the bag of food, and her stomach growled loud enough for Sagan to hear in the vacuum of space. "Is that chocolate?"

Sagan laughed and held out the bag to her bestie. "How long has it been since you ate anything?"

Rayne shrugged. "The Martyr Complex kept me hydrated and nourished—Oh my god." She closed her eyes and moaned. "This is so good."

"Xelan demanded you wake up when he first found you like that." Sagan blurted the words out with little thought, but was glad she told her. "He—I've never heard a sound like the one he made."

Rayne looked away. "I... can't imagine it."

"I'm naming our daughter 'Echo.' I have a slight crush on my mother-in-law. And I know what Nox did to you."

Sagan's confessions made Rayne look up. Her voice was soft, almost lost to the vast nothing around them. "I know you do. You told me in Korac's Verse." Softer, she said, "That was between Nox and I."

Sagan frowned. "I'm sorry. I hate knowing without telling you, and since reading all these Verses, I'm so confused about it. If Nox had resurrected instead of Xelan, I'd want to kill him all over again or leave him in an infinite conduit loop. But the Icarus he was to Korac... and the way he wrote to you... Rayne, I don't know how you manage your confusion."

Okay. Enough with the prying confessions. Sagan stopped herself from blurting out more things she wanted to say over the last few years and examined her girlfriend.

Rayne floated within the abyss, not alone and afraid, but with love constellated in her bright blue eyes. She smiled, and it was brilliant. "I think you'll find I'm less confused than I ought to be, but don't let that upset you. I want to meet Echo and I can't believe you named your daughter after me. I feel all honored and shit. What does Korac think of it?"

No hesitation. "He loves it."

The smile crooked into a smirk, confident enough to give Korac a run for his credits. "I'd like to have a few words with him before he goes off and asks you to marry him. You know? Lay down a few ground rules. Like, whenever we're admiring a beautiful view in space, I get to kiss you."

Rayne buffeted closer, cupped Sagan's neck with both hands, and brought their lips together. Soft and sure, Rayne's kiss took Sagan's breath away. After a few seconds, they separated by only centimeters, enough to appease the fuse.

To that end, a tear rolled down Rayne's cheek. "Worth it." Azure pulsed under her skin, and another tear fell. "You need to get back to the others."

Now Sagan was crying. "I wish I could stay with you."

Rayne shook her head. "You won't miss anything up here. All the action is happening down there. And I'll see you again when you bring Tameka. I owe her a hug, remember?"

Sagan fought against the lump in her throat to get the words out. "I love you." A conduit opened behind her.

"I've never and will never love anyone more than you, Sagan. I'll see you soon."

When Sagan stepped back into the conduit and it began to close, she swore Rayne started talking to her shadow cast by Enki's sun.

{ENKI | TORRENTUS}

Tameka faced a hurricane. It was wet and windy. Especially sixty-five feet into the torrent. She stood in the fleshy palm of Torch's hand, wondering if the treads of her combat boots were uncomfortable on his pitch-black skin. She hazarded a glance back at the half-Lyrik, half-Gargantuan Tritan to check.

With those narrowed sapphires of his, Torch frowned as he concentrated on the fire barrier engulfing them. A gift from his mother.

Tameka grinned. She couldn't wait to bring Pehton's children home, and she hoped Caedes was looking forward to co-opting Pehton. Time spent with the new boyfriend and time spent with the lost children. It sounded complicated, but Tameka had a feeling the Lyriki General would make it work.

With a natural affinity for it, Aria decompressed to her full height and bent to scoop Aya in her hand. With more ease than her brother, the Siren's gale formed around her.

Wow.

Both Gargantuan Lyriks flared blue gliders, closed their hands around their precious cargo, and flew into the storm. Northeast, specifically. They were headed for the eye of Torrentus. The Siren's Gale evaporated the stinging rains and shielded against the winds. While they ascended, Tameka prayed to Elden Xelan and Korac had ordered the troops into the Pantheon. That they found Rayne. And mostly, that they killed Celindria and rescued Pax.

Tameka also hoped Lucy and the Medical Bay distracted Enki's defenses enough to let the armies gather and allowed Lance to free the innocent Tritans from their pods before Enki suffered a major remodel.

"Your thoughts take you far from here," Torch observed.

Tameka shrugged. "It's a coping mechanism."

The Gargantuan Lyrik smiled at her, and she wasn't even as tall as one sharp tooth.

A thought occurred to her. "Why haven't you tried to fly through the conduit?"

He shook his massive head. "So high, even our shields cannot shelter against the winds. We faltered."

Tameka peered at him, curious. "But you said you've been to the eye before?"

Torch nodded. "Amber glass and circuitry. Lower altitude than the conduit. You'll see. We will arrive shortly."

The strain around his bejeweled eyes told Tameka he was struggling to concentrate against the winds. She settled securely into his palm and abated from asking further questions.

Not long after, the rain stopped, the wind ceased, and an eerie silence settled in Tameka's ears. She could hear her heartbeat for the first time since falling through the conduit.

The Sirens' Gale abated, and Torch announced, "Welcome to the eye of the beast."

Aria emerged beside him through the bands of rain and peered serenely as she relieved herself of the Siren's Gale. They all stared at the round wall of cumulus clouds before gazing at the nacre-glass sphere in its center.

Tameka asked, "How long ago did you discover it?"

Aya answered for her gods. "Not long after all the children matured. Aria and Torch discovered it on their own."

Torch swooped below the sphere, and Aria followed. The segments of the sphere weren't sealed. They flew inside it, and Tameka could make more sense of the situation.

Black fire was spilling in an infinite cascade in the center.

She swallowed before asking, "You touched it, yes?" The two giants set down their charges.

Torch and Aria nodded. Him, with an amused lilt to his lips, and her, with placid composure.

Tameka wasn't sure what to think of that. So far, everyone involved with Cascading Light was a villain to some degree. But there were exceptions, such as Andrew, who obviously fought on the side of good. And Pax...

Tameka sighed.

Aya reached out to touch the flames, and Aria stopped her with a touch of her hand. She shook her head, and for the first time, the serenity faded. There was sadness in those sapphire eyes.

The Caprent girl saw it and lowered her hand with a gentle smile for her deity.

This was too much, and Tameka pushed it all aside to focus. She stepped through a hallway and almost walked through the finest filament she'd ever seen. Wires so thin they were sheer, stretched floor to ceiling along the amber-glass corridor. Tameka narrowed her eyes and caught the light glint on the near-invisible material. She almost gasped. "Gold."

"Arteries."

Torch had shrunk to seven feet before peering around the corner at Tameka.

Arteries.

Veins.

Tameka called, "Aria, with Aya. Be ready for the Siren's Gale. Torch, with me."

He glided up next to her and peered down at her, blinking. "What will you do?"

She bit her lip before saying, "I want to feel its heartbeat."

Tameka didn't need a mirror to know her eyes went Atramentous. She felt it when her ability coursed through her. The well opened. Through it, she sought a source. What made Torrentus breathe?

Beside, her Torch lit like a beacon. A source of unspeakable energy, and it nearly blinded her.

Focus.

This was Torrentus' nacre.

Gently, Tameka reached out and touched one circuit—

The floor beneath them trembled, and the sky cried. Torrentus felt... sick.

Tameka muttered to the creature, "What's wrong? Tell me. Let me help you."

Again, the sad wail in the atmosphere.

It was drained. Someone had already emptied the impressive creature of its nacre energy.

Tameka knew what to do. "Torch?"

"Yes, Fury?"

How did he know—

Curse Cascading Light.

Tameka's voice came out in three pitches. "Tell Aria and Aya to hang on."

Torch asked with naked curiosity. "What ails the beast?"

"It's hungry, and I'm about to feed it."

That got him moving. He went into the main chamber with the others while Tameka reached out and gently gripped the circuits like strings on a harp. This might be an uncharted continent, but they were still inside Enki.

Tameka reached out to a star she knew well and came to love, and siphoned its nearly endless energy. With her eyes closed, she transferred it through her fingers into the golden circuits of Torrentus and opened a channel through her.

After two heartbeats, the sky groaned.

More.

Tameka fed the light of the sun into the eye of the storm.

Torch called through the Cascading Light chamber. "It moves!"

Yes, it did.

The violence of the wind buffeting her hair lessened, and the air smelled different. Less of ozone and rain, more of... fresh air. All around them, the barrier of cumulus clouds thinned. No longer a hurricane, reduced to a summer rain.

There's the signal, Xelan.

Torrentus was replenished and returned to terraforming the continent, determined to finish its purpose.

Tameka muttered, "Malfunction my ass."

Aria stepped into the room, followed by her brother and Aya. All of them shared a similar trait in their expressions: hope.

In three pitches, Tameka ordered, "Get your people. I'm taking you home."

Now it was time to locate the bridge.

{ENKI | PANTHEON}

Kyle knew without looking that Silence, Lucas, and Smith were hovering above the Pantheon. He could feel the familiarity of her memories and the presence of theirs beside her.

Why didn't he alert someone?

Because Kyle was waiting to talk to Andrew about it while they reaffirmed his purchase on this Probability.

So now, inside Andrew's memory scape was the right time. Only...

In this panel of his memories, Andrew held Rayne with the warmth from her magnesium field. It was uncomfortable, but so important. Softly, Andrew admitted, "She's almost too brilliant to touch."

Staring at it, Kyle muttered, "She always was just outside of arm's reach." He finally blinked and looked away, still keeping his eyes from meeting Andrew's gaze. "Hey, man. I've been meaning to say something but—"

"Silence, Lucas, and Smith are watching us." Andrew did not sound alarmed.

It made Kyle search his best friend's—really, his brother's—eyes. There, he found the answer to his next question. "Oh . . . " Of course. "In how many Probabilities are they up there?"

"One."

The finality in Andrew's voice sent a chill down Kyle's spine. One? "Shit."

Andrew nodded his agreement and sighed heavily. A sigh Kyle really identified with. Andrew said, "I keep trying to test it with my coin, but . . . I think I'm too close."

Right.

A thought occurred to Kyle. "Do you think that's why they're up there? Because they know you wouldn't be able to hunt for concrete outcomes?"

Andrew shrugged, and it was sad. "I don't know."

Kyle wanted to rally his brother. To assure him Silence and Lucas were capable of better than that and would never mistreat them that way. That they both came to their senses when they protected Para and Karter and set Rayne free.

But when Kyle opened his mouth, no words came out.

Instead, Andrew wondered aloud a question they'd all been thinking. "What did they gain by letting Rayne out? Why would Imminent bring her here in the first place?"

It was Kyle's turn to shrug, maybe a little sadly. He said, "You know? They want the big boom, and they want her to die with it."

Andrew's eyes widened at the same time as Kyle's, and they both blurted, "They want *us* to die with it."

The memory scape bled away into bright white surroundings and the milling of armies around them.

"It's about time you two came out."

Andrew and Kyle startled and whirled to find a teary-eyed Sagan standing over them. They sat, surrounded by soldiers in the center of the battleground, near one of her conduits. She pointed at it with her thumb. "C'mon. Xelan wants us all there for Tameka's signal."

Been there. Done that. Still freaking out over it.

Andrew took her hand, stood, and looked down at Kyle. "This time it's for real."

Ah. Matrix knowledge. Kyle took both their hands, and they pulled him off the ground. "Let's do this. Again."

It *did* feel different this time.

F8, Pehton, Iuo, Legir, X, Kombuchi, Lamassau, Tumu, and Xelan all waited at the window.

They were the people to inform of Silence's presence. Kyle glanced over at Andrew to find him staring back. He shook his head as if to answer the question Kyle had yet to ask.

Not yet.

"What's bothering you?" Lamassau asked when he nudged Kyle.

Deflect. Kyle rubbed the back of his neck awkwardly and came up with a lame cover. "Just a little overwhelmed is all. What with the billions of people swapping places here and there. I'm not even sure what I should be doing."

Pehton humphed like she was her boyfriend or something. "No shit. I'm making things up as I go."

"That's not exactly a mindset we want to share in front of our allies, Warden." Warm humor lightened Tumu's words. "Scratch that from the record, Iuo."

"Hah! No way." They all turned to look at the Lamian Prince, recording on his stenography device. "I want history to know Imminent lost control of the Vast Collective to this confused band of fugitives."

Kyle noticed Xelan's grin broaden. He was proud of them, and it affected Kyle despite their usual differences.

Rayne was back. Tameka was apparently on her way any minute. Things were looking up for team Shadow.

"Amos, I'm ready. Over and out."

Sagan opened a conduit, and Korac stepped through. Although he muttered for her ears only, Kyle couldn't help but overhear. "You're right. Triss won't let us in. Pablo says any minute now."

A smile tugged at Kyle's lips. Sagan would make an exceptional mother. Still a little iffy as to Korac for a father, but the daughter of Triss and Razor could certainly do worse for a paternal figure—

"Rayne says she wants to have a word with you," Sagan whispered to Korac.

"No." Kyle didn't care if he was being rude. "There's no way you get to see her before I do."

Pehton laughed, incredulous. Andrew groaned and rolled his eyes. Xelan, Tumu, and Lamassau all ignored him. F8 watched the interactions with barely veiled curiosity. Kombuchi, Iuo, X, and Legir had already placed bets on which "K" would see her first.

That reminded Kyle. Gently—oh, so gently—he skimmed Sagan's most recent memory of Rayne—

And shut it right the hell down.

Kyle's ears burned, and he kinda wanted to apologize for intruding on that intense kiss—

The people in the shrine stopped snickering and fidgeting to collectively stare at F8. The Monarch 3 Queen took a step toward the window. Then another.

Xelan peered at her as she passed him. "F8?"

Tumu frowned with his lack of prominent features and also took a step forward, staring out the window.

Were they seeing something Kyle had missed? And Xelan—

Nope, Wingmaster saw it, too. He had the same expression on his face, head full tilt, staring sideways at the view.

"There!" Sagan cried, pointed, and jumped up and down.

The eye of Torrentus... it moved.

Which could only mean that Tameka was alive and taming a hurricane.

{ENKI | MEDICAL BAY}

Curse the Aegis delivery for preventing a Cesarean. Pablo clenched his jaw to keep from swearing. Triss was bleeding faster than Bethany could transfuse, and their supply of Aegis blood wasn't eternal.

C'mon, baby Echo, crown.

A cloth touched his forehead. Pablo refused to look away, but he gave a grateful nod to whoever dabbed at the sweat.

And there *was* sweat.

The salt of it stung his eyes, which was something Pablo hadn't experienced since receiving his nacre. Unless he wanted to count the extremely exerting sex with Lynn involving a trapeze before Sagan Seamswalked in and made it one of the funniest memories of Pablo's life.

To this day, Sagan still stopped him now and then to ask, "But how?"

Triss screamed and drew Pablo's attention back from those more pleasant thoughts. Retreats from his present stress.

Elden, there was so much blood. Yellow and orange mixed and dripped from his elbows. The air smelled of kerosene and potassium. Occasionally, a sound came from inside Triss: meat tearing. Like a percussive ripping of wet cardboard.

The doctor might have blanched a few times, near vomiting. Thank Elden for nacres.

Qas mumbled the least reassuring thing he could have said right then. "Her blood pressure is failing."

Pablo called, "Lynn."

His wife nodded and said, "Got it." To Triss, she added, "Listen, crazy bitch, no one here really wants you to survive this—"

Triss growled in Lynn's face, and it carried the lilt of a whistle.

"—So do what you do best and fucking disappoint me. You promised Razor—your god—you'd live to see him during this delivery, remember? Or was all that just big talk?!"

While Lynn taunted Triss to maintain her will to live, Bethany emptied the last of the Aegis blood bags into the canister. Wordless, she shook her head with a curiously empty expression on her face.

This was bad—

What...

Was that...?!

Pablo about punched the air with a 'yes!' "Crowning."

Qas sighed with relief.

Triss bore down and screamed—

No, screeched.

Some mutated vibration that made the wavelengths visible in the air until all the surrounding glass shattered.

Pablo grabbed onto infantile shoulders and pulled baby Echo the rest of the way into this world.

Nothing tracked after that for Pablo because the adrenaline was too high. He didn't remember forming the thought, but he said the words, "Scissors." Someone cut the umbilical cord and handed him a towel.

Toes.

Fingers.

Feathers.

Pitch black skin. Bright white fuzzy feather-down mixed in with soft strands of matching hair. Little diamonds stared up at Pablo. Small black lips opened with a bright pink tongue in a toothless mouth.

One cluck.

Two chuffs.

Then, the baby cried a song in the most melodic voice Pablo had ever heard. "Hello, baby Echo. We've been waiting for you." His tears fell onto the blanket of the swaddled infant cradled in his arms.

Only then did everything return to him in a sudden assault of the senses and immediately overwhelm him.

Lynn was trying to tell him something. Her face blanched, and her lovely eyes filled with tears. Not happy ones like his. But sad.

What...

She said something as if she had repeated it before, but Pablo still didn't hear it.

A hand gripped his shoulder, and he faced Qas' grave voids.

Why . . .

Pablo frowned and wondered why Triss hadn't asked to hold her baby yet. He stood, ready to hand Echo over to her mother, and—

No.

Oh, please no.

Triss lay back with orange and yellow blood smeared all over her black face, gone pale. Her lips were gray. Her yellow eyes stared up at the Medical bay's ceiling, unseeing.

"No."

Lynn reached for Pablo, trying to take Echo away. "Please, baby. Just for a second. You're going into shock."

Was he?

"Yes," Qas answered, as if he heard Pablo ask the question.

Oh.

He handed Echo over to Lynn and stared anywhere but at his patient.

Bethany busied herself at her station, detached, drawing more of Pablo's attention than necessary because he found it too painful to look at Triss.

A villain.

A vile woman with a history of the worst atrocities.

But she was Pablo's patient, and this felt wrong.

No.

Pablo rushed around the bed to her side. "I refuse to let her die. Any minute now, Korac will show up with Razor upcycled, and this family will spend one precious moment whole. Then everything will fall away as it should, but I will not stand by and do nothing while that moment falls apart. Qas."

The sorrow in Qas' voice hurt Pablo's resolve. "Yes, doctor?"

"Is there anything I can use to defibrillate her?"

Lynn gently rocked baby Echo, who bubbled in her arms. "Triss lost too much blood."

Pablo closed his eyes and counted to ten. Of course, Lynn was right, but they were all out of blood—

No. Not all out.

"Miy!"

The Lyriki warrior called up from the tier below. "Yeah, doc? What's going on up there?"

With renewed hope, Pablo asked, "Would you donate for a transfusion? If so, get up here."

Lynn and Qas exchanged a look Pablo couldn't miss. They were concerned he wasn't handling the loss well, and they were right. But as far as he was concerned, it wasn't a loss yet.

Miy stepped up into the bay with them and… stopped. She stared at a woman who'd caused her a lot of pain and suffering, but who also practically raised her. The history with Triss and the Lyriks was complicated, and Pablo expected any of them would respond likewise to the news of her death. Relieved and saddened.

Miy licked her lips before saying, gently, "Dr. Suarez, she's…"

Pablo shook his head. "There's a faint pulse. Please."

With one last look of doubt, Miy sat down beside Triss, and Qas set her up for the transfusion.

Meanwhile, Lynn cooed at Echo. "She's so beautiful. Do you want to see her, Miy?"

"I expect to have a hand in her upbringing, so yes, but not right now."

Miy looked a little ashen. Shock would do that to even the pitch dark complexion of a Lyrik.

The orange blood flowed into the clinically dead woman, and Pablo went to work setting up the device to defibrillate and started. He muttered for his own benefit more than hers, "C'mon, Triss."

Nothing.

A few more heartbeats passed, increasing the risk of brain damage.

Please—

Qas' voice was soft, kind, and almost too much for Pablo to bear. "The blood isn't strong enough. She needs Aegis blood. I'm sorry. Even if you could revive her, she would only fail again without more of it."

No.

Pablo pounded his fist on the device. "No."

Miy stared at him with something too close to admiration, making him look away.

Lynn, holding an orphan in her arms, reached out to him—

It was all too much. Pablo needed—

He needed—

Bethany.

Pablo stared down at Kyle's little sister, who held a bag of Aegis blood in her hand. "How..."

Lynn answered for her, "She squeezed all the residual from the mostly empty bags and managed a full one."

"Thank you, Bethany... Thank you."

Pablo emptied the bag into the canister and, on the first defibrillation attempt, Triss sat up and gasped for air. Miy stepped back with tears in her eyes, giving Lynn a wide berth to hand Echo over to her biological mother.

Triss cradled her daughter, weak from blood loss and nearly dying. The hard citrines of her eyes bled orange tears from Miy's donation. Her voice was hoarse, but full of warmth as she said, "Hello, my darling girl."

Lynn nudged Pablo and muttered, "You did that."

He smiled and let the tear roll down his cheek.

Yeah. He did.

{ENKI | CINDER'S SHRINE}

Torrentus wasn't just moving. It was disseminating into separate cells of gentler storms. The kind perfect for terraforming.

The signal.

Xelan turned—and yes, maybe there was a happy flare to his coat—as he addressed his Generals. "Let's find the helm of this ship and commandeer it."

Korac pinched between his eyes and groaned into his hand. "Why are you *still* like this?"

Kyle and Andrew exchanged a glance before looking away, fighting a snicker.

Sagan smoothed her hand over Korac's shoulders, the highest she could reach. "I know, baby."

"No, you don't understand. He's always like this, amos."

There was that involuntary twitch in Xelan's eye again.

Lamassau barked out a laugh as if he'd caught it, making Xelan's face burn.

Pehton swatted the green Tritan, who stood four feet over her head.

"Ow. Yes, ma'am. I'll behave."

Tumu met Xelan's eyes and lifted his lipless mouth with a barely visible nod.

Iuo recorded every moment while Legir, X, and Kombuchi signaled their return to the Pantheon, laughing.

F8 glided back to the conduits, shaking her head like she was impressed. "The Shadow." Before stepping through a conduit to the Pantheon, the Monarch Queen smiled all those sharp teeth in a genuine beam, her multifaceted eyes sparkled. "Go retrieve our Empress, your majesty."

Xelan blanched.

Empress.

Sagan and Kyle whirled on Xelan, who held his hands up in surrender. As they fired at him like a duck in a carnival game, he started pacing and biting his thumbnail. Over their heads, Korac smirked, enjoying this punishment.

Kyle bit out, "So that's what Tameka doesn't know?"

At the same time, Sagan sounded so concerned. "What will they expect her to do?"

Andrew gently touched their biceps, shaking his head. "It's okay. It'll turn out all right for everyone."

Sagan's anxiety visibly calmed, but Kyle still looked tense.

Tumu asked an important question filled with warmth and confidence. "Ask yourselves, do you think Peaches would decline such a station?"

That was the question Xelan had asked himself a million times while he brokered their allies for troops. He stopped pacing. It was time to confess. "I was meant to ascend to Emperor over the Vast Collective once we defeated Nox."

All three Progenies' eyes widened. Even Iuo's black and blues doubled in size.

Only Pehton looked unaffected, standing with the mask of a professional. Of course, she already knew as one of those allies.

Korac's mouth gaped open.

How unrefined of the Silver General. It was almost enough to make Xelan laugh, but the subject at hand wore him down. He said, "Before Imminent amplified its exposure, the greatest threat to the Vast Collective was Nox and the Icarean armies. F8, Kombuchi, Legir—All the planetary allies I've made over my travels—my journey to defeat my brother—backed me under one condition."

Sagan said, "You would unite the Twelve Worlds."

When Xelan smiled, the bitterness reduced it to only half his mouth. "With the Progeny behind me, I never imagined I wouldn't survive it."

Watching the implications wash over them twisted Xelan's stomach. He wet his lips before saying, "My motives in training you were never ulterior, I swear. I didn't want the title or the responsibility that came with it. I wanted to live on Earth and watch the Progeny progress. A small life—That's not what I was granted."

Lamassau glanced at Tumu. "Is that why you had a commission for his arrest?"

Tumu nodded.

Korac finally closed his mouth to say, incredulous, "An empire?"

Xelan cursed and looked away.

Kyle surprised them all by saying, "Let's leave it to Tameka to decide how to go forward." That brought Xelan back around, staring at the young man, who continued. "You're her partner, and she is damned capable of handling anything, including how to even approach this topic. Right now, we need to focus on if we're to defeat Imminent in the next few hours. Like Rayne said, Enki doesn't have long."

Andrew patted Kyle on the back. "Hell yes. Let's go find Tameka."

Sagan opened a conduit, and they all stared at it. Xelan noted a flinch in her eyes, and she touched a delicate hand to her temple. The strain was costing her.

She said, "This is about where Razor's map leads us. The bridge. Who's coming with?"

Lamassau took Tumu's hand as he turned to him to say, "I'll play General. You go be the first Tritan on Enki's bridge." They kissed before he stepped over to the Pantheon conduits.

Pehton stepped up, still professional. "I'm with you, your imperial majesty."

Despite how awful he felt, Xelan smiled at Pehton's wink.

Xelan wasn't surprised when Iuo followed in line with all his stenography equipment. "As if I'd miss seeing the bridge."

Kyle ran a hand through his curly hair, clearly frustrated still, but matured enough to do his part. "Me and Andrew will go to the Pantheon. Once you reach the bridge, we imagine that's when the fighting will start. Maybe I can crash the memories on those Weapon clones."

Xelan was very proud of the man Kyle had become. The most recent strife was too fresh between them, but soon he'd tell him.

"I'll see how much *suggestion* I can influence over them." Andrew sounded confident, and he walked away, waving with his coin. "We're on the right track, people. Good luck, all."

Sagan waved to her unrelated brothers with teary eyes, holding Korac's hand.

Lam waved with his Pil gauntlets as the three of them stepped through the conduit to the Pantheon.

"Is there anything else before we meet Peaches?" For the first time since Xelan could remember, Tumu sounded overwhelmed.

Xelan could relate. Weapons weighed down his belt, and he was surprised his pants could stay up. The sickles on his hips, Tameka's chain dart—gold tipped, of all things—on his front, and the whip at his back.

Oh.

Sheepishly, Xelan held up a finger. "Uhm. One more thing." He retrieved the whip from beneath his coat and, even though Korac had relished in Xelan's misery, he still handed it over. The bigger Icarus.

Korac stared down at it in his hands with some emotion behind his facade. It was there in his eyes. The Icarean General swallowed before asking, "Where did you find it?"

"Celindria's lab. She'd kept some trophies, apparently."

Xelan didn't understand the significance of the whip until reading Korac's Verse. A gift from Nox. The same whip the General used to punish Celindria some millennia ago. Once upon a time, Xelan would've left it in her lab, but lately, he'd begun to value that people, places, and even Weapons were made of more than one side of their stories.

Sagan sidled up beside Korac and squeezed his arm. The smile he gave her was familiar, and it was private, so Xelan glanced away as Korac retrieved his brother's gift.

With one dramatic flick, Korac popped it, and the crack reverberated in their ears throughout the shrine.

So dramatic.

"Thank you."

That startled Xelan back to meeting Korac's eyes. Love. That was the emotion. It was familiar and long-missed. But it was also too much right now, and so Xelan said the only thing he thought appropriate for the moment. With a grin, he assured, "I got you."

Korac groaned and pinched his eyes again. "Seriously?!"

Xelan laughed all the way through the conduit, flare in his coat and all.

FIVE

MANAGE YOUR EXPECTATIONS BEFORE SOMEONE SUBVERTS THEM

{ENKI | BRIDGE}

ENKI'S BRIDGE WAS A SERIES OF GLASS WALKWAYS CONNECTING MASSIVE TERMINALS, PRECARIOUSLY SUSPENDED OVER A BEAUTIFUL NIGHTMARE. An ocean of Cascading Light pooled below them and funneled into a whirlpool of black flames. It spun in a quiet maelstrom, draining away into a cylinder of nacre glass positioned under the central terminal of the bridge.

Korac grew dizzy from staring at it. He shook his head and tried to focus on anything else in the space, but everywhere he looked, ghosts haunted him. Translucent men and women with white hair, white eyes, and white skin wandered the rail-less gangways, inputting data from the terminals into projections of keys on their palms, arms, and bare stomachs. Anywhere skin showed, their devices projected an instrument for calculations.

If Korac closed his eyes, he knew the faint echoes of their voices would increase with clarity and volume, taking him away in the spell cast by his people. Their immortality imprinted in him forever. One trace outline walked toward him and into him. Korac turned to watch them walk away toward one of the many entrances to this place.

There, in the firm light of reality, Sagan stood with love in her gentle eyes.

It was almost enough to make Korac cry. "I love the way you look at me."

Her smile shone brighter than the fires below. "Then I'll never look away."

"I can't tell if they make me want to gag or coo. What about you?"

Korac and Sagan both looked at Pehton, all of four-foot five, staring up at thirteen-foot Tumu, waiting for the answer to her question.

Tumu said, "I find it's best to look elsewhere. Don't you agree, Xelan?"

Korac tried very hard not to glance at Xelan and failed. The Prince of Cinder stared down at the funnel of Cascading Light, tense shoulders affecting his royal carriage. The Icarus really should consider stretching that out soon. Stress lived in Xelan differently than it did in people without his unique family history for insanity and carnage. Not much separated a 'Xelan' from a 'Nox.'

As if he also noticed it, Iuo stepped up to Xelan and whispered something in his ear. The Icarus looked up and met the Lamia's eyes. A wordless exchange took place, but eventually, the trademark grin emerged. Xelan said, "Thank you," with a good deal of sincerity.

Great.

Now, not knowing whatever Iuo had said would bug the shit out of Korac until he discovered what it was. A nudge drew his attention downward. Pehton stood at his elbow, smiling up at him with those garnet eyes. She said, "We're close. All of us. Somewhere in here is the answer to what happened to my children."

Sagan hugged the tiny Lyrik from behind and rested her chin on a pitch-black shoulder, peering at Pehton. "How are you in hanging in there?"

Pehton shrugged, and it nudged Sagan's lips closer to hers, momentarily filling Korac's head with an image he'd best keep to himself. Pehton said, "I'm ready to know, either way. I have so much more to live for than ever in my life, and if that good news includes some way to save them or simply an answer to the unknown, I'll find closure."

Xelan leapt across the glass gangways with only his coat acting as wings, while the hungry maw of the Cascading Inferno beckoned below. "Let's get your answers. Tameka will be here any minute."

Sagan and Pehton—*Korac's* fan club—both grinned at the Prince of Cinder, eliciting an eye roll from Korac.

Show off.

Tumu simply walked across the expanse with one great stride.

Now, *that* was impressive.

Iuo stretched out his body to twice its typical length, still clothed, and slithered down one ramp. Korac glimpsed Sagan and Pehton giving Iuo the once-over before meeting each other's eyes and bursting into a fit of feminine giggles.

All the men, except Iuo, rolled their eyes.

"Silver General, this is Doc. Over."

Korac controlled a small bout of panic. If something was wrong with Karter or the delivery, Dr. Suarez wouldn't sound so damned pleased. It could only mean… "Doc, is it good news? Over."

"Indeed, it is." His grin sounded through the comms. "Baby Echo is with us and healthy and full of surprises. Over."

Sagan leapt into Korac's arms, and he spun her, laughing out their joy together. All around, the Shadow celebrated. Xelan punched the air, Pehton cheered, and Iuo hissed an emphatic, "Yesssss!"

Tumu startled Korac by dropping confetti IN HIS HAIR.

Sagan gasped with a hand cupped over mouth. Xelan pointed and laughed full-heartedly. Pehton muttered to Tumu, "Run."

Iuo took out a small fan and blew the confetti from Korac's hair, saving Tumu's existence.

Well wishes poured in over the earpieces from all across their fronts in Enki. Ross, Devis, Twenty-One, even Caedes.

T.A.O. came on the mic next. "The brightest fire. Like you, Korac. Bright and blinding. Too beautiful to look at. The worlds melt when she smiles."

Korac's heart warmed, grateful for his old friend's freedom and hopeful for her future.

All of it paled compared to the next voice. "Hug your little girl for me, Sagan. Korac. I'm still so flattered you named her after me. Over."

A lot of the huggy shit which the Shadow got up to sorta poured off Korac like water on feathers, but everyone reacted the same way to Rayne's voice. He actually choked before swallowing and getting the words out to say, "Will do, War King. Over and out."

Family.

Sagan's hand slipped into Korac's. He gazed down at her, and she looked up at him. "Ready?"

Ready.

Korac took her with him to the main terminal, where he stopped. Everything. The only thing he focused on was his heartbeat and his lungs exhaling and inhaling. Ghosts brushed against him and through him, but he sought one face. One calculating mind.

Razor came to him in his mindscape, chained to the floor, saying, "*Brother.*"

The word sounded profane from his lips, and Korac shook off his initial disgust to negotiate. "We made it to the bridge."

The twin crescent pupils glinted. "Triss?"

"I'll be honest with you. When Dr. Saurez told me Echo was born, I didn't bother to ask if Triss survived." Korac didn't care. "Frankly, I want this business on the bridge finished so I can hold my daughter. If you don't mind..."

Razor shook his head. "You broke your end of the bargain. I was to be there for the delivery, for Triss."

Korac growled. "Shit happened. The baby came sooner than expected, and Remorse stole Pax. Tameka's on her way here, and we need your help—"

"Where is Sagan?"

That made Korac clench his jaw tight. He hated whenever Razor so much as breathed her name. Now he was demanding to know her whereabouts. "She's here. Like me, she's waiting to hold our little girl."

Razor nodded. "Good. She brought the dossier drive like I told her, didn't she?"

"Yes."

On his knees in the metaphorical space, Razor stretched his neck until it cracked, followed by his knuckles on long fingers with no nails. "Complete the upcycle. I'll bring the bridge online."

Korac narrowed his eyes. "Razor."

"*Brother*, dear?"

Goosebumps broke out on Korac's arms, and his hackles raised. If his wings were out, the pinions would rustle. "Don't try anything. Xelan, Tumu, Iuo, and fucking Pehton are out there. They won't play your games, and I don't want my body destroyed. I like my fingernails."

The laugh Razor gave was bitter and tinkered like broken glass. "Complete the upcycle."

Upcycle complete.

Razor opened their eyes, and they looked down immediately at Sagan. Korac hated the way her entire body changed. Tense, recoiling away. Her eyes too wide—Now they were in extreme Atramentous. Solid black with purple slitted pupils. But Korac's girl held her ground, and he loved her for it.

Sagan said, "Razor." His name left her on a steady note, low, almost a growl.

Razor nodded Korac's head at her and checked out the rest of the space. "Seamswalker, Prince Xelan, Primary Tumu, Prince Iuo, and Peh Peh." The last, he sweetened his voice like a poisoned berry.

Inside the mindscape, Korac's voice was icy. "Leave her, Razor. Pehton's been through enough."

Razor smiled. "Quite right." Outside to the others, he said, "Let's get down to business." He faced the translucent terminal with its bank of projectors. "Seamswalker, the dossier drive, please."

Sagan hesitated only a second before retrieving it from her pocket and pointing at the terminal. "Here?"

Razor nodded and stepped a little to the side, giving her space. Something Korac wouldn't credit him for if not for their last conversation.

"You broke her heart, and I hate that you ever possessed enough of it to hurt her. She wanted a friendship with you, and you betrayed her. There is no coming back from that, and I think it strange you want to at all. I'm almost convinced, after spending this time with you in my bones, that you don't pursue her to hurt me. I think you pursue her because you realized what you lost, and you're desperate to get it back. Like with T.A.O. *If that's the case, do the right thing. Help them. Help Sagan save Rayne and finally finish Celindria's game."*

Korac still felt this was true, and the slight gesture from Razor only affirmed it.

Sagan used the space to step against the terminal, reach with all her five foot, three inches of height, and secure it in the slot Razor had designated. She even stuck her tongue out, a cute habit of hers when concentrating on a task—

"I can feel your love for her."

Korac was a private Icarus. The idea of Razor sharing even that much grated on him.

He continued, "Imagine your world without her for an instant."

Imagining it wasn't necessary. Korac knew. When Razor pushed Sagan into the Seam and she was trapped there for a week, Korac knew a world with only her desperate cries for help. He asked, "Are you saying that's how you feel about Triss?"

Razor said nothing.

This prompted Korac to push. "Triss wanted Echo for you. She gave everything for that little girl, and now she's here. Are you regretting asking Sagan to raise her—"

"No."

Wow, Razor didn't elaborate. The man who'd fallen in love with his own charisma declined an opportunity to talk. Again, the hackles raised on the back of Korac's neck. "What do you want now, Razor?"

Through Razor's eyes in Korac's head, they focused on Sagan. Small and sweet in front of him. Her short blond hair, those anxious Atramentous eyes, the blue halter top and black leather pants, leaving much of her tan, freckled skin exposed. She rubbed the tension in her neck before turning slowly, as if she sensed his gaze on her.

Korac didn't like this. "Razor..."

Razor took a step forward in Korac's body and swept around Sagan without a word. Instead, he focused on the terminal, which projected onto Korac's arms. There, he pressed a sequence of functions before glancing once more around the less than friendly faces in the room.

With some of his usual showmanship, Razor asked in a dramatic voice, "Is everybody ready?"

They all nodded, slow with the tension.

Something felt wrong—

The drive sank into the terminal—

"Razor!"

Everything went black.

{ENKI | PANTHEON}

Bones was having a good day. The Shadow recovered Para, Karter, and Chris; Rayne reunited with their family; and baby Echo arrived early, but healthy. A truly beautiful day.

Then the lights went out in Enki.

Beside him, Kombuchi called into the inky abyss, "Is it everywhere?"

Kyle returned through the still open conduits—kick ass, Seamswalker!—and confirmed, "Yeah, I think it's everywhere. Follow me."

The leaders of the Twelve Worlds followed Story Taker into Cinder's Shrine. All the armies had finished migrating a half hour ago, so they were alone with this terrifying view.

A dark Dyson's Sphere.

No ancillary lights or ambient glow. Just the light from the star which barely reached out this far. On top of that, it was cold. Like vacuum cold and getting colder.

Into the dramatic silence, Bones followed his instincts and asked, "How much air have we got?"

X swatted him and groaned in a whisper, "You know we don't need air like that. Nacres."

Andrew smirked.

Kyle rolled his eyes.

Bones shrugged. "It's what you're supposed to say in the movies."

Legir, the grown adult, who fathered the most famous brothers in the galaxy gently admonished, "We must focus on the advantages this affords our enemies."

F8's regal voice sliced through the darkness. "This is when I'd find it most advantageous to stage troops on the front. Under the guise of darkness."

The pitch darkness yielded a certain kind of protection, for certain. A grand entrance. "No." They all turned to Bones even though they could hardly see him. He finished his thought. "A grand entrance isn't enough for Imminent."

Kyle said, "He's right. They'll strike in the dark."

"Get back to the Pantheon," Andrew ordered.

The leaders rushed through the conduit into a din of confusion.

Icarean eyesight was sharp enough to make out thin lines of contrast—shapes—but not so much as to identify them. In the abyss, Bones could see silhouettes attacking the front line. L. Capra's army.

"Bones."

He knew what Kombuchi wanted, and he gladly circled his arms around—

"This is Andrew, dude."

"Oh, sorry." Attempt two. He shifted to the next person at about the right height. "Kombuchi?"

"Hurry." Right.

Bones grabbed the Caprent in his toga and flew into the air with him. Over his troops, they made out the struggle of conflict and the puking gag of acid. Shrieks followed.

Kombuchi ordered, "Caprents, cease acid fire."

Over the earpieces, Kyle announced on all channels, "Fighting has commenced on the Pantheon front. No visuals. Repeat, no visuals. Over."

All around, generals and planetary leaders called for their soldiers to engage.

Flares shot in the air in blues, greens, and reds, illuminating the endless swarm below. Lamias, Drones, Caprents, winged-Icari, and jellyfish Luk wearing black and white gear assaulted the Vast Collective armies with a terrifying distribution of Weapons in the guise of Nox and Rayne.

Millions of them.

Still in his arms, high above the badly lit fray, Kombuchi convulsed and gulped. Bones turned his head away and squeezed his face tight. "C'mon, man. Do you really gotta—"

With a belching gag, green Caprent acid rained down from Bone's passenger onto a pair of Weapons. Bones almost cheered for the disgusting win, but Kombuchi watched carefully, apparently duly cautious.

The acid and skin melted off the amber shells of the copies, who turned hollowed eyes up toward the sky.

"Fuck!"

"Get us out of here, Bones!"

Kombuchi's voice increased in pitch and volume as the two shells ascended. Cussing the entire way, Bones flew to find cover as the flares died in the sky.

"I thought Rayne said those things couldn't fly."

"They can't. We just pissed them off that much."

Kombuchi was right. Two Imminent Icarean soldiers launched the Weapons like people missiles, while Vast

Collective soldiers fell to the superior opponents below. They needed help.

They needed—

Their pursuers plummeted out of the sky.

In fact, all the noise stopped. The fighting ceased on both sides.

Bones landed and released Kombuchi near the conduits. That's when he realized what was happening. Andrew's Atramentous eyes were black with a teal pupil. He took calm, even breaths, seemingly blind to everything around him. Sweat broke out on his brow.

Kyle explained on behalf of his brother-in-arms, "He can't hold them for long."

F8 asked, "What are we hoping for?"

Lamassau suggested with less irony than expected, "A miracle?"

Kyle shook his head, and the next word out of his mouth gave Bones goosebumps.

"Silence."

{Enki | Bridge}

Sagan came to, confused. Why was she lying on the glass gangway with a raging migraine? How was her head hurting with a nacre? What happened—

In the dark, white eyes with twin crescent pupils stared centimeters from her face, set in Korac's face with a finger pressed to his lips.

Razor.

Free.

A scream crawled up Sagan's spine, but she swallowed it when she saw the lack of menace in Razor's eyes. He nodded and left her on the floor, crossing the room to check on Pehton. Then Iuo who'd fallen beside the terminal. Tumu—

Sagan startled with a gasp.

Without lights, she made out the Primary hanging halfway off the gangplank, arms reaching for the endless swirl of Cascading Light.

Razor shocked her by dragging Tumu's significant heft onto the main floor with ease. He went to Xelan last, who lay face down on the floor. Tenderly, Razor brushed aside all that black hair until none covered his face. He gazed a second longer at the Icarus before returning to the main terminal with a spring in his step.

With his back to her, Sagan reached for her axe—

Gone.

Sagan peered over to find both of them and the whip holstered on Korac's belt. Under her breath, she muttered, "Fuck me." And instantly regretted it.

Razor spun and pegged her with a stare, one eyebrow raised. "I'm feeling magnanimous, so I'll leave that one untouched. Clearly, you're under the influence of this ensemble." He gave a sweeping gesture over Korac's belted robe and leather pants. Specifically, lingering his fingers along the open front. "Did my baby brother leave all this exposed for you or for our fiery Peh Peh?" He smirked before gazing back at Xelan. "Or perhaps an admirer with more history?"

Through gritted teeth, Sagan confessed, "I wouldn't mind either way."

That brought Razor's eyes back to hers. He smiled. "You *are* perfection." When he turned back to the terminals, he instructed, "Get on your feet. We have work to do, Seamswalker."

"I'm not doing a damned thing until you tell me what's happening." Her voice carried through the dark in three pitches.

With his back to her, Razor raised a hand to run through his hair in frustration, stopped like he remembered it wasn't his hair, and chuckled at the novelty of it. In response to her demand, he said, "There's not enough time for detailed schematics. The blackout is Sphere-wide, and your *family* is in danger." He said 'family' like it was a dirty word. After pressing a few more projected keys on Korac's arm, he faced her. "You'll just have to trust me."

Sagan stood and shook her head. "No fucking way."

Razor pointed at Korac's face, pointed at himself. "You won't hurt me while I'm in this inferior body, and I'm intrigued enough by something your lover said to summon Ishkur as promised. I still want in the Hall of Dead Kings, or did you forget about our bargain?"

Summon Ishkur? Ishkur was a person?

Shaking her head, Sagan focused on her immediate dilemma. Somehow Razor had shut down power to Enki and laid her team out, including Korac. He was steering a precious vessel, all while claiming it in the name of good.

What choice did she have? "What do you want from me?"

Razor sighed from Korac's lips in relief. "Good. First—"

"Sagan, this is War King. What's happening out there? Everything's dark. Over."

Razor's eyes widened in Korac's face. To Sagan, he said, "You found her."

Sagan wet her lips, itching to answer Rayne but not wanting to draw more attention to her best friend. "Yes." Some part of Sagan worried Rayne would kill Razor in Korac's body simply to end his existence. They couldn't have that.

To her surprise, Razor nodded as if that was well and good without contributing a scathing remark before saying, "Answer her, then take me to Triss."

Eager to see Echo herself, Sagan said over her mic, "Just some difficulties. We'll figure it out. Over and Out." She opened the conduit to the Medical Bay. Korac's hand lightly touched her bicep, and she jerked away like it burned.

Shrinking from her lover's touch was a step backward.

No.

Sagan returned to his proximity and glared at Razor.

He searched her eyes before confessing, "I only wanted to say that I'm afraid."

She recoiled. "Of what?"

"If Triss yet lives, she'll insist I hold the child."

Still not following, Sagan frowned her confusion. "And?"

The twin crescent pupils in his eyes shifted, staring at her like the situation was obvious. Razor clarified, "Once. Only once will I get to do this. What if once isn't enough? What will my existence be like after knowing I can never do it again?"

Oh.

Without waiting for her reply, Razor stepped through the conduit.

By the time Sagan followed through, Pablo, Lynn, and Dr. Qas all stood on red alert. Beyond them, Bethany stared upside Korac's head with hungry eyes. Emergency glow orbs illuminated the bay, scattered all around.

Uncertain what else to do, Sagan held up her hands, staving them. "It's okay. We made a deal, remember—"

Did Bethany just lick her lips like a hungry kitten?

Whatever. Focus. Sagan opened her mouth to ask if Triss was alive—

"Razor?" Beyond them, Triss let out a faint call again, "Razor?"

Korac's face frowned, and Razor's eyes glanced at Pablo. "Dr. Suarez?"

Pablo nodded, understanding and looking a little grateful. "She's been calling for you since the lights went out." He glanced Korac up and down before asking Razor, "You wouldn't have anything to do with that, would you?"

But the body of Sagan's lover had already stepped around Lynn and the doctors to kneel at Triss' side. The others watched in horrified fascination. Sagan stayed put and, from her vantage point, watched Triss' withered gray hand reach to caress Korac's face.

Resist the urge to kill.

Sagan bit her tongue and eavesdropped on the moment.

"I knew you'd come for me." Triss sounded like shit, all dry and breathy.

A tear—an actual tear—fell from Razor's bizarre eyes. "Always." The genuine emotion coming from Korac's voice made Sagan clear her throat and lower her eyes.

The two gazed at one another for an eternity before Triss said, "She's here. Our girl... Dr. Suarez?"

Pablo muttered to Sagan, "She's in the next bay on this tier. Caedes and Miy are with her. You can bring her in." His smile was full of a love only near-siblings shared, and Sagan would take it.

She found Caedes making faces into the medical bed. Miy watched Sagan enter with a hand on her hip and a brow curiously quirked. Sagan smiled at them both.

The gruff Icarus straightened and let his features fall into his grumpy resting face. "Ahem. She's all yours."

A tiny lilt of a musical note came from the bed as Sagan approached, nervous and excited and sad Korac wasn't with her. Especially once she glimpsed inside.

Sagan cupped a hand over her mouth and stared down at the beautiful Aegis-featured, Lyriki-complected infant. "Hello, Echo." She tried to exclaim softly, but the baby startled and turned to her, poised to cry.

What should Sagan do? Tickle her? Feed her? "Is she hungry? Does she need changing—No, that's pre-nacre babies. What do I do?"

"Pick her up." Miy sounded so bitchy, but also gentle. It was a complex way to communicate.

Sagan lifted baby Echo in her arms and blinked through her tears as the newborn calmed down. Did everyone's voice change to the same pitch and softness when talking to babies? "Hi, there. Hello. I'm—" Sagan choked. Swallowed. Tried again. "I'm your mommy."

Echo squeezed her finger in greeting, and Sagan got moving. One day in the future, when she and Korac recounted this day to their little girl, Sagan didn't want to say she failed to get Echo to her birth parents in time. Rounding the corner, Pablo looked on the verge of a breakdown, spurring her to rush to Triss' bed—

Oh.

Elden.

Triss was a nightmare Sagan would never forget, thinned to ruin and covered in yellow and orange gore. The once pitch-black skin, now gray, had shrunk into the angular bones of her face. Her yellow feathers fell out from her scalp.

Only her eyes, hard citrines, shone with their usual beauty.

And Razor gazed at her with nothing but adoration. The god turned acolyte. "She's here, Triss. Hang on for me, please."

In that weak, raspy voice, Triss begged, "Hold... her. Razor. Please." All the melody had left her.

Razor reached out to Sagan and met her eyes for one crystalline breath. This was him at his most human. He was afraid. Afraid of losing Triss and afraid of falling in love with his daughter.

Sagan pitied Razor.

As if he had held a million babies in his lifetime, the Pain Curator expertly cradled Echo in Korac's arms—an obscenity, given Korac had yet to do so.

But again—Sagan reminded herself—this was about Echo.

Razor gazed down at his daughter, who reached tiny hands to Korac's face. He bent to let her cup Korac's jaw and kissed her. "She looks exactly like her mother. She's beautiful, Triss."

Echo clucked and gasped on a whistle, the only sound in the room aside from Sagan's heartbeat.

"Triss?"

Razor whirled in a gentle spin, remembering the baby in his arms and...

Sagan saw what he saw. So distracted was she by him holding her daughter that they'd both missed it.

Triss' last breath was at least two minutes ago. She was white as a sheet, her lips lilted in a ghastly smile. Her fingers unfurled from where she'd clenched them in the blanket. A quiet passing, basking in the moment.

A heartbreaking sound brought Sagan back to Razor in Korac's body.

He hugged Echo to his face and muttered, "No.

"No.

"No, no, no."

Meanwhile, Echo twirled a strand of Korac's hair around her finger and played with it.

Sagan took a step toward the emotionally crazed man holding her infant daughter in her lover's arms. "Razor. I'm sorry." She actually meant it. As horrific as Razor and Triss were to Sagan and Korac—the entire Vast Collective—this was a nightmarish way for their relationship to end. Especially with Razor's existence leaning toward the long-term.

So, Sagan took another step, reaching out.

Razor brushed Echo's down-feathers and gazed at her, long and unblinking. Sagan knew he was afraid to look away, afraid to get another glimpse of his lover in this state. Understanding, Sagan gently took the blanket from Triss' grip and, with as much sensitivity as possible, shrouded the dead woman from her lover's eyes.

Emotionally keyed up, Sagan wasn't sure, but she thought Razor croaked softly, "Thank you."

Instead of asking for confirmation, she held out her arms for the baby. "Please, Razor. Please."

He met her eyes then with his, full of tears and...

Fear.

"She looks just like her mother. Do you know how impossible that is? Aegis genes are dominant."

Sagan swallowed and tried again, firmer this time. "Please. Give Echo to me."

Razor looked from Sagan to Echo and grimaced in pain. The kind that affects the heart, deep and potent. Sagan was familiar with it because Razor and all of Imminent had put her and family through it repeatedly, but now her enemy stood here, utterly affected, and all Sagan wanted to do was cry with him.

"Please."

Razor handed Echo to Sagan, staring at the young woman the entire time. He said, "You'll make an exceptional mother, Seamswalker."

She swallowed, unsure of what to say. At least Echo looked equally perplexed. Gently, Sagan insisted, "We should get moving before the others wake. They won't be happy with you, and I doubt you'll get this 'work' you spoke of done so easily, then."

Razor stared nowhere—not seeing the room, the blanketed body in his periphery—miserable. "Yes. You're right."

Pablo met Sagan around the bed, equally miserable. He was crying, his eyes red from it. "I'll take her. I could use the comfort."

Sagan smiled pityingly for him and kissed Echo before letting the doctor have her. "Thank you, Pablo. For everything."

"Yes." Razor sounded scooped out and empty behind her. "Thank you for your excellent care, Dr. Suarez."

It wasn't unusual for Razor to be full of compliments. He was rather well known for being a fair, if interesting, employer, recruiting into his cult of vice brokers with sweet words and smooth deals. But something felt different here.

Sincerity.

Razor had hit rock bottom, and Sagan was the only thing keeping him upright. "C'mon."

They stepped through the conduit, returning to the bridge. Everyone was still unconscious, much to Sagan's disappointment—

The floor switched places with the ceiling, and Sagan fell into the terminal beside her.

Razor was there, present, but not touching her, scanning her with his bizarre eyes. "Seamswalker?"

The concern in Korac's voice was comforting, and she craved his presence after Triss' death. A tear fell from her eyes as she tried to wave him off. "I'm fine."

"You're over taxed."

True, but their enemy didn't need to know that. Distract. Change the subject. Sagan straightened and asked, "What's your aim, Razor?"

Razor went back to the terminal and projected the Dyson's Sphere into a three-dimensional rendering over the whirling nightmare below. More to himself, he said, "I told Korac vengeance was a hungry master. Of course, I was referring to Nox at the time, but we're all guilty of it."

Appeal to his ego. Sagan licked her dry lips and pressed, "Isn't vengeance beneath you?"

He laughed, but said nothing further on the subject.

Get him talking. She asked, "What intrigued you?"

"Hmm?"

Sagan finally felt stable enough to stand while clutching the terminal. She tried again for a diverting subject, buying time for the others to wake. "You said, 'I'm intrigued enough by something your lover said to summon Ishkur as promised.' What did Korac say that intrigued you?"

Razor faced her as he said, "'Remorse stole Pax.' That was never in our plans. Celindria always raised him with Nox. However, Xelan's resurrection inside Gait instead of Nox—a finer choice, in my opinion—and the only way Celindria would let Pax go would be over her dead body, so . . . It was an intriguing revelation."

Sagan's face scrunched with the frown. "But what does that have to do with your plans and vengeance—"

Lights.

Razor powered the lights back on.

"It means I get to be the hero for once."

That wink frightened Sagan more because he'd meant to be reassuring.

{ENKI | BRIDGE}

Thank Elden for nacres with perfect recall. Razor's map proved useful for traveling across the Torrentus content with no guides. It was a wasteland eroded from constant weather. Alone, Tameka traversed the conduit labyrinth until she entered a globe of clear, seamless glass suspended over an ocean of Cascading Light. That's when the lights went out. She lingered there, wings retracted, afraid to move or risk falling. When the lights returned moments later, she followed the glass gangways, which brought her to the final conduit. Through there, if Razor had told them the truth, Tameka would enter the bridge.

"Please Xelan already be here. Rayne and Pax, too."

With another brief prayer to Elden, Tameka crossed the final threshold and stepped into a confounding scene. Xelan lay closest to her, luo was on the ramp beside Pehton, and Tumu was stretched across the central hub. All of them were unconscious. Only Sagan and Korac moved around the space, hovering over a terminal.

From across the way, Tameka heard Sagan say, "Razor, you can't be a hero and seek vengeance at the same time. We learned that from Nox and Korac."

"Sagan." Tameka tried to keep her voice neutral because, despite the present chaos, she was thrilled to see her best friend again. "What's happening?"

Razor cursed.

Sagan spun and cried out, "Tameka!" She Seamswalked across the planks and pulled Tameka into a weak embrace, almost leaning into her. The hoarseness of her voice didn't stop Sagan from her excited burst of words. "I held Echo, and she's beautiful. And oh my god, Rayne. She found us. Her frequency is zero zero twelve. Oh, and Celindria's dead. Remorse killed her—"

Razor interrupted the reunion with a silken laugh, like a proper villain.

Both women turned to him. In the motion, Sagan stumbled and Tameka took her weight. With a brow raised, she pushed. "Do you have something to say?"

He went about his work, unsupervised, which really grated on Tameka. He asked, "Who told you Remorse killed Celindria?"

Beside her, Sagan frowned. "Xelan."

"Ah. Yes. Well." Razor sounded bemused and incredulous all at once. "Don't mind me. I'm just operating a Dyson's Sphere."

Tameka held her hands up in a stopping gesture. One thing at a time. Staring only at the impossible view below, she asked, "Where is my son?"

Sagan winced, leaving Razor to answer with a curious lilt to Korac's voice. "Remorse took him."

"Tameka?"

It was Xelan.

Sagan straightened and nodded. "Go to him."

Tameka went and knelt beside him, noting someone had already brushed his hair away from his face. She said, "I'm here."

Xelan squeezed her hand weaker than usual. His voice was soft, faint. "Korac was right."

She leaned down to make sure she heard him correctly. "About what?"

"You're alive."

The relief in his voice made her eyes squeeze shut. He'd thought Torrentus had killed her in the firestorm. Tameka kissed Xelan's cheek and promised, "I'll never leave you."

While Tameka comforted the love of her life, something was taking place behind her. She glanced over her shoulder to find Sagan held in Korac's arms, only centimeters from falling into the maelstrom. Tameka asked, "Sagan?"

Razor was still at the steering wheel, carrying the Seamswalker like a princess. "She's struggling." The concern in his freaky eyes grossed Tameka out as Razor said, "She needs blood."

That was enough. "What. Is. Happening?"

"Yes, Razor." The strength had returned to Xelan's voice with a dash of sexy anger. "Give me one good reason to keep my end of the bargain and load you into the Hall of Dead Kings after you've pulled this stunt." He stood, lifting Tameka with him.

Sagan, barely conscious, stared into his face with all the love meant for Korac—Delirious.

Razor looked into that expression, saying, "I have only ever known the love of one and the friendship of another." He glanced at Xelan. "Correction, two others."

Tameka tried hard not to look at Xelan. His past relationships were none of her business, no matter the implications of said relationships.

As if sensing Tameka's patience, Xelan looped his arm around her waist and pulled her tighter against him.

Razor continued. "Since occupying space behind Korac's conscious I've... gleaned emotions. Not exactly eavesdropping, although, let's face it, I am not above that, but more impressions of warmth and acceptance unlike anything I've ever experienced, even among my own people. Triss was all there ever was for me. She's gone now, Xelan. She passed only minutes ago."

Xelan swallowed audibly beside Tameka, and she sensed the loss affected him more than he'd expected.

Later.

They could share mutual grieving later.

"But the epicenter of this phenomenon comes from her." Razor gently gestured with Sagan in his arms. After another heartbeat of him staring at her and creeping Tameka out, he confessed, "I have something to prove."

Xelan asked an important question. "Where is Korac?"

"When he wakes, he'll blame me for the nacre concussion and cycle me before I can complete my purpose. But I swear to you, the effect was unintended."

Tameka had been through a lot today. This was one more thing too much. She squeezed Xelan in a side hug before letting go and crossing the space to stand in front of Korac's body with Razor's eyes. "Why did he upcycle you rather than Zero or anyone else?"

The Aegis entreated her with unmasked sincerity in his gaze. "Father wanted no one to find Ishkur. He was adamant to the point of risking his demise."

Behind her, Tumu said with a groan, "It's true. The Primaries tortured him often over it. He wouldn't give the bridge up either."

She glanced away from Razor to check Tumu with her own eyes. He stood and went to the others, helping to roll Iuo onto his tail.

Meanwhile, Razor frowned. "Where did you get Aegis blood on you?"

Tameka scowled when she realized he was talking to her. "What?"

He pointed to her shoulder, stained with a drop of Celindria's blood. Originally crimson, then cobalt, now it was canary yellow. Tameka peered at it, confused. "I backhanded Celindria. How—"

Razor laughed that silken note again, with Sagan still dazed in Korac's arms. "You are most impressive, Fury."

"I think it's time you put Sagan down."

The Pain Curator handed the Seamswalker over to Tameka. He said, "Yes. My brother will wake soon."

Although Tameka was more than strong enough to bench-press three Sagans, they were nearly the same in height. It made the princess carry a little awkward. "Xelan?"

He was already there and took Sagan from her, staring at Razor. "How much work remains?"

"I've nearly summoned Ishkur and mapped the route for power. Here." Razor swept over to the terminal. "I even revived the nacre radars so you can locate Remorse and Pax. Bol is here. Near the Pantheon."

Tumu cursed. "You don't want him involved in that fight and... are those—Those aren't our troops." He pointed at the millions of dots veiling the southern portion of their Pantheon clearing.

Razor shook his head. "Those are Imminent soldiers."

Iuo lost some color. "The fighting... it's already commenced." He adjusted his earpiece, presumably to the other channels.

Tameka followed suit and flinched at all the noise on the other end. "This is Bones with the Pantheon team. Code Red. I repeat, Code Red. Bridge team come in. Over."

Xelan answered them. "Pantheon. What's your status? Over."

"Oh thank fuck, Wingmaster. We're barely holding on out here. There are millions of Weapons. Conscience amped up his *suggestion* to full-on volition control, but he can only hold them if we don't touch anyone. That's everyone, good and bad guys. Over."

Iuo responded, "This is Bridge team. This is a good news/bad news situation. Fury is back—That's the good news. The bad news is that Seamswalker One is fainting. We'll recover her and update you ASAP. Over and Out."

Transport.

They needed transport.

They all turned and looked at Sagan near passing out in Xelan's arms.

All except Razor.

Tameka *hated* this. "I take it Korac is still unconscious?"

The Pain Curator nodded without turning around.

"Feed her."

Just saying it made Tameka's skin crawl, but dammit, they were out of options and time. She knew from personal experience that clinical feeding was never completely clinical. For an Icarus-blooded being, sharing blood was an intimate act. When Caedes and Tameka lived together for two years in Enki, he let her feed from his wrist out of necessity, but he still purred as an autonomic response.

Xelan wasted no time kneeling to make Sagan more comfortable. Razor went to Korac's knees and bit into his wrist, letting the yellow blood flow. It dripped onto her lips as he sealed the vein to her mouth.

No remarks.

No looks.

The Pain Curator was neutral, staring out into the room without seeing it. Razor didn't even watch Sagan's mouth latch onto the sensitive skin or her throat convulse when she swallowed.

It worried Tameka more than if he was scathing about it. The bastard was planning something.

"What the fuck?"

All of them, including Razor, looked in Pehton's direction. She was cradling her head, glaring and frowning in confusion, looking mostly hungover. "What did I miss?"

Tameka smiled at her. "A lot, but once Sagan's mobile, you're coming with me."

Xelan asked, "Where are we going?"

"To see Rayne. We need her blood to be at our best, and I can't wait for her to meet Razor."

{The Heart of Enki | Within The Previous Hour}

Calibrated.

Optimized.

Stabilizing...

Unable to stabilize.

Warning: Nine hours and seven minutes until maximum destabilization.

"Elden, I need your help."

The nacres laid on their pedestals in the amber dome, playing sentinel over Cinder's failing prosperity. The same ancients who'd witnessed the fall of the royal family. All those tribulations and losses, never once interfering.

Not until the girl who stood in the chamber's center swallowed Nox's nacre under Li's bloated sky. Now Rayne had returned with more prayers. Elden permitted her to hold his chipped nacre in the small palm of her hand, squeeze it inside her fist, and—

A splinter cracked and laid in her hand, further diminishing the white pearl.

Much like when she retrieved Night Killer, Rayne punched a hole in her own chest. Distracting from the agony, she muttered, "One splinter for the Icarean Royal Family. One splinter for me. But," her voice squeezed tight as she gasped out, "Unlike Umbra, I'll share mine with you—"

Chink.

Rayne entered her chest with one white chip and removed her hand—healing the wound instantly—with one of amber glass. She fixed it to Elden's pearl and kissed it before restoring the ancient nacre to its pedestal. "I'll keep my promise."

Over the last hour, Nox witnessed Rayne lie to the people she loved. The martyr knew no ultimate way to survive the Weapon detonation, but she may have afforded herself some hope with Elden's nacre.

Why had Elden helped Rayne keep Nox's nacre separate from hers? Did the ancient Icarean deity and his reincarnation share an accord?

It was an impressive, if desperate maneuver, which left Nox more than a little curious as to Rayne's kinship with his ancestor. Curious as to how she impacted her relationships and engendered so much loyalty and trust even among the ancient and powerful—

And now Rayne was kissing Sagan after returning to the heart of Enki.

Nox turned all the way around and busied himself with the three-dimensional rendering of their fronts.

Calibrated.

Optimized.

Stabilizing . . .

Unable to stabilize.

Warning: Seven hours and twenty-two minutes until maximum destabilization.

Nox winced even as Rayne said, "Worth it."

He'd be damned if he didn't smirk, which quickly vanished as the Seamswalker and the War King exchanged heartfelt goodbyes.

Inside her head, with his back to her, Rayne's voice was thick with emotion, the tears audible in her words. "Please don't pity me. I couldn't bear it right now."

Nox shook his head, whether or not she could see him. "I could never pity you." Because he loved her too much not to do something about it. "Look."

Behind him, Rayne straightened herself. He knew because when she appeared beside him, the evidence of her tears was mostly gone. "What is it?" Her voice was still heavy with sorrow, but filled with the light familiarity she'd found when speaking with him lately.

Nox would take the good with the bad. He pointed, "This is the projection of the rogue half of Gait if Enki's predictions are accurate. It will impact the hull in three hours. If you keep physical contact to a minimum—"

"We could make it. I can refill at the battleground and not have to explode Enki, myself!" Rayne gripped Nox's wrist while she hopped up and down with excitement. "Here's to Matt and Lucy!" She released him to punch the air.

Damn Nox, but he grinned down at her, the enthusiasm infectious. Not to mention, surviving this would be nice. Although, they'd have to create some protocols for her privacy. A way to dismiss Nox for intimate moments. If they lived through this, he'd be fine with that.

Azure pulsed under her skin again.

They stopped celebrating as Rayne stared at her arm outside her head. "Nox?"

He hated the finality in her voice, and he wanted to remind Rayne of her strength. "Yes, your majesty?"

She pushed her hair behind her ears as she said, "We can fix this, too, right? Me and Silence with Ishkur—whatever Ishkur is."

Comfort. Rayne needed comfort, and Nox wasn't able to give it more than the words. "I believe we can. Without further obstacles, the teams will be successful and Gait will destroy Enki without endangering you to the brink of destruction, but these variables are unpredictable. The situation is fluid and outside of our control. Either in or against our favor, this delicate balance can tip at any moment—"

Enki went dark.

Rayne gaped and laughed incredulously. She looked him up and down, accusing, "You did that."

Nox opened his mouth to say he obviously did not, but thought better of it and closed it.

Over the private channel, she said, "Sagan, this is War King. What's happening out there? Everything's dark. Over."

Sagan responded, "Just some difficulties. We'll figure it out. Over and Out."

How should Nox approach informing Rayne that her lover had just lied to her? Sagan's voice sounded frenzied with an edge of panic. Was it even worth mention—

"She lied to me."

The azure pulse came again, the frequency increasing.

Rayne sighed, heavy with exasperation.

Nox would try some diplomacy. "Without knowing her, it might seem unfit for me to advocate. But knowing what I do of her, I can vouch that Sagan would never lie to you unless she wanted to prevent this exact frustration and impotence you're feeling because of your distance from the fronts."

Rayne looked away from him and spoke to the view. "Nox, you lived my life with me. You know her as well as I do, and that's why I know you're right. Only... I don't want her to keep things from me. Damn it! I can still fight."

Staring at her profile, he pointed out. "Without her or T.A.O., you are immobile, cut-off up here. Let her manage, and I'm sure she'll return to you promptly."

Unexpectedly, Rayne laughed and turned to Nox with humor glittering in her vibrant eyes. "'Promptly.' Yes, I guess if Sagan's anything, it's 'prompt.' Thank you, Nox." She went back to staring at the dark view.

Nox returned to his calculations, and after a time, the lights returned. During their lull, the azure light had pulsed twice more under Rayne's skin. Each time, her brows tightened, and she swallowed, choked with apprehension. This isolation wasn't benefiting her fear. Nox didn't ask why she kept her comms on the private channel. If anything happened below, Rayne couldn't help them. The ineffectualness would simply drive her mad until the situation worsened to the point of Sagan fetching her from this important task.

Calibrated.

Optimized.

Stabilizing...

Unable to stabilize.

Warning: Six hours and forty-nine minutes until maximum destabilization.

A conduit opened.

Nox narrowed his gaze at the timing as a parade of familiar faces emerged. Rayne contained herself as Sagan, Xelan, Korac, Primary Tumu, and a Lyrik, who could only be Pehton, stepped through. It was the last person entering the space who decimated Rayne's self-control.

"Tameka!"

Rayne flew to her, and they embraced tightly. The King of Earth and Cinder muttered to her friend, "You smell like home. Elden, I missed you."

"Oh, I have so much to tell you. I can't wait for you to meet Pax officially."

Calibrated.

Optimized.

Stabilizing...

Unable to stabilize.

Warning: Six hours and thirteen minutes until maximum destabilization.

Nox winced.

Rayne choked on a gasp and separated them, brushing the tears from Tameka's face before letting her go completely.

Sagan shared, "Echo's here."

Nox stifled a cheer. By Elden, if he'd possessed a body, he'd wrangle Korac into an uncomfortable hug and demand to hold the child. As it was, Rayne cheered for them both. "I can't wait to properly meet them! Congratulations, Korac—That's not Korac."

No. Those eyes were all wrong.

The man dressed in Korac's skin took a step forward before Xelan stopped him with a magnificent sweep of his ridiculous coat. "That's close enough for me, thanks."

Pehton snickered and whispered something to Iuo, who shared a grin over his stenography equipment.

Tumu looked disconcerted by the situation altogether.

Rayne smiled at her guardian and shook her head at how seriously he still regarded his role. Inside her head, to Nox, she said, "He still thinks I need protecting."

"You always will to him." And Nox knew this to be the truth.

A tiny flicker of love flashed in her eyes before she returned to the present assembly.

Korac's hand waved at her while the man inside him spoke. "Hello, Rayne. I can call you 'Rayne,' can't I?"

Rayne's response brought a smile to Nox's lips. "Only if I get to call you 'Three Two Four.'"

Even Xelan grinned with a touch of pride.

The Pain Curator's eyes tightened slightly. "I want us to be friends."

Pehton raised a brow and jabbed, "I'm not sure if the King of Earth and Cinder is interested in your idea of friendship."

Tameka got to the point, a trait Nox admired about her. "Rayne, those Weapons you told us about, they've arrived, and Xelan told me about your plan. I'm down, but we need ideas on how to fight them. All I can come up with is more of your blood."

Tumu's voids scanned Rayne before meeting her eyes. "I'm not so sure powering up the Weapon inside your nacre is a good idea."

Pehton pointed out. "It's the only one we've got."

Sagan asked, "What about the blood, Rayne? We'll have to touch you for it."

Rayne looked at Nox. He said, "It should be doable."

To them, she said, "You can have it. It won't impact the fuse. Much."

Xelan looked unconvinced, but stayed the course. "We'll bring Pablo immediately and load up—"

The azure pulse came again, and everyone stared in silence.

Rayne shrank inside her head, her eyes widening on the brink of tears.

Nox ran a hand through his hair, seeking the best approach. Eventually, he settled on, "Look in their eyes."

She nodded.

"See all the love there just beneath the concern?"

Again, the nod, but this time Rayne's shoulders loosened with it.

"Hang onto the warmth, Rayne. I know it's impossible to imagine at this moment, but they act out of love. Not pity. They don't think you're a freak or a monster. Those were my fears. Don't let them be yours."

Rayne shook herself, inside and out, and targeted Razor. The man watched the strained encounter with unveiled curiosity. She said, "I assume you serve a purpose. I'm still waiting to speak to my General. How much longer will you inhabit his body like this?"

Nox nodded with approval. "Very good."

It snapped the others out of their staring, and some of them looked away, dealing with their shame and concern. Sagan and Tameka hovered closer to Rayne. The three powerful women who held the Vast Collective above water while the floods rolled in would learn to traverse emotional currents beneath the surface of their warrior facades. Together.

Razor, who noticed the power stance, smirked at the females. "Your majesty, Seamswalker, and Fury—I promise to return him moments from now. I call to Ishkur to relieve your nacre of its ailment. And what a nacre the Tritans gave you. Tumu, was it difficult for them to part with Primary Des?"

Tumu glared at him. "Watch your words, Pain Curator."

"Two nacres would've done the job."

Razor's words widened Nox's eyes.

Rayne breathed inside her head, "Does he know?"

Nox had no assurances to offer her. "The Aegis were phenomenal beings. There's no limit to what he can discern simply from looking at you."

Razor pressed on, turning to Xelan. "And you, dear Prince. Did you ever learn how your first nacre found its way to Gait? Instead of Nox's?" He winked at Rayne.

Shit.

"He knows," Nox and Rayne exclaimed at the same time.

But Tumu surprised them by saying, "I will knock you unconscious for Korac's sake if you continue to antagonize us." The Primary gave Rayne a look with reassurance in his voids.

Xelan glanced at Tumu, and Rayne noticed the question in her guardian's eyes.

She asked Nox inside her head, "Do you think..."

Did Tumu substitute Xelan's nacre for Nox's? Could the Primary also tell Rayne was carrying Nox's nacre with her all along?

Nox let out an incredulous laugh. "At this point, nothing is beyond anyone. Focus on the war at hand, your majesty."

"Right." Rayne returned her focus to Razor. "Stop deflecting and do your part to fulfill whatever bargain you've made with the Shadow."

Again, Nox approved.

Razor straightened Korac's body and pounded a fist to his chest in salute. "Right away, your highness. By the way, you are simply stunning in person."

While Nox agreed, the naked admiration in Razor's eyes boiled Nox's blood—

Pehton flicked Korac's ear, barely able to reach it.

"Ow!"

Nox and Rayne both laughed.

Sagan left Rayne's side to smooth Pehton's back. "I know. I know. But leave his beautiful ears alone, okay?" She opened the conduit.

Pehton agreed as they stepped through it. "Fine, but they both deserve it."

Tumu laughed and joined them.

Iuo paused to wave at Rayne on the way through. "It was nice seeing you." *For the last time hung in the air*, and it was there in the sadness of his two-toned eyes.

"I'll see you again," Rayne called with a wave before the Lamia disappeared with his stenography equipment to the bridge.

Tameka and Xelan remained.

The amount of people who cared about Rayne overwhelmed Nox, but not more than the power radiating from this couple. Together, they exuded confidence, hope, and consternation.

Tameka promised, "We'll be back for the blood."

Xelan's eyes held so much concern. "If you need anything, tell us. You know our channel frequency."

Rayne inhaled a shaky breath. Nox knew what she needed, and she was out of time. So he offered, "Only an hour from now and Gait will crash into Enki."

She nodded and pushed through the grief. To Xelan and Tameka, she assured, "Let's get everyone prepared with my blood, and we can start the power transfusions whenever you're ready, Tameka."

Xelan reached to touch her hair. She shook her head, and he let his hand fall without showing the loss in his smile. "I got you."

Inside her head, Nox watched, impotent, as Rayne's heart broke while the couple stepped through the conduit.

Tameka lingered long enough to say, "I love you."

"I love you!"

Then they left Rayne alone to her tears.

Not alone.

"Rayne."

A shiver passed over her, head in her hands.

"Rayne."

Nox waited until he drew her out of the shelter of her palms. He wanted to touch her, but resisted lest he trigger old trauma. Rayne met his eyes finally with hers constellated in pain. He said, "Talk to me."

A couch appeared behind them in the construct of her mind. Rayne fell onto it and pulled her knees to her chest, hugging them. She swallowed before saying, "Please, sit with me. I don't want to be alone right now."

Nox sat on the couch beside her.

They stared out at the sight of Enki and the continents and oceans of its Sphere. The star in the distance, blocked by a massive structure to provide shade and the semblance of night. It revolved around the nameless star as the moon revolved around the Earth. Day. Night. Shadow. Light.

Silence.

"They love me."

"They do."

"I love them."

"I can see why."

"I hope we win."

"I know we will, your majesty."

"Thank you, Nox. Just . . . thank you. I'm less scared with you around."

"So am I, Rayne. So am I."

Calibrated.

Optimized.

Stabilizing . . .

Unable to stabilize.

Warning: Five hours and fifty-one minutes until maximum destabilization.

SIX

OLD WOUNDS CAN'T HEAL WITHOUT FRESH BLOOD

{ENKI | GAIT'S SHRINE}

THIS WAS A ROUGH RIDE. Where was Justice Lee taking Lucy this time?

"Ugh."

"She's waking up." That was Yito's voice.

Oh, wait. Lucy remembered. Abresson had drugged her, and her new boys came in to save her.

The Ultimate Mission.

But now where was she?

There was a light whirring sounded around her, and she was stuffed in a cramped space. The other Tritans' voices sounded teeny on the speakers.

Praw said, "We have to hurry. We have two hours before Gait collides into the hull. I'm surprised Primary Rem hasn't blown the damned thing yet."

Lucy almost laughed. About that...

Stressed, Dolton said, "Eminent Lance will need our assistance with the pods once we reach a breakaway point. There's simply too many for one person to open."

Yito ordered, "Dolton. Praw. Take the others and go. Lucy and I can retrieve the demolition team together. Right, Lemonade?"

Stupid nickname. Lucy smiled at it in her half-awake state.

Yito's return smile was in his voice. "That's right."

Praw suggested, "We'll rendezvous in the Pantheon once Gait hits. I'm looking forward to ending this. Good luck to you."

"And to you, old friend."

The other voices stopped.

Lucy opened her eyes. Space. Were they in space? The shrine to Gait lingered in the middle of nothing outside the windows of the single pilot cockpit. Her voice came out softer than intended. "Matt."

The rogue half of Gait came into view, and Yito assured, "As fast as I can, Lemonade. We've been rescuing the demo team with Pil platinum magnets." He shifted storage to let Lucy sit up while he opened the retrieval protocols on the terminals. Into the comms, he urged, "Demolition team. The magnets are on their way. Set all equipment to next phase parameters and the suits will do the rest. You have twenty minutes. Good luck. Over and Out."

Even woozy, Lucy still managed to repeat the process for the next hemisphere. On the private lines, she asked, "Ginger. This is Morning Star. Are you and Puk all right? Over."

Through the seamless glass of the transport ship's windshield, Lucy stared out at the hurtling chunk of planet so near its destination. This was the plan. Set up fake charges to buy Rayne an exit from a fate promised by the Probability Matrix. No "alone and afraid." The Shadow wouldn't let that happen. Instead, Gait would destroy Enki as was poetic justice. The Dyson's Sphere eliminated by its own prison.

Lucy bit her lip, considering the Tantamount. It was the only unexpected flaw in their plan. Imminent had stolen the colossal Tantamount from Earth's Volcano Day battle and, as far as she last knew, they were planning to anchor it onto Gait. They wanted to guarantee Rayne resorted to her fate.

Concerned by the uncertainty, Lucy asked, "Do you know if they were successful with the Tantamount?"

Yito shook his head. "No, I'm sorry, I don't know. Try Matt again."

She did. No answer.

Her new Tritan friend smiled. It was a little scary, with all the sharp teeth in his head on display. "He's okay, and look!" Yito pointed. The retrieval ships were transporting people, magnetized to the vessels, back to Gait's shrine.

Please. Let them be safe.

Lucy was feeling more herself, but the question of the Tantamount wouldn't rest. "Eminent Lance, this is Morning Star. Come in. Over."

Lance sounded busy, but patient. "Morning Star. How can I help you? Over."

"The Tantamount. Do you know if Primary Rem's team affixed it to Gait?"

"I don't know. I'm sorry, but I believe he would have detonated it by now. Rem fought the hardest against the Aegis for Enki, and if he could, he would stop Rayne to save it. Keep that in mind. Over and Out."

Right—

"There, the Emporium!" Lucy shouted and pointed excitedly.

Yito shot her a knowing smile because, of course, he knew where to look for Matt and Puk.

Speak of the devil. The closest blip on the screen matched Puk's biorhythmic tag. "You've found them."

The smile on the Tritan's face tightened a bit. "Puk. I found the Mon3 drone. His vital signs measure larger on the scanner than human. It's having some trouble finding Matt—Incoming."

Yito brought the small vessel to hover over a demolished, stacked building which resembled a parking deck on Earth. Matching the rotation of the planet strained the vessel, and it groaned under the stress. He told her, "Press the projection key, and it will activate the magnets."

Worried for Matt but excited to play with a spaceship, Lucy pressed the light key.

Anything containing even trace amounts of Pil platinum should adhere to the surface. It was a rare and expensive metal. They used it for the soles of the demolition team's boots to capture them in sweeps like this one.

Both Yito and Lucy stared out of the cockpit, searching. Hoping. A significant thud resounded and shuddered the ship. Followed by two smaller thuds before Puk walked upside the ship's view screen and waved at them, looking ridiculous with his headgear fashioned to accommodate his needle-nose. He smiled and waved, multifaceted eyes shimmering.

Lucy pointed to his comms.

Through the glass, Puk made a cutting motion at his neck and mouthed, "Not. Working."

Shit.

Again, Yito assured Lucy. "Don't worry. We'll find him, then we'll join the fight in the Pantheon. I've got this." He held up a device. "It monitors the charges on Gait and the planet's trajectory. We'll know if it explodes or if it careens into Vi's Ocean, but we'll need help to evacuate these people."

"A Seamswalker." Lucy knew it was the only way. "Either of them will help. I'm sure..." She heard her voice trail off, staring out at the scenery as the radar swept for signs of life. There was only one thing on her mind now. The man who'd set Lucy on her mission which ended with the ultimate target not even an hour ago. The man who believed in her, who gave her purpose. Her best friend and soul mate.

"Matt, where are you?"

Yito sat up and tapped on the radar. "There."

Lucy sprung to it. "Did you find him? What is it?"

"It's human life."

"Thank Elden."

{Enki | Medical Bay}

Bethany relived Echo's memories of being born repeatedly. It wasn't intentional. The little girl was trying to sort out how she came to be cold and facing a bald, frowning man when she only recently was so warm, fed, and safe.

It happened when the brown-eyed man pulled her free of the warmth and cut away her source of nourishment. Then came the yellow-eyed, crying woman. She smelled familiar, and her smile made Echo feel safe. The baby tried to squeeze the woman's finger extra hard to tell her so. Then they placed her in this box with blankets, never quite warm enough, and a man peeked in from time-to-time with a different frown.

One eyebrow up. Both. Sometimes he upturned his nose with his thumb and stuck out his tongue.

That one made Echo laugh.

But still... cold and hungry. Mommy. Echo wanted her mommy—

"She's through here, Tameka. Xelan."

Sagan's voice startled Bethany out of her memory walk with Echo. She entered the bay soon after and smiled brightly in Bethany's direction, leaving her feeling guilty for intruding. Xelan with his fancy coat and Tameka in her pretty clothes followed, both of them walking in quiet steps as if afraid to wake the fully conscious child.

Bethany should excuse herself, but an abomination stepped through the doors.

Razor in Korac's body.

The Pain Curator. *"It's okay to cry. But you're old enough now to know it won't do any good except to upset you further. Do you understand?"*

King of Broken Promises. *"A little more then we can stop for the day. Does that sound good?"*

The Last Aegis. *"Tonight, you feast on your rescuer, and all outside communication privileges are permanently revoked. A lesson for those so eager to leave. Don't endanger your families."*

Razor, himself, had stood in Bethany's cell until she ate all three servings of ground Mon3 drone.

When he emerged in the Medical Bay wearing the only man in all the Vast Collective who understood her trauma, Bethany laughed. The entire party stopped their trek to Echo and stared at her. Xelan's eyes filled with empathy. Tameka glanced between Bethany and Razor with contempt. And Sagan took a step toward the teenage girl, reaching out.

"It's okay, Bethany. Korac will return soon. Have you been looking after Echo?"

But Bethany couldn't stop laughing. Should she kill his baby? Would that be retribution enough?

No.

No.

Those weren't her real thoughts or feelings.

Bethany went quiet and gripped her head, rocking.

She loved Echo. Loved the story of her birth, and Bethany was actually happy to salvage enough Aegis blood for Echo to experience her mother's arms.

But why was Razor here?!

Bethany slammed her fists against the wall on either side of her. He didn't deserve to breathe near Echo, let alone touch her. He deserved for someone to feed her heart to him—

No.

No.

Bethany sank down the wall, covered her head, and screamed into her arms.

Meanwhile, commotion erupted around her, but she couldn't hear or see it. Hands touched her gently, and she jerked away—Singed. Oh, Elden, she was sure that was Xelan's voice trying to soothe her, but for all the world it might as well have been gasoline thrown on a fire.

Stay away!

Dark. Bethany needed the dark. Where was her hood? Why was there so much light—

"324."

That name out of that voice.

Bethany stopped breathing. The Nice Man. He was back.

"Bethany, it's Matt. Everyone else left the bay. We're alone." His voice was a pleasant tenor, empty of everything—Pretense, coaxing, ulterior motives. Everything about Matt was safely empty.

She lay in a ball on the floor, unaware of how she had contorted this way. Slowly, she unfurled her arms and legs, stretching out to her petite size. Bethany wasn't ready to open her eyes yet, so she kept one arm thrown over them. It was too bright.

Matt groaned as he sank down to the floor and stretched one leg out, leaving one bent for his arm to rest upon. She peeked through her arm to watch him play with his overgrown fringe in that nice auburn shade which complimented his freckles. After another heartbeat, he said, "You're doing a great job guarding Echo."

Pride suffused Bethany.

Matt filled her in on some of the commotion she'd checked out of earlier. "The Shadow are gathering Rayne's blood for the battle currently on pause. I'm glad I didn't miss it." He grinned, and it was cute. It faded when he glanced down at her as if he knew she was looking. "Are you joining in this time? I think you ought to."

Bethany? In a fight?

Matt shrugged like he sensed her doubts. "I'm sure I can convince your brother and sister it's a good idea. Everyone should get a chance to say they fought in the great battle for the Vast Collective." Again, that grin. "Me and Lucy have a celebration planned for after, but you don't need to know about that. Do you wanna see Lucy? She and Puk are here along with some new friends."

Yes. Bethany liked Lucy and Puk. She nodded.

Matt whistled, and the blond girl accompanied by the Mon3 drone stepped into the bay. Both of them smiled affectionately at Bethany. She liked it.

Puk beamed at her. "So, what do you say, Bethany? Do you wanna drink some of Rayne's blood and kill some bad guys with us?"

Lucy's eyes weren't dead like Matt's. The deep blue sheltered mysteries beneath the purity. Those mysteries liked the sound of Puk's plan because her eyes sparkled. "We'll look after you," Lucy promised.

Bethany dropped her arm and sat up, peering at them. Such a strange group of people, but they'd survived Gait together, and that was some bond.

Dry.

Sore.

Bethany's voice was untried, even so, she tried to ask, "Can... I... eat them?"

The group exchanged looks, not one of them in shock or judgment. More like they were intrigued and entertained. They settled their gazes on Matt, who turned to Bethany and shrugged. "Sure. I don't see why not."

Puk extended a hand, and Bethany took it to stand.

"Just be sure to floss after, okay, kid?"

Bethany nodded.

{ENKI | MEDICAL BAY}

Razor tried not to look at the woman glaring at him. He kept diverting himself with instruments around the medical bay, noting Dr. Suarez had yet to dispose of Triss' body. Meanwhile, he couldn't touch his own child for the traumatized girl in the next bay, who was dangerous in her own right.

Memory was a tricky thing, and broken people made regrettable mistakes.

Sagan sounded incredulous. "You have some nerve suggesting Bethany might be a danger to Echo. After everything you put her through, you'd think you could find *any* trace of compassion for another being who wasn't infatuated with you. *Anything*, Razor."

Her disappointment gave weight to the words as the Seamswalker expected human emotions from the least human of all beings in the galaxy.

The only living person who'd ever understood that and might plea a case for him was ferrying Tameka, Xelan, and Dr. Suarez to Rayne for vials of blood.

Rayne.

Razor shook Korac's head, a tad overwhelmed. He hadn't imagined it. The stories of Night Rayne—Rayne and Nox's fabled romance—were rooted in more reality than he thought. Tumu had to have seen it, but none of the rest of the Shadow seemed to know.

Somehow, by some Aegis-level miracle, Rayne had retained both her and Nox's nacres separate from each other. Mostly. There was some merging, and oh, that would produce some interesting results—

The splinter of fractured tangents in Razor's mind allowed him to momentarily escape the Seamswalker's mighty judgment.

Razor tried for reason, keeping his voice nonthreatening and bland to avoid allegations of manipulation. This was too serious to risk on games. "It is only right for that girl to take her vengeance out on me, and my greatest vulnerability is the baby Triss gave her life for. Don't you see?" He took a step forward before realizing he'd moved and stopped himself from encroaching further. "It's why I never wanted children. They pose risks and weaknesses I can't afford. If 32—Bethany ever wanted to repay me, that's the only way."

Sagan listened. He saw her following his logic in the frown which scrunched her freckled nose. Saw the frustration in her as she stood and touched her forehead, rubbing it. Still overtaxed despite the blood donation, which was more than a little difficult to remain neutral during. Tameka looming over him as a constant threat was enough to make Razor behave. As a being born without a nacre, he'd yet to experience a power drain, and he respected Tameka because he knew she was likely the only person in the room who wouldn't hesitate to lay Korac out.

Matt, of all fucking people, stepped into the bay, occupied privately by Razor and Sagan. The human ginger looked quite relaxed and at home with the situation. "Hey. I got her to calm down."

A feat only possible because Razor had put Bethany and Matt together, but he didn't expect to receive any credit for it.

Matt folded his arms, leaned against the threshold, and continued with the update. "Bethany left the bay with Lucy. Xelan and Tameka are in there with Echo now."

"Lucy's a pretty name."

Razor stated it as a point of fact, but Matt and Sagan both turned their attention to him slowly, as if they knew he'd meant more by it. The younger man smiled the same congenial threat he and Razor had shared in the past.

It brought up old slights. When Razor had employed Matt at his Emporium of Exotic Experiences, he'd considered the human with an extraordinary gift for violence as a protégé. The betrayal was beautiful and bitter all at once. Staring into that familiar face, Razor considered the circumstances and held out Korac's hand. "I would have done the same, and I appreciate your style."

Matt's smile broadened into a grin. He stepped up to Razor, clasped the extended hand, and kept his eyes on his adversary the entire time with that dead spark in them. "It was Lucy's style, but I'm glad you're coming around, boss." Their hands dropped, and Matt waved at Sagan. "See ya, Seamswalker. We're heading out to join the games."

"Thanks, Matt. Tell Lucy I'm glad you're both okay."

"Will do."

Razor couldn't help but notice how Sagan beamed around the people she loved. Her eyes were bright, her smile open, and her face beautiful. She'd looked at Razor like that before he'd ruined her.

The Seamswalker devoured another nutrition ration, pacing when she should be resting. She slumped against a wall and gripped her hair, sighing.

Without asking, Razor knew she was impatiently awaiting Korac's return. He offered, "Not much longer now."

She shot him an accusing glance. "When we return to the bridge, Xelan will monitor all of your actions from hereon. We'll let you finish with Ishkur. Then I hope it's a while before I see your eyes again, Razor."

Razor opened Korac's mouth, thought better of making a joke, and closed it again in time for Xelan and Tameka to return.

The young woman went first. "Rayne donated enough blood to refill everyone's pendants."

The Pain Curator conceded to the Shadow. Those small Pretiosum Cruors were a brilliant strategy, completely undetected by Imminent.

Confusion passed over Sagan's eyes. "What about the shield virus?"

No doubt Xelan had an answer for that. It's one trait Razor liked most about the half-Icarus, who looked happy to say, "The vaccinations prevent us from contracting it. Our nacres will remain viable to upgrades even after drinking Rayne's blood."

Tumu rounded the corner. "T.A.O. is transporting them to the Pantheon team now. We should finish with Ishkur while Andrew still has control."

Tameka glared at Razor as she crossed the room to Sagan. "Here." She clasped one of those chains around Sagan's neck. "For in case you pass out again. We'll give Korac one after Razor's gone." So much distaste in such a pretty voice.

Xelan shot Razor a look that was ninety percent consideration and ten percent sympathy.

Sweet Prince.

Razor shoved Korac's hands into the pockets of his leather pants and shrugged innocently. "Shall we?"

Sagan opened a conduit for them to file back into the bridge. There, Razor rushed to the main terminal with

Xelan close by, watching more with curiosity on his face than suspicion.

Tameka announced, "I'll work on the power transfers to Rayne." Then sat in a meditation pose to concentrate, her eyes in Atramentous.

Pehton and Iuo followed from a separate conduit, and Razor ignored the sliver of concern for Sagan's capacity. Instead, he reveled in the activity while he operated the bridge.

Not long now.

"I've been observing you with the interface."

Xelan. Clever, brilliant Xelan. Of course, he'd catch on.

Razor kept his eyes on the controls. "Yes?"

The Traitor Prince's voice was quiet as he relayed his assumptions. "The Aegis have a beautiful way of naming things."

Well, that wasn't what Razor had expected him to say. "We did."

Xelan turned, planted his ass against the terminal, and folded his arms, staring at Razor. "'Monarch Hall.' 'Feast of Roses.' 'Opal Mezzanine'—Yes, I've been there. Quite lovely."

Razor's concentration suffered under Xelan's careful gaze. The man was measuring his worth. "What is it, Xelan?"

"What better name for a bridge than the 'Hall of Dead Kings.'"

Fuck.

Razor almost closed Korac's eyes and cursed aloud, only it would confirm Xelan's suspicions.

Xelan leaned closer, appearing outwardly as old friends talking, but his eyes—

There was nothing friendly in them.

So close. Razor was almost done. "Xelan, I need to upload to interact with the internal interface. You'll never see Ishkur without it."

The Icarean Prince nodded, intelligence in his gaze. "What happens to your place in the Atheneum?"

This time, Razor cursed aloud. "Damn it. I'm sure you've already guessed." A few more sequences and functions.

Xelan's voice softened. "You know we're destroying Enki one way or the other. Don't you?"

"Yes."

"And you'll never escape alive?"

"Yes."

They both stopped looking at each other and stared at Tameka, Sagan, and Pehton, who were teasing luo and Tumu. Happy even amid this chaos because they knew the righteous would win this day.

Xelan asked, "What about T.A.O.?"

Razor's laughter was bitter, and Korac's voice conveyed it well. "Don't worry. I won't leave without my grand exit. Farewells for all."

The last sequence.

Xelan said, "You were wrong for so much, Razor." He met Xelan's eyes again, and they stared at each other with the last key between them. "I wasn't aware or here for most of it, so I have this weird sense that I'll miss the Razor I knew. Like the Triss I knew."

The Pain Curator experienced an emotion he couldn't quite identify at the Icarus' words, but Razor knew what to say. "I'd prefer you remember me that way."

Xelan nodded in Sagan's direction. "Say something to her before you complete the sequence. Sagan's experience with you is so terribly complicated. I don't want one of my closest friends regretting anything unsaid between you."

Again, that bitter laugh. "I'm sure it's only fair to let her say 'I hate you' one last time."

Shaking his head, Xelan stepped away from the terminal, saying, "She never hated you, Razor. That's what haunts her. You're her brother-in-law. Fucking act like it."

Razor shot Korac's brows up high. Xelan never swore. The Prince crossed the room to Sagan and called her over. In the meantime, Razor digested his words.

What was the value of relationships to a being like Razor?

Triss? T.A.O.? Xelan, Korac, and Sagan? If not for her affiliation with Zero's youngest son, Razor would never have hurt Sagan in the first place—

But was that true?

T.A.O. was hurt simply by proximity to Razor's world. The life he led couldn't shelter innocents.

Haunted.

That was the word Xelan had used, and it was the shade in Sagan's eyes as she approached. Razor glanced down at the final key and back up into her timid eyes. "Seamswalker."

"Xelan said you wanted to say something to me."

That Sagan stood there at all to hear what Razor had to say…

Make it count.

Razor took one step toward Sagan and gingerly took her hand. When she controlled her apparent urge to flinch, he brought her knuckles to Korac's lips and kissed them. Before he'd destroyed her, it was a gesture of affection between them, and it affected him because she allowed it.

One last time.

Over the Seamswalker's small fingers, Razor said, "Forgive me, Sagan. When he asks, I hope you say 'yes.' I would be proud to call you 'family.'"

Razor completed the sequence.

{ENKI | MEDICAL BAY}

Ross stood with Jack, who knocked on the medical bay's threshold. The highest tier contained the two Valkyrie and their human lover. Karter and Para had come down a few times to take the pulse of the situation, but while they socialized, Chris remained upstairs. And, well…

Ross wanted to talk to him.

"Come in."

The army veteran from Earth sounded much better than he had only a few hours ago, as Jack and Ross stepped into the space. Chris sat with his back to them, zipping up his black and blue combat suit. Like Jack's.

Even though Ross had to stop remembering the bruising on her thighs from Chris' hands, she took Jack another step forward.

Grateful, the younger man asked, "Are you joining the battle?" He sounded hopeful.

Without turning around, Chris confirmed, "All vaccinated and ready to fight." Still, he concentrated on his gear.

Ross remained quiet, letting them have this moment, while Jack awkwardly worked the kinks from his neck, saying, "Do you want to be on the same squad? Like Volcano Day?"

Chris groaned, leaning down to slip on his combat boot. "That may not be for the best, kid."

Ross hated the way Jack's face fell. She knew this was about what had happened to her, and she wouldn't let it go on any longer. Softly, she pressed, "Jack, can you give us a minute alone?"

Chris went stiff at the sound of her voice.

Jack glanced from Chris to her, and she let all the reassurance show on her face. No one was worried Chris might hurt her again, but it was so hard to approach this topic.

"Sure. I'll be on the stairs."

Ross squeezed his hand. "I'll get you, I promise." When Jack disappeared down the staircase, she bolstered herself for a hard conversation and refused to have it with the back of Chris' head. "Please, look at me. I understand why you don't want to, but I have a lot I want to say, and I'd like to see your eyes for it."

They were warm eyes, Ross knew. A brown like oak trees in the autumn. Kind. She'd always liked them.

When Chris stood and turned to face her, all the warmth had seeped from his eyes. They were shards of brown ice with a hint of fear around the edges.

It was enough to make Ross cry. She looked down and wet her lips, afraid of all the emotion. But the caring man who'd screamed in his own head not to hurt her was worth a little discomfort.

Ross faced him again without tears and told him the truth. "I know you didn't want to hurt me. It wasn't you. I need you to know that, and that's not the confession of some inexperienced girl. Razor once spent thirty minutes touching me—"

Chris winced.

"—Without getting nearly as physically close to me as you were. What he did left far more lasting harm than . . . " Ross swallowed and continued. "I know you think you unwillingly left some psychological scars, but you didn't. I promise I'm fine, and Jack just wants things back how they were if you can find that in you to give. We're here for you Chris. We're waiting to have our family back together whenever you're ready. If you're ever ready. I understand."

"We've both been through enough." Chris finally said something. "About the kid... I'm willing to try, but I can't promise I won't PTSD my way through this battle. Or what comes after. I..." It was his turn to swallow and try again. "These things take time, and it's kinda known the Shadow never really get enough of it to fully heal. But I'll try, Ross. Coming here and talking to me was brave—"

She shook her head.

"—Yes, it was. You may have had it in your head the entire time that I wasn't in control, but there will be always be some part of you that will never react to me the same way again." He wet his lips, choked, and tried once more. "We'll never recover that, but I think you're right. We can move on. Send Jack in for a bit, will you? I want to tell him some things."

Crushed with relief, concern, love, and confusion, Ross turned to head for the stairs.

"Ross?"

She stopped and glanced over her shoulder.

Some of the warmth had returned to Chris' eyes. "Thank you. Thank you so much for knowing."

Ross nodded and grabbed Jack. With only a look, the young man rushed up the stairs to talk to his guardian, while Ross went looking for Bethany. She rounded the corner and nearly ran into T.A.O.

"Sorry." Ross tried to go around her, but T.A.O. stepped back in her way. The woman was nearly a foot shorter than Ross, so it wasn't a matter of intimidation but curiosity. "Do you need something from me?"

The tiny woman with her strange eyes smiled, and it was sweet. "She will feast."

Ross wasn't sure her eyes flared wide enough to hop out of her head, but that's what it felt like. "Uhm..."

T.A.O. continued, "You will let her, and she will save us all."

This wasn't a drill, and T.A.O. meant every word. Ross agreed. "I will let her."

"Good."

The tiny woman stepped out of the threshold to the next bay, where Matt, Lucy, Puk, some Tritans, and Bethany lounged like lions in a cave.

"Hi." Ross waved.

Puk waved back, grinning like a big goof. It was infectious. Lucy smiled sweetly, her fingers drawing circles on Matt's arm, who seemed to enjoy it given the goosebumps.

Then Matt grinned at Ross. "Hey, we'd like permission to take Bethany out to the Pantheon for the fight, and since Kyle is already there, that makes you her chaperon."

Bethany punctuated his words with a big grin of her own and an emphatic nod.

Ross blinked.

Lucy explained, "T.A.O.'s Seamswalking us there in a minute. Our team has some soldiers to meet and form our own squad. We'd like it if Bethany would join us. We'll look after her, of course."

Puk looped an arm around Bethany's smaller shoulders and squeezed her into his muscular heft for a convincing side hug, ruffling her hair. "She'll be perfectly safe."

On a battlefield.

Ross glanced downstairs at the pile of bodies. Was she any safer here? And Bethany looked so excited to go.

"You will let her, and she will save us all."

With a heavy sigh, Ross said, "Sure. Check with Kyle when you get there, so he doesn't kill me."

Lucy hopped out of her seat and skipped across the room to Ross, wrapping her in a warm embrace. "Thank you. She'll be safe. I promise."

Right then, Ross wasn't worried about them keeping Bethany safe. Ross was worried about Bethany becoming like them. But as Imminent had proven repeatedly, there were worse ways to turn out.

{ENKI | BRIDGE}

Korac fell to the floor as Pehton rushed over to help Sagan hold his head up. He was far too tall for both short women to keep him upright. Pehton peered at Sagan over Korac's unconscious body.

There had been a recent development. Pehton could see it in the tears streaking the Seamswalker's face.

Pehton reached for Sagan's hand. "What's wrong—"

"Hello, all those not currently possessing a Dyson's Sphere."

Razor's actual voice came from an all-comms system. It was Everywhere.

Tameka, Pehton, Iuo, and Tumu looked properly panicked, but not Sagan and Xelan.

"I'll be your guide to Enki for the next two hours before your expulsion. In the meantime, enjoy the fireworks. The Pantheon is currently providing one phenomenal display, and I have the perfect soundtrack for it."

Music with a heavy beat pulsed through the surrounding speakers. Rousing violins joined in a dramatic overture to battle. Why were the Aegis and half-Aegis such big drama queens?

Tameka whispered to Xelan, who seemed rather calm about their current situation.

Pehton left her earpiece open to the Pantheon team, and Kyle sounded a little concerned. "What the fuck is that? Over."

Now wasn't the time to laugh at the mundanity of communication protocols, but it was super tempting. Instead, Pehton said, "I'll find out and provide you an update ASAP. Over and Out."

Sagan was also talking to her comms. "Yes, War King. That's Razor—"

Xelan crossed the space and knelt to check Korac's vitals. He looked into Sagan's and Pehton's eyes, no doubt filled with concern, but not the Prince. He assured, "Korac will wake any minute. Try not to stress yourself too much, Sagan."

Tameka grumbled something about being in communion with a star and needing to concentrate, despite all this drama.

Pehton glimpsed Tumu standing in the center of the bridge, gazing around it. Colored lights transitioned in time with the music. Ambiance. Razor was giving them atmosphere for some grand display of his—

Korac stirred at last, and Pehton pinched his arm.

"Ow!"

She let him have it. "General, you have no idea how badly you worried Sagan."

Xelan chuckled.

Tameka muttered, "Thank Elden."

Iuo took a picture of the group all crouched on the floor over the tall, fit specimen of Icarean and Aegis breeding, laid out with his hair fanning him like some pale halo.

Would Pehton ever get over him completely?

Korac cupped Sagan's face, and she smiled despite her puffy eyes.

Tumu was the only one not having a good time. "Star, what did Razor say to you last?"

They all stared at Sagan, who looked less happy now. A little confused, she said, "I'm not sure, but I think he said 'goodbye.'"

Pehton stepped back to give Korac room to stand, and she settled beside Iuo while the others talked. Korac said something about not sensing Razor anymore, but Pehton was rather distracted with the picture of them in Iuo's latest entry.

"Wow, Iuo, I can't remember looking so happy. Ever."

The Lamian Prince shown her a winning smile. "I think you look prettiest this way." She blushed a little, especially as he went on. "And if you and Caedes ever want a film—"

"Peh Peh."

Pehton whirled to find a life-size projection of Razor's Aegis form, complete with a three-piece suit, a cane, and a fucking top hat.

The Lyriki warrior exclaimed, "Hey, team!"

The others stopped talking and stared. Even Tameka finally gave up on her task to gawk.

The Razor projection waved. "I am the eyes and ears—really the heart of the Dyson's Sphere now. Try not to break me. At least not for another two hours."

Pehton glanced at Wingmaster. There was something to this. He didn't look concerned or confused, but more like he'd expected this much.

But time and place. Pehton asked, "Why are you asking for me?"

Razor smiled, and it was made of light. "I may need your help."

Pehton didn't have to laugh in his face. Tameka did, and it was full of incredulity.

The Aegis fixed his alien gaze on the redhead, and his smile crooked into a smirk. "I *know* I need yours, Fury. You're the key to Ishkur."

Well, that got everyone's attention.

SEVEN

WONDERS NEVER CEASE IN SHADOW

{ENKI | PANTHEON}

"WHERE IS UNCLE NOCK?! You promised to take me to him and Auntie Rayne."

"Not much longer now, son."

That was the twenty-eighth time Remorse had repeated the line during their swift journey through Enki's labyrinth of conduits. He'd reduced himself to half his height, now at thirty feet, to fit through rifts of energy, while keeping compression enormous enough to carry the child in his hand.

Bol.

That Primary had sided with his brother and partner in all endeavors since Rem had betrayed Quet. Primary Bol was the only one being left in the Vast Collective with the reinstatement of the Tritan species as their highest priority. The three of them—Bol, Rem, and Pax—would escape Enki with the evacuated stock of Weapons and return to the Vast Collective, prepared to reconquer it in the name of all things Tritan.

Pax was instrumental to this revivification. Without him, they wouldn't contain the necessary genetic material to create brainless receptacles for procreation. Surras without the intelligence.

Yes.

That was the key.

Let Rayne wipe out Enki and take their enemies with her. Xelan could burn for all he'd betrayed Remorse's gifts. Razor made for a better son in more than surrogacy. Even Vi would have approved of adopting the Aegis prodigy—

Where was Bol?

Primary Rem arrived at his brother's sanctum to find it empty.

Pax squirmed and huffed. Bored children made for quite the bother. Pax asked, "Where is Skylence? I like her."

Did the boy know by saying it in such a way, he was alluding to not liking Remorse?

The Tritan grandfather hated to admit the sting was lasting. "That's a good question, Pax. You're such a smart boy."

Midnight blue bled into the child's eyes, and his voice triplicated in pitch. "I knew all things which occurred that led to my making. Who I was and who I would be in multiple strands of reality. I saw across the flaming vista to Rayne's end and felt cold beyond it. I was afraid without Celindria's guidance." Pax hyperventilated in terror. "What happened to her? I don't believe she would retreat without me. And mother. Where is my mother? Father? Uncle Nox? You are *not* my family. You are a parasite which preys on us. Mother? Where is she—"

The boy fainted in Remorse's hand.

Primary Rem needed to find some of Rayne's blood before Pax awakened. It was the only way to guarantee a defense against his draining ability. He'd need enough for both him and Bol, and possibly the soldiers. There was no way to predict how malleable Pax would be, especially with this unexpected burst of consciousness.

Where was Primary Bol?

"Hello, all those not currently possessing a Dyson's Sphere."

Razor.

"I'll be your guide to Enki for the next two hours before expulsion. In the meantime, enjoy the fireworks. The Pantheon is currently providing one phenomenal display, and I have the perfect soundtrack for it."

Music played over an all-encompassing communication system Primary Rem had never known existed. It could only mean the Shadow had uploaded Razor to the bridge.

A victory for Imminent, and it had arrived with a hidden message.

Remorse left Bol's sanctum and headed straight for the Pantheon. If the Shadow had amassed their forces there, Bol would meet them, if only to take samples of the greatest among their enemy.

Silence was most likely there as well.

Rayne.

Yes. Once they collected the necessary samples, they could evacuate the Tritan bulls from Enki and start fresh. Before the two hours ended, they'd also detonate the Tantamount and destroy Gait's rogue half. Perhaps he could contact Razor and figure a way to download him out of the Dyson's Sphere. Hopefully, Abresson was already there and could update Primary Rem on how the depository evacuations went.

Surely the Eminent wouldn't risk his life by failing Remorse again.

{ENKI | PANTHEON}

Korac ducked his head for Sagan to give him a Shadow chain. In his hand, he held a vial of Rayne's blood, which they trusted to him. He'd come a long way since Invasion Day.

Meanwhile, Razor, freed within Enki's mainframe, explained how Ishkur required a power infusion. "Do you think you're up for it, Fury?"

Korac appreciated that their future galactic Empress never looked to Xelan or Tumu for permission or confirmation. Fury simply said, "If I find you're manipulating us, Razor, we won't have to wait for Gait to impact Enki's hull. I'll destroy you, myself."

Sagan's eyes sparkled with pride as she glanced at Korac. He smirked back.

Yes. Tameka would do nicely, and oh, to be a fly on the wall for the conversation where Xelan confessed it all to her.

The image was enough to revive Korac. He didn't even groan as he stood. Truth be told, without the Shadow asking, Korac had already prepared to upcycle Zero in case things went sideways with Razor.

It felt weird expecting aid from his father, but here he was, waiting for dad to bail him out if things got too tough.

Korac *was* getting soft—

Tameka crooked her finger at Korac, asking him to join her across the room. He quirked a brow. Even higher as Sagan, Xelan, Tumu, Pehton, and Iuo all exchanged glances. Straightening his robe, Korac answered her summons.

The redhead with her killer complexion and enviable freckles stared up at him, green eyes filled with purpose. "I have news for you and Pehton, but I can't share with—" She pointed at the terminal, meaning Razor. "Listening. Watching."

It must be important for Tameka to spend one-on-one time with Korac. He would've suggested the Seam for privacy, but Tameka couldn't go there, and asking Sagan for more Seamswalking while she'd already strained her ability wasn't happening.

Tameka continued. "I'll brief you on the situation when the time is right. I just didn't want you to think I kept it from you intentionally. It's good news, I promise." Wonder of wonders, she smiled at him. It was genuine and bright.

Korac wanted to repay her confidence, seal an accord between them, finally. He retrieved the amber glass box from his pocket and held it out where only she could see.

The smile fell from Tameka's lips while her eyes filled with wonder. On a gasp, she asked, "Really?"

A cool composure was Korac's trademark, but as he asked for Tameka's blessing to marry her best friend, he found himself nervous. Again, soft.

But when Tameka looked up from the ring to Korac's eyes, he decided soft wasn't so bad. That was a smile to fight alongside. A thousand-watt beam. "She'll love it." As if she saw through to Korac's fears, Fury gripped his shoulder. "She'll say, 'yes.' *Believe me.*"

Korac did.

Tameka's smile crooked into something cheekier as she said, "By the way, Xelan told me you were the one who convinced him I was still alive."

Korac chuckled. "That's because I knew."

Tameka put a hand on her hip, sassy. "What did you know?"

"No storm could take you out."

"Damn straight."

One glance at Xelan, pacing and biting his thumbnail, told Korac it was a bad idea to bring up the Empress deal, but since Tameka was so forthcoming, it seemed unfair to keep it from her entirely. Korac fought a wicked smirk as he said, "Xelan has a secret he's afraid to tell you."

Tameka glanced over at her future galactic co-leader and clicked her tongue. "You're not planning to tell me, are you?"

"Nope."

She sighed, and it held the weight of someone who'd fought a storm this day. "How did you ever get him to stop being so mysterious with you?"

Now Korac's laughter was rich. "Believe me, Fury. You don't want that level of detail into our relationship. I had my ways." He walked back to Sagan, leaving Tameka blushing in his wake.

Sagan smiled with a hint of strain in her eyes. Keeping conduits open all over Enki was eating away at her reserves. Although Korac wasn't happy to learn Razor had donated blood to her, Korac was glad Sagan had fed recently.

The Seamswalker held a hand out to him. "Someone's waiting to see you."

Without question, Korac took her hand and—

Vertigo hit him pretty hard as they stepped into nothing. Space. They were in the heart of Enki.

"Open your wings."

Rayne.

Korac opened his wings and used them for stability in the abyss. Sagan held his hand the entire time, patient.

After an azure light pulsed under her pale skin, the King of Earth and Cinder said, "I'm so happy to see you as yourself again."

Rayne looked, as always, beautiful, but in an untouchable kind of way, and Korac supposed that was painfully close to the truth. Any contact with her would diminish the frightening fuse. All the times Nox had shied away from contact—Even thinking of what a lonely existence his best friend had led choked Korac. And now that burden fell on Rayne.

On the topic of his half-brother, Korac said, "As am I, your highness. I'm sorry you ever had to meet Razor."

The signature brightness of Rayne's eyes faded for a moment. It returned as she said, "I trust you to keep him in line while he operates Enki for the Shadow."

Sagan took in the scenery, saying, "I can't believe you can hear Razor out here."

Rayne looked withered by the vast emptiness surrounding her. Still, she sounded in high spirits when she said, "I suspect we'll hear more from our 'guide' in the next two hours."

Okay. Korac wasn't imagining it. The brightness in her eyes faded again. He kept his frown off his face as he formed a hypothesis. Now Korac wanted to test it. "This…" He swept a hand to indicate the view. "It reminds me of the stories of the Valkyrie—" AKA, his own mother, "—Fighting in the rings of Thailea."

Rayne's eyes definitely shifted down a notch to a regular dim. Then the brightness returned. She said, "It didn't surprise me to hear Amolot was too afraid to fight beyond the stratosphere."

Korac used every ounce of his control not to open his mouth and gape at Rayne.

No one living knew that precious detail. Nox had hauled the confession from Amolot during a shouting match after she'd caught the boys during one of their pranks. Korac was the only witness.

Rayne smiled at him, waiting for a response, commiserating with impossible specifics. More than anything, Korac wanted to ask her if somehow—someway—she'd made the legends of Elden's Verse viable.

"Take the warrior you fell to victory with you."

Was Nox in there?

Rayne glanced at Sagan, then back at Korac. As azure pulsed under her skin again, Rayne gave him the most indiscernible of nods and, with it, confirmed all of Korac's hopes.

He actually had to clear his throat before saying, "Yes, your majesty. I understand you won't be joining us on the battlefield, but I will retrieve you, myself, before we evacuate."

The brightness in Rayne's eyes was on full power. "You got it. Besides, I refuse to miss whatever wedding we all know you have planned."

With a wink, once again, Rayne nearly leveled Korac.

Sagan beamed at him. "One can only hope."

Tameka came over the earpieces. "Seamswalker and Silver General, we found Primary Rem, and we're about to begin. Over."

Sagan confirmed. "On our way. Over." She opened a conduit back to the bridge.

Rayne...

Korac almost shook his head with the awesomeness of it.

Rayne's eyes dimmed as she presumably spoke to Korac's best friend inside her head. Then she smiled. "We'll see you soon."

Yes.

They would.

{ENKI | MEDICAL BAY}

With their new Rayne chains, Chris and Jack descended the stairs after communicating a better understanding of each other. At the bottom, they found Karter, Para, and Ross waiting with T.A.O. Gratitude filled the veteran soldier, melting the ice Celindria had left behind. He loved this family of theirs.

Dressed in Valkyrie combat gear, Karter embraced him, and Chris found everything he needed in her arms. She purred against him, and the sensation overwhelmed him. It thickened his voice with the effort to put his feelings into words. "Thank you."

Para scoffed. "As if we'd go to war without you."

Chris widened his arms to include her, and the smallest Valkyrie joined the throuple snuggle. Jack pulled Ross against his side for a hug, and their team basked. It was a good moment.

So when T.A.O. spoke into her earpiece, their nosy asses took notice because it wasn't on the Pantheon team frequency, and Chris presumed it was on her private line.

T.A.O. sounded happy to hear from her caller. "Your voice reminds me of home." She paused, listening, fidgeting with her Rayne chain. "Yes, there is one additional star in Enki, and she will burn through the cosmos." Another pause. "I see it. Yes." With the call evidently over, she faced Chris and team once more. "Last chance for abandon. Your post will belong to another."

Karter shook her head, assuring, "No one is abandoning their post today. Please take us to the Pantheon."

They linked hands and followed T.A.O. into—

A head trip.

Was Chris hallucinating the armies poised on the brink of fighting, frozen?

All the soldiers on the front line were posed mid-punch, kick, stab—In the air. On the ground. Everywhere Chris looked. Lamias, Luks, Dwarves, Mon3 Drones, humans,

Icari, Caprents, Lyriks, and Tritans. Scattered among them were the haunting edifices of Rayne and her greatest adversary, Nox, with their skeletons made of nacre glass and powered by Aegis blood.

They sure would give the Terminator a run for its money.

All the Shadow hung back in awe, grouped near the conduit to Torrentus. Ross found Bethany hanging out with Matt, Lucy, and Puk—All wearing chains. She checked on her sister, who pointed to their left. Kyle, Bones, Caedes, and Lamassau all stood beside Andrew, distress had contorted his entire body under the strain of his ability. Every single one of them were staring up at the sky.

Chris had never met Silence, but the woman hovering up there with Lucas and Smith could only be her. Her blue wings matched the stripe of blue at the front of her hair and the Atramentous of her eyes. An azure light pulsed under her skin twice during the time Chris examined her. She was gorgeous, and a little similar to Karter in complexion and facial features. Although, Silence kinda looked similar to a lot of Icari, if Chris stared long enough. Only one flaw diminished her ethereal effect.

The woman above them looked lost. Lost in what she wanted and lost in what brought her here. Her foundation was rocked and shaken. Silence directed this existential crisis at Kyle, who looked like he was waiting for a response.

"Won't you answer me?"

Yup. He was waiting for a response.

In the sky, with Smith on his back, Lucas said something to Silence, too far away for them to hear. Chris didn't need anyone to tell him that anything involving Lucas would hurt Andrew. Conscience swallowed and choked on it, coughing and nearly stumbling. Kyle and Lamassau saved him. To Chris' surprise, Lucas lost his serene composure for a moment and flinched.

What the hell was happening here?

With Andrew leaning on him, Kyle called up to them, "You know this isn't what you wanted! You can break nacre glass. Fight with us!"

The three in the sky talked amongst themselves. Silence never took her eyes off Kyle. Maybe Chris had spent enough time around Icari to read them, but he suspected Lucas wanted to join the fight. It might have something to do with his boyfriend—ex?—turning the color of a parfait down here, but those were Chris' assumptions.

The alien light pulsed under Silence's skin again.

In the most terrifying display of power Chris had ever witnessed, Silence lifted her open palm in front of her, squeezed it into a fist, and sent every single Rayne and Nox copy to the floor in a crumpled heap of concaved nacre glass.

Godlike, Silence stood on high, hands on hips, and quirked an angled brow, letting her actions speak for her.

"Sorry. She gets like this when she's gone too long without sex." They all looked at Smith. "It's really best just to stay off her radar."

Yeah. No shit.

{ENKI | BRIDGE}

"I'm sorry, Kyle, can you repeat that? I thought you just said Silence decimated the Weapons with a gesture? Over."

Xelan and Tameka shared a bewildered look as the Shadow on site confirmed it.

Razor's projection appeared over the center of the maelstrom near the main terminal where Xelan, Tameka, Tumu, Sagan, and Korac waited for his next instructions. Pehton stood on the highest glass gangway with Iuo, who recorded every word and gesture like his race depended on it.

The projected rendering of Xelan's old friend smiled. "You missed one glorious display. Silence is quite the wild card. Now, Tameka. Are you ready?"

"I hate to do anything you say, but yes. I'm ready."

Xelan understood her reticence, but they all trusted Korac's contingency, which he shared in code to avoid detection by the all-seeing, all-hearing Aegis in the room. The Prince glanced at his General, who nodded. He never trusted an expression as much from any other person in the Twelve Worlds.

Good to go.

Tumu turned and monitored the projected screens, expanding them until the empty display stretched thirty feet wide and tall over the swirling black flames. The old Primary asked, "Okay, Razor. What're we looking at?" There was something inauthentic about the question that Xelan couldn't place. Almost exaggerated curiosity, but Xelan ignored it for now.

The Bridge Team stared up at the blank projection, displaying absolutely nothing.

Xelan was the only one who spared a glance behind them at the life-size light show which was the Pain Curator. The Aegis tipped his top hat and winked at him.

Without glancing away from the screen, Korac asked, "What're you playing at here, Razor—"

Sagan, Tameka, and Pehton gasped, bringing Xelan's attention back to the display. The image stopped his heart.

Impossible and enormous, the exterior hull of the Dyson's Sphere encompassed the better part of a solar system surrounded by asteroids and a rainbow of gas clouds. The manifolds of sun-sized light fixtures—currently off—were nestled along various circuitry, paneling, and nacre glass domes. Peppered along the screen, tiny satellites orbited the massive structure, which was how they could view it from the exterior.

Enki was beautiful.

"This is Ishkur."

Razor smiled at them as all but Tumu faced him with varied expressions of confusion. His smile deepened for Sagan, whose nose was scrunched with her frown. He sighed, ecstatic with the grand demonstration. "I never tire of your inferior capacity to appreciate the totality of Aegis engineering and scale. Allow me to formally introduce you to Enki's twin. My brothers—Zero's sons—wanted to replicate the success of Enki, so they built a second Dyson's Sphere. Enki is a machine of defense. Ishkur is the paradise we sought to protect."

Without turning from the image, Tumu muttered, "He never meant for us to find it, and I never believed I'd live to see it with my own eyes."

Xelan stared at Tumu, finally understanding. "Your people fought to take Enki because you knew Ishkur existed."

Tumu met Xelan's eyes. The Tritan looked weary. "Not all of us, but Remorse, Quet, and Bol—Yes. They thought the Aegis were greedy."

"We were."

When everyone glanced at Razor, he shrugged, taking ownership of a vice he vouched for in the Aegis.

Iuo said, "In all this time we've taken record within the Vast Collective—official and unofficial—no one mentioned a second Dyson's Sphere."

Pehton nodded in agreement. "That's right. We defended Enki for the Tritans across millions of years. I don't think even Gale knew this place existed."

"That's because it isn't finished." Tameka stepped closer into Razor's personal space than Xelan ever saw her do before. She stared him down with an icy understanding in her expression. With a nod at Sagan and Korac, Tameka said, "We heard the entire story you gave them when you uploaded into the Atheneum. The incident you caused that led to..." She glanced at his hands, perched on his cane, with their nail-less fingers.

Razor's eyes narrowed at the reminder.

Tameka pressed, "You said by calling multitudes of your brothers from various Probabilities that you were trying to help them with a project, and you accidentally caused pandemonium when the copies and your brothers fought in the confusion. It stopped the construction on Ishkur, didn't it?"

Oh, but that made so much sense. Even as a bitter smile spread across Razor's lips, confirming Tameka's assumptions, Xelan made so many more leaps in the story, biting his thumbnail as he considered the possibilities.

"Wingmaster, we're losing you."

Korac.

Xelan snapped out of it as Tumu said, "That's why you need Peaches."

Razor chuckled, and Tameka glared at him. He gave a cavalier shrug and offered, "What? The nickname is cute." He waved her off. "Yes. Yes. It is. I disrupted their attempts to generate power, but even without my interference, there were other concerns."

Pehton folded her arms and glared at Razor's projection. "Such as?"

He raked his gaze over the orange-feathered Lyrik and smirked. "Peh Peh, have I mentioned recently how much I admire your fire?"

Xelan opened his mouth to redirect the Pain Curator's attention deficit when Korac groaned, pinching the bridge of his nose, a new habit of his lately. The General admonished, "For the love of Eternity, answer Pehton's question without objectifying her? I can't believe I'm related to you."

Razor's head ticked to the side. "Jealous someone is paying our Executive Warden her due attentions?"

Korac glared at his brother.

Xelan cleared his throat and walked between them, facing Razor. He gave the devil a discouraging shake of the head. "You're stalling for something."

Razor recoiled as if struck, hand flattened to his chest. "How could you accuse me of such underhanded—"

"Primary Rem is making his way to the Pantheon with Pax," Tumu called from the terminal, voice flat and unhappy. "Bol is nearly there. If the Primaries enter the fray, we'll lose the advantage Silence afforded us."

Sagan, paler than her usual tan, fumed despite her apparent weakness. "Pick a side, Razor."

"Now." Tameka sounded equally displeased.

Xelan faced the man he once considered a friend, and a heartbeat passed between them in measuring silence. Two.

Then Razor finally said, "Power. The star was significantly weaker than Enki's, even with its nacre. They could never siphon enough power to keep Ishkur operating, but I believe we have the solution to that problem." He let his twin crescent eyes settle on Tameka.

She asked, "How?"

Xelan knew the answer. "Enki's star. You can open a feed between them and sufficiently power Ishkur's sun."

Razor grinned at Xelan. "Genius is quite attractive on you."

Sagan turned and held off Tameka *and* Korac. She soothed, "I know. I know."

Tumu rolled his eyes and mumbled about "Xelan's admirers."

Iuo and Pehton looked ready to find some popcorn.

Xelan sighed and shook his head at Razor. "Incorrigible doesn't begin to cover it."

The projected Aegis looked so pleased with himself until Xelan took Tameka by the shoulders, kissed his lips against her ear, and whispered, "Let's finish this, save our son, and christen every continent on Ishkur."

They pulled apart and stared into each other's eyes for a moment. Tameka nodded and looked at Razor. "How will I get there?"

A conduit split the bridge. Through the wavering energy barrier, they saw an identical space, like a mirror image of where they stood.

"Welcome to Ishkur."

Welcome to their new home.

{ENKI | PANTHEON}

Without a Seamswalker, Silence would resort to flying through Torrentus. There, she'd reach the bridge and the presumed entrance to Ishkur. By now, Three Two Four would have opened it for the Shadow thanks to the Atheneum. It was only a matter of getting there.

The cursed azure light shimmered under Silence's dark gray skin, a more frequent reminder of her dire circumstances.

But…

Kyle stared at her from below, impressed and happy to see her. Only a little sadness shaded those foresty eyes of his. Ones which looked as beautiful open as they did closed in ecstasy.

Silence wanted more.

"There isn't time." Lucas was right.

His lover looked on the verge of collapse, held fast by Kyle and the green Tritan.

Silence carried so much respect for these people, a family not meant for her.

As if hearing her thoughts, Smith asked, "Why not tell them?"

Lucas answered, his voice appropriately grave. "It's a choice between Silence and Rayne. Who do you think they'll choose?"

Only two people in the entire galaxy carried dual nacres powerful enough to destroy Enki, and Silence was no martyr. She chose the Probabilities which would lead her to happiness, and she refused to lose it. Cascading Light *owed* her a promise.

True still, how could Silence live with herself once Rayne died that noble death? Would her grandsons tolerate her presence? Would Kyle turn away from the sight of her?

The least Silence could do was level the playing field. In her creation, the Aegis had meant for her to mold nacre glass for machinations before they offered Project Surra to the Tritans. Her affinity for the atomic structure of unbreakable bones was circuited throughout her nanites.

Why not destroy all the nacres of the Imminent army?

That was the difference between a pane of glass and the computer functioning inside of it. It was far too complex.

Technically, the Rayne and Nox abominations were still alive and conscious in their little bundles of foiled bones. Their nacres were untouched. Fortunately, they were mute.

"You're stalling."

Damn Lucas—

The lines between universes blurred and multiplied.

Smith hissed, "It's a cosmic event."

And no simple event. Where hundreds of thousands of Probabilities were typical, this new development issued millions of Probabilities here on the brink of Rayne's end.

The azure pulse came and went.

Silence gripped Pax's chain around her neck, noting the Shadow below had donned new ones. It was a brilliant strategy with Rayne returned to them. For now.

Gripping Lucas' back, Smith announced, "It's time, Silence."

Yes.

Silence expanded her wings, alerting the Shadow below. No more words. They soared to the conduit, prepared to face any resistance in kind. The bridge was online, and an Aegis had opened the conduit to Ishkur. Nothing could stop Silence now.

There, the properties of Ishkur's hull would render the Weapon in Silence's nacre inert.

She'd finally know peace.

The shimmer of azure light traveled down her arms and through her fingernails to remind Silence—This was no way to live.

They stopped.

Kyle hovered over the conduit, flanked by Bones, Caedes, Jack, and an Icarean female who could only be the Atheneum's mother, Karter.

Silence finally broke her namesake. "Your wings?"

Kyle looked like he'd expected the question. He held up the spent chain of Rayne's blood. An offensive maneuver.

Tired.

That's how Silence felt. Exhausted in her old bones. She would know peace. Happiness. There was little concern about knowing love again. It burned in Kyle's eyes.

Silence tried Smith's tactic. "Let us pass to Ishkur."

When the azure light passed over her body, Kyle's gaze followed it. Saddened, he said, "I can't let you go in there without knowing why and if your reason harms our people."

Lucas looked at Silence, begging something of her—Communication, logic, a paradigm shift?

She couldn't feel it or see it. All Silence could see was the Probabilities where Kyle ended her in battle.

Was this it?

No.

Enki would not be Silence's grave.

EIGHT

NOTHING SPARED IN YOUR TRIALS AND THE CONSEQUENCES OF WAR

{ENKI}

"T.A.O., **ONCE REMORSE AND BOL JOIN THE BATTLE, I WANT YOU TO FIND SOMEWHERE SAFE.** Worry about yourself before anyone else. Tell me you understand."

Razor knew better. There was something angelic about Seamswalkers. Perhaps it was their access to so many worlds and so many peoples—an overexposure to life—which left them atypically compassionate.

The Afflicted One answered him on her private frequency. "There is no mistaking your heart in the warning. I will miss you, friend."

There.

Such an open kindness. It left Razor overcome. He said, "Not as much as I have you these last few years. I am happy for your freedom, but do not waste it saving some hug-happy Shadow cultist. Heed me, little sister."

She hesitated before asking, "What about the Silence in our Stars? Mother wants Ishkur."

No doubt. When Razor opened the conduit to Ishkur, all of those Imminent had witnessed the fractured glass of their reality, the likes of which the Matrix couldn't fathom.

Not since Elden drank Razor's blood had an event opened so many Probabilities. And Elden's attack was an unexpected miscalculation still costing Razor seven million years later. Fucking Progeny...

Except for the Seamswalkers, of course.

Razor said, "Let Silence and the Shadow contend with one another. All that matters is Echo's safety. I entrusted her to Sagan, and I still believe I made the right decision."

"Agreed. A breeze of fresh air over your desolate bone yard. Over and Out."

T.A.O. left the Pain Curator to his thoughts. That's all he was now. Thoughts and circuits and light. No corporeal body to speak of. For now, entertaining himself with his three-dimensional renderings would suffice, but if Razor expected to live long term as a Dyson's Sphere, he'd require a mechanized form. Perhaps the Dwarves of Pil would have some ideas.

Of course, none of it mattered. This existence was temporary. In an hour, Gait would plow into the hull and take Enki out. Or some time after, Rayne would explode. The Weapon army was no longer a secret. There was no way in the Wrong Side of Eternity that the Shadow would leave Enki intact with the depositories stationed on every continent but Torrentus.

Rayne.

Nox.

If Razor still possessed a head, he would've shaken it in bewilderment. What a fascinating discovery—One Rayne was keeping from those she held dear. Within the first three minutes of realizing her nacre trick, Razor envisioned two million, three hundred and eight thousand ways to capitalize on it. He could groan at the wasted potential if only he had a throat.

Fuck it.

The Pain Curator had lost enough to mourn today without grieving imaginary losses.

Triss.

Razor wanted to laugh bitterly because, even without a physical heart, his still felt broken. No one would ever place their faith in his hands like Triss did. The perfect trust which came from knowing and understanding him completely. All of it—Gone.

Maybe they weren't the Eternal Bind after all, but Razor would make sure history remembered them.

The Pain Curator manifested his projection beside Sagan, who sat cross-legged on the gangway furthest from Ishkur's conduit. She was snacking on a nutrition ration. He appeared sitting beside her. "A Dyson's Sphere is a great place for a little girl to grow up."

Sagan startled and dropped the ration.

He made to catch it, but it fell through the light of his hands into the swirl of Cascading Light below. "Oops." Razor tapped his cane on the gangway for emphasis. "Apologies, Seamswalker. Still skittish, as always?"

'Pain Kitten' still suited her.

Sagan blinked, processing his first words. "You mean raise Echo in Ishkur?"

"I do. I think all of you—the entire Shadow—could be quite happy there. The King of Earth and Cinder included."

Razor let her sit with the idea for a minute, both of them in an unexpectedly companionable silence. They watched on as Tameka stood before the conduit with her wings out and accessed the astonishing ability within her. Razor saw it in the Atramentous of her eyes, concentrating and transferring energy from one star to another.

It wasn't flashy. There were no lightning bolts or streams of energy, but the woman trembled with the enormity of it until a black color swallowed the solid green of her eyes.

Xelan observed Tameka from close by. He was the first to notice Razor in the room, after that inquisitive mind of his had made a sweep of his surroundings. The half-Icarus possessed so many endearing foibles.

Including that dorky wave.

Razor suggested to Sagan, "Keep thinking on it," before appearing beside Xelan. "Yes?"

Korac noticed him then, and his cool exterior bristled ever so slightly, much to Razor's amusement.

Xelan saw the friction and ignored it for a more productive subject, eye on the bigger picture. "So Torrentus malfunctioning wasn't an accident. It was intentional to secure the bridge and prevent anyone from accessing Ishkur. But who drained the storm of its nacre energy?"

Sharp. Razor liked him so very much. "Our father. After... " He held up his hand, letting his empty nail beds finish the sentence. "The Tritans arrived, and the Exalted learned of my friendship with Remorse—"

"Friendship?!" Korac scoffed.

Razor placed both hands on his cane and leaned on it. After a curious examination of his relationship with Remorse, he confessed, "No. You're right. It was more like a surrogacy. Primary Rem treated me like a son, and he was more of a father to me than Zero could ever claim to be."

Lifting his head from the terminal, Tumu asked, "Iuo, how many children did Remorse father or surrogate according to your records?"

"Eight hundred and ninety-two."

Semantics couldn't change the long walks and talks with the Primary, but something was wrong...

Remorse stole Pax.

Razor said, "Those were numbers—Seedings for the breeding program. None of them were special interest cases—"

"What about my children?" Pehton's orange gliders flared along her forearms, matching the anger in her voice. "Experiments, right? And you knew. Knew how he treated his children. *My* children."

"And me?"

Xelan.

He was a special case, but...

Remorse stole Pax.

Why?

Why did it upset Razor so?

He met Korac's measuring stare from across the room. The Atheneum said, "Let's face it. I'm the only family you have left."

Tameka called out, "Hey, team?"

They all looked through the conduit to see Ishkur's bridge illuminated in an uninterrupted continuation of Enki's helm.

Razor muttered, "Let there be light."

It was working.

{ENKI | PANTHEON}

Tameka had never felt so alive. The power of a star flowed through her and into another. No one could understand the raw energy and unbridled fire burning in her nacre. Well, except maybe Rayne.

"It's working, Fury. Keep it coming."

The War King sounded as exhilarated as Tameka felt.

Razor told them the property of the hull surrounding Ishkur should negate Rayne's fuse. She might never leave the second Dyson's Sphere, but it was more than enough to keep her occupied for a few million years. That's what Tameka wanted. Her entire family—all the Shadow and all their allies—living in Ishkur.

Safe.

Thriving.

Peoples united and working together to make the Vast Collective a rich and diverse community of peace. Tameka wanted to tell Xelan about it so badly, but there wasn't exactly a window to share her vision. Or to share the intelligence on Gait's children.

Ugh, Tameka actually felt bad for keeping something from Korac.

How things changed.

Pehton's children had asked to remain a secret. They wanted a big reveal for their mother, and who was Fury to stand in their way?

With no one near enough to overhear, Tameka muttered into the exclusive frequency on her earpiece, "Aya, we're still on the bridge. Standby until the battle recommences. Over."

Aya's voice shivered with excitement. "We eagerly await your signal, Fury."

All good.

Now, for Razor.

The Pain Curator hovered and buzzed about the bridge, engaging in one-on-one conversations with their team. There was no telling what he could affect in Enki. Anxiety buzzed in Tameka's veins. She couldn't trust him, and she resented that anyone in their group felt compelled to do so now. They were vulnerable, and he was pretty much a god.

"Razor."

He answered Tameka's summons by flitting his projection to her side. Why not exercise her multi-tasking skills by interrogating him while powering Ishkur's star?

After considering her words, Fury decided to kick diplomacy out the window and asked him directly, "What are your motivations?"

"I'm curious, myself," Xelan confessed without looking away from the radar screen. He gestured at it. "Rem and Bol should've arrived at the Pantheon by now, but look..."

Tameka glanced at the screen and watched one blip run into a conduit meant to take it straight south, but somehow it rerouted to the west.

Korac stared at the image with hard eyes. They softened when Sagan stepped up to his side and snuggled in, careful for their axes. That vein strained in Xelan's forehead again. Tameka understood it. Some people might assume it was a jealousy thing, but it was actually hard on Xelan to adjust to the idea of his student being in love with his ex-partner and best friend.

Tameka got it.

They all turned and looked at Razor beside Tameka when the blips rerouted once more.

The Pain Curator played with the gem adorning the top of his cane. After a heartbeat, Razor shrugged as if they'd caught him in some mischief and he wasn't ashamed of it. "I've redirected a few conduits."

Iuo paused from his stenography equipment and gaped. Pehton crossed her arms, hard carbuncle eyes narrowed at him.

Tumu peered at him with a contemplative frown on his featureless face. "Why?"

Razor sighed, and it was heavy, especially for someone without lungs. "I wanted to prolong them from reaching the Pantheon while I consider my options, and because it's funny to listen to them cuss up and down the corridors."

Was a smile trying to tug at Tameka's lips?

Xelan lost any resistance and grinned.

Sagan's voice was soft as she asked, "What options?"

Korac chafed her arms like she'd experienced a sudden chill.

Razor took his top hat off and dusted it against his knee, dodging eye contact as he continued with the unexpected confession. "I want you to raise your son, Xelan, and I want Echo safe more than anything." Again, he sighed, meeting their eyes for the next. "But I don't necessarily want the Tritans to fall. The hubris of my people fueled the war more than Tritan arrogance. Those are my motivations, Fury. That and how to repay Primary Rem."

That popped her brows high.

Tumu turned away from the radar and scanned Razor with considering voids. He pointed at a squad of nacres at the Pantheon battleground. "Those are the Tritan race. All the remaining young males Lance released earlier, thanks to Matt and Lucy."

At the mention of Matt's name, a smirk tugged at Razor's lips.

Pehton pressed, "But if Remorse finds them fighting alongside the Shadow, he'll rationalize killing them. Then he'll find himself at the same square one when the Aegis killed the Tritan females—Blaming someone else for a problem he created."

Korac nudged her with a smirk. "Well said."

Tameka let them carry on a bit as she stared at Xelan. They were engaging in a conversation without words. Her quirked brow asked, "Should we trust him?"

The small dip of Xelan's chin said, "I'm considering it."

Then came the buzzing of anxiety again.

Iuo spoke up next. "With Ishkur, the Tritans will thrive, and the Aegis will live on in Echo, raised as a Shadow."

Razor met Sagan's eyes. Every time he did that, a strange current of something passed between them, confusing Tameka. It wasn't love or sexual attraction. It was more like fate. The Last Aegis held an affinity for Seamswalkers.

Tameka didn't like it.

Korac didn't either by the flicker in his icy eyes—A threat for his older brother.

To Sagan, Razor said, "I know you'll keep her safe."

The Seamswalker, all serious with her leveled stare, said, "I'll stake my life on it."

That was it.

Razor turned to Xelan and asked, "Are you certain you want Remorse dead? After all, he is your father, and I want no regrets between us."

Tameka's eyes widened at the offer which was implicated by the question, and she looked to Xelan for his answer.

Xelan met Pehton's gaze. She nodded, firm and without question. Then he met Tumu's eyes. The two, Tumu and Rem, were Primaries and relatives. The last of the Gargantuan Tritans. If anyone had a right to object, it would be him.

Tumu confessed, "I should have eliminated him long ago."

Tameka couldn't agree more, but it wasn't helpful to voice those kinds of thoughts. See? She was maturing.

Xelan looked back at Razor. "Considering how much Remorse has fixated on my family, I don't think Pax will ever be safe while the man still breathes."

"For Nox."

Tameka surprised herself by muttering the words, but they were true. So much of what befell the brothers happened because of Primary Rem.

Although Korac wasn't smirking, a hint of it was in his voice. He said to Tameka, "*Now* you can give a speech at our wedding."

{ENKI | BRIDGE}

Tameka amazed Xelan.

Powering a star and a Weapon. Defeating a hurricane. Diplomacy. Leadership.

All while their son was in the hands of their enemy.

Xelan kept busy while Razor prepared the epic surprise for Primary Rem. The Prince of Cinder monitored the situation, fielded communication, and designed plans for Ishkur, but now and then, he stopped and simply admired the mother of his child.

Empress Fury would suit her just fine, and Xelan knew she'd welcome the role. Maybe with understandable hesitation at first, but she'd take to it so naturally. And as long as Tameka was by his side, Xelan would fulfill his promise to their allies and unite the Vast Collective.

Easily.

"I'm so lucky."

"You're damned right you are." Korac stealth-approached from behind.

Xelan spun with an intentional flare of his coat. He enjoyed aggravating his best friend with it.

After rolling his eyes, Korac said, "Not that I mind hanging out with you and Fury in this mind-fuck . . . " He pointed to the funnel of Cascading Light below their feet. "But I don't feel quite copacetic about leaving my soldiers on the front line without their General."

Xelan grinned. The king of aloofness wanted to fight alongside his mother and needed to know the situation here was under control before abandoning his post to join her. It's not that Korac was transparent by any means. It's that Xelan knew him so well. He said, "I understand, but Gait should crash into Enki within the hour. Fighting may not be necessary."

Sagan joined them, looking a little worse for wear. "That's a good excuse for me to switch places with T.A.O."

Concern tightened the corner of Korac's eyes as he looked her over.

Xelan leaned back against the terminal and bit his thumbnail, considering her strained capacity. "Are you sure you can evacuate everyone on impact?"

Despite her weariness, Sagan nodded, confident. "I'll drink my vial of Rayne's blood and scoop them with a conduit to Ishkur, like butterflies in a net. But if I do it before Andrew releases everyone's volition, then I'll inadvertently evacuate Imminent's armies as well. It's best to wait it out until we can separate them."

Korac added, "And if Gait doesn't collide with Enki, at least we'll be there to corral Remorse for Razor's insane plan."

Pehton sidled over. "I'm game. I'd like to get a few searing kicks in."

Xelan nodded, agreeing with them. "I hear you loud and clear. Let me check in with Bones." Over the earpiece, he asked, "What's the situation, Pantheon team? Over."

Bones came on the line. "Silence is still deciding how badly she wants to go through us to get to Ishkur. I think she's waiting to see if Gait will hit Enki. Over."

Tameka called to Xelan from where she stood at the conduit to the second Dyson's Sphere. "If Remorse was planning to blow Gait, he would have already, right?"

Xelan looked across the room to Tumu for the answer. The Tritan shook his head. "He has time yet to decide if he wants to let his home be destroyed by Gait or by Rayne."

Iuo spoke from his equipment. "There are over three hundred thousand instances of Remorse proclaiming his fondness for Enki. It stands to reason with his Imminent foresight into the Probability Matrix that he's struggling with this decision. We'll see."

Razor, in all his three-piece light show glory, appeared on the central gangway. "It's time."

Xelan switched the comms to 'all' on the main terminal. Everyone in Enki would hear him, including the Primaries. Confident in their team's ability to pull this off, Xelan announced, "I want my son, Remorse. No more games. We're rerouting a direct course for you to the Pantheon. I'll meet you there."

"I'm coming with you."

To beautiful effect, Tameka's clothes swept around her as she walked over. Sagan and Korac stepped to the side, letting her into their huddle. Xelan noted the hint of respect in Korac's eyes and the naked admiration in Sagan's. Even Pehton nodded with approval.

Xelan didn't doubt Tameka, but, like Sagan, he wanted to check her capacity. "You wanna go with me to fight a deity while powering an entire Dyson's Sphere and Rayne's nacre?" He stepped close to Tameka until he looked straight down and she looked up to maintain eye contact.

"You got it, mister."

Unable to help himself, Xelan grinned as he retrieved her weapon from beneath his coat. "Then you'll need this."

Tameka beamed at him. "My chain dart!" She jumped up and held on while they kissed.

Around them, several throats cleared, and some people shuffled awkwardly. Xelan couldn't care less. When he and Tameka broke away, it was still too soon.

"Ahem."

They both looked up to find Razor waiting. "Endearing and all, but Remorse is nearing the Pantheon."

Tameka asked, "Is it all right for me to move from this location?"

Razor's projection nodded with a tip of his hat. "Absolutely. As long as a conduit is open to Ishkur, you can maintain the transfer from any location."

Tumu rushed down two levels of gangplanks. "We're all going. Like you said, Wingmaster, you need a Primary to win this fight."

Iuo frowned. "But how will I monitor Gait's impact?"

"Ah." Razor held up a hand before changing the display projection and several of the same image opened on multiple screens all around them. "Satellite feeds. I'll project these to all parties." He glanced at Sagan. "Including Rayne."

With some hesitation, Sagan muttered, "Thank you."

Korac did *not* like that. Oh, how tempting it was to needle Xelan's best friend in payback. Instead, he adjusted the lapels of his coat and nodded at Sagan. She opened the conduit, and they Seamswalked to the Pantheon.

Gait would make planet fall and destroy Enki's hull. Then Sagan would evacuate them all to their new home, where he and Tameka would raise their son and serve the Vast Collective. It was all working out.

Rayne wouldn't die alone and afraid this day.

{Enki | Medical Bay}

Lynn and Pablo spent a little time here and there between patients looking in on Echo's crib. Miy and Twenty-One were guarding her after staying behind when T.A.O. migrated the Tritans, Caedes, Bethany, and the rest to battle. Qas joined the war effort to act as a field medic.

It was quiet.

Damn, Lynn wanted to fight, but…

Bags puffed under Pablo's red-lined eyes. Rivers of tears stained his cheeks, no matter how much he wiped them away. Those strong shoulders sagged with grief. He caught her looking and offered a pale imitation of his usual smile. Triss' death weighed down on him like an anchor.

How could Lynn contribute to Pablo's full plate by stacking additional concern for her safety?

Plus, well…

Look at that adorable baby Aegis-Lyrik.

Watching over Echo gave Lynn enough to think about for their future to distract her from the fear of missing out. Though she definitely planned to have a Cesarean delivery. No way was she about to push a baby out after the nightmare that was Triss' labor.

"Are you cold?" Pablo asked, chafing her arms after Lynn apparently shuddered.

'Yes, so please warm me up,' but that wasn't appropriate to say, so Lynn lied. "I'm fine."

Pablo's eyes ignited with a brown fire, letting her know they were on the same wavelength. He pressed the most wonderful lips to her ear and whispered, sending different shivers down her spine. "If I thought I'd be quick, you know I would, but I'd need you for too long. After Gait breaches the hull and we evacuate to wherever, I'll spend a few weeks seeking solace in you. But until then, we should be ready for anything—"

In the center of the bay, a screen appeared and flickered until it displayed an impossible rock careening through space.

Miy pointed and asked, "Is that Gait?"

Twenty-One beamed. "There's our King's salvation."

"May I see my daughter?"

Lynn and Pablo whirled to find Razor's projection behind them. He looked so spiffy, which felt so alien tonally. She spared a glance at her husband, who nodded with consolation in his eyes.

"Of course."

Razor flitted his image to Echo's bedside. He reached out, stopped, dropped his hands through the bed, ineffectually.

Miy laughed, capturing Razor's attention with a brow drawn high. She said, "You can't possibly expect me to feel sympathy for you." Her orange and black gliders flared and the matching streaked feathers rustled.

With a silken tone bizarrely contrary to his words, Razor said, "I will not lower myself to contend with a discarded instrument. I've lost too much, especially today, to lose my self-respect as well."

"No matter how much you lose, it will never be enough to make up for the trauma you left behind."

Pablo made to step between them, but Lynn squeezed his arm gently. "I'll handle it." She put herself in the middle and glared at both of them. Neither were good people, but they were trying to improve, supposedly. And perhaps it was a little late, but the Shadow would take them as allies. So Lynn would try her hand at diplomacy. "I don't care about the fucked up history between the two of you, but I won't have you disrespecting this medical unit under Pablo's supervision. Look at him."

Her husband shrank under the spotlight, but both Razor and Miy did as they were told.

Lynn continued with her point. "That man delivered Triss' baby earlier with the utmost regard for his professionalism and compassion, and he's only twenty-one years old and from pre-nacre Earth. The two of you..." She paused until they met her eyes. "Are millions—possibly billions of years old, in Razor's case—and 'higher beings' at that. The least you can do is respect this medical space, even if you are incapable of respecting each other."

A tense heartbeat passed where Razor and Miy stared at Lynn. Then Twenty-One chuckled, lending to Pablo beaming at her.

Miy sighed and muttered, "Yeah. Whatever."

Razor smirked at Lynn, saying, "I like you, Chief Suarez—"

"Renee," Lynn corrected. "I kept my family name."

Twenty-One lost control and laughed from his gut while Razor's smirk widened into a grin. "Yes, ma'am, Chief Renee." He glanced over at Pablo. "You did well, Dr. Suarez."

Finally, Pablo's eyes sparked with life as he kept grinning at Lynn. "That's just the tip of the iceberg."

"Speaking of iceberg." The wonder in Miy's voice made them all turn and stare at the projection of Gait. "Look at that thing spin. I can't believe Matt was clinging to it."

Twenty-One asked, "Do you think it'll hit?"

Lynn took Pablo's hand. With an inherent confidence gained from being in the Shadow, she said, "Absolutely."

Pablo squeezed, prompting her to glance at his face. He was staring at the screen, but not with wonder.

With concern.

Well, that was certainly a blow to Lynn's morale.

Was Rayne not out of the woods yet?

{THE HEART OF ENKI}

Calibrated.

Optimized.

Stabilizing...

Unable to stabilize.

Warning: Seventy-one hours and fifty-nine minutes until maximum destabilization.

Something.

Stabilizing...

Unable to stabilize.

Warning: Thirteen hours until maximum destabilization.

Was wrong.

Stabilizing...

Unable to stabilize.

Warning: Forty-five hours and twenty-eight minutes until maximum destabilization.

With Rayne's fuse.

The malfunction had begun with the first infusion of power from Tameka. With everything happening on all fronts, Rayne didn't want to mention it to her team, hoping it would settle down after the first bursts of power. Unfortunately, it was still going berserk.

Would this be it? How Rayne succumbed to her fate of dying alone and afraid, but—

"Rayne."

The way Nox said her name could make her cry. Why did he say Rayne's name like it would be the last word he ever said?

"Tell them."

Nope.

Nuh-uh.

Rayne shook her head—metaphorically and physically. "Their hands are pretty full, and the fuse will right itself."

Nox reasoned—not argued—with her as he asked perfectly good questions. "But what if it rights itself with only a minute to spare?"

The instant panic ignited by this last question emblazoned white light from her eyes. It was bright enough to flare to the sun. Hot enough to warm the surrounding space.

Rayne's nacre was on fire.

And god damn it, she couldn't contain it. Her power spilled out of her in showers of flames like Cascading Light. So bright was it that she struggled to see Nox through the glare, even in her consciousness.

Distraction.

Rayne need to distract from the anxiety. "Why didn't you let me tell the others about you? I understand why you wanted Korac to know, and I think he figured it out from our hints, but..."

Nox's voice was so steady that it calmed Rayne's nerves instantly. "My brother—the others—they will need easing into it. By Korac's own admission in his Verse, he'll make for the best ambassador to vouch for the situation. Already he takes cues and follows them."

"That's true." Rayne finally relaxed enough to see Nox again. "Did you see the look on Korac's face when he figured it out?" She couldn't help but grin at the memory.

The matching expression on Nox's face suited his features, making them more handsome than cruel. "I did, and there's no mistaking it. He knows—"

The stupid azure light pulsed under Rayne's skin, and another one of her flares ignited through the heart of Enki.

Rayne gasped from the panic. "I can't—"

Electricity scored her veins, bowing her spine, and drawing a scream from her. The magnesium field leaked out as far as the sun before Rayne could breathe again.

They were heavy, measuring breaths, meant to remind Rayne of her mortality. Each power feed from Tameka humbled Rayne. After she gulped down a breath, two, she muttered, "I don't remember Tameka's ability hurting this much."

Nox lent his quiet strength in these moments because what other choice did Rayne give him other than repeating the same question?

Why not ask the Shadow for help?

Because Rayne feared she already knew the answer—

"Quite the light-show up here."

A projection manifested in the space before Rayne. It was Razor in a fancy getup. With a smile, he swept off his top hat and bowed to her. "Your majesty."

Nox growled, summarizing Rayne's feelings succinctly.

Straightening, Razor returned his hat. "Ahem. In exchange for not ousting your little secret, I beg an audience."

Azure swam under Rayne's pale skin, and she wondered why she carried on with the secrets at all. Who was she protecting? Herself? Nox? How much longer would it matter—

No.

The last thought was fatalistic, and Rayne would be damned if she gave in to that mindset.

Metaphorical and physical fists clenched, she demanded, "What do you want, Razor?"

The Pain Curator gestured to thin air where a screen formed, displaying—

"Is that Gait?"

A little too delighted with her surprise, Razor nodded. "I promised our mutual friend I'd treat you to the view."

Inside her mind, Rayne asked Nox, "What do you think?"

The enormous Icarus glared at the Aegis in their company. "I despise him. He's a danger to you and our people."

Nox referring to the shadow as *'our'* touched Rayne. She couldn't agree more. Aloud, she asked Razor, "Must you be here for it—"

From her toes to every follicle of her hair, Rayne surged with energy galvanized enough to break every bone in her body.

Rayne left, knocked from the physical world. Her heart beat all around her, throbbed and echoed. It was warm here, and the light didn't burn. In the distance, Rayne's mother called her name.

Someone stood between Rayne and the conduit from where the voice came. Their back was to her, displaying the most extraordinary curtain of hair down to their knees. Each strand was two colors: the underside was black, and the topside was white.

Rayne's heartbeat slowed.

Tall and imposing, the figure cast a shadow in the bright white light, but it was no ordinary shadow. Different silhouettes formed in never-ending multitudes of men and women, stretching on and on. In the furthest distance, Rayne recognized a shade of unmistakable size, looming without meaning to.

Nox.

The next figure stood beside him, pensively biting his thumbnail.

Xelan.

Beyond him was Celindria, outlined by the multiple textures of her beautiful hair. A few silhouettes down the line, Rayne's shade knelt with her arms out to what could only be Pax's tiny shadow.

A legacy of strength, power, and sacrifice.

"Elden?" Despite all their nacre construct education, Rayne had never actually seen him. Only heard him speaking in her mind. "Is that you?"

Rayne's heartbeat slugged by as the figure turned an inch, then another so slowly revealing a trail of gilded tattoos along his arm—

"Rayne," her mother called again

Another heartbeat.

"Rayne!"

Thump thump.

"Come back to me, Rayne!"

That wasn't Michelle Callahan screaming for her. That was—

Nox's face was a shadow hovering over Rayne. Her chest hurt where he'd compressed to revive her. His mouth left hers as warm as the afterlife she'd experienced, fresh with the oxygen he'd breathed into her.

"Nox..."

Oh boy. Rayne's voice sounded like Shit with a capital "S."

Razor asked from a respectable distance, "Is she all right?" They both looked at him, and something about the view made him snap his fingers. "If I'd only known sooner. I could've made you a fortune with the franchise and myself a nice percentage off of it."

Rayne groaned, exhausted, but doubly energized.

Nox snarled at the Pain Curator.

Calibrated.

Optimized.

Stabilizing...

Unable to stabilize.

Warning: Sixty-four hours and one minute until maximum destabilization.

Stabilizing...

Unable to stabilize.

Warning: Two hours and seventeen minutes until maximum destabilization.

The King of Earth and Cinder released a second groan for good measure. This was too much. With all her bones healed, Rayne sat up, ready to stand. Nox stayed close, but never offered to help. It was no longer disturbing how well he knew her.

Honestly, Rayne was grateful. "Thank you, Nox."

In his shadow form, his smoky eyes flashed chrome—Atramentous. The sudden glimpse of it, and its emotional implications, took Rayne's breath away—

Razor sighed, shaking his head and muttering to himself about 'missed opportunities.'

Once Rayne was back on her feet, Nox said, "I should return."

This truth made her sad, and the sadness meant something, didn't it? Clearing her throat, Rayne said, "Right. Thanks again."

Nox walked around and stepped back into Rayne until he was back in her mind. There, he said what he wouldn't say in front of Razor, "It's my council that you should notify them before..."

It kills you hung in the air.

Rayne listened to every word and considered them carefully, staring at the image of Gait hurtling toward Enki. So close. To Nox, she said, "I'll tell them once we see what happens with Gait. I promise."

Nox narrowed his eyes at her. "No matter the outcome?"

Rayne wouldn't answer that—Couldn't answer that. She knew what was coming. It crackled around her like kinetic electricity, waiting to strike.

Fate.

Beside her, Razor mused, "The Hall of Dead Kings."

"What's that?"

When he turned and looked at Rayne, the significance in his alien eyes shocked her. "Nothing, your *majesties*."

Inside her head, she confessed with a touch of concern, "I don't like the way he said that."

Nox shook his head, staring at the Aegis until Razor turned back to the screen.

C'mon, Gait.

"There!" Razor pointed to the sudden cloud of dust and dirt emanating from all around the planet's bulky half. "Those are the charges." His grin was genuine when he faced Rayne again. "They failed."

Inside her mind, where her reactions weren't subject to scrutiny, Rayne jumped in the air, cheering. "Woo! Matt and Lucy, you two are my heroes!!!"

Sagan came on the private line then. "Do you see it, Rayne? Did Razor get you a view screen?"

Rayne glanced at the Pain Curator before answering, "He did! Thank you!"

"It was his idea, but yay! Matt and Lucy pulled through!"

There wasn't time to notice the Pain Curator swallow and duck his gaze in humility. Rayne was too busy celebrating, watching the planet fling closer and closer until—

Gait busted into thousands of chunks.

Razor shouted, "Fuck."

But Rayne wasn't sure she heard him or anything else for the buzzing in her ears. Sagan was on the comms and exchanging words about the Colossal Tantamount and Primary Rem. Other people came on the line and said things.

So many things.

Rayne took a breath. In and out. Another one. The fuse continued to fritz, and the azure light passed under her skin again, but she couldn't take any of it in.

"Rayne."

Yes?

She couldn't form the word aloud for Nox, as she watched the bits of Gait fall safely into the ocean.

All those Weapons.

Inside her mind, Nox stepped between Rayne and that view. "Elden will not fail you."

Rayne stared at him, blinking. Her voice sounded far away. "Elden?" Did Nox see him, too?

"Not alone and afraid. With the shard from Elden's nacre, you won't be alone, and you've never feared anything in your life."

Elden.

Yes.

"Yes."

Nox was right.

Rayne faced Razor to find him genuinely contrite. It shocked her, but still she asked, "Razor, your plan for Primary Rem. How long will it take?"

He seemed surprised at the change of subject. "Less than an hour."

Rayne could hear the earnestness in her voice. "Get Pehton and the Lyriks to help you."

Razor tilted his head in bewilderment and incredulity. "If she will."

"Tell her it was my idea, and she will."

His next question held enough gravity to weigh down Enki. "What will *you* do, your majesty?"

Rayne held up her finger and spoke into the comms. "Tameka, keep the power coming. We won't lose this, do you hear me? It's working."

Tameka sounded invigorated. "You got it. Get ready for some Imminent army energy."

"I'm ready."

Rayne meant it.

She was ready.

Calibrated.

Optimized.

Stabilizing . . .

Unable to stabilize.

Warning: Two hours and eight minutes until maximum destabilization.

NINE

SHARE IN HOPE AND HOLD ONTO IT THROUGH THE END

{Enki | Pantheon}

Operation Gait had failed.

There was no way for Matt and Puk to prevent Imminent from stealing the Tantamount and employing it in what remained of the rogue planet's core. Beside him, Lucy sniffled, and he pulled her in for a side hug without thinking.

Not only had their team failed, but they failed someone important to them.

In the middle of the Pantheon, Matt gazed around at the soldiers frozen on the pale, glowing battlefield. He said into his earpiece, "War King, this is Ginger. There wasn't anything we could do. I'm sorry. Over."

Puk gave him an approving thumbs up, blades glinting on the knuckles of his hand-to-hand weapons. His Rayne chain was longer to accommodate his bulk, swinging as he turned back around to face the front line.

Beside the drone, Bethany glanced Matt's way, big honey brown eyes blinking with the world trapped inside. Hearing her talk again was great, but her brother and sister might not like what she had to say. She was safer with Matt and Lucy's group, Rayne chain at the ready.

All the Tritan guards and bulls were gathered here. Even Eminent Lance threw off his robe to reveal ample and sinewed muscle under his combat suit. He came armed, carrying one of those inside-out guns.

Lucy had snitched herself a scalpel from the medical bay. She vibrated with excitement against him, eager to try it.

Matt looked down at his bare hands. These were all he needed.

Rayne came over the Vast Collective frequency. "Don't you dare apologize, Ginger. You and Morning Star had better make me proud on the battlefield today, and don't worry. I'm not finished with Enki yet. Over and Out."

The unfrozen Shadow squad cheered and grunted. Anything to celebrate Rayne's infectious determination. Puk punched the air with those bladed fists. Bethany grinned, danger behind her eyes. The Tritans all pounded a fist to their chests.

Arkansan accent thick, Matt replied, "Yes, ma'am."

It made Lucy smile up at him. This was the morale boost they all needed.

Wingmaster came over the line, entering the Pantheon with the rest of the bridge team. "What's your plan, Callahan?" Only Xelan could call Rayne by her last name now.

Rayne answered, "I'm sticking with my initial plan. I'll use the Weapon in my nacre to destroy Enki and escape before the fuse sets off, like when I killed Nox. There was a window after I tore out his nacre—I'll use my own window to heal and survive if a Seamswalker can snag me in time."

Sagan didn't hesitate. "You got it, babe."

Puk called to Matt, "That's what we call a 'high risk operation.'"

No shit, but it's not like their team left Rayne with much choice. Matt said, "We'll support her any way we can."

Yito, off to the side with Lance, echoed, "Yes. We will."

Meanwhile, Andrew held the armies steady, exhausting his reserves with an unspent chain around his neck. Above them, Kyle and Silence stared each other down. Smith and Lucas faced off with Caedes, Bones, Jack, and Karter. Xelan and Tameka flew up to meet them.

Silence kept her eyes on the power couple.

Wingmaster handled the conversation well, considering Silence was supposedly his long-dead grandmother. "Will you fight with us?"

Matt narrowed his eyes at the blue light pulsing under Silence's skin before she answered, "My destination is Ishkur."

Tameka offered, "Why not ask us to help you?"

Smith threw up his hands, exasperated. "That's exactly what I've been saying."

Lucas shushed him.

This drama was distracting the Shadow from unfreezing the fight, gnawing at Matt's less than savory craving. Even so, he noticed the way Silence raked her gaze over Tameka before saying, "You're everything Elden wanted for his people."

Both Wingmaster and Fury looked taken aback.

Kyle asked, "Isn't that a good thing?"

No shit. Wasn't Elden *the* role model? The Icarean messiah? Matt had certainly adapted to using his name for swearing—

Andrew shouted, drawing their attention to him as he collapsed to his knees.

Lucy cried, "Look!" She pointed to the front line.

Perfect.

The action recommenced all around them. Blows connecting, weapons impaling or exploding, and blood spraying.

Matt grinned, ready to break into it—

Lucy bolted into the fray ahead of him, calling, "First one there gets to be on top tonight!"

Well, that was a win-win.

Matt raced after her and punched his first opponent, a Caprent in Imminent black.

The bastard took it in the jaw, hard enough to shatter the bone. Enraged to the point of foaming acid, the Caprent swung with those backward-bent joints, and Matt clutched the limb. With a satisfying pop, he bent his opponent's elbow in the human direction.

Landing a good headbutt, Matt thanked his dad for a thick skull and used the Caprent's disorientation to shove him, head first, into the Imminent drone behind him.

Both the drone, the Caprent, and the Lamia beside them went down.

Strike!

Matt was ready to take on all three when they screamed at once—Every Imminent soldier surrounding him screamed at once.

Lucy stopped slicing up a Luk to stare at the spectacle. Puk gawked, too.

All around, Imminent soldiers went down. At least three thousand soldiers bled from their noises and eyes in their rainbow of sanguine colors, dying. Blisters formed on their exposed skin like someone had poured boiling water on them. Or sugar...

"What the fuck—"

A teeny grunt made their team turn to find Bethany behind them. Her Rayne chain was spent, and her eyes had shifted into Atramentous. The sweet honey brown shade consumed the entirety of her eyes, but that wasn't what told Matt she belonged with their troupe. It was the wicked smile on her face as she exposed her enemies to the tortures of her past.

Lucy was beaming when she said, "You'll need to tell her the rules, Matt."

That's right.

Bethany could hang with Matt's crew after he taught her the homicidal commandments.

Thou shalt not harm the innocent.

Thou shalt not copy another's signature.

And, most vitally, thou shalt not claim another's kill.

Amen.

{ENKI | THE PANTHEON}

"Execute formation 'Acid Rain.'"

Korac ordered over his earpiece and provided the coordinates while he spun with his axe, slicing four Imminent soldiers and cutting one in half. Above, four hundred Icari carried as many Caprent partners over the throng, who regurgitated acid once the Vast Collective's black and blue troops cleared the target zone.

A chorus of Imminent screams sang Korac a much anticipated melody. "Excellent, troops. Prepare the lures for the Luk traps."

For the first time in battle, strategy wasn't Korac's primary mindset. Instead, other external factors muddied his train of thought. T.A.O. was talking to Razor occasionally. Korac could tell by certain words she had used in the past. It made him itchy, allergic to his brother's bullshit. Razor's ambiguous aims troubled Korac's thoughts, among other things.

The weight of the ring box in his pocket.

Echo.

And Rayne.

Korac didn't buy Rayne's declaration over the comms. There was something missing in how she described Nox's end, aside from swallowing his nacre. Something she wasn't sharing with the rest of the group, and Korac feared it. Too many people's happiness relied on a healthy, living Rayne. Xelan, Sagan, not to mention Nox. Plus, Korac had grown terribly fond of the Sprite over the years.

Sagan Seamswalked into Korac's quadrant, much to his relief and delight. They clasped hands, used the momentum to switch places with each other, and swung their twin axes.

Enemy heads rolled.

As the couple beamed at each other, a lieutenant answered, "Lures are ready, General."

Glowing like a Valkyrie in battle, Sagan gave the order. "Go ahead." Breathless, she beamed at Korac.

This was it.

In the midst of war, with her violet eyes bright and her tanned complexion flushed with adrenaline, Sagan was gloriously beautiful to Korac and now was the right damned time—

Screams erupted around them, followed by excessively loud slurping sounds as Imminent soldiers fell into Luk electric webbing and survived long enough for their insides to jellify while X and his troops consumed them.

Not exactly the soundtrack Korac wanted for this, but it was better than the electronic symphony Razor played over the mass comm. Korac reached into his pocket, saying, "Amos, I have something to ask you, and no, it can't wait for a better time."

Sagan peered at him across the clearing before her eyes went wide. "Down!"

Korac ducked without hesitation and recognized the familiar sound of an axe thrown overhead, reminiscent of their fight in her school cafeteria. When it struck its target with a wet thud, Korac stood and retrieved it from the dead Lamia's chest. "Nice throw." He turned back around to find Sagan had crossed the clearing and was standing right in front of him.

"You wanted to ask me something?"

Did Sagan know? Her eyes searched his, and tears pricked the corners. Of course, she'd guessed. His girl was brilliant.

Korac smirked as he took her hands, wet with the blood of their enemies. "General Sagan Sterling . . ." He released one small hand to retrieve the box, sweep his hair aside while she gaped, and drop to one knee, gazing into her eyes with their sweet tears. She cupped that trademark hand to her mouth, and he nearly choked on his next words. "When I say 'give to me what you want; take from me what you need'—Those aren't just words. Those are vows Icari make under Elden to union with you until Eternity takes me. And Sagan, if you'll have me, I'm yours until that day comes. Will you share those vows and union with me?"

It occurred to Korac they had gone an awfully long time without an interruption, and he spared a glance away from Sagan to see their soldiers pressing the enemy back from their small clearing. Not just any soldiers.

The Lyriks.

Waving caught his eye, and Korac found Pehton giving him a salute. She mouthed, "Good. Luck."

"State your terms."

That spun Korac's attention back to Sagan. Even with tears swimming in her eyes, her smile was playful and so very sexy. He smirked. "An Icarean ceremony with you in full garb. Do you know what that means?"

Sagan shook her head, still beaming at him.

Korac would enjoy this explanation, and he let the enticement into his voice. "Those ribbons Rayne sometimes wears on her biceps and hips—We'll wrap you in those for the union, waiting for me to unlace them with each shared swell on our wedding night. The more lacings you tie, the more faith you place in me to achieve this synchronized chorus.

"And amos, even though we'll bind you entirely, it still won't be enough."

{Enki | Pantheon}

Sagan shivered in a good way, surrounded by war, standing before the half-Icarus of her dreams and negotiating the terms of their happily ever after.

What a life she was leading.

On his knees, Korac trembled, waiting for her answer with love in his eyes. Sagan was crying, and the shimmer to the snow in his gaze made her heart stop. Although her lover had spent most of his life as Cinder's General, he'd never forgotten his humble beginnings as a slave. And in this moment, she saw his fear.

Sagan would never turn Korac away, and she knew the perfect answer to signify this. Breathless and trembling with tears, she said, "I consent, Master."

Korac grinned, radiant and perfect. He swept her into his arms and spun her around the battlefield clearing. She closed her eyes to drown out the spinning sea of faces in combat. He set her down, and it was only as he placed the ring on her finger—with shaky hands—that Sagan realized what it was. A band of nacre glass inset with a single yellow stone—

No.

Not a stone. It was blood.

It was Korac's half-Aegis blood beneath clear, breakable glass. He fidgeted a bit in a nervous display which nearly floored Sagan, as he said, "Dr. Suarez helped with it. It's for emergencies, like when we lost you in the Seam."

It was so considerate and so beautiful. Sagan opened her mouth, but she didn't have the words—

"Congratulations, you two. That was probably the sweetest thing I've ever seen."

Korac and Sagan blinked at each other. "Rayne?" The question came out simultaneously.

Over her earpiece, Sagan asked, "Uh. Thanks but how…"

The genuine happiness in Rayne's voice meant the worlds to Sagan as she said, "Razor cast the display up here and, I assume, all over Enki." Rayne's voice tightened, but she was still upbeat. "Now *that's* what I call a morale booster."

Korac pointed up, and Sagan looked to find themselves projected in the sky, like a couple at a baseball game.

Razor's words came back to her. "*When he asks, I hope you say 'yes.' I would be proud to call you 'family.'*"

More congratulations flooded Sagan's private lines. They watched on the feed as Pehton ran over to them. The couple turned to her in time to catch the jump she made into their arms, forcing them both to lean down for a three-way hug.

The tiny woman confessed, "I have never been so happy and so jealous all at one time."

Korac pulled them apart to kneel, smirk, and cup the Lyrik's chin as he said, "You're still my girl, General Pehton, we just have to stop carrying on like this or Caedes will find out. How could he ever hope to compete with Sagan and I?"

Oh, that got Sagan. At Pehton's pretty face all agape, the Seamswalker giggled hard, hugging her sides—

"Incoming!"

Bones shouted loud enough to reverberate throughout the Pantheon, but it wasn't necessary. Sagan recognized the familiar jarring of the ground in spaced intervals, spaced in time to footsteps. Each one vibrated her skeleton under the muscle, which tightened in primal fear.

Flight or fight.

All around them, the fighting had stopped. Both sides were preoccupied with staring sixty-five feet above them. Sagan had never met Primary Bol, but she knew he wasn't her ol' buddy, Remorse. Too pale, almost withered like Eminent Wiw.

The Gargantuan Tritan blinked with filmy membranes over his lidless voids.

Frozen.

Everyone was very still as not to attract Bol's attention. Those man-sized voids searched the crowd, pausing at Tameka, who waved and nearly made Sagan snicker if not for the goosebumps on her arms standing on end in terror.

Then Primary Bol's indecipherable stare settled on Silence. "Project Surra." He said the name like it was profane. "You owe us much. Will you settle it? Come with us and return to your place in our labs. We will release these . . . " His voids swept across the crowd before he said, "Substandard creatures to continue breathing and breeding."

"Yes."

A second voice.

That voice.

Sagan whirled to find Remorse standing behind her, compressed to seven feet of his height. The bastard Tritan held Pax in his arms, unconscious. In the middle of a battlefield.

"Pax!"

Tameka's cry broke Sagan's heart. Korac pulled her closer to him, as if he felt it shatter.

Xelan shouted, "Remorse, our unfinished business doesn't need to involve my son! Return him to us."

Primary Rem was listening, but he was staring at Sagan. Once up on a time, he'd disguised himself as a prisoner in Korac's cell block, and she'd liked him then. Both he and Razor played her, but...

Sagan asked, "Did I get through to you, Remorse? Will you do the right thing and give Pax to us unharmed?"

"Yes. I will." At his words, Sagan's heart skipped a beat, but then he continued with nothing in his eyes. "As soon as Abresson arrives, and you evacuate us to Ishkur. As Bol said, we'll require Surra, but then you'll be rid of us and free to evacuate from Enki."

Korac tensed beside Sagan at the mention of Abresson's name. She was there for Matt and Lucy's briefing, but not everyone knew he was dead. Nerves forced Sagan to wet her lips before breaking the news to Rem. "The Eminent attacked Lucy, but she defended herself and survived the attack. Abresson did not."

Primary Rem called out, "Three Two Four, did you hear that?"

Did he figure out the Last Aegis was in the Dyson's Sphere main frame?

Razor came across the mass comm. "Yes, Primary. A fitting end."

"I'd say so."

Well, at least Remorse agreed, but the ice in his voice sent a chill down Sagan's spine. The Shadow could never lose one of their own and react so distantly. Was that why Imminent was losing? Detachment?

Bol called, "Primary Rem."

"Yes. Yes." Remorse nodded at his kin before giving the full weight of his alien stare back to Sagan. "What do you say? Help us evacuate for old time's sake." He shifted Pax in his arms like he was ready to hand the boy over.

Tameka and Xelan both inched forward as if to take him, despite the distance between them.

Sagan looked from Pehton to Korac, then back to Rem. Learning to trust again was an important element to her recovery. Forgiveness, too. But… "Andrew?"

After a second, Andrew shouted loud enough to be heard across the battlefield, "He's lying!"

In the same instant, Remorse cursed and deactivated his compression field, growing and growing with Pax in his hands. On cue, the fighting continued.

"Look out!" Korac snatched both Pehton and Sagan out of a Caprent acid attack and flew with them to meet Xelan and Tameka—

Something slammed into them, sending them spilling into the crowd. Sagan's scream was involuntary as she careened into two of their Lamian soldiers and one enemy drone. Tumble, tumble, tumble into a wad of limbs and a needle nose. Sagan punched the drone hard enough to dent his skull as she climbed out of the tangled mess. When she stood, all the blood drained from her.

Remorse.

He jeered down at her, lifted a foot, and dramatically hovered it over Sagan. She stood in its shadow, paralyzed with fear. All around she heard people scream, yelling at him to stop and yelling at her to Seamswalk away, but wow, this was one hell of a way to go—

The foot stopped its descent.

Why…

Sagan stepped out of its shadow to see Silence holding Remorse's kneecap. Glaring at the Tritan, the Mother of all beings snapped his knee sideways.

Remorse bellowed and busted Sagan's eardrums. When he fell, the crowd bounced some three feet off the ground.

"Run!"

That came from Lucas.

Sagan whirled to find him hovering nearby with Smith. They were right. She opened her wings, hardly used, and joined them in the sky over the battlefield. Korac and Pehton hovered across the way.

Tameka shouted at Silence, "Stop! He has our son!"

Xelan tried to reason with the Primary. "Let Pax go. You can't win this. Don't hurt him."

Gasping in pain, Remorse said, "Once I release Pax, you'll drain me dry. While he's in my hands, I'm immune to you."

Loping thunder drew their attention westward where Bol ran into the fray, squishing Imminent and Vast Collective troops alike.

"Fuck!" Korac always knew what was on Sagan's mind.

Remorse recovered quickly and stood once more, kicking Silence back from him and into the crowd as Imminent's Gargantuan Generals surrounded the Shadow's leaders in an unfair standoff.

Unfair until the flames.

{Enki | Pantheon}

Tameka hauled back as flames erupted around Remorse's feet. Off the ground and into the sky, the Shadow soldiers surrounded him.

T.A.O. pointed and cried in delight, "Toasty toes!"

Across the way from Tameka and Xelan, Korac raised a brow at Andrew, who mouthed, "Toasty. Toes." It was some inside thing Tameka wasn't privy to.

The shouting Gargantuan Tritan danced away from the blistering injuries with her son in his hand. She ordered, "Lamassau, be careful of Pax!"

With Bones cheering him on, the Chef gave two thumbs up before spewing another round of fire at both Primaries.

While they dodged flailing blows, Xelan muttered something reassuring but also terrifying. "They won't hurt Pax. They need him."

Need her son?

That was enough.

Tameka opened the bottomless well inside her and drank deep of Imminent soldier nacre, Bol's nacre, and Enki's sun. Charged with vibrant electricity, she fed it to her people, to Rayne, and to Ishkur.

Lam's flames flared, and Bol collapsed into them. In the same instant, Tumu decompressed to his Gargantuan size, facing off with an agitated Remorse, untouched with Pax in his hand. Every one of Imminent's troops toppled around them. With no one left to fight, the Shadow faced Primary Rem, and this was the time.

Tameka stopped basking in the power surge and said into her secret frequency, "Aya, Now."

Kyle frowned at her without taking his eyes off Remorse. "Who's Aya—"

"Look!"

Caedes nodded toward the Torrentus conduit, where hundreds of thousands of Remorse's victims emerged. Those who could fly carried those who couldn't. All of them were dressed in their dead, even the two leaders, who decompressed immediately upon arrival and raced into the fray to fight their father at full height—

Pehton's startled cry pierced the battlefield. The two Gargantuan Lyriks with pitch black skin and blue feathers looked at their mother, who was small in the air. Caedes flew to her side with his quiet way of showing support, because this was a bizarre reunion.

"Aria. Torch." Remorse dared speak their names. His children met his voids with their sapphire eyes. He held up Tameka's son in his hand and said, "Join me. With him, we can rebuild a new race on Ishkur."

Tumu, at sixty-five feet tall, looked between Gait's children and Remorse. Bol remained down for the count and slightly charred. The rest of the Shadow backed away from the confrontation, preparing for the scale of whatever came next.

The smell of kerosene fumed from Torch before he said, "Give us Fury's son, father."

Aria was less civil. "We'll see you in pieces, tyrant—"

Her cry thundered through the Pantheon as she fell to the side. Bol stood and lifted Aria by the leg he'd gripped and flung her Gargantuan body over his head, slamming her into the battlefield on the other side, flattening Vast Collective troops by the hundreds.

Torch, with full Siren's Gale, jumped on Bol's already charred back. With Remorse distracted, Tumu punched him in the throat.

Razor hijacked their earpiece frequencies to say, "Get Pax away from Primary Rem, and I'll deliver the coup de grâce." Screens of the Primaries' fight appeared in the Pantheon's sky. That soundtrack of his blared louder from everywhere, building to a crescendo.

Tameka turned to ask Xelan about evacuations—

He was ghastly white and staring at the Gargantuan Lyriks, a tear streaming down his cheek. Frozen in shock. So much so that when Bol picked Tumu off the ground and threw him, he aimed for Xelan.

"No!" Tameka darted at him, knocking them both out of the air in time to escape Tumu's fall. "Xelan!" She cried in his face, climbing off of him. "Talk to me."

When Xelan spoke, what he said crushed Tameka. "They were dead. They told me I killed them. They were—"

"Shh. No. They're not." Tameka sat him up with a hug, holding him. "I know you didn't know. It's okay. We need to get our son. Are you… Will you be all right until then?"

He wrapped his arms around her and squeezed. "That depends on what other surprises you're hiding."

Tameka laughed—in the middle of all this—she laughed. "Uhm. I think just Aya, but that's a surprise for Korac. Can you stand?" She pulled from their embrace and held out her hand for him to clasp.

When he did, they stood together. Xelan brushed pale dirt from his wings. "You're a marvel, Tameka Phillips. Let's save our son."

They flew back into the sky in time to avoid Remorse taking a step backward on them as Aria uppercut her father. Tameka bet that felt great. She was actually jealous she couldn't join the fight properly, but hey, at least she'd take credit for bringing the lost children some resolution—

"Silence!" Kyle shouted her name across the battlefield.

Tameka followed his line of sight to see Silence, Smith, and Lucas soaring for the Torrentus Conduit.

Sagan Seamswalked beside Tameka in thin air before she yelled to Kyle, "We've got her!" Sagan took her best friend through a conduit and cut-off the fugitives' mid-flight.

In their wake, Tumu grappled with Remorse, cautious of Pax. Both of them were careful not to harm him. Xelan was right. The Tritans wanted Pax.

But that had to wait.

Tameka gave the ancient woman her best withering glare. "Silence, that's your great grandchild. You broke a Primary's knee like it was a matchstick. Get in there and save Pax."

The same azure light which was under Rayne's skin pulsed under Silence's deep gray complexion. Once. Twice. Many times and quickly.

While Silence stared wordlessly at Tameka, Lucas entreated Tameka with golden eyes and a reaching hand. "Please, Fury. She'll die if we don't reach Ishkur."

Silence turned sharply to glare at him, light pulsing ever faster.

Sagan shook her head. "I'm sorry. It's really hard for us to imagine trusting anyone from Imminent."

Tameka's feathers rustled. "Exactly. Don't give me the same sweet eyes you gave Andrew before you crushed him—"

Lucas winced, and Smith patted his shoulder.

"—And you, Silence, you'll wish you were dead if you survive and Pax doesn't. Tell me I'm wrong."

Even though Tameka meant every word, some innate portion of her brain distressed at the thought of hurting Silence. She created their species, she was Xelan's grandmother, and Kyle...

There he was. Behind them, fighting Remorse. All the memory Progeny—Ross, Kyle, Devis, and possibly Bethany, judging by the look of concentration on her 'too young to be fighting a war' face—They exposed the Tritan to his and their worst memories or overloaded his nacre banks to the point of malfunction and repair. Very useful distractions—

Remorse shook his Gargantuan head, stunned by Bethany's ability. Nasty blisters erupted along his blue skin. He snarled, but was too distracted to block Tumu's next blow while Xelan made an attempt at the enemy Primary's compression orb.

Please don't let them accidentally hurt Pax.

Frustrated, Tameka turned back to Silence. "Please. I know you can save him. It's what Elden would want." While she waited for the answer, she drank from the star to feed Rayne and Ishkur.

The stadium lights lining the Pantheon's artificial space dimmed, casting them into darkness. Only for a moment, but when they returned, Silence was nearly to the conduit.

"Shit," Sagan said, before grabbing Tameka's hand. "Hang on."

They flew through one conduit, slammed into Silence midair, and rolled into a second conduit to—

"Where the fuck are we?" Tameka shuffled herself upright in yellow sulfuric silt. It stank. She called, "Sagan?"

Her best friend was on all fours, concentrating on her breathing. Little drips of red blood splattered on the shifting yellow dirt beneath Sagan. She muttered, "Gimme a minute."

"You intend to kill me." Silence stood there, majestic and unaffected, sounding more intrigued than angry. "The Shadow would see me dead?"

Tameka shook her head. How was this getting so messed up? "I want your help to save my son. Then we'll take you to Ishkur."

The warrior waved a hand down her body, indicating the pulsing light. "How much time do you suppose I have to waste around—" She sniffed the air. "Monarch 1?"

Monarch 1?

Sagan gulped before asking, "This is Monarch 1? I always called it 'Hell.'"

Tameka's eyes widened. "Hell—"

A howl resonated through the columns of yellow rock, followed by the thunder of many feet on the ground.

"Sagan?" Tameka was proud that her voice was steady despite the concern.

The Seamswalker finally stood, a little shaky. "The Petrified."

Silence studied Sagan and smiled at the last.

Tameka understood. "Agree to help us, and we'll return you to the Pantheon."

More howls and baying announced the creatures Sagan once told Tameka about.

"Remember the day everything went wrong on Cinder? Korac made me abandon Rayne so he could take her to Nox, and then I found you weeks later. Well before I figured out my ability, I spent my twentieth birthday with the Petrified in Hell. I was trapped there for days."

"What are the Petrified?"

"Monsters made of calcified bone. Rock solid and starving."

As described, the two-headed behemoths charged toward them on taloned feet with weapons in all three of their arms. Their fists were the size of tires, and they towered over all three women—

Nacres.

Tameka could feel nacres inside them. What a relief. She wasn't sure Sagan was capable of a speedy escape just yet. Still, she asked, "What will you do, Silence?"

But she wasn't paying Tameka any mind. Silence was staring at the monsters with... sorrow in her eyes. The strange and ancient woman walked into their path, went to her knees, and kowtowed before them.

So weird.

But even more bizarre, they stopped, staring at...

The Mother.

Silence straightened, walked over to the closest Petrified, and pet its goblin head. Tameka had never heard such profound sadness in another's voice until Silence said, "My fourth batch. The Petrified, as you call them, saw more success in some Probabilities than others. Remorse told me he'd incinerated them from the surface of Monarch 1, but..."

Like the Icari.

That monster answered any of his problems with burning an entire race off the face of their planet.

The azure light strobed under Silence's skin now, another of Remorse's victims. Tameka tried, but she couldn't keep the tears out of her voice. "Silence..."

"Take me back, Fury. Seamswalker. Take me to Remorse."

{The Heart Of Enki}

Calibrated.

Optimized.

Stabilizing...

Unable to stabilize.

Warning: One hour and forty-three minutes until maximum destabilization.

Nox knew why Rayne wouldn't tell Xelan and the others. He felt it in the light separating her atoms. He felt it in how that separation broadened.

Bright.

So bright.

With each of Tameka's infusions, Rayne burned. Her screams would haunt Nox into the next life. And there was nothing he could do. In the telling of his life, he knew of only one moment like this.

The instant Nox died.

Every particle in him had blazed with the same phosphorous brilliance glowing in Rayne now. So much like the storm in her, Rayne's reactions were tempestuous—Crying with joy at Sagan and Korac's engagement, laughing at the Primary's emblazoned feet, cursing the Gargantuan for hiding behind Pax, and demanding to join the fray. She cycled through these emotions, sometimes all within seconds.

Resuscitating Rayne terrified Nox, and he worried that with each surge from Tameka came the time to do it again. But what if this time he couldn't draw breath from the oxygen in her blood to breathe into her lungs? Or if he lost his semi-corporeal form entirely and couldn't perform the chest compressions? What were their options then?

Razor?!

Oh, and the Pain Curator enjoyed this. Nox saw the glint in his bizarre eyes every time Rayne's spine bowed, and Nox despised himself because he'd been nearly the same in his lust for coaxing pain—

"You've gone away again."

Rayne.

She sounded so lonely in her torment and fear.

Nox peered around the mindscape. Where they stood inside her mind was black and empty, focused on her external senses, including the view from her eyes. Behind them, the storm assaulted the ocean as waves crested to trade blows with the clouds. His lava fields pooled into the foam, steaming into solid rock below.

There was a metaphor in there somewhere.

Nox confessed, "I want to take you away from this, but I can't imagine anywhere which wouldn't revive some painful memory."

Externally, Rayne wiped fresh blood—bright and crimson—from her lips and under her nose.

Razor said, "I'd offer you a handkerchief if I were corporeal, your highness, but alas..." There was a shift to his eyes as he watched her.

Nox didn't like it.

Internally, Rayne muttered, "Where did you have in mind?" She managed a weak smile for Nox.

A place to dazzle her, distract her from the burden.

The salt capital of Lacceirus-Capra? No. It was underground and claustrophobia-inducing. Lukemore's sky temple? No. It was a little drafty, and Nox found it dull once the novelty wore off—

"Nox?"

He glanced down at her. Rayne stood beside him, looking out of her external view. She was trembling. Nox swallowed, prepared to give her anything she asked. "Yes?"

"Take me home."

Rayne stared down at her hands, the azure light strobing along her skin. Another promise of the end.

Nox constructed a replica of her house in Little Rock, Arkansas, a modest two-story, three-bedroom home which had served the Callahans well. Before he'd invaded Earth and wrought destruction on the planet. On Rayne.

Her smile was stronger now as she stared up at him with appreciation in her bright blue eyes. Nox swallowed and gestured for her to join him—

A surge of power went through Rayne, separating the bonds keeping her together. Light escaped in between and threatened to rip her apart. It was another significant dose, leaving her gasping for air when it receded. Her molecules were stitched back together through nacre repair systems.

Nox couldn't help her from inside her mind. Instead, he waited until she got back on her feet. When Rayne glanced externally at Razor's eyes, Nox could see that knowing shimmer, and he growled in his chest.

Rayne asked the Pain Curator, "Are you enjoying this?"

He shrugged, casually, and assured, "I'm here to help, but I might as well appreciate your performance. Agony becomes you. I can see why Nox tortured you so—"

"Shut your mouth." Rayne cut the air with her hand. "You know nothing about Nox. Or me. So you can shut the hell up about a franchise you didn't profit off of. Instead, reflect on how Sagan would feel about your line of thinking."

That made Razor straighten off his cane and stare at Rayne with an eerie stillness.

Nox's chest swelled at her defense of him. Again, maybe two other people in existence would ever vouch for him in that manner, and one of them had raised her to kill Nox.

After a few moments, Razor grinned and tipped his hat at her. "My apologies, your majesty. Sagan's estimations of you were accurate."

Rayne tilted her head to the side, waiting for him to elaborate.

"You really don't tolerate bullshit."

Her laughter was genuine and infectious. Both men in her company shared in it, irritating Nox despite the smile on his face. She said, "No, I don't. I love Sagan. I know why she was willing to give you a chance, but Razor, if you were corporeal—"

"I know. I know. You'd decimate me." At least Razor sounded as if he took this seriously. "But it isn't necessary. She split me in half with a conduit, and I deserved it."

Rayne pointed at the screen. "She brought Silence and Tameka back."

Razor was still grinning. "Between the two of them, they could bring anyone back from the brink."

The truth in the statement left them all in a companionable silence.

Rayne returned to her mindscape with a clap. "Let me introduce you to the place where I dreamt up all your deaths, Nox."

He didn't wince or flinch. Nox smirked. "Lead the way, your majesty."

While Rayne toured her living room and kitchen, meant for video games with Jack and strawberry ice cream, Nox considered why he wanted to wait for the Shadow to know he was in Rayne's mind. As she absorbed blast after blast of nacre radiation, it occurred to him...

Nox never thought they'd survive Enki.

Not really.

And why disturb Korac, Xelan, and the rest with the news of his second existence if it was an existence so short-lived—

"You've gone away again."

Nox looked up at Rayne, where she stood at the top of the staircase to the second floor. He'd paused at the bottom, lost in his thoughts. "I'm sorry."

Rayne's smile was soft and a little sad. "It's okay. I've been thinking a lot, too, but that's why we're on this little tour. So I don't have to think. With you, I'm not alone."

Nox climbed the stairs with his shoulders spanning the breadth of them, and thought to ask, "Are you afraid?"

Again, that sad smile. Rayne brushed her hair behind ear as she said, "Well, you know, after nearly dying from that one infusion, I was scared."

Nox stood one step down from her. At this angle, this close, Rayne looked altogether more delicate, not less. Or maybe the situation made her more frail to him. He asked, "And now?"

"I know there's nothing to fear. Everything will be all right."

Rayne was right, and Nox would see to it.

TEN

IN PEACE, THE PAST MAY HAUNT YOU

{ENKI | PANTHEON}

REMORSE REFUSED TO LOSE THIS FIGHT, ESPECIALLY NOT TO HIS CHILDREN AND TUMU. And while he traded blows with lesser beings, he might as well eradicate those who defied him. Each footstep—every knock down—crushed hundreds of soldiers. He rolled often to eliminate a few thousand more. Anything—anything—to validate his reasoning.

Primary Rem was *right*.

Righteous even!

With Three Two Four's fall, the Tritans assumed the mantle as the paramount species in the galaxy. Razor would see to the inheritance of his successors. Without a doubt, that brilliant Aegis was calculating an escape plan for Bol, Remorse, and the Tritan males still on their side. If all turned traitor, the two remaining Primaries would construct new ones as they'd made the Lyriks, using Pax's graduated Tritan cells for mortar.

All these thoughts occurred to Remorse in the instant he dodged a fiery blow from Torch and his Lyriki Siren's Gale. The disgruntled father spat, "Such a disappointment."

"I agree, cousin." Tumu punched Rem with his insufferable, yet persistent, and enormous fist.

Stars burst in Remorse's vision, coalescing into coffee grounds, then momentary darkness. It was a concussion his hard tissue repair system addressed quickly.

While Remorse was down for the second to recover, Bol uppercut Tumu hard enough to send him flying into the crowd.

Good.

Remorse's vision returned to normal in time to see Torch swing his sister, Aria, in a swinging kick. He stepped back, avoiding it, while grabbing her by the waist and yanking them both across the battlefield.

Every step thundered and bounced the small creatures around them. Those in the air narrowly rode out the shock waves from each blow. All the while, Three Two Four somehow timed the beat of this infernal music to every move of the brawl. Remorse could watch the entire battle in the view screens he'd never known existed in Enki during the hundreds of millions of years he'd lived here.

Three Two Four would upload into Ishkur and teach the Tritans how to run it with his genius.

Nothing would stop them.

Now, Remorse wasn't truly committed to this fight. How could he be with his grandson in his hand? He was careful with Pax, who was still unconscious from earlier.

As if reading the Primary's mind, Xelan shouted, "Remorse, think of my son! Return him to his family for Elden's sake!"

With one good kick square to the middle of Tumu's chest, Primary Rem growled and whirled on his wayward son. "Will I ever escape your Icarean dogma?! Let me educate you about Elden, *my son*. No Icarus was more selfish, more shortsighted than your precious messiah. His relentless pursuit of Surra savaged this galaxy."

Xelan's eyes widened.

Remorse noticed the fighting had stopped momentarily and all the armies stopped fleeing to listen. He continued, "Elden took the reins of Surra's glorious armies and prepared to wipe entire civilizations off the map to find her. He attacked Razor for information, ready to tear down Enki itself for love. So we put him down, and, with Umbra's puppet leadership, assumed control of Cinder. And that's the truth, Xelan. Your martyr was nothing more than a lovesick fool with a gift for pretty speeches."

"And I was wrong to leave him."

When the heart stops, there's a euphoric pause to existence until the lungs force air to draw again and the chambers and valves pump once more. The arrhythmia left Remorse choking as he turned to face his end.

Yes. There in her blue Atramentous eyes, Remorse saw it. Silence had finally discerned the path to her happiness lay through him. He'd never seen her so resolute and so focused, and she was the only fighter who wouldn't care for Pax's safety. Remorse doubted if the Shadow even realized this fact yet. It was best to try some damage control.

"Surra, please. Think of the boy—"

Vi.

Savis.

Remorse's two greatest loves flashed before his eyes as Silence delivered a blow to head his head which splintered his Gargantuan skull with that tiny fist of hers. He focused on the eyes of the women from his past, so similar in severity. Their lips set in a frown of perpetual disappointment. Eternity, help him if they smiled at him. They'd derived happiness only from his misery.

These thoughts were so comforting as Remorse went down. Xelan and Tameka shouted at Silence to stop, but those were distant sounds. Primary Rem's slowed heartbeat was louder than their voices, rushing black blood through his ancient veins.

Dying proved rather painful.

Before Torch delivered a severing kick to Remorse's head, Bol intercepted, turning the Gargantuan Lyrik's momentum against himself and swatting Silence into the distance. Tumu and Aria helped Torch back onto his feet while Bol tended to Remorse.

"Stand."

Yes. That qualified as tending.

The nausea subsided enough for Primary Rem to push himself up. Pax was still alive, his tiny heart pulsing in the Gargantuan Tritan's hand. He held the boy out for the Shadow to see.

Remorse addressed them, "If you want to kill him, then by all means, proceed with your attempts to murder us in our own home. But I'm keeping Pax safe because I love him. Don't make me responsible for his death."

Xelan and Tameka exchanged a glance before Fury asked, "What will it take for you to return him to us?" She sounded so incredulous it was amusing, if not for Primary Rem's recent near-death experience.

He considered the best options to afford both Primaries some time. "Safe passage to anywhere in the galaxy of our choosing via conduit."

Xelan pressed, "And Pax?"

What words could Remorse say to feign convincing forfeiture of his greatest asset? "Silence has convinced me it's in my best interest to return him to you." That should fool the intention reader.

As if reading his thoughts, Sagan asked, "Andrew, what are you getting?"

While the young man didn't sound entirely convinced, he confirmed, "What he said is the truth. Silence convinced him."

Manifested by their conversation, the truly majestic creature who was Project Surra returned to the fray with an expression made of ice. She wanted another round.

Xelan and Tameka conferred before she said, "We want our son first."

Fools.

Three Two Four would save both Primaries. Remorse only need hold out until then and try to resist the urge to crush Pax in the meantime.

{ENKI | PANTHEON}

Xelan hated that Tameka was trembling beside him in impotent rage. He hated he was doing the same. Only a clear head would see Pax through this.

The Shadow hovered in a ring around the Primary fight. Pehton's impossibly gifted children and Tumu squared off with Bol and Remorse. All around, Imminent and Vast Collective forces alike sought shelter from the Gargantuan battle currently paused for negotiations. A demand for concessions to spare Pax's life.

Remorse, holding Xelan and Tameka's son in his hand, looked apathetic to the situation. His voice boomed in its ear-splitting depth when he asked, "You want me to relinquish my grandson without assurances? Bol, does that sound reasonable to you?"

Xelan had never heard Bol sound so unhappy. "Rem, however you've entangled us into this quagmire, I leave it to you to see us out of it."

In a surprising lack of decorum, Tumu spat black blood at Bol's feet. "You continue to perform for our audience that you didn't know Remorse was corrupt, rather than contend with your complicity in his actions. As I've done."

Bol glanced at the splatter of blood, and his featureless face rippled with disgust. He wiped his own blood on his wrist. "I think I'll stick with my kind, you traitor."

Since Xelan was declared the Traitor Prince, would that make Tumu the Traitor Tritan?

Kyle beat him to it. "Traitor Primary has a ring to it!"

Across the way, Xelan couldn't miss Silence's grin, despite the light strobing her skin.

So close.

They were so close to happily ever after.

Tameka leaned in to Xelan and whispered, "Follow my lead."

He didn't hesitate. "Always."

Tameka straightened and flew closer to Primary Rem. "You won't release Pax because you know I'll drain you, and then the others will kill you?"

Remorse narrowed his eyes at the last. Arrogance dripped from his words, as he said, "As if *you* could kill *me*, but yes. I don't want you to steal my nacre energy and feed it to the War King so she'll destroy my home."

Home.

Enki was no one's home now. When Rayne finished with it and they evacuated to Ishkur, it would be nothing.

Raising Xelan's curiosity, Tameka slipped off her Rayne chain and held it out to Remorse. "Drink Rayne's blood, and you'll be impervious to our abilities."

Xelan trusted Tameka.

Bol asked, "And the conduit?"

Razor announced over the mass comm, "I'll create the conduit myself so the Shadow won't know its destination. It will take me some time to route it. Once you make the exchange, I suggest evacuating the armies on both sides. I'll need Xelan for that and Tameka to power the conduit reserves. Naturally, Pax will join them on the bridge."

Bol asked, "And *my* chain?"

Xelan slipped his off. It wasn't like he'd looked forward to drinking Rayne's blood, anyway. "Here." He flew out to the Primaries.

Andrew muttered, "What? No 'I got you'?"

Glaring at Remorse, Xelan said, "I save that for family."

Across the way, Korac's smirk was audible.

Sagan snickered.

Primary Rem was so dispassionate of the situation, he showed no response.

Tameka nodded at Silence and Tumu. The Tritans might take advantage of Rayne's nanite infusion, the power within it, and recommence with the fighting. It was up to the two strongest fighters to take them down in that case.

Silence mouthed, "Easy."

Tumu nodded, one finger subtly pointed at Lamassau, ready at his feet.

Xelan and Tameka held out their respective chains. The Primaries took them, tentatively. Rem opened his fist finally, allowing Tameka to snatch their son into her arms and fly back to their ring of friends. Xelan lingered, watching the villainous Tritans toss the entire necklace into their mouth and chew. Both their voids widened and their spines straightened as Rayne's nanites imbued them with her power to unknown effect.

All of it played on those screens with a rising string score to mark the moment. There was a good reason Xelan and Razor got along. The Prince of Cinder called, "Razor! We're ready for those evacuation conduits. Let these people go home."

Sagan and Korac circled the ring of fighters to open a conduit for Tameka, Pax, and Xelan into the bridge. Kyle, Andrew, Silence, and Pehton maintained positions. Tumu and the two blue Lyriks stayed right where they were, poised for further mayhem.

Tameka muttered to Xelan as he made his way to her, "Are you sure you can trust Razor?"

To answer her, Razor opened a conduit to the bridge in their path.

Xelan hoped the Pain Curator would keep his word and disappoint Imminent one last time.

{ENKI | PANTHEON}

Silence grew more impressed with Fury's leadership at the passing of every given moment. The entire scenario occurred as the young woman had predicted. Remorse was intimidated into freeing Pax. He and Bol were already deteriorating. And Three Two Four persisted with his attempt to reconcile with the younger Seamswalker, to the Shadow's advantage.

Small conduits opened all around, leading to unknown locations, because anywhere was safer than here. The villainous Primaries were intentional in their collateral destruction. Gait's children were reunited with their respective planets. The Vast Collective soldiers returned in formation through Sagan's conduits, back to Cinder's shrine.

Meanwhile, Silence reserved the chain she took from Pax for the last moment. The light under her skin was strobing now, but soon it would blur into one beacon and disintegrate her. At least, that's what Quet and Remorse had told Silence all those millions of years ago.

Lucas hovered beside Silence, with Smith on his back. The loyal Icarus' attention was never in the fight. He stared without looking at Andrew across the way. Silence knew because she stared without looking at Kyle beside his brother-in-arms.

If it weren't for the pulsating light beneath her skin, she'd say this was ridiculous.

Smith muttered to the other man, "You two are ridiculous." Both Silence and Lucas glared at him, but as always, Smith refused their attempt to deter him. "I mean it. They're right there. You're fighting on the same side. Say something."

Halfwit.

He knew it wasn't that simple—

"Hey!"

Stilted and slow, Lucas and Silence looked away from Smith and across the way to where Kyle was waving like the sexy goof he was. Beside the wild man, Andrew's normally golden complexion paled in mortification to the same shade as Lucas' skin. Even the Gargantuans stared at Kyle, perplexed.

Silence couldn't help herself. She laughed. She laughed harder when Kyle nudged Andrew beside him, saying, "See? I still got it."

Smith grinned beside her, and despite himself, Lucas gave a small smile under the blush to his cheeks.

"How unfaithful of you, Surra." Remorse went and ruined the moment. She glared at him, not willing to waste her words, but incidentally prompting him to continue. "Elden tore the worlds apart to find you, and you moved on so soon after waking."

Tumu's voice was firm. "That's enough, Rem. Don't take advantage of the armistice."

But the vicious Primary's words had already performed to his liking. They needled into Silence's guilty conscience. She fell in love with Kyle while her memory had evaded her. Elden was far from her mind then. Even so, the love of Silence's life was long gone, died defending his people as Rayne would soon do. And how would Silence ever confess to Kyle that she knew all along there was no hope for his close friend—

"Hey... If you need to frown, that's okay, but don't let him get to you."

Kyle.

The memory Progeny had flown across the battlefield to console Silence. She stared at him, unsure what to say or think. Lucas and Smith were her only constants since she disobeyed Elden's only wish.

"Save this world."

Silence closed her eyes. Softly, she said to no one. "It starts with *him* and ends with *her*."

"What did you say?" Kyle sounded properly confused, and Silence opened her eyes to find a confounded frown on his face. He wet his lips before asking, "Can you repeat that?"

Silence knew the invocation appeared throughout Nox's and Korac's Verses, but it was so much older. Of course, Savis had learned it from Cascading Light and passed it on. Only, it saddened Silence how badly it was twisted around Rayne in recent years. Looking into Kyle's concerned eyes, she supposed she owed him something in explanation. "It's the first thing I retained from the Probability Matrix. I'm not sure of its full context."

Beside Kyle, Andrew's face fell. Both men looked as if she'd kicked their favorite Hell Kitten. Expecting answers to make sense of this ever-tangling web which brought them together was courting madness. Only an Aegis could interpret threads as complicated as these.

Silence reached a hand out to brush Kyle's arm, her own swirling with light in beat to her imminent death. The act of comforting him was worth pushing fatalistic thoughts aside. Instead, she offered, "We can find its meaning together."

Kyle stared at her in disbelief while Andrew perked up. The intention reader looked beyond her, presumably at Lucas. After a tense moment, both men grinned, and Silence's heart thrilled with hope.

Please.

Let this be the Probability to happiness.

{ENKI | BRIDGE}

Tameka half-expected the conduit Razor provided them to send them falling into an ocean filled with sharks or more of those leviathan things. It took them right to the bridge and the swirling vortex of black fire. With Pax in her arms, she saw the maelstrom in a different light.

Imminent had put their hands on Tameka's son.

For good measure, she took another draw on Enki's star and split it between Ishkur's sun and Rayne. She needed to check on her best friend after they sent Pax somewhere safe.

But before Tameka could do that, she needed to swallow her pride and try not to vomit as she mumbled, "Thanks, Razor." Fast. Done.

Xelan was by her side for it and didn't give her any shit about it, as he helped Tameka lay Pax out on his pirate frock, of all things. It provided soft cushioning against the glass gangway. He checked their son's vitals, while she oscillated between hovering over him and giving him room for air.

The smile Xelan gave her was kind and the perfect reassurance. "You're doing great, and so is he. I think he expended his ability during the fight with Celindria and Remorse earlier." With a crooked grin, he chuffed Tameka under the chin. "Our boy's just tuckered out after a hard day of work."

Tameka couldn't see through her eyes for the glistening of tears. Happy and relieved, she pulled Xelan in for a hug over Pax's sleeping figure. No longer a cherub, he was the size of a seven-year-old Earth child with a million-year-old mind for all Tameka knew.

Shoo. This would take some adjustment.

"You're welcome, Fury. Prince Xelan." Razor's magnanimity had limits. His voice took on some urgency as he declared, "I've found something which might interest you."

Tameka swallowed a little more pride and admitted to herself that it was generous of Razor to let them have this moment alone as a family, but the gesture didn't stop her from shuddering at the sound of his voice. It did keep her from glaring at him when he appeared in his projection beside the terminal with a gloved wave.

Xelan stood and took Tameka with him, nodding over to the screens. "Let's look."

Razor projected various images.

Tameka frowned and took a step closer. "Is that water peeling away from Enki's hull—Is that an ocean?!"

Xelan bit his thumbnail, staring in silence with an occasional glance at Pax behind them. He looked concerned. Eventually, he asked, "Where is this occurring?"

Razor answered while flicking through other images of similar activity. "All across Enki."

On the continents, anything without roots floated away from the surfaces. Boulders, animals, the atmosphere—Everything moved in the same direction.

Like a demented professor, Razor explained, "Enki is losing enough power to the transfer that the anti-gravity is failing across the Sphere. The continents and the oceans will shut down first. Then the Primary Sanctums, the Shrines—Eventually the Pantheon and the Hall of Dead Kings."

Tameka knew this was true based on the visual, but it wasn't a complete explanation. She looked at Xelan for confirmation.

He nodded at her and glanced at Razor. "This isn't all." Firmer than concrete, he was dead certain, and the demand for the rest was in his voice.

Razor smirked more at Xelan than Tameka. He shook his head as if lamenting a loss before sighing and completing the lecture. "There's a competitive source of gravity within the Sphere, and it's winning." He looked between them and something like contemplation crossed his projected face before he said, "Rayne."

Tameka scoffed. "What do you mean? For her to have any sway over gravity in this place with a sun, she'd need to gain mass by the millions, and unless my best friend has gained a significant amount of weight in the last hour, you're making this up."

Gently, Xelan squeezed her bicep, making her turn to him. Concern warmed his midnight eyes. And guilt. There was a drop of guilt in there.

The Weapon project. Tameka swallowed her initial instinct to ask, '*What did you do?*' Pushing aside the accusation, she said, "Please. Tell me." She trusted him to deliver the truth.

Out of her periphery, she saw Razor flit away as Xelan said, "Her nacre is the perfect Weapon. The blast I performed in Umbra's Spire to spare you and the Progeny from Nox and Korac was nothing compared to what Rayne can do."

Tameka shook away her initial confusion and denial. Why would Xelan create something so dangerous? No. No. She understood. He wanted to stop Nox, but...

"Can you give me an equivalent?"

Trust Xelan.

Love Xelan.

Don't doubt him now.

"An Mton hydrogen blast of solar system proportions."

Tameka gripped his stupid signature black tank top and rose to her tiptoes, putting her face close to his as she begged an answer from him. "Why?" Her voice broke on a desperate sob.

Xelan cupped the sides of her face, pressing moisture from fresh tears into a long day of salt on her cheeks. For the hundredth time today, tears glittered on his lashes. "You know why. I was blind to so much, and I was wrong. Out of the three of us—Nox, Korac, and I—The actual monster is the one you fell in love with."

It wasn't self-pitying. Xelan believed it. He'd trained them to kill his own brother without informing the Progeny of his familial relationship. To what end?

Choking on the truth, Tameka asked for more. "If you could create something like that, why did you need us? Kyle, Andrew, Sagan, Rayne, and I?"

Xelan brushed a coil of her red hair from her vision. She watched the gesture in the reflection of his eyes, so shimmering were they. His voice croaked as he confessed, "I was alone."

Tameka's head felt heavy, and it bobbed with the shock. She was boneless.

With no effort, Xelan lifted her to him in a hug. On instinct, she wrapped her arms and legs around him and gripped the sturdy Icarus like a koala, crying what remained of her makeup onto his shoulder.

The man kept explaining himself, as if once the dam was unlocked, he couldn't stem the flow of truth. "Hollow soldiers with atomic bombs in their chests don't make for a revolution, and I'd lost myself to the mania of research. I was dehydrated without connection. My cause needed a people. Without a doubt, Nox would come for the Progeny—*My* Progeny. When the Tribunal exiled me to Earth without contact, it wasn't because of the cataclysm on Thailea. It's because I'd learned too much of their relationship with the idea of Imminent. I'd learned what they'd used me for—what the Vast Collective groomed me for—and they discarded me."

Weary still, Tameka pulled back to search his eyes.

Finally.

More explanation would come later in his Verse, but she needed at least this much to move forward. And one more thing. "What made you break your exile in the end?"

Xelan swallowed as if this answer proved difficult. There was so much sorrow in his voice when he said, "Rayne."

The power surged throughout the bridge.

Tameka realized she was still clinging to Xelan in the middle of a battle under the watchful gaze of the almighty fashion victim. She patted him until he set her down. He looked bruised, and she knew how that felt. Taking his hand, she assured, "I still trust you, Wingmaster. Do you think you can put that giant brain of yours to use and think of a way to spare Rayne from . . ." Although she tried for cavalier, Tameka couldn't finish the sentence.

Xelan cupped the nape of Tameka's neck with his warm, reassuring hand. "I got you." Tameka swatted him, as he looked at the terminal and asked, "Razor, what's the ETA on the final blow?"

"I'll need Peh Peh's help with the rest. I'm looking forward to asking. The Primaries will require distracting. Rem trusts me to perform to his expectations, but he will tire of standing in unfriendly company. In other news, Ishkur is seventy-five percent online. I can route additional evacuation conduits from Cinder's shrine to the Pantheon equivalent in Ishkur, if you'd like? It will spare the Seamswalker the extra effort."

Tameka and Xelan shared a knowing glance. Why the Last Aegis sought validation in Sagan baffled Tameka, but as long as it served the Shadow, they'd take it. And maybe part of her saw what Sagan wanted to redeem in him. Fat chance, though.

The screens continued to play the pull of water from Enki's interior.

Softly, Tameka asked, "Should I stop feeding Rayne power?"

Xelan massaged her shoulders, saying, "You can always ask her yourself—"

"Mommy?"

"Pax?!" Tameka bolted to her baby boy and swept his reaching arms up around her, crying again into his neck. "Pax. My son. Pax."

Muffled against her chest, Pax cried, "You did it! You came back for me!"

"That's right, baby. Nothing in the galaxy will keep me from you."

{THE HEART OF ENKI}

Calibrated.

Optimized.

Stabilizing...

Unable to stabilize.

Warning: One hour and twelve minutes until maximum destabilization.

The light cascaded under Rayne's skin, faster and faster, until it nearly formed one solid beacon. Razor's screens displayed various views of Enki's ruin around her. Tameka fed her spine-bending power infusions.

And Rayne barely noticed any of it.

"This last one you should know from sharing my experiences with me. Can you guess?" Plucking it from her bed, Rayne held up a stuffed panda missing one button eye and flattened from her nightly snuggles.

Nox leaned against the far wall, one arm folded and supporting the other while he bit his thumbnail. Like Xelan. Rayne could tell Nox was concentrating on his memory banks because he narrowed his eyes thoughtfully. He stopped biting his thumb and used that hand to fire a finger gun at the panda. "Galena."

Rayne giggled hard enough to bounce her bed, sitting on the edge reminiscing of all the times her mom nearly caught her and Sagan making out. Remembering the hours spent stitching a cut or icing a muscle after training with the Progeny and Xelan. Catching Jack 'borrowing' her music without permission. All the sleepovers. Birthday parties. So much makeup.

"Now *you've* gone away."

Rayne smiled under Nox's gentle scrutiny. After everything they'd been through, he knew her better than Xelan. He knew she'd lied to them, and he was decent enough not to call her out on it.

Rayne needed a hug, and Ms. Galena wasn't up for the task. She stared at the floor and squeezed the barely stuffed panda, anyway, before asking, "Did you construct the training ground, too?" She met his eyes as she finished.

Nox gave a silent nod and stepped to the side, letting Rayne pass him through her bedroom door with only the slightest of brushes. He was simply too massive for her room to move around him without contact. Even though this was inside her head, the small connection made her pause and glance at him.

The chrome Atramentous flashed in his gaze, granting her a reflection of a young woman with haunted blue eyes and a smile to pity. As the mirror faded, Rayne forced her back straighter, her shoulders squarer, and her chin higher. She would not die a pitiful girl. Rayne was made of better stock than that. She came from a long line of Progeny, Icari, and, somewhere in there, a bit of Tritan, like Tumu. Pride suffused her veins.

Descending the stairs two at a time, Rayne called to Nox over her shoulder, "Shall we?"

Nox followed her like he would do so until the end. A privacy fence separated the Callahan's property from the trail to the training grounds. It was the same fence Rayne had vaulted the morning of Invasion Day. He dissolved it, and they found the obstacle course Xelan had built in the undeveloped woods beside her neighborhood.

Home.

Rayne sat on the picnic table, where her adorkable guardian had insisted they gather for rests. Butt on the tabletop and feet on the bench, she leaned back and stared at the nothing, wishing for stars—

The entire table thudded when Nox climbed on, mirroring her. It was jarring enough to make her smile. "Do you think—"

"Hey, War King. This is Wingmaster on your private line. You there, Rayne? Over."

Optimism radiated from Xelan's voice, full of hope and relief—Could it be? "I'm here. Please tell me you have good news! Over."

Again, Rayne heard the grin in his voice. "We have Pax, and he's safe. Over."

She and Nox shared the same smile as she said, "That's the news I wanted to hear. Give him a hug for me. Over."

"You'll give him a hug yourself as soon as we finish with Remorse. Until then, I wanted to see how you were doing up there. Over."

Nox raised a brow.

Should Rayne tell the truth? Lying to Xelan, even to protect him, sucked. She settled for something in the middle. "Wingmaster. Complete evacuation within the hour. I'm nearly ready. Tell Tameka to keep the power surges coming. Over."

She hated that some of Xelan's joy left his voice when he said, "Ten-Four. Hang in there, Callahan. I'm not leaving you. Over and Out."

To keep her promise, Tameka sent another surge through Rayne, and it immobilized her—

How did her arms and legs work? Her brain was full of static. What was the name... the name of...

"Galena."

Nox's voice brought Rayne back to her consciousness, followed by a painful needle-tingling in her fingers and toes. Static shocks electrocuted the feeling back into her extremities—

"I'm half-tempted to tell Xelan, myself." Razor reappeared, violating her intentional self-isolation. "If he knew I was keeping this from him, he'd shut down Enki's circuitry and kill me properly dead."

Rayne heaved air into her mouth, gulping great lungfuls of it to make sure she didn't forget how. It burned, while the rest of her sparked with energy. On a groan, she said, "Don't. They can't help me, and all you'd give them is an hour to feel helpless about it."

The Pain Curator tipped his hat to her, conceding the point. Still, he pressed, "Why not tell them about the great King Nox? Play the Atheneum game and let him speak to Xelan before the end."

Back on the picnic table inside her mind, Rayne glanced at Nox. She'd hate to admit it, but Razor made a good point. "Is that something you want?"

Nox ran one enormous hand through his long hair in a gesture he'd developed when taxed. "If there's any love for me left in my brother, then he would suffer twice the loss this day. I find that unkind. Not to mention, an hour is an awfully short time to force him to decide how he feels about me while also negotiating his impending loss of you—No." He shook his head, then added, "But I appreciate you keeping your vow."

Rayne spared him an understanding smile before answering the voyeur in their midst. "Nox said no. Bad timing and all that."

Again, sadness stole Razor's smile and left his eyes old. "You have much less time to tell them now. Call if you need me." With that, he flitted away.

For a long moment, Rayne gazed around the cognitive puzzle of her mindscape. Dark in some places, yet on the horizon, a storm harassed an ocean while a volcano cooled in the salt before the segmented scene ended in the training grounds.

She pointed at the three-meter wall of wooden planks. "The first time I vaulted that, I knew I'd defeat you."

Nox chuckled, shaking his head—Not incredulous, simply happy. "That *is* quite impressive for your height."

"Damn straight."

They carried on this way for a while, discussing training from throughout their lives, personal bests, etcetera. During the conversation, the storm in Rayne's heart raged with the occasional bolt of lightning from Tameka. It became easier.

Nox made it easier. He made Rayne laugh, and she needed it so badly. When Rayne would give anything to hug Xelan, Sagan, Tameka, Andrew, and Kyle, Nox's quiet consideration of her was almost enough to make her forget. Forget how they got here, forget what was coming, and forget how little time she had left.

With Nox around, how could Rayne die alone and afraid?

A thought occurred to her. Ashamed of her selfishness, Rayne blurted, "Nox, what would you want to do with your last moments if you weren't stuck here with me?"

Rayne expected him to look bewildered or startled by her outburst, but Nox simply reminded her, "I've had my epitaphs. When I wrote the Verse for you, I knew you would end me only days later. Here with you is no punishment. It's an honor to finish Enki at your side."

Rayne swallowed, apparently audibly, because Nox tilted his head curiously at her. Unable to unpack his sentiments right at this moment, she tried for some levity. "Do you think it's too late for me to start writing my Verse?"

"Rayne, with or without one, the Vast Collective will never forget you. Your legacy will end syndicates and create worlds. Entire solar systems will be named after you. You'll get your Verse. I promise you."

Recommendation: Attain minimum safe distance.

Warning: One hour until maximum destabilization.

ELEVEN
ONE MAN'S END IS ANOTHER EMPIRE'S BEGINNING

{ENKI | PANTHEON}

ONCE AGAIN, ANDREW SCANNED PRIMARY REM AND BOL'S INTENTIONS, AND ONCE AGAIN, PRIMARY REM GLARED AT HIM WITH DISPASSIONATE VOIDS. It was weird how the Tritans could sense if Andrew and Kyle used their abilities on them, and also weird that they couldn't affect Lyriks at all. Humbling was the word.

The second the villainous Primaries' intentions shifted from staying the current course, Andrew would sound the alarm. Imminent's own people fled, evacuating for fear of their leadership. As for the Vast Collective troops, Razor opened some conduits to Ishkur within Cinder's Shrine, which was still available through Sagan's conduits. It boggled Andrew's mind to imagine there was a second Dyson's Sphere. Across the way, Sagan and Korac conferred with F8, Legir, and X to supervise the Vast Collective's mass exodus for the new world.

One hour.

That's how long Xelan said Rayne gave them to leave.

And Andrew was a reprobate because he wasn't concentrating on any of it. Every fiber of his being vibrated this close to Lucas and his golden eyes shyly averted like Andrew's. Yet both men pretended they were holding their positions in this fight. With every peripheral glance from Lucas and ever amused smirk by Smith, Andrew knew the truth.

Beside them, Silence and Kyle communicated similarly. They were happy to see each other, if their grins were any indication. It was an awkward but anticipated reunion.

"Keep your faith in me a little while longer."

A long talk. That's what they needed.

Everything was so tense that Lamassau nearly startled Andrew as the Tritan came over his private frequency. "Hey. This is where I get to say 'I told you so.'"

Andrew didn't need a refresher on what the good Tritan referred to.

Pax.

Lam was right about him.

Elden, how many *days* ago was that? It felt like a lifetime.

The toddler was playing in the Villa's tree, and he made a few references to things he shouldn't know. Lam came in and accused him of being an evil genius.

Andrew responded discretely, "It's looking like you exaggerated a bit."

The fire-breathing Tritan ignored the semantics to say, "I also won the engagement pool. You, Bones, Kyle, Twenty-One, and Iuo owe me twelve thousand credits. I knew he'd propose in battle."

In the background of Lamassau's mic, Andrew overheard Iuo say, "I'll swing you and Tumu a free film instead. Unless he plans on being decompressed, then the production costs go up."

Bad images. Bad, bad images.

When Andrew stopped rubbing the obscenity from his eyes, he glanced to find Lucas staring at him, bemused. The golden-eyed Icarus asked, "Was it Lamassau or Bones?"

Blinking, Andrew said, "Lamassau. How did you know?"

The other man smiled, and it sent an electric current to Andrew's toes. He barely heard Lucas answer, "You only do the eye rub when you're talking to one of them, and they suggest something salacious."

Andrew gave himself permission to chuckle. Just a little. "Yeah. One of Iuo's 'films' for Lam and Tumu, decompressed."

Lucas' eyes widened.

Smith recoiled with a puckered face.

Kyle gagged behind Andrew.

Silence said, "I'd pay for that." All the men gave a slow turn to stare at her in disbelief. She shrugged, utterly unashamed, and confessed, "It would be a sight these ancient eyes have never seen."

Bewildered, Andrew shook his head, blinking. It made some sense, but wow.

Another voice came over his earpiece. It was Razor.

"Shadow, this is your only warning. Vacate the Pantheon post haste. Seamswalker, make the sweep. Pehton and Miy standby. I'll need my birdies to sing the Primaries one last song.

"Their requiem."

Down came the first drop of rain.

{ENKI | PANTHEON}

"Well, fuck."

Kyle appreciated his influence on Silence's vocabulary, and he appreciated that Tameka apparently gave her an earpiece along with the two Gargantuan Lyriks, who shared an "oh shit" look. Like seriously. What kind of warning was that? With drizzle glistening in his hair, Andrew communicated wordlessly with Lucas, trying to keep Remorse and Bol from noticing. Unfortunately, the two Primaries were glaring at Silence after her outburst.

With the villain's backs turned to her, Sagan drank her vessel of Rayne's blood.

Through the rain, Kyle reached out his hand to Silence, for all the life in him trying to convey with his eyes, "Hang. On." Shit. Primary Rem saw everything.

"What do you think you're doing?" His voice boomed the question throughout the Pantheon, disrupting the surrounding droplets.

Diverting his attention, Tumu asked, "Have you forgotten what comfort and warmth look like, Remorse?"

Primary Rem humphed. "This looks more like fear to me. Fear of what—"

"Remorse." An enormous three-dimensional projection of a man who could only be Razor appeared in the sky, wearing a fancy suit and a cavalier expression. Despite the lack of a corporeal body, rain poured from the brim of his top hat.

With relief in his deafening voice, the evil Primary asked, "Razor, is the conduit ready?"

Razor cocked his head to the side, staring at the Tritan with his bizarre eyes, remote. "There's been an unforeseeable delay."

Kyle's mouth fell open. Was this for real?

Remorse sounded disappointed, but not surprised. "Ah. The Seamswalker got to you, didn't she, son?"

The Last Aegis tapped his cane on an invisible surface, splashing a puddle. He lowered his head until the brim of his hat hid his eyes, considering. "'Son.' A word with so much significance. With that one word, you destroyed the last vestiges of my relationship with the Exalted, my people. With it, you convinced a child to condemn himself to a lifetime as your Weapon, so he could grow strong enough to protect the family you and I ruined. Now, you call your malleable grandchild 'son,' scheming to turn the boy against his father. Well, old *friend*, I don't see that in your future. I see the end." With that, Razor neatly tucked his cane under his arm and opened an umbrella. "This time, the flood comes for you."

Lightning fast, Tumu snatched Primary Bol's robes and headbutted the bastard. The Gargantuan enemy went down, unmoving.

Kyle whooped, grinning until he saw the look on Silence's face. She was staring at him with so much... sorrow. Blazing like a beacon, she soared into the fray.

"Silence!" Kyle wanted to know what the look meant. Wanted to know how close she was to the final stage of her nacre's expiration date. But Andrew grabbed his arm, while Lucas and Smith formed a blockade. All three faces were grim.

No.

Kyle wasn't having it. "What's she doing?!"

Smith answered, "Her job."

Silence flitted into Primary Rem's face and knocked the monster a good one in the temple with a satisfying crack.

Meanwhile, Bones flew in and activated Tumu's compression orb, since the big guy was staggering between Aria and Torch after the noggin knocker. On the wet ground, Lamassau swept his damsel in distress into his arms and made for one of the many evacuation conduits. The two Gargantuan Lyriks compressed without orbs as far as Kyle could see, and followed the other Tritans through an octagon of conduits. Sagan was really pressing her advantage with Rayne's blood. And there. The sweeping conduit scooped troops and Gait's Children alike into an energy net, transporting them presumably to Ishkur.

After listening to his earpiece, Andrew tied back his drenched hair, muttering, "Sagan's coming to get us next."

"But Silence... " Kyle watched her battle the man responsible for so much pain her in life, delivering skull-shattering blows and working through some trauma in time to the lightning strobing the dark sky. "How will Sagan snatch her without grabbing Remorse?"

Lucas and Smith shared a look before the golden-eyed Icarus assured, "We won't leave without the Mother. We'll stay by her side."

Kyle didn't like the sound of that. Like they planned to stay back and die with her to keep Remorse pinned to some invisible target, but even as he considered it, the pair hovered away, giving space for—

The Seam, all purple and happy—Then rolling onto a glass gangway over—

Whoa.

The swirling black flames below flashed Kyle back to the epic swirly from his first solo Icarus fight on Invasion Day, but on a much less survivable scale. Travel by rolling conduit sucked. It left his stomach with the same feeling as driving too fast down a hill. He groaned—

Someone pulled him to his feet with ease.

"Hey." It was Tameka. "Welcome to Ishkur boys."

Andrew asked before Kyle got the words out, "What about Lucas, Silence, and Smith?"

Tameka frowned, puzzled. "What about them?"

Kyle said, "I think they're on some suicide mission. They stayed behind, fighting Remorse."

Xelan was beyond Tameka, playing with Pax and settling people into the new Sphere. Tameka turned and gazed at them. Kyle feared she was soaking them in. When she faced Andrew and Kyle again, Tameka's eyes were fierce. "I promise. I'll bring her back." She stepped through a permanent conduit leading to an identical platform. Through it, Kyle heard Tameka say, "Razor, open a conduit back to the Pantheon."

"Fury, I can't guarantee your survival."

"Oh, you'd just love that, wouldn't you?"

Then the future Empress of the Vast Collective stepped through a conduit to save the Mother of the galaxy without informing her husband, her son, or even her best friends.

Andrew was so helpful. "Xelan will be pissed at you if she dies, dude." And so right.

"Shit."

{Enki | Pantheon}

Pehton didn't find this hard to believe at all. Razor would totally kill his former ally out of jealousy and cumulative resentment. Finally, the great Pain Curator recognized he was as manipulated as Quet, Nox, Pehton, and anyone else Primary Rem crossed paths with. Thank Elden she'd given him that copy of Nox's Verse.

Flying with the flock through the storm, Pehton and the Lyriki army followed the Gargantuan Lyriks' compressed figures to a conduit leading to Cinder's shrine. From there, she'd follow into whatever conduit they took to Ishkur. She didn't care where it went. Pehton remembered her children. Their names, Aria and Torch. Their faces and beautiful coloring, such an exotic combination of their parents' genetics. And their hugs and smiles in the sunshine.

Pehton's children.

Caedes kept up beside her with his brand of support, strong and silent as a column—

Pehton's palm vibrated, startling her. Only the Primaries communicated this way—

A little three-dimensional rendering of Razor appeared in her hand. "Peh Peh, it's time."

"Hah! As if I'd go along with your plan."

The tiny figure smirked. "Triangulate the chorus, and we'll both finally be free of Remorse."

Where Pehton paused in the rain, she looked up to see her kids move further away from her. Her army lingered at her side, ready for orders. Droplets momentarily disrupted Razor's image while he waited for her answer.

A galaxy newly united and free of Remorse.

Pehton swore loud enough to reverberate through Cinder's shrine. She really was about to go along with this! "I'll do it, but I don't know how you have the power with the atmosphere and gravity slipping."

With one of his infuriating smiles, Razor admitted, "This will use the last of Enki's reserves now that Fury dimmed the sun for Ishkur."

But if Enki lost all power… Pehton narrowed her eyes at the transmission. Did Razor know the implications for his chance of survival? Not that she cared. She said, "Get ready."

"I always thought Gait was lucky to have you." The sincerity confused Pehton before he added, "Over and Out," like he found it amusing and disappeared.

Caedes, cute when drenched in the rain, did not sound amused. "Can you trust him?"

Pehton laughed again. "Absolutely not. I hate the man."

"You wish you did."

"Ugh!" That deserved an eye-roll. If Razor could invade the private frequency of Pehton's earpiece, why did he appear like a message from R2D2? "You might want to stand back." She nodded at Caedes, who did as he was told—With the sexiest smirk, distracting Pehton momentarily.

Stop that.

Focus on triangulating the galaxy's most deadly Weapon of mass destruction.

On Pehton's signal, all the Lyriks drank Rayne's chain. The War King's nanites suffused with Pehton's nacre, and a sun blazed in the Lyriks. Pehton sang with it. The others joined and matched in pitch. It rose in volume. Kerosene fumed from their blood, blurring Pehton's vision. Flames erupted beside her. Torch and Aria returned to join in the song. Despite the loud foot stomps of combat boots, the sound left the room in a vacuum, only filled by their chorus.

Before Razor traveled on the frequency of their voice to join in the interface of their constructs using the satellites they activated, Pehton prayed to Elden Sagan had truly gotten through to the Last Aegis.

{ENKI | MEDICAL BAY}

"Miy, can you acknowledge me?"

Pablo was trying to reach the thorny Lyrik, who was singing in the middle of their evacuation. Even with the power outage and lack of gravity, he refused to leave her.

T.A.O. waited with Twenty-One and Lynn, holding Echo, while Pablo tried to break Miy's programming mid-float.

Something flit in the corner of Pablo's eye, announcing Razor's arrival before the Pain Curator said, "I'm afraid it will be another moment. Once I complete the chorus using our lovely Lyrik here, she'll be free. Don't waste a second to evacuate. Rayne's accelerating."

Pablo and Razor turned and looked toward the bay housing Triss' body. In a deep voice filled with sadness, Razor said, "You must leave her behind with me. Tell Echo of her parents' last moments. Together."

Lynn surprised Pablo by saying, "We will." Twenty-One stared at her in disbelief, and she shrugged. "Woman-to-woman, what Triss did was incredibly selfless, and if you're coming through for the Shadow, Razor, then you earned Echo knowing your part in the fall of Enki."

The Pain Curator's responding smirk was bitter, sad, and proud before he flitted away.

"He is why I'm here," T.A.O. confessed.

Although Pablo had been curious why the ancient Seamswalker came to their rescue, he didn't dare pry. "Thank you." He glanced from her to the massive Icarus at her side. "Twenty-One?"

"Yes, Dr. Suarez?"

Pablo wet his lips, and the act of it squeezed his heart because he knew Lynn watched it closely. Resolute, he said, "I'm breaking my vows, and I need your help."

Lynn cried, "What?!"

Twenty-One called, "Say no more. See you in Ishkur or Eternity."

While Lynn panicked with Echo in her arms, Twenty-One took hold of Pablo's wife and Razor's daughter. T.A.O. dragged them through a conduit to Ishkur. It closed behind her.

Pablo swallowed hard, hoping it wasn't regret. "I won't leave you, Miy. Razor said we'd have one second to escape, and if we don't—Well, at least I saved Echo and Lynn."

Miy continued to sing, non-responsive to his words.

Closing his eyes, Pablo prayed to Elden that Razor pulled through, so Pablo and his wife could get to work on having a dozen babies of their own.

{Enki | Cinder's Shrine}

Anxiety buzzed through Ross, and people's histories leaked into her.

First kiss.

First sex.

Sports win.

What they ate for breakfast before the battle.

A Monarch 3 tree colony in flames, millions of drones dying. Blistering. Melting—

Ugh, this was awful. Ross would start attending therapy sessions with Korac after this. If Jack was secure with it, of course. Aside from the resilience of sheer appreciation for the half-Aegis, half-Icarean male, Ross was over Korac. Apparently, so was Pehton. Mostly.

Why was Ross standing in Cinder's shrine, wasting thoughts on this in the middle of an evacuation? Because if she didn't, she'd freeze everyone while absorbing entire lifetimes. Maybe drinking Rayne's chain was a bad idea.

Chris called attendance, "Jack. Karter. Para. Devis. Andrius. And Ross."

"Here."

For about twenty minutes, their team brought some order to the remnants of the Vast Collective's forces and led them through Sagan's conduits to Ishkur. The curtains of energy separating these spaces from the Seam had flared when she drank Rayne's chain, but now they were diminishing.

Ross and Jack volunteered for the Mon3 troops. Considering the wide variety of drone warfare memories, maybe Ross should've gone with Yun's army. Nevertheless, the last of them trickled through, and now the team reassembled for their own evacuation—

"Harder, toy. I'm so close."

Ross' knees buckled and her stomach lurched with the need to vomit—And it wasn't her need to do so. She tried—oh, Elden did she try—but she couldn't help glancing at Chris, who flocked to her side as soon as she went down.

Something must've shown on Ross' face because Chris recoiled.

Karter caught on, saying, "It's okay. We know you didn't mean to Ross. Devis, can you help her?"

Ross was gasping from the reverberation of Chris' worst memories and desperately wanted some kind of help.

Para encouraged, "Deep breaths."

Andrius offered, "I can *suggest* her to sleep."

Jack looked both pained and kind as he consoled Ross. "We'll get you to Ishkur first. Razor said we didn't have time."

Devis reached a hand out for Ross to clasp. "Hold on to me. We'll try some meditation that helps me, but Jack is right. It's time to go."

The lights flickered in the shrine, and everything got much lighter. As in no more gravity lighter.

Floating.

They were floating.

This both did and didn't help with the anxiety. On the one hand, zero gravity was fun. On the other hand, the shrine was failing.

Chris recovered and started swimming toward the nearest conduit. "We're out of time. Evac, now!"

Andrius and Devis imitated him.

Karter clutched Chris against her, using her wings to fly them in front of the conduit.

Para followed, calling back, "You got your girl, Callahan?"

On Ross' nod, Jack gingerly wrapped his arms around her—

"Jack, I'm worried about those guys I saw you with yesterday."

Jack stood in Rayne's shadow. Even though she was shorter than him, she had this presence which loomed. Could she see through him to the drug deals, the gambling, and the lie about being a virgin? Would she judge him—Was she standing in judgment of him now?

Angered by his own shame, Jack snapped, "Mind your own business, big sis. It's best you leave me alone."

"Are you threatening me?" When someone says that, they usually sound mad. Rayne didn't sound mad. There was disappointment in her eyes. When Jack didn't respond, she backed off, saying, "If you ever need to talk, I'm here for you, lil bro."

Fueled by stupid teenage hormones and an entitled sense of rightness, Jack shouted, "I wish I was an only child!"

Saddened, Rayne said, "One day you might get your wish."

"Oh, Jack," was Ross' last thought before Andrius *suggested* her to sleep.

{ENKI}

Razor routed a few satellite feeds to Ishkur, which wasn't completely within the same internal interface, and therefore limited, but he wanted the galaxy to witness his last feat. After all, it had been a long road to this moment, and he'd enjoyed the ride immensely. Everyone deserved to witness it.

Silence battled Remorse in a storm which raged over the Pantheon, making herself a target. Yet without her, nothing would prevent the Gargantuan from a last-minute escape.

Still...

"Dear, Silence."

Shining like the sun in the rain, she finished delivering a blow to the Tritan's solar plexus and turned to face Razor in the gray sky. "Yes, Three Two Four?"

Razor grinned. "I hope you survive."

The woman's smile was truly fantastic as she said, "May the stars shine on us both."

Drenched, Lucas and Smith waved from the sidelines. "We hope so, too." "They'd fucking better."

Black blood spat from Remorse's mouth and poured from his eyes. He grunted through the agony of breathing and cursed, "You haughty, overbearing, racist, female-murdering, filthy Aegis—"

Razor's grin crooked into a smirk. He bowed under his umbrella. "May you find Vi in Eternity, Remorse. And may she kill you again."

Beyond the Pantheon's stormy sky, light triangulated into one central column and unleashed on Razor's oldest and dearest friend. For one dazzling moment, white light engulfed both Primaries—

"Silence!"

Was Razor dreaming, or was Tameka jetting in to—

No.

Xelan would never forgive Razor.

Lucas cried, "Tameka!"

Smith called, "No, it's suicide!"

But it was too late.

Tameka flew into the light at the exact moment the Chorus fired, claiming the target area in brilliant disintegration.

The second the explosion cleared, Razor released several projections of himself to locate any sign of a body. Hers or Silence's. He wasn't alone. With Smith still on his back—the longest piggy-back ride in history—Lucas also searched the area.

The dust cloud made it difficult for his limited vision. Amid the clearing debris, Razor asked, "Do you see them anywhere?"

Lucas shouted from across the battlefield, "No, but—There!"

As the blow back dissipated, Razor made out two forms on the ground. He flitted another projection closer to find they were indeed Tameka and Silence.

They'd survived the Chorus.

In all his projections, Razor shook his head. "Progeny women are so impressive." But his relief was short-lived.

Silence was holding Tameka in her lap, shaking her. "Wake, child. The new galaxy awaits you. Wake." She searched the men surrounding them. "We can't let this be."

Lucas pointed at Silence's chest. "That should do it."

For the first time since Razor could remember, Smith frowned.

Wow. Why was this so monumental? Razor asked, "Am I missing something?"

Silence looped the chain over her head and stared at it in her glowing hands. Quiet.

Lucas answered for her, "She was planning to use it to prolong her nacre's expiration until she arrived in Ishkur."

So bright was the light emanating from Silence that she formed a starburst halo, making it difficult to see her. Resolute, she said, "My time is over, but not hers." She fed the drop of Rayne's blood to Tameka.

Fury sat up, gasping for air. "Did I save her? Did I—Silence, we need you—"

Silence fell over, and Lucas finally alighted. Smith hopped off his back and checked her pulse. He said, "She's almost gone."

"No. No. I came here to save her." Tameka lived up to her namesake. "Razor, open us a conduit to Ishkur."

The Pain Curator winced, sincerely. "My apologies, but I've no more power to give." Not exactly the truth. "The last conduit to Ishkur is on Enki's bridge. I don't know if she'll survive long enough—"

"She will." Tameka lifted the woman in her arms. "Anything between me and it?"

"Besides the continent of Torrentus, you might want to know Rayne is in the final stage. Enki has minutes left."

A strange expression crossed the future Empress' face, as if she warred in some internal conflict. Begrudgingly, she asked, "What happens to you?"

Razor didn't answer.

Lucas did. "The captain goes down with the capitol of his people's empire."

Smith saluted Razor.

Again, came that unfamiliar feeling...

No.

There was no need to examine it now. It was far too late for him. Razor gestured to the Torrentus conduit. "Go now. You haven't much time."

Tameka swallowed hard before saying, "Thank you, Razor."

"Go."

They left Razor with his thoughts in his failing Dyson's Sphere. At least he wasn't completely alone. In the heart of Enki, Rayne did the galaxy a favor. What a complex on that one. He thought he knew what a martyr was before he'd met Rayne Callahan, but now he was certainly educated. He had a few parting words for her—

"My lonely friend."

T.A.O.'s voice was soft from within the Seam.

The words touched Razor. "It's good to hear your voice." He wished he could see her solid Atramentous eyes one last time, but... "It's not safe, as you know. Stay away."

T.A.O. said, "Safe in the birdcage, all gilded in blood. Years without you. My friend. Now no more years."

If Razor weren't a projection, he would consider crying. He cleared his throat of emotion before saying, "You have Korac and my daughter. Look after her. She'll be small like you. Like her mother..."

T.A.O. sniffled, and he knew she cried for him. She said, "Eternity is glass with a view of all your best deeds. This will be your largest window."

It was too much. "I have little time remaining..."

Understanding, the ancient Seamswalker said, "Go. See her. Not alone and afraid. Goodbye, friend."

"Goodbye, T.A.O. Thank you."

The Seam grew cold without her warmth, like a part of Razor's heart when she'd left so long ago. How so many things could've been different...

Razor emerged in the heart of Enki. Rayne was a sight to behold. Like Silence, light emanated from her skin in a blinding brilliance. But unlike Silence, Rayne was separating on a molecular level. The light permeated between each atom of her making. And it hurt.

She was gasping when she said, "You did good work... soldier."

Razor tipped his hat to her. "You're a wonder, and I'm not entirely sure you plan to die. If that's the case, you'll need this." He held out his hand, glowing with interface computations.

Rayne's light dimmed and then recharged as she conferred with Nox. She asked, "What is it?"

With a flare for the dramatic, Razor pressed a key on his palm and let the pictures flash on a screen. "This contains the dossier Sagan sought with Imminent's proximal vendors and benefactors. By touching my hand, I can transfer it to your nacre's memory banks."

For a moment, Rayne contorted with pain, and the light spread nearly to Razor. He flitted back an inch and waited for the spasm to pass.

When it did, Rayne asked, "How did you know?"

"Oh, you're a paragon. No matter the fate of Enki, you always planned to finish what Nox started."

Again, the light dimmed. Then, "Go ahead."

Razor tilted his head. "You aren't afraid?"

The King of Earth and Cinder's voice was crystal clear when she challenged, "What's left to fear?"

Admirable.

Before the others arrived to make their goodbyes, because surely they would, Razor clasped Rayne's shining palm and transferred the dossier to her. The glow of the computations traveled across her skin and disappeared beneath her clothes. This close, looking into her eyes, he saw pure determination.

Brave soul.

In consolation, Razor assured, "I'd like to present you with a choice. And you, Nox. The others will come for you, either to force you to leave with them or to say farewell. With my help, you can offer them an interface upload of Nox's nacre for them to resurrect. I'll do this free of charge."

Something flickered in Rayne's eyes, and a tightness consumed her features that wasn't about physical pain.

"Are you offering to separate our nacres and take Nox's so that if I die, at least he lives?"

"Yes."

Rayne asked an important question. "Why not both of ours?"

Razor shook his head, genuinely dismayed. "Your nacre has breached beyond its stability. Some time ago, in fact. Perhaps from the moment you stepped out of the Martyr Complex."

Rayne winced at his words, but she nodded her understanding. After which, her eyes dimmed. They stayed that way a long time as Razor watched her discuss the option with her... Mate? Adversary? Partner?

Partner sounded good.

After another second, Rayne's voice held a great deal of awe when she said, "No. He asked to stay."

Wow.

Bewildered and impressed, Razor tipped his hat once more. "Very well." He glanced around the space before settling back on her dissipating form. He asked, "Was it worth it?"

Despite the pain, Rayne smiled. "You tell me."

Touché.

Razor spun his cane and tapped it once. "See you in Eternity, War King."

"I'll look you up in the section for martyrs."

Nearly smiling, Razor flitted to Triss' final resting place. Here, he'd ride out the last of Enki's apocalypse in peace—

"Razor, is that you?!" Dr. Suarez asked from around the corner. What was he doing here?

"It is. But—"

"Oh, this is rich." Miy sounded bitter. "*He's* our last hope?!"

Would Triss want Razor to waste his final moments holding her lifeless hand? Or would she rather him save the doctor who treated her with respect and kindness in the least friendly of company?

Razor laughed, readily and gladly. Yes. Indulging in Miy's misery would have to serve as an emotional palette cleanser. "I'll be your knight in shining armor."

Dr. Suarez said, "I didn't want to leave her—But Echo's safe with Lynn."

"I wouldn't dare keep the two of you apart." Razor meant it, but this was it.

The end.

Three Two Four, the Last Aegis, and the Pain Curator used Enki's remaining power to open the conduit for Dr. Suarez and Miy. She slipped through without a word, but the good doctor paused on the threshold. With sincerity in his eyes, Dr. Suarez pounded a fist over his nacre. Then they were gone.

Enki's dying breath.

Destroyed by Tameka and obliterated by Rayne.

Razor's final moments were full of thoughts—of windows—but the last was his best. No longer removed from greatness. With Remorse's death, Razor finally eased the Vast Collective of its troubles. Diminishing in power, he made it to Triss' bay and reached for her hand before Eternity claimed him.

"The Eternal Bind, my lethal siren... Yes... They will never forget us..."

TWELVE

NO SOLDIER LEFT BEHIND;
NO SHADOW WITHOUT LIGHT

{Ishkur | Pantheon}

Lucy threw her head back and cried out as Matt finished with her. Wet. She was slick with the blood of their enemies, and he kissed her through it, pressing her to the wall. Behind Matt, Lucy could see Puk's back where he stood watch from their corner in wherever the evacuation conduit had taken them to. Beyond Puk, the little devourer of memories, Bethany, was letting Yito teach her some takedown maneuvers. They weren't close enough to see or hear the couple copulating.

It was fine.

With a groan, Matt separated them and let Lucy's shaking legs go. She needed his help to steady her, and it was delicious. Wetting her lips under his enraptured stare, she admitted, "Maybe we shouldn't work separately for a while."

His grin was male and all satisfaction. "Agreed."

Puk called over his shoulder, "Don't forget to fix your hair this time. Both of you. It was so embarrassing that one time at The Brethren's conference. And don't act like you don't know what I'm talking about. We can all smell lemonade."

Lemonade.

Lucy smiled. So that's why.

The couple straightened their clothes and their hair. She fixed Matt's fringe from his near-black eyes, all sparkling in his strawberry and cream complexion—

"Lemonade, Lucy! Lemonade." Puk groaned. "Sheesh, you two never stop. If you're quite finished, I'd like to go over and teach our new members a proper guarding stance. Yito wasn't meant to be a soldier." As he said it, Praw gut-punched Yito despite his demonstration for Bethany. Dolton pointed and laughed. Lance looked stoic. Maybe stoic was his thing. Or maybe he was lamenting the loss of Enki.

Lucy took Matt's hand and pulled him toward their team. The surrounding space was white, empty grounds like the Pantheon, but it smelled differently. Untouched.

Puk held up his fists and positioned his feet, holding his core tight. "Like this."

Bethany mimicked him with a wide grin. There wasn't a drop of blood on her. Why would there be? The young girl didn't 'eat' her victims. She fed on their memories and left them empty. Like Tameka with nacre energy, but more specific. It was a terribly useful skill for Matt and Lucy's line of work.

Lucy leaned into Bethany, delighted when she didn't flinch, and whispered, "Stomp his foot and uppercut him. Your brother taught you, right?"

The girl nodded, smiling.

Puk asked, "What're you saying—"

Bethany stomped hard enough on the drone's combat boot for him to yell, "Yowch!"

While he was stunned, she knocked him a nice one under the chin.

Yito barked out a rich laugh through scary Tritan teeth.

Puk's teeth chattered together, and he staggered back. "Ow. I think I'm bleeding."

Lucy smiled sweetly in his face. "You're an excellent teacher."

The drone shook off the daze as his nacre lessened the pain. He asked Bethany, "Were you holding out on me?"

Matt smiled down at his protégé. "Bethany here was taught by her brother long before the Invasion. Great job."

Bethany beamed.

Lucy had always wanted a little sister—

"Shadow, this is Bones. I'm with F8, and we're taking a head count. So far, we've sustained minor casualties in what I'd call the weirdest battle since Nox 'invaded' Thailea. We have about ten thousand fatalities to honor, but... I think we can claim victory in their memories. Report back from your respective teams. Starting with Ginger. Over."

Matt faked the pride in his voice when he said, "I'm glad to say we're all here, including the Tritans. Not one loss on our team. Over."

Lucy smiled at him, ignoring the rest of the check-in to consider their lives instead. What was next for them? If the entire galaxy moved to Ishkur, it would make it easier for their hunts and familial obligations to the Shadow. All those bad men and women—their prey—would be centralized to one dominion of space.

What about kids? Were children in their future?

The way Matt beamed at Bethany was as close to genuine as his feelings for Lucy. It stirred something warm in her, but not entirely maternal instincts. Besides, their lives didn't lend themselves to healthy parentage.

But maybe one day.

Until then, Matt and Lucy would carry on with the mission he'd set her on so long ago. Hunting to make the Vast Collective a safer place, one glorious massacre at a time.

{ISHKUR | PANTHEON}

Chris was overwhelmed. Leadership—Xelan, Korac, Tameka, Kyle, Andrew, and Sagan—weren't answering their comms. T.A.O. had disappeared. Andrius and Devis were worried to the point of silence. And the Icarean female under that name was also missing. As were her companions.

While he counted off his team, Chris nodded at each of them. "Bones, we've got Jack, Ross—she's unconscious but coming around, Para, Karter, Devis, Andrius—Don't know where T.A.O. is—Lynn, Echo, Twenty-One, and a good Tritan named Qas. He's looking for Pablo and Miy, who… may or may not turn up. I'm sorry I don't have better news to report. Over."

Karter pulled Para against her and hugged the smaller woman like she was a teddy bear. The little Valkyrie gave in as if accustomed to this. It made Chris smile despite the earlier reminder of his captivity with Celindria.

Poor Ross.

Jack sat on the pale ground and held Ross in his lap, gently brushing his fingers through her mass of brown curls.

But the concern marring Jack, Devis, and Andrius couldn't compare with the distress in Lynn's eyes. She paced, staring into nothing with baby Echo cooing in her arms. Twenty-One tried to take the infant from her, but that was a no-go. He didn't look happy either, with Miy missing. The friendly Tritan, Dr. Qas, also offered to hold the half-Lyriki, half-Aegis, all-perfection baby, but still there was no response from Lynn.

On top of that, the stricken Chief kept muttering, "'Never endanger this. Never risk yourself without me. Never leave without coming back.'"

It hurt Chris' heart to see the young woman so distraught—

"Lynn, this is Miy. I don't know your private frequency, so I'm interrupting the head count to say, 'We're alive, and Pablo's coming through from Enki now.' Over."

Lynn gasped and nearly fainted. The only thing which stopped her from passing out with Echo in her arms was her nacre and Twenty-One's burly biceps. He steadied her as she started talking.

"Yes, baby. I can hear you. Oh, Pablo. Don't you ever do that again!"

From the ground, Jack said, "He must be on her private frequency."

Karter clicked her tongue and folded her arms. "Elden have mercy on him once she comes down from the adrenaline high."

Para nudged her. "You'd forgive Chris."

Chris and Karter shared a look over the small woman's head. They'd spent two months trapped in Hell. Unable to save each other. There was some healing ahead of them. Chris wasn't sure how long before he'd feel up to the physical, but when he got there, he'd make it the best lovemaking of her long lifetime.

Ross stirred in Jack's arms. "Where are we? Did we make it?"

The kid smiled down at her. "We did." He glanced up at Lynn. "We all did."

Almost all.

Chris got back on the mic. "Bones, I'm happy to report Pablo and Miy turned up on the comms. Still no sign of T.A.O. Over and Out."

Where was she?

{Ishkur | Pantheon}

This had been a *day*.

Bones wanted to soak in some hot springs while eating a slice of Colton's famous cheesecake with Cheeto's on the side. Maybe some Yun nectar.

Yeah.

That sounded like the perfect remedy.

Instead, Bones was standing in a bare Pantheon-looking landscape. Identical, even. He wondered if he went far enough in any direction, if he'd find stacks of books like in Enki. The trouble with a barren tundra was determining which direction to go. If this was a perfect mirror to Enki, maybe he should go through the Torrentus conduit. But what if the conduit didn't go to a continent housing the bridge?

What if something lived there? Unknown life forms with ferocious appetites.

Surely not. Bones and the others had been watching too much Sci-Fi.

He reported, "We got Caedes, Pehton, Pehton's long-lost children, the Lyriks, Tumu, Lamassau, good ol' Iuo who owes the Chef some money, Colton, Cypher, Tempest, Dolor, X, Legir, Kombuchi, and I already mentioned F8—"

The Queen nodded at him, consulting with her Mon3 forces.

"—No sign of our Generals here either." Bones sighed before continuing, "I want us to centralize for when the Seamswalkers return, but I have no idea which way to go. Stay put until then. Over and Out."

After working the Chorus magic, the Lyriks were resting off to the side. Razor's generosity in sharing the spectacular event with Ishkur over the screens meant the movie would be more accurate when Bones was finished with it. A truly fantastic explosion. And there were no two more deserving souls in the entire Vast Collective.

Caedes hung out with Iuo, Lamassau, and Tumu. The cheeky Icarus kept sparing glances at Pehton, who was sitting on the ground meeting her kids. Tears were in her eyes the entire time. Bald and smitten looked good on Caedes.

Bones was waiting to see Para himself. He was so relieved to hear she'd survived and escaped just fine. Their team, in particular, had endured enough.

Tumu came over to Bones, suggesting, "We could try sending flyers to circle out."

"Yup. That's what we'll have to do. You can take your sixty-five foot ass out and search, too."

The old Primary—the *only* Primary—chuckled.

Wow. "Tumu, I don't mean to be rude or bring up any negativity, but are you really the last Gargantuan?"

More cavalier than expected, Tumu shrugged. "Perhaps it depends on your definition." He nodded toward Pehton's kids. Riiiiight. The Tritan continued, "They're new. No compression orbs required. But they're still Gargantuan. I'm proud to call them Primary."

"They need more clothes, though." Lamassau prowled his way over and circled his arms around his taller partner.

As someone who saw up Torch's white loin cloth more than once during the fight, Bones had to agree—

T.A.O. Seamswalked into the clearing near Pehton's circle.

Bones flagged her down. "Hey—Whoa!"

She popped right in front of him with her permanent Atramentous eyes, sharp and avian—Hey, were her cheeks tear-stained?

"Now."

The Afflicted One's cryptic speech rose the hackles on Bone's collar, so he was grateful when Tumu pressed for more information in a gentle voice. "What do you mean, T.A.O.? What's happening 'now?'"

"Enki's last words."

THIRTEEN
GOODBYE TO TEARS, TO LIGHT, AND TO ME

{Ishkur | Bridge | A Few Minutes Earlier}

"What do you mean, Tameka went back to Enki?"

Sagan was glad Kyle was breaking the news to Xelan instead of her. The Seamswalker was failing, barely holding it together. There were too many conduits open and millions of people evacuating through them. No amount of blood could replace good rest and recuperation.

Plus, Kyle assured them, "Razor was helping her." He offered this information hesitantly, like he wasn't sure if he could trust it.

Sagan saw his point. She struggled to believe Razor was actually helping them—

"Look!" Andrew called out and pointed at the center of Ishkur's bridge.

A screen appeared. The soldiers and Children of Gait rescued by Sagan's sweeping conduit moved closer to see. Pax tucked in beside his dad. Razor's screen displayed Silence fighting Remorse.

Beside Sagan, Korac's brows went high, impressed with Silence's craftsmanship.

Transfixed, Kyle muttered a private comment aloud. "That's my girl."

Light beamed down on the Primaries in a glorious column, backed by Razor's exhilarating score. Only...

Frowning, Xelan used Pax's hand to point. "Did you see that?"

Kyle swallowed loud enough for Sagan to hear across the gangway.

Andrew whispered, horrified, "Was that flash Tameka?"

At the same moment the blast connected, a streak of black and blue knocked Silence out of the column of light.

Without hesitation, Korac gripped Xelan's shoulder. "Remember."

She's not dead.

"I remember." Xelan picked up Pax and let the boy twist a finger in his hair. He glanced down at Sagan. "Can you?"

Kyle and Andrew looked at her expectantly, but Korac knew. He didn't even glance at Sagan for confirmation. She hated to admit it, but... "I only have enough left in me to rescue Rayne."

Andrew frowned. "What about T.A.O.?"

Kyle said, "I just tried. The comms are down."

Sagan hated the stress in Xelan's eyes as he searched hers. She'd do anything to alleviate her guardian of this decision, but it was *his* decision.

Rayne or Tameka.

Pax squeezed his dad's hand and gave a bounce. "Did mommy leave me again?"

Sagan's heart broke. How was there so much left to break?

Into the vacuum, waiting for an answer, Xelan said, "No, Pax. She went to run an errand, and she's on her way back. Until then, would you like to meet Auntie Rayne?"

Again, the little bounce. "Oh, yes! She has castles in her dreams—"

Coffee grounds encroached on Sagan's vision, and when she took a step, it felt all airy.

One round trip. Please. A little more...

She opened the conduit and the founding team stepped through—

Into blinding white light.

The heart of Enki smelled like a family beach—all sunscreen and surf.

While Xelan shielded Pax's eyes, his son cried with glee, "It smells like ice cream cones, daddy!"

All of them hid their faces from the glare.

Did Sagan accidentally take them to the sun? No... This was right where she left—

Rayne.

The light receded into the King of Earth and Cinder. It wasn't her magnesium field either. This phenomenon abated into the seams of her making. It was her nacre, expanding inside her. Through her.

"Rayne!"

Sagan flew to her, ready to Seamswalk to Ishkur—

Stopped.

A firm hand gripped Sagan's bicep and kept her from going to Rayne's side. She turned back, gasping, "Xelan?"

His eyes were Atramentous and shining. He said nothing. Only shook his head.

Even Pax sniffled quietly beside him.

Beyond the father-son pair, Korac stared unblinkingly at Rayne, eyes narrowed inquisitively. He called, "Sprite?"

Sagan could see Kyle was itching to fly forward as he asked, "Rayne, can you hear us?"

Andrew asked, "Why would the light make her deaf, Kyle?"

The other young man scoffed, "Get off my ass, Andrew—"

Gesturing at Rayne, Andrew argued, "I'm just saying, *Story Taker*, it doesn't look like anything is wrong with her ears."

That escalated things. "Well, Conscience, why don't you flip that coin of yours and fix this before I shove it up your—"

"I'll miss this."

"Rayne." Sagan made to fly toward her again, but stopped at Xelan's words.

"What do you mean 'you'll miss it?'"

The words sunk in one syllable at a time. Miss. Absence. Loss.

Grief.

With her heart in her throat, Sagan cried, "Rayne?!" Korac was there instantly and pulled Sagan into his warmth while she repeated Xelan's question into her General's chest. "Why? Why will you miss us?"

Rayne's voice harmonized in three pitches, soft and sad. "I can't go with you to Ishkur."

"No." Kyle blurted, and Andrew grabbed him around the waist as he continued, "No. You have to."

Korac kissed the top of Sagan's head and rubbed soothing circles on her back, but she couldn't stop crying. Rayne was so bright and so fragmented. Sagan shook her head against him, saying, "No. I won't leave you. I'll drink another chain and sweep you into a conduit—"

"We have to," Xelan said.

Sagan's mouth fell open, as did Kyle's. Even Korac stared hard at Xelan's back, with his eyes flicking between them. Only Rayne could see his face, and whatever was on it made a bright tear streak a shadow down her cheek.

Softly, Xelan asked, "How long?"

Rayne swallowed against a spasm of pain which racked her entire body before saying, "Ten minutes."

Elden, no. No, no, no—

"Say goodbye, amos. Don't waste a second or you'll regret it for the rest of your long life." Korac gently pried her away from him. He cupped her chin and placed a kiss on her forehead. "I'll wait for you here."

Without thinking, Sagan's wings took her close enough to Rayne that it hurt to open her eyes, but Sagan stared through the blaze. Andrew and Kyle flanked her, both looking as miserable as she felt.

Elden, why?

"I'm sorry," Rayne said with so much sincerity, as if she of all people had anything to apologize about.

Sagan shook her head. "No. Don't. You're saving us from

so much wrong in Enki. Who knows what else Imminent stored here? I only wish Tameka…"

When Sagan couldn't go on, Kyle finished for her. "She saved Silence when Remorse died, and she's on her way back." He gave a half-hearted smirk, pained as it was. "We'll never hear the end of it from her. Remember how long she went on about missing the plane crash in Siberia?"

How could Sagan forget? It was outside Enki's conduit on Earth. Amid all the wreckage, it was the same day Sagan had learned about Korac and Xelan.

She spared Wingmaster a glance, but couldn't see his face. He was staring at Enki's south pole with his hair shading his eyes. Pax mirrored his father. It was a precious second wasted, and Sagan refused to waste another. She met Rayne's eyes and let everything go. "I love you, and I will always love you. Korac's in my heart, and we'll raise Echo together, but you came first in my life and always forever after. So, please—Please… Don't make me say goodbye."

If Sagan had been standing, her knees would've buckled. As it was, she went completely slack, exhausted almost to the point of passing out. During the outpouring of her words, the boys flew a step back, giving her privacy. Now they seemed poised to catch her for a fall without gravity.

Tears poured shadow lanes down Rayne's beautiful and fractured face. "I wish I'd gotten the chance to see her. You two will raise one spectacular and capable little girl. But I can't stay, and that's why I'm sorry—" Her face twisted in pain, and the light surged brighter.

Bright enough to force them back toward Xelan, Pax, and Korac.

In a fast burst, Kyle said all at once, "I'm sorry we never fully reconciled, and that I found my wings without your permission. I'm sorry for everything, Rayne. I'd hoped to earn your forgiveness before either of us saw an end. More than anything, I wanted to see you happy."

Andrew added, "And a hug. He hasn't shut up about the hug." After Kyle shot him a truly nasty look, Andrew said to Rayne, "You were a pillar in my confusion, a guidepost to find my way. Always, you chose the path of goodness and family. There will never be anyone like you, Rayne. And I know that for certain." He held up his Probability coin as proof.

The King of Earth and Cinder trembled with sobs and anguish, crying from eyes fixed forward while her body was torn asunder. There was pain in them, sadness, and love. There wasn't a trace of fear.

Sagan would never forget the moment she let the boys pull her back and let Xelan and Pax fly forward. The sinking feeling of permanence, and the spiral of the indefinite what-ifs. What if she swept Rayne away now? What if Korac fed her his half-Aegis blood? What if something in Ishkur could save her?

What if...

What if...

When Xelan finally looked up, Sagan knew.

No more what ifs.

No more Enki.

No more Rayne.

{The Heart Of Enki}

Eight minutes to Eternity, and there was no way back. The end of Enki smelled like salt water and sandcastles. The view would leave an impression forever burnt in Xelan's mind. Never would he forget Rayne asunder in space.

Softly, almost unable to speak, he said, "Pax. This is your Auntie Rayne."

As if sensing his father's turmoil, his son solemnly reminded him, "From my dreams... 'Member?"

Of course. They knew each other.

Xelan cleared his throat and let himself look into Rayne's eyes, brighter than ever. "Don't worry about Tameka. She'll regret missing this, but I'll make sure she knows you love her."

Stiffly, Rayne nodded.

Pax squeezed Xelan's hand and nearly broke him. To Rayne, he asked, "Can you speak?"

As stilted as before, she shook her head and winced from whatever pain it caused.

Seven minutes, thirty seconds.

"Even if we had the next millennia together, I wouldn't have enough time to tell you how proud I am of you and how much I love you. I owe my life to you, Rayne. And now, so does the entire Vast Collective. I'll never let them forget you..."

Rayne nearly doubled-over, but Xelan caught her face and pressed his forehead to hers. Her skin burned his, searing but not blistering. In her sobbing fit, he hushed her gently. "No. No. I got you, but I need you to open your eyes and look at me. Look at me, Callahan, that's an order." Xelan hovered lower to look her in the face. Pax peered up, too.

Because it was important—*so important*—Rayne look him the eye for this next bit.

There. So much pain and so much love. Xelan couldn't bear it.

"There's no way in the Wrong Side of Eternity I'll believe for one second you intend to stay dead." Gasps came from all around, but Xelan ignored them. Speaking directly into her eyes, he kept going. "I know you, Rayne Echo Callahan. You're the best of me. Saving your life saved me, and I won't ever accept you're gone."

Six minutes, forty-five seconds.

Someone grabbed Xelan by his coat, pulling—But not yet. Not yet.

"I love you, Rayne. You're not alone, and please don't be afraid. I'll find you—

"I'll never stop looking for you—"

{ENKI | TORRENTUS}

Tameka flew as fast as she could across the continent of Torrentus. Pretty certain Razor had lied to her about the last of his energy reserves. Also pretty certain someone could've found a Seamswalker to help her by now. But that was fine, because here they were.

Smith and Lucas kept up, fueled by the occasional bursts of energy from Tameka's overflowing well. No dramatic speeches. No light-hearted comments. Only pure adrenaline was between them.

With Silence haphazardly in her arms—Elden, this woman was tall—Tameka flew into a glass dome, obviously housing the bridge as nothing else was out here. They followed the gangways, trusting her innate sense of direction until lights appeared along them—No, not all of them. At each junction, only one path was lit. Less begrudgingly, Tameka said, "Thank you, Razor."

Lucas muttered similar praise.

Smith smiled with delight.

Whatever Sagan had done to that man, Fury wanted it bottled and packaged for all their future enemies—

No.

No more enemies.

Only the future lay ahead.

And that's what Tameka was soaring toward. Her son. Her love. And her family—

A bright white light from behind cast their shadow ahead. It grew longer still as the light expanded. As if seeking them, it followed Tameka, Smith, and Lucas through the paths of the dome, and it moved much faster. All three surged forward.

Keep moving.

Don't think about what it meant for Rayne.

Pax.

Xelan.

Ishkur.

"Silence, hang on. We're taking you home."

{ISHKUR}

Korac felt like a villain for dragging Xelan's grieving carcass away from Rayne's lonely side. Beside Korac, Sagan trembled from shock. Andrew and Kyle stiffly backed away, mumbling about watching for Tameka. Pax stayed with his father, refusing to release his hand.

And it was a good thing, too, because the Traitor Prince was an agitated mess. He'd fallen to the gangway with his head in hands and wept, quietly. Korac thought the volume was for Pax's sake, but their leader was taking a well-deserved mental break before the show was over.

Sagan left the conduit open.

On the other side, the impressive Sprite hovered in space, forming a sphere of light, paralyzed. As they watched in a mixture of horror and fascination, the sphere expanded.

With a heart-wrenching gasp, Sagan turned her face against Korac's side. "I can't watch." She sobbed, and the sound broke him. He wrapped his arms around her and held her tight so she didn't have to look—

What... was that?

Something moved on the other side of the conduit. Korac could swear it did—

There.

Again.

A flicker—A shadow. With eyes.

Not just any eyes. They were mirrors reflecting Korac's image back to him.

Nox gazed at his General through the conduit, half-formed in the shade of Rayne's glow. Solemn and grave, Nox mouthed something.

What was it?

Nacre.

Nacre what—

The conduit closed before Korac deciphered it, and Sagan sagged in Korac's arms. "Babe. Amos, talk to me." He checked her vitals. Her pulse was fluttery, but present.

"She succumbed to exhaustion." Elden, Xelan's larynx had seen better days. His voice sounded worse than Hell Kitten shit as he said, "She needs rest. We all do, but…"

Not until Tameka emerged. Korac assured him, "Any minute now."

Yes. Any minute now, Fury would run through the last remaining conduit to Enki with Silence, Smith, and Lucas, having saved the day.

And then the impressive Sprite would die and take Enki with her—

What the fuck had Nox tried to say to him?! It would haunt Korac for Eternity—

"No sign of her, yet," Andrew announced before he flipped his coin. Under his breath, but loud enough for Korac to overhear it, the Progeny said, "C'mon, girl. Give us something."

Kyle stood beside him, quiet and pale.

As Korac laid Sagan on the gangway to Ishkur's bridge, he admitted, this was a bitter victory for the Shadow, and only Tameka's timely arrival could sweeten it.

Pax patted Xelan's back, where he still knelt on the floor. "Mommy will come, daddy. She said nothing would keep us apart—"

"Incoming!" Kyle shouted as he and Andrew ran from the white light seeping out of the conduit.

On the heels of the blast was a wall of flames, hurdling straight for the bridge to Ishkur.

{The Heart Of Enki | A Few Minutes Earlier}

Recommendation: Attain minimum safe distance.

Warning: Four minutes and twenty-two seconds until maximum destabilization.

Nox stood on the training grounds under the ocean's storm. With her energy extending outward toward the explosion, Rayne's mindscape waned, collapsing scenes into one another. Imploding. And there, the greatest warrior in the galaxy stood with her fists clenched and her eyes squeezed shut. Tears spilled from them and transformed into gems of light, floating around her.

When the powerlessness of grief had crumbled Xelan's composure, Nox had shed tears for Rayne. How could he possibly help her?

That's when he noticed Korac watching through the conduit. While the others mourned Rayne or fretted over Tameka, Korac kept his eyes on the War King. With Rayne's permission, Nox had taken shadow form and allowed her to transmit a message through him.

Now they waited for the end.

Inside her mind, Nox stood in front of Rayne, consoling her with his presence—The reminder she wasn't alone. "Rayne."

She trembled, but didn't answer.

"You are disarming your enemies even now. By your own admission, you aren't afraid and you aren't alone. You're strong—"

"I'm so sick of being strong." Rayne's voice broke, and when she turned her eyes up to Nox, there was the warrior he loved. Lightning struck the sky, and it couldn't match the storm in her eyes. "This isn't fair. I know. I know. What is 'fair?' Right? But I've done enough. Haven't I?" She hiccuped on a sob, but kept going. "I was too paralyzed to say I love them—to say goodbye to them. I want to meet Echo and play with Pax. Introduce them to strawberry ice cream and boardwalks. Toss them in a pile of dried leaves and climb the most interesting tree Ishkur has to offer. Is that so much?"

Rayne's chin trembled, and Nox had never felt so close to another person. He wanted all those things with his niece and nephew. Hunting trips in Cinder's blackened forest. Lava surfing in the Ignis Desert. Cliff diving from Li Mountain onto soaring wings—The places they would fly.

Despite Rayne's contingencies, Nox knew. There were few powers in the galaxy which could recover from atomic disintegration on this scale.

Rayne knew it, too. Which was why Nox said, "Punch me."

"Wh-what?" The frown she gave him was so pretty.

Nox lifted her hand and balled her slender fingers into a tiny fist with stellar power. "Hit me, Rayne."

"No." Rayne wrenched her hand from his and stepped back. "No, Nox. All your life people beat down on you—Took their smallness and rage out on you. I will never—*ever*—be like them."

Rayne shamed Nox. Of course, she was better than that. How could he even suggest—

"Don't do that either." Rayne recovered the step and surprised Nox by taking his face in her hands. She forced him to meet her eyes. "Don't retreat from me. It's not your fault. I appreciate the gesture more than you know, but you're worth more to me than a punching bag. You mean more… to me."

Nox stared at the King of Earth and Cinder as Rayne finished her sentence, with something new constellating in her eyes. Something brilliant and soft. He searched them, trying to decipher it. What was she trying to tell him? "Rayne—"

"My, you are taking an awfully long time to die."

That voice.

Stilted, they both turned from each other to look outside Rayne's external vision. Neither moved aside from that.

Celindria, in an elegant white gown with gold dripping like venom from here and there, had somehow manifested—alive—in the heart of Enki. "Little King, are you still alive in there? But of course you are. Our father wouldn't design this death to be kind."

Rayne winced.

Nox ground his teeth, ready to snap Celindria in his jaws. A dragon devouring a leviathan.

Celindria said, "Remorse said Nox was in there with you, doomed in an eternal Hell, subjected to your righteous sanction. He's mine, you know?"

A shudder claimed Nox, and he noticed the same response in Rayne.

Celindria dipped her chin, conceding a point. "It's true. During your first consummation concourse for all of Cinder to see, I'd glimpsed an attraction—A connection, even. But it can't compare to the Eternal Bind." She peered through the windows of Rayne's eyes, almost as if she could see inside. Whatever she found there didn't satisfy her. "You've deteriorated beyond seeing. No matter. I'll find another way to revive Nox. There is plenty of historical data to reconstruct his nacre. And with Enki's end, you'll finally stop interfering."

Interfering?

Nox and Rayne simultaneously turned and stared at one another. She was still holding his face, angled down for her. He was still leaning down to accommodate her height.

Interfering.

Rayne dropped her hands as if they burned—Burned as bright as her cheeks and her eyes.

"Enjoy dying alone and afraid, little King. I'll deliver word of your last moments to our father soon." Celindria waved before melting into a shadow cast by Rayne's light.

What followed next could only be described as a culmination. As if Celindria's presence had held it at bay, the end came to claim Rayne in racking waves of self-loss and crippling spasms.

Rayne screamed internally, no longer able to let it out. Gasping, she fell to her knees. Nox knelt with her, finally experiencing a fraction of it.

There.

He knew what to do.

As Rayne eased down into a ball from the last spasm, she stared at him, chest heaving from the aching breaths. "Not long now. But I won't let myself pass out. I want to see it. I want to see Enki end."

As did Nox. "Dying hurts, your majesty." He spoke from experience which was cut short for Rayne sparing him the complete nacre disintegration the last time.

She gave a painful laugh. "I'm getting that."

He held out his hand. "It doesn't have to."

Despite the agony, Rayne frowned. "What are you saying?"

"Take my hand and transfer your nerve responses to my nacre. You've done enough."

A quiet followed, one in which Rayne searched his eyes with something akin to awe in her own. "Nox..."

In his last moments, Nox wanted this. He wanted to do the right thing. "No more being strong for everyone. No more martyrdom. If this is truly my final act in these worlds, let me spare you. Please. Take my hand."

{The Heart Of Enki}

Recommendation: Attain minimum safe distance.

Warning: Two minutes and three seconds until maximum destabilization.

"Take my hand."

Something stirred in Rayne, here on the brink of Eternity. Something warm and full of life. It was familiar and lifted her soul.

Nox, enormous as he was, held out his hand, greater still for the pure kindness in his offer.

And what an offer. It was freedom from a torment so visceral Rayne would've sworn she was born with it. Lightning struck beside them, a spark echoing the significance of the moment inside her.

Nox's rehabilitation was complete, and it killed Rayne that he'd never get the chance to reconcile with his brother and reunite with his best friend. It killed Rayne that she'd never see her brother or best friends again, either.

All those smiles and hugs they'd never have...

"No more being strong for everyone. No more martyrdom."

Nox loved Rayne, and she understood. The ocean tempered the volcano, and with the fusion, created something new.

Rayne took Nox's hand.

The massive warrior squeezed his eyes shut and clenched his teeth, groaning on the edge of a scream and clenching his fists. He gave an unexpected laugh. "You were holding out on me."

Her laughter was hesitant and pitying. "I guess I was." She'd been enduring the pain for so long, she'd acclimated to an extent. Easily, Rayne settled in beside Nox, staring out at the horizon. "I won't leave you."

But Nox was already failing. He opened his eyes, and the mirrors in them reflected a blazing sun. "What does it look like? Tell me. What does the end of Enki look like, Rayne?"

"Water is coming in from Enki's oceans, littered with rocks and other debris from the continents. It's gathering around us, collecting in a helix swirl. I think the orbit is wonky because we're unstable. The light is spreading. It's beautiful and deadly. Everything it touches—the satellites, shrines, clouds of gas—disintegrate into nothing. Soon, the phosphorous fireflies will come. Like when you died. I can feel them waking, taking me away."

Recommendation: Attain minimum safe distance.

Warning: One minute, thirty-eight seconds until maximum destabilization.

Nox shouted out in agony and on the edge, he asked, "Have I... ever told you... that you're a sight worth dying for?" All his muscles—and they were truly many and substantial—twitched and jerked involuntarily to the suffering.

Rayne smiled in her tears. "Yes, you have. Long ago when you were the King of Cinder and I was Earth's General."

Abruptly, Nox grabbed her hand. "You saved them then. You've saved them now." He growled into the pain. "They'll sing songs about you. Write literature on your deeds. You'll never be forgotten."

Rayne knew the end was close. The phosphorous fireflies had arrived. Bits of her escaping. She said, "I don't want to be remembered."

Nox licked blood from his lips and asked, "What is it you want? After everything you've done... All the lives you've saved. What is it the martyr wants?"

It was funny how little Rayne was asked what she wanted out of all of this. And sad.

The blood pumping in her veins slowed, her heart with it. The paralyzed muscles relaxed, but were no longer mobile. Her failing body took a shuddering breath, and Nox along with it, patiently gazing up at her for the answer.

"Right now? More than anything in the worlds, I'd take it all back for a hug from my mom."

Rayne didn't feel the final explosion.

Rayne didn't feel alone or afraid.

The last thing Rayne felt was Nox's arms pulling her in for an embrace.

FOURTEEN

VICTORY, BITTER AND SWEET, SHOULD BE FILLED WITH GRATITUDE AND OPTIMISM

{ISHKUR | BRIDGE}

THE EXPLOSION DIDN'T INFILTRATE ENKI'S CONDUIT ONTO THE BRIDGE. It roared its ineffectual violence into the vastness of the Seam, unable to reach. The final shockwave was on its way. It would take days to reach Enki's hull from Rayne's position in the Dyson's Sphere. It would take out the sun.

Xelan stared into the flames after Andrew took Pax from him. The older Progeny was demonstrating to the youngest one how Ishkur's interface projected onto his beautiful brown skin, so like his mothers. His freckled cheeks formed dimples as he smiled at the glowing symbols. Red curls bounced when he hopped in delight.

Other people were on the bridge, but Xelan forgot them. Everything aside from Pax and—

A shape appeared in the cloud of debris and fire, a silhouette. Shorter than himself and shapely. Fast, soaring, and… carrying something.

Tameka.

Red curls, green eyes, and legs that could break a grown Icarus' sternum—Fury flew toward the conduit contained in a nanite barrier, and Lucas was fast behind her. The blast swirled around them, yet couldn't reach them.

The wonders surrounding this woman never ceased. Xelan wanted to grin for her—to let her see his relief and love, but the hole which had pitted in his heart wouldn't let him operate the corners of his mouth. Instead, he shouted, "Everybody, incoming!"

Tameka barreled into Ishkur's bridge, repeating, "Silence, don't die. Don't die. Don't die." She didn't acknowledge anyone else, not even when Pax cried her name. Xelan was worried until he saw the way Fury gingerly laid his foremother onto the gangway. "Please." Her eyes were haunted when she searched the faces around the room. "She saved us."

Xelan let himself feel a little relief when Tameka allowed him to pull her up and against his side. Pax ran across the rail-less paths and adhered to her leg like a bear cub to a tree. Muscle by muscle, she relaxed from the adrenaline between them.

After stripping the last of his robes off, Korac formed it into a pillow for Xelan's dying foremother and checked her pulse with a curse. Smith finally detached himself from Lucas and lowered his head. Lucas closed his eyes and muttered what Xelan recognized as an ancient prayer to Eternity. Beyond them, Andrew flipped his coin.

Kyle knelt beside Silence. "Are you sure the barrier was her?" He gazed up at Fury for the answer.

When Tameka met Kyle's eyes as if she actually saw him, Xelan knew she was coming out of the shock. Especially as she reached out and brushed Pax's curls, taking comfort while explaining, "I—The barrier... I don't know where else it could've come from."

The smile Kyle gave her was reassuring and brotherly. "Yeah. She's full of fantastic surprises." He turned and looked down at the unconscious Mother of their galaxy. The next he said with the confidence of someone who'd lived a much longer life. "That's why I know she'll survive this."

Xelan asked her two comrades, "Why did she need Ishkur? Specifically?"

Lucas ran a hand through his hair, looking as exhausted as Xelan felt. The golden-eyed Icarus said, "This Dyson's Sphere is her best chance of survival." He knelt across from Kyle to face him at eye level. "The hull can nullify certain nacre attributes. She needs a medical bay and blood."

Kyle bit into his wrist without another word and poured the crimson liquid into Silence's non-responsive lips.

Smith smirked.

Korac checked her pulse again. "It's already stronger."

"Phew." Half the room turned and looked at Andrew, who said, "Don't mind me. Just gambling with the Probability Matrix over here. Carry on."

Tameka muttered, almost in disbelief, "She'll... live?"

Korac nodded at Lucas, who turned and looked up at Tameka, where she stood behind him with Xelan. The golden-eyed Icarus said, "Another miracle of the Shadow. You brought her here in time. You saved her, Tameka."

"Mommy's so cool." Pax stopped clinging to her leg and went to play under the main terminal.

Xelan chafed Tameka's arm, where the color was already returning to her complexion. Tears of relief and exhaustion pricked her eyes. "Thank Elden."

Yes. Ishkur was a miracle. Remorse's death was a miracle. Rayne...

Numb.

Stay numb and optimistic in the moment. Let this be about Silence's recovery—the liberation of Project Surra—

"Where's Rayne? And oh my god, is Sagan okay?" Recovering from the shock admirably, Tameka rushed to the unconscious Seamswalker's side.

As Korac followed her, he kept his eyes on Xelan mid-stride. It was a pointed look filled with pity. "Tell her," it said. Korac answered Tameka's second question. The easy one. "Sagan will be fine after some rest, Fury."

Now it was Xelan's turn to answer the hardest. He glimpsed Kyle wearing the same pitying stare from

Silence's side. Andrew also wasn't volunteering, keeping his eyes down. Lucas looked the question at him, and Xelan couldn't even shake his head in answer. Which was more than enough for both men. Smith put a fist to his chest and lowered his head.

How did Xelan tell Tameka Rayne couldn't avoid the explosion and likely had never planned to? The martyr deep in her veins wouldn't allow anything less. And did he share the survival theory with Tameka? Should Xelan tell her he believed his deactivated nanites from when he'd fed Rayne years ago—months for him—in Iona-01 would alter the Weapon and let her survive like Xelan had survived his self-destruction on Cinder. Or was it too cruel to hope—

"Auntie Rayne esploded."

The room held a collective breath.

Tameka turned from Sagan to stare at her son where he played. "What did you say?"

Pax was drawing on the terminal using a marker from his bottomless pockets and played on without looking at his mother, saying, "I got to meet her. She's pretty, mommy."

Xelan was paralyzed as Tameka, wide-eyed and horrified, met his stare. She bolted from the floor and went to him with an edge of panic in her voice. "You went to see Rayne? Did you rescue her like we planned? Xelan. Xelan, where is she?" The tears returned.

Craving her warmth, Xelan clutched Tameka and pulled her against him, holding her through a violent sob.

"No. No. Please tell me. Anything but this. Please."

Xelan met the eyes in the room, clung to his mate with her sorrow seeping into him in an extension of his own.

Tameka's voice was muffled and warm against his chest. Her nails pierced his skin where she gripped him and held on for dear life. "Why?! We just got her back!"

No.

Xelan wouldn't tell her about the nanites. He wouldn't share the feeling in his bones that Rayne could never stay down—

Tameka startled him by pulling away and blurting, "No. No, she'll come back. Like you. There's no way she'll stay dead."

There was Xelan's Fury.

{ISHKUR | BRIDGE}

"We don't need to talk about Rayne anymore, because she'll come back. And that's the end of this discussion."

Tameka knew this was what Xelan needed to hear. Not getting to say goodbye to Rayne would haunt Tameka's dreams and the corner of every quiet moment. Not one breath would she take that Tameka wouldn't think, "No one was there for Rayne's last one." But Fury knew her best friend. Knew that martyr to her marrow—her soul. Rayne would want them to continue leading the Vast Collective in her name. The galaxy was made safe by one girl—and a truly extraordinary one at that.

Tameka wiped the tears from her raw and scalded cheeks, suddenly wondering what her hair and makeup must look like. Her clothes were singed and torn after the battle and rescuing Silence. She could feel the bruises under her eyes.

Xelan brought her back to him for another hug and whispered in her ear, "You look beautiful, Fury."

A warmth adhered to their sides, and without looking, Tameka knew it was Pax. Their family was whole again.

Tameka wanted a long vacation, but so much work lay ahead of them. Oh! "Wingmaster, I have this crazy idea, and I'd like you to hear me out."

It broke her heart to hear Xelan sound so scooped out and empty, but he didn't hesitate. "I'm listening." He also didn't let her go.

Tameka had so many ideas and knew exactly where to begin. Throw herself into rebuilding and save grief for later. "We have work to do. Now. We need to terraform Ishkur's continents and oceans—"

"Razor uploaded Torrentus here at my request." Xelan was on the same page.

The thought of adopting the creature lit Tameka's darkened heart. "That's great. We'll need it to make these people some homes and start restoring the planets they're from, including Cinder. I'm pretty sure I can reverse what happened to Li—"

Xelan separated them enough to crush her mouth with his in a hard and desperate kiss. It tasted of gratitude and loss.

Pax gasped, "Daddy!"

They stopped and looked down to find Pax red as a beet before he snickered and ran under the terminal to continue playing.

A little breathless and feeling less bruised, Tameka asked, "What was that for?" She glimpsed Korac, sitting shirtless and cross-legged at Sagan's side. He'd heard what she said about Li and nodded in deep regard.

Xelan asked, "What do you think about becoming the leader of a galaxy?"

That brought Tameka back to Xelan's eyes, blinking. "What? Like President?"

He chuckled, and it reminded her of broken glass. Fractured but repairable. "No. More like Empress."

Her eyes widened. "Oh, you're not joking."

While Xelan shook his head, Tameka thought about how much this man confounded her. Leader of a galaxy. One in need of healing and growth, a mixing of cultures and a blending of histories.

In Rayne's name.

Tameka smiled. "I've got a better idea." She climbed onto her tiptoes and whispered in his ear.

When she set back down, Xelan grinned at her, and it was more his true signature one than a ghost of it. After which, he said, "I got you."

Tameka returned the expression. "Let's start by restoring the comms. We should be hearing from people by now."

Hand-in-hand, they walked over to Pax's playground. Quick to focus on something other than grief, Tameka's man fell into the task and traversed the Aegis technology with ease. While Xelan worked, there were so many questions Tameka wanted to ask him. About his past and how an empire came to be his future. But even as she considered those curiosities, her body ached for sleep. True rest and a good meal. Some amazing sex. And a healthy amount of crying in each other's arms—

The conduit to Enki was still open. There was nothing on the other side. The first bridge was gone, destroyed in Rayne's destabilization. It was the past.

Gently, Tameka tugged on Xelan's fancy coat. He glanced down, and she gestured toward the conduit. He let out a shuddering breath before pressing a key projected onto his arm and closed the way to Enki forever. She tucked in closer to him and felt Pax hugging him from beneath the terminal.

"She's coming around," Kyle announced from his vigil over Silence.

Smith beamed nearby.

Lucas stood beside him, pretending not to glance at Andrew. He said, "There's much to rejoice."

Distracted, Tameka almost didn't notice the lights on her skin. Symbols and shapes. She looked up at Xelan. "What?"

He smiled, proud and cool. "You'll need to learn how to run this thing. Press this button." He pointed at the u-shape on her forearm. "It'll release the signal dampener and allow us to communicate."

Tameka's grin was a fragile thing, but she was happy to make it for Xelan. She pressed her arm—

"—Hear us? Over." Bones was on the all-frequency.

"This is Ginger. T.A.O.'s just arrived. Rendezvous in three minutes. Over."

Chris came on next. "Okay. Us next, and then we'll be gathered for when leadership returns. Over."

Miy asked, "Has anyone seen a trace of Imminent's army? Did Razor send them here with us? Over."

"That's a good point." Xelan bit his thumbnail before selecting a few more projections. "Here Tameka, this one will show us destinations of Enki's last conduits from the archives."

Still delighted with the novelty of Aegis tech, she pressed the button on her bicep. A report appeared over the swirling black flames below. The information in it stunned her. "No fucking way."

Xelan had 'I told you so' face.

Korac was looking at it as he stood and crossed the room to them. "Does that say Razor routed those conduits elsewhere on Enki? So those Imminent soldiers..."

Were all dead. Rayne killed the last of Imminent in the blast. No one needed to say it aloud.

These quiet moments of shared grief would never go away.

Tameka stared through the glass floor at the maelstrom below. Cascading Light spun, endless as the time ahead of them. Softly, she asked, "Were either of you ever tempted to touch it?"

Korac shook his head and looked behind him at Sagan, unconscious, and laid out comfortably on his clothes. "She was unexpected. A complete surprise. Everything made sense the moment she hit me. Seeing into the Probabilities—the futures—would take all the unforeseen away." He smirked. "Never."

Tameka smiled and wasn't at all begrudged to say, "Congratulations."

Korac nodded. "Thanks. I'd better go coordinate with Bones on the comms." He stepped away to give them privacy.

Tameka's eyes went to Xelan, and she quirked a brow.

He was working through some function on his forearm when he said, "I think by knowing the future, we try to manipulate it to our end and possibly make it happen."

"Self-fulfilling prophecy?"

Xelan smiled at her and nodded. "Exactly. You?"

Tameka glanced at Andrew. "I used to." Then she looked down at Pax, playing at their feet. "Hey, kiddo?"

Pax peered up at her with a grin.

"When did you first see the Probabilities?"

Without turning away from his drawing, Pax said in three pitches, "When I first existed, I knew. When I first opened my eyes, I saw what the others saw. I knew and could see everything at the time they knew and could see. But not what happened next. I needed the black fire for that. I was the last of myselves to touch it, late because I wanted more time with father. More time with you." He punctuated it with a giggle and a snort.

Both parents exchanged a look.

"Okay. That'll take some getting used to."

{ISHKUR | BRIDGE}

"Bones, this is Silver General. Leadership is on the bridge and back online. Report. Over."

Korac sat his half-naked ass down by Sagan's side, where it belonged.

Overtaxed.

That's the word. They were all overtaxed.

"Silver General, it's good to hear from you." Korac could hear the genuine relief in the Icarean warrior's voice. "We're in what looks like the Pantheon, and we've got some people in need of medical attention. Oh, and don't worry. Chief Lynn and the Doc have Echo. She's fine. Over."

Korac shut his eyes. "Thank Elden." Sagan sighed in her sleep as if she'd heard, and he brushed his knuckles against her cheek. "Shh... She's safe." Into the comms, he said, "Bones, the bridge is hazardous, but I'll give you the coordinates for T.A.O. to locate us. Bring everyone. Let's debrief all at once." He gave the location then 'overed' and 'outted' that shit.

It was about to get really crowded in here.

Not that Xelan would notice. Korac fought to keep a smirk off his face as he glanced once more at the Prince. He was fucking devastated, but he was also giddy with all of Ishkur to design. It was exactly the kind of work the manic-obsessive scientist needed to cope with losing Rayne.

And Nox, though Xelan didn't know it—

Nox stared at his General through the conduit, half-formed in the shade of Rayne's glow. Solemn and grave, he mouthed, "Nacre—"

Nacre what?!

Korac shivered. An Aegis impression walked over his grave and made its way to an exit. There weren't as many here as on Enki. Likely because it was unfinished. Wait...

One impression stood on the highest gangway, back against the far wall. He was younger, smaller, with his hands tucked behind him like the apparition was told not to touch anything, but didn't trust himself not to do it, anyway. If Korac looked hard enough...

The eyes.

Twin crescent pupils.

The youth watched expectantly as his older siblings rushed about. He tried to call to one, but they brushed by him. The next one he flagged with no response. The smallest Aegis fidgeted and waited... waited for his chance at greatness.

After everything Razor did for them this last week, Korac planned to have a long conversation with their father about right, wrong, and the gray area in between.

Commotion drew his attention to an alcove. It was T.A.O., leading a chain of people through a conduit. She was followed by Bones' team and Chris' team after that. The Matt kid with Bethany and their team. The chain ended with Chief Lynn. And she was holding Echo.

The groups collided into a mingling mess. Lots of relief. Lots of huggy-huggy shit. His priorities were Karter and Pehton. Most of all, Korac wanted Sagan to wake with their daughter by her side.

But how to make the crowd part for him? "Excuse me. Gorgeous shirtless warrior coming through."

Bones chuckled and stepped aside to reveal Pehton's tiny dark self standing behind him with wide, blinking eyes.

Korac chuffed her under the chin. "Wake up, groupie. You can't let Caedes catch you drooling—Whoa! What's this?"

Someone latched onto him. They'd better have a casket picked out, trying to rope him into the hugs—

Oh.

"Bethany." Confounded, Korac let her cling to him, not sure what to do with himself.

Behind her, Matt and Lucy were snuggled up, watching the event with psycho cheerful smiles on their attractive faces.

The young girl gripping onto Korac looked up and flashed him the smile of a satisfied carnivore. "Thank you, Mr. Korac."

Bethany spoke.

Korac relaxed and let his hand fall to her back. He patted her, saying, "You did all the work. Remember that. You brought yourself to this moment. Be proud of it, Bethany."

The wattage on her smile went to full beam. Then she abruptly separated herself from him to join the crowd, locating her brother and sister.

Beside him, Pehton muttered, "Wow."

The warm and fuzzies.

They burned.

Korac shuddered them off. The Shadow couldn't have him. Not fully.

Pehton laughed, and the joy in it brought him back to the main mission.

Kissing her feathers, Korac muttered against her dainty ear, "I'm glad you're still alive, Lyriki General. Echo will need a godmother." Then he dramatically abandoned her mid-gape to locate his mother at Chris' side.

That human was seeing some ghosts of his own. Korac almost shuddered again at the thought. Celindria's captive for months—Horrifying. The couple had made their way to Xelan, who pulled Jack aside. Korac captured the Prince's gaze to offer him some courage.

No one wanted to break the news to Rayne's sibling. No one.

Near an exit, they were far enough away that Korac couldn't hear the exchange. Xelan said some words while Jack's eyes, growing wider, looked around the room. Anywhere but into the concern and kindness in Xelan's expression. Until the Prince stopped speaking. Jack squeezed his eyes shut and wrenched out a sob loud enough for everyone to hear.

Conversation ceased, and the room watched on as Jack gripped Xelan's coat and begged for it not to be true.

Korac swallowed his own grief and lowered his eyes in respect. He'd held the sprite in high regard, but never got to know her. Never got to ask about her and Sagan growing up. Or talk about training under Xelan. The resonance of losing those conversations and moments had branded Korac. And losing Nox a second time—

Mirrored eyes.

Words mouthed.

Nacre. What?

Charades with a specter.

Korac sighed, and it blended with the voices surrounding him. Grief. Exhaustion. And so few of them knew the magnitude of the work ahead.

Tameka brought Pax over to hug Jack with Xelan, offering a maternal touch. Korac glanced over at Karter, where she stood with Chris, Ross, and Para. They were waiting to support Jack with their family forged in battle. The tall Valkyrie glimpsed Korac staring. Her smile was sad, but filled with infinite warmth.

Love.

Korac would catch up with her after everything settled down. Right now, he needed—

"Korac?"

He turned to find a young Caprent woman with curly green hair. She asked, "Do you recognize me?"

Yes. A ghost which had haunted his Verse. But alive. So very alive, smiling, and relieved. Korac breathed, "I never knew your name."

"It's Aya, and I'm so glad to see you again." She held out her hand.

Korac took it in both of his and squeezed. This reunion deserved more time, but right now…

Aya said, "It's all right. We can catch up later. I can't wait to read this Verse I've heard so much about."

Overcome, Korac reached out and patted her shoulder. "We will find time. I promise. Until then have you seen…"

Aya pointed, and he turned in that direction.

There.

Chief Lynn was near the front of the crowd with the rest of the pre-Volcano day team. The originals. With respect for the moment, Korac gently pushed through the crowd to her.

Lynn spied him halfway and readied Echo, muttering, "Daddy's on his way."

Wow.

Just like that, Korac's grief and confusion dissipated for one shining moment.

Dad.

He was a dad.

Echo cooed a little whistle and reached her pitch-black hands out for him. Her white feathers arrested him every time he laid eyes on her. With diamond eyes, she took his breath away.

Of course, Echo couldn't see him yet. But as Korac took her from Lynn, there was a spark of recognition. She knew his scent.

Dr. Suarez put his arm around Lynn's shoulders, whispering, "She didn't fuss once during the evac."

Korac swallowed before saying, "That's my brave girl."

The warmth in which he said it made Lynn and Pablo share a look. It expressed healing and a future to look forward to.

Warm and fuzzies.

Before they claimed him, Korac nodded gratefully to the two and went to Sagan's side. Sometime during his errand, she'd rolled over to her side and hugged his robe, breathing in his scent. Like Echo was doing now. The tiny bundle in his arms occupied her time by curling and uncurling her soon-to-be-mighty fists.

It fascinated Korac that something so sweet and harmless could come from two people so... paradoxical. Thinking on it, he laid Echo against her mother and spread out on the floor beside her, nestling the infant between them. He took turns brushing his knuckles across their cheeks.

The others resumed restoration talks, tiptoeing around the subject of Rayne.

Half-listening, Korac overheard the good Doctor talking to Pehton and her two lost children—now recovered. He said, "Well, Wingmaster and I have spent the last few months researching the Weapons—" to cure Rayne "—And I think we can apply some of it to Silence and the others from Gait. Only if they're willing to volunteer."

Torch said, "Perhaps. Many were left unfinished."

Aria asked, "Mother, do you trust this human?"

Without hesitation, Pehton said, "Completely."

Korac could hear Pablo flush from across the room, and he wasn't the only one blushing.

Lucas was sitting with his legs hanging off a walkway, communicating without words with Smith beside him. When Andrew made his way over, Smith grinned like an idiot and excused himself. The remaining pair blushed and tried their best for eye contact, but it was slow-going. Not that it was Korac's business, but the Shadow would make for a great soap opera.

Pax zoomed by, pretending to be an airplane.

Korac was wondering if anyone had checked on Thubgy guarding the Villa when a pair of combat boots stepped into his line of sight. The hem of a ridiculous coat brushed them. Korac dragged his eyes up long legs and a straight back to find Xelan smiling down at him.

Elden, he looked broken.

The Traitor Prince could fool Tameka and everyone who trusted him to lead, but there was something missing in his eyes. Korac hoped Xelan found peace in rebuilding. For now, he asked, "What? No government bodies to assign preposterous names? Let me guess. You're naming the capitol 'Iona's Alcazar?'"

With a conceding tip of his head, Xelan admitted, "Actually, I like the sound of that."

Korac groaned and pinched the bridge of his nose. Echo cooed at the noise, and he pecked her a kiss, waving for Xelan to continue.

"I'm about to give the address. I'll need you to work with Tumu and organize the other Generals. Are you up to the task?"

It was a heavy responsibility for a War Criminal. Echo captured his finger in her fist and squeezed with all her might. Korac smirked. What a ride it had been. "I'll follow you anywhere, your majesty. Where Cinder goes, I go."

No truer words had ever been spoken.

{ISHKUR | BRIDGE}

What smelled so good?

Frost and untamed wilderness.

"I'll follow you anywhere, your majesty. Where Cinder goes, I go."

Sagan opened her eyes and smiled. In a world without Rayne, Echo lying between Sagan and Korac was enough. The certainty in his eyes while swearing his fealty to Xelan was enough.

This future was enough.

Korac looked at Sagan like she'd said it aloud. He was lying on his side, face propped in his hand, and he looked secure and comfortable with...

Wow, there were a lot of people in here.

Sagan's throat was still sore from crying. Her voice sounded worn as she asked, "How did I sleep through this?"

In answer, Xelan nudged her with his boot. "Being a superhero is tiring." He grinned—oh, the haunted shadow of his signature expression—before saying, "Glad to have you back, General Sterling. Just in time for my address. If you'll excuse me."

Xelan's face transformed. Opening his eyes wide and lolling his tongue out, he gave a silly wave to baby Echo.

Sagan giggled, and the infant smiled. Beaming with success, the Prince—no—the King of Cinder headed over to Tameka and Tumu, who waited at the main terminal.

Korac watched Sagan through the entire exchange, focusing on her face. Her smile for him was weaker than she wanted, but the day had been long, with much left to do. This little bubble with him and Echo—Sagan could stay here forever. Safe and happy.

Careful not to squish her, Korac leaned over Echo and kissed Sagan on her nacre. "Amos."

A blush crept onto her cheeks, and he smirked in response. Flustered now, she said his line, "I love the way you look at me."

He vowed, "Then I'll never look away."

Sagan closed her hand and allowed herself to feel the ring on her finger. It was already feeling like home. Korac stared at it, quiet. Almost at peace.

Xelan's voice popped the bubble as he spoke over the mass comms. "The Vast Collective." He said it with so much authority and so much promise. After a pause, he continued, "A galaxy free of Imminent. Free of Remorse. And as of today, a galaxy free of slavery in all its forms. The mines, the mills, the vice—All of it changes today. With Ishkur's technology and resources, we are free."

With a smile for Tameka, Xelan stepped back and let her speak over the mic. "Lacceirus-Capra, Lukemore, Pil, Reipon, Yu, Monarch 3, Earth, and Cinder, your home is here, if you wish it. We welcome and honor you. Your sacrifice and promise will forge Iona Pax, the Concerted Empire. We invite your elected leadership to design a home here in Ishkur. One which is most suitable for the needs of your people. While you occupy a habitable space here, we can restore your worlds damaged by this war. Repair our people and our planets."

They switched places again, and Xelan said, "F8, Legir, X, 2Lip, and Kombuchi—I expect to hear from you soon. Welcome to the tomorrow we promised you. Welcome to Ishkur."

The crowded bridge thundered with applause and rejoicing.

Sagan grinned at Korac, who was still rubbing his temple at Xelan's name for the empire.

Iuo shouted, "Reipon is ready, your imperial majesties. Welcome to tomorrow!"

Tumu called, "It'd better be tall people friendly. Everything Aegis so far is short."

Lamassau slapped his ass. "Bend over more often."

"Oooo," Twenty-One and Bones harmonized.

Tameka covered Pax's ears and glared at the Chef.

"Sorry, Empress Fury."

Xelan tried to flag him over her head, mouthing, "No. Don't."

Too late.

Tameka put a hand on her hip and sassed it out. "That's *Emperor* Fury."

Sagan watched Korac's brows go high at the announcement to which he shouted, "Here, here!" The rest echoed him. He gave Sagan a 'what' shrug before admitting, "She's too bad ass not to celebrate."

Going native looked cute on Sagan's man.

Even Echo waved a little arm in jubilation.

Miy and Pehton shared their first agreeable look, and it was all female empowerment.

Caedes beamed at Fury.

It warmed Sagan's heart to be surrounded by so many incredible men and women willing to fight together and die together...

Rayne.

As if overhearing her thoughts, Jack raised a drink ration into the air. Everyone went quiet. Rayne's brother said, "For those we lost." He gestured at Silence. "And those we won." He met the stares of the people on the bridge. Xelan and Tameka with Pax. Korac and Sagan with Echo. Pehton and Caedes. Pablo and Lynn with Dr. Qas and the new Tritan allies. The power group of Kyle, Silence, Smith, Lucas, and Andrew. The 'get it done' squad, with Matt in the lead. Twenty-One, Iuo, and Miy. Bones and Para snuggled where they thought no one could see. Chris and Karter leaned on each other. Gait's children smiled with a bright future filled with hope. And Ross gazed at Jack with pride and affection.

"We will always remain."

No one cheered.

No.

Everyone put a fist to their nacre and lowered their heads in deference.

The Shadow, the Twelve Worlds—They'd lost so much to make it here. Billions of lives and entire worlds ruined by Imminent. Now with Tameka, Xelan, and the Concerted Council leading the way, tomorrow never looked so bright.

Would it be easy?

No.

But what worth fighting for was easy?

Now more than ever, the Shadow faced monumental challenges and weighty decisions. They would build new homes for the people and honor the lost forever. Everyone would know the names of the fallen.

Sagan gazed at Echo and the lives which led to her making.

Razor.

Triss.

Nox.

And Rayne most of all.

FIFTEEN

REST AND PEACE ARE NOT ONLY FOR THE FALLEN

{Ishkur | Gale's Iona | Six Months Later}

"General Warden Pehton, report."

Pehton stretched under the sheets, careful not to wake Caedes. She was sore inside and out, and it was lovely. There was no cause for the irritatingly silken voice calling over her palm device to wake them both. Naked, she tiptoed to the closet for something—anything—other than her armor to wear—

"Yip!" Pehton clutched the nearest clothing item to her chest.

Projected in her hand, Korac's eyes went wide before he shut the visual link down. "Sorry. I saw nothing. Elden, you're not out of bed yet?! I'm getting married in nine hours." There was an edge of panic in his usually cool voice.

Rolling her eyes, Pehton slipped on a t-shirt and brought the visual back online to let him see the lack of amusement on her face. "Not everyone needs twelve hours to primp."

Best man.

Best man.

What a stupid Earth custom, and she was twice the fool for agreeing to be one for such a high maintenance, boujee, prima donna—

"That post-coital glow looks good on you."

Could Pehton's cheeks burn any hotter without activating the Siren's Gale?! She threw the nearest object at the projection. It went through, of course, but she felt better. "Does Sagan know you talk to me like this?"

"Hi, Pehton!"

Korac was smirking. "That would be her in the background."

Again, the General Warden rolled her eyes. "Aren't you two supposed to be separated or something for the night before 'the big day'?"

The smirk increased in wickedness. "Good luck keeping us apart."

Sagan's face appeared in the projection. Wow, speaking of glowing. "I'm heading out now if he'll ever let me go to Tameka's."

There was the definitive sound of an ass being slapped at the same time Sagan, "Yipped," and disappeared from the projection in a fit of giggles.

Pehton sighed and let them carry on like this. Every phone call. For six months now. She wasn't begrudging them at all. Everyone had earned their peace.

The daily occurrence had become standard operating procedure since Korac appointed Pehton the General Warden of Planetary Security. With the appointment of elected officials—F8, Legir, X, luo, 2Lip, Tempest, Lamassau, and Jack Callahan—the Concerted Empire accepted the offer from Co-Emperors Tameka and Xelan to transport their populations to habitable continents Ishkur-wide. For now, that was the continent of Cinder II, the planet before Li's expansion. This arrangement was temporary until Xelan and the terraforming engineers in charge of programming Torrentus prepared estates for all the represented peoples.

The migration from planet to Dyson's Sphere was purely voluntary, but when it became clear the less savory types were choosing to stay behind, Korac hired Pehton. Funnily enough, most of the unsavory types were old contacts of hers from Gait. How convenient.

But Pehton didn't mind. General Warden suited her just fine. She even got her own Iona. Xelan let her name it after Gale. This embassy was in the sky, accessible via flight and conduit. The air always smelled of spring meadows here—

Pehton sniffed. That wasn't spring meadows. The smell was...

Ignoring Korac and Sagan being utterly adorable on their well-deserved union day, Pehton followed the scent out of her closet. The bed was empty and made, and the bedroom door was left open. Sounds came from the kitchen and the delectable smell of...

"French toast."

"He'd better deliver it to you in bed."

Korac's voice broke the spell, and Pehton, wearing only a t-shirt, mused, "Wouldn't you like to know?"

Sagan cackled in the background before the door closed on their side of the call.

"Morning, Iona General," Caedes called from the stove, accustomed to Korac's inappropriate calls. "Happy union. Stealing Pehton early, I gather?"

Pehton sighed and went into the kitchen so the men could talk while she poured herself a glass of Yun lichi juice.

"I am, soldier. I am." Korac always grew more solemn and serious around other people. It made Pehton cherish their friendship more that he opened up to her, and simultaneously sad for the other people who couldn't experience it. The General continued, "How is the latest case?"

Caedes "humphed" without looking away from the divine smelling skillet.

Pehton smiled at his taciturn ways before pointing an accusing finger at Caedes by the stove and Korac's image. "No work talk today."

"Yes, ma'am," Caedes said, perhaps a little too readily and firmly.

Korac chuckled.

Oh, the jokes about training the man or keeping him on a tight leash—They would never end. Not since that one time Korac walked in on her and Caedes.

Stupid spiked collar.

Pehton padded back into the bedroom and scrounged together some pants. She said to Korac, "I'll be there in two steps. Just let me eat breakfast and put on some pants." She snatched the 'best man' kit, including her ensemble for the wedding.

No comment about her pantlessness. Korac never went for low-hanging fruit. Instead, he said, "Echo's looking forward to seeing you."

Bless.

Any mention of the sweet angel melted Pehton. Stupid secret weapon. "See you in thirty."

"See you." Korac disappeared to prep for this momentous occasion.

Rushing.

Always rushing.

"Let's see. Pants on. Check. Kit complete with gear. Ready. Feathers… Better do something with them." Pehton fretted all around the open living space until she heard Pil porcelain sliding across Cinder Ignis granite. The smell alone would revive her from the brink of death. "Thank you, Caedes."

Everything fell to the wayside as Pehton took her seat at the bar beside her lover, partner, and coach. Rather than speak, Caedes purred briefly at her gratitude, making Pehton smile into her bite of French toast.

So far, so bliss. The only thing they'd yet to agree on was a drawer for his things. She was several million years older than him, but Caedes still thought a drawer at six months was too fast.

When Pehton had asked him, the gruff Icarus said, "We just established John's Iona, and I'm its Major Officer. I'm needed there."

Still, he spent every night in Pehton's bed at Gale's Iona. Clearly, both of them felt responsibility for their dead. But come on. It was only a drawer.

Despite this one point, they respected each other enough not to go on about it. Instead, they found sanctuary in quiet moments like these.

"Try it with a strawberry in the same bite," Caedes said, while raising his fork for Pehton to indulge in his request.

She did, and maybe teased him a bit about it. Eye contact could do wonders at the right moment. His gaze was intense, dark green eyes locked on her lips.

Cardamom.

Pehton let Caedes' scent fill her, and if there'd been more time, it wouldn't be the only thing of his inside. "It's delicious." She kissed his lips with the syrup and strawberry still on hers. "But I have to go. You're heading to Bones', first, right?"

A terse nod from the Icarus with a knowing smile threatened to melt Pehton on the spot.

No.

No time for sex.

Pehton laughed. At her, at Caedes, at how happy she was. "Stop trying to cause trouble. I'll see you there." Then she made a mistake. She gave him a goodbye kiss.

Caedes roped her to him and propped her onto his thigh until she was firmly planted in his lap in a searing kiss. His hands marked their territory, claiming her shoulders, breasts, waist, and hips. Lower—

"Caedes, put your hands down." Pehton's Icarus did as he was told. "Let me go." He gently set her aside with an intensity darkening his eyes to near black. "Behave yourself today. For Sagan's sake."

"Yes, ma'am." Caedes accepted his orders with a regarding smirk. The man enjoyed being told what to do.

Pehton enjoyed every second of it. "See you there." She left him to clean up the kitchen, while she traveled from one hall of the Iona prism to the next. The conduits took her to the outside, where the sky greeted Pehton with a spring breeze.

There was another reason she was excited about the wedding. Aria and Torch. With her work off-Sphere, Pehton found herself gone for weeks at a time. Co-Emperor Tameka and Co-Emperor Xelan asked Pehton's children—both Primaries—to guard the imperial family. They accepted and lived on the Palatial Grounds full-time.

Sure, Pehton got to visit her kids to her heart's content, but it wasn't often enough given how much time they needed to make up. Still, she knew they'd get there. Today was another excuse to see them.

Below, specially engineered machines tilled and harvested the Vittle fields, Yun crops, and Lukemore cotton, contributing to the fresh smell. Nets emerged from crimson lakes filled with fish packed with proteins and omega fats suited for all races. Wild Hell Kittens bounded alongside Petrified hunting packs, tamed by Silence's intermediary communication.

Between Pehton and everything below, Overseers, zipped by, filled with passengers. All of them were on their way to the wedding from all over Iona Pax, not only Ishkur. Xelan opened conduits to all the planets in a hundred thousand locations. The Overseers moved through them, carrying non-flying entities to their destinations.

Not Pehton. She slung the kit over her shoulder and scanned her blood at a super secret conduit. It led to a plain shrine with multiple shimmering veils. It was super secret because these conduits led to the Shadow.

Pehton took the second one on the left and emerged in a snowy glade surrounded by capped evergreens. It smelled like—Well, it smelled like the master of its dominion. She knocked on the grand entryway to a Reipon glass and Cinder log chalet. She called, "Korac, I'm here—"

Pehton gripped her sides in laughter, dropping her kit.

Korac answered the door in a silk robe with a toothbrush in his mouth, foam separators between his polished toes and rollers in his drying hair. A team of stylists followed him, positively distraught by his mobility during their work.

High. Maintenance.

The Icarus removed the tooth brush to put his face in hers and said, "You're next."

Pehton swallowed. Surely Korac was joking.

Surely.

{ISHKUR | TEETH'S IONA}

"I'll bet two hundred credits that General Korac is already awake and getting ready."

Bones loved it when Para laughed at his jokes.

As she snuggled closer in bed, she said, "Surely not. It's hours away."

He chuckled. "And I'll raise you another one hundred credits that he's already gotten Pehton out of bed."

The swat from the tiny Valkyrie's pillow was hard and uncalled for. Not to mention all the static cling shocked him as Para pulled it away.

"Foul," Bones called before retaliating with his much bigger, firmer pillow.

They played. Kissed. And took part in play of another nature.

This was peace, and they'd earned it.

Bones loved his job, overseeing the migration of Iona's planets to Ishkur. It meant he was away for work a lot, so he cherished these moments with Para. She lived with Karter and Chris, but on Bones' home rotations, she always made time for him. Every night in each other's arms, preceded by poker with the crew.

Game Night was a security nightmare. Colton griped incessantly about it while prepping a cheesecake for each event. Iuo, King Elect of Reipon, came up on breaks from sorting the fictional and accurate histories between all the races. During Bones' last trip home, Iuo hooked him up with a film session as a surprise for Para. Bones still owed the virgin Porn Baron a bag of Cheetos for that one. Twenty-One was head of rehabilitation services as a living example of his own methods. Caedes, gruff as ever with his new responsibilities in treatise, thought he was smooth, leaving every game night for Pehton's place.

As if.

Move in already.

The crew hesitated to let Smith return at first, but his perpetually smiling face was too familiar to reject. And what a wicked poker face. Lamassau let no one call him King Elect. He accepted nothing less than Chef Royale.

Kyle and Andrew were harder to sync schedules with, but they made it to every game.

During the last few games, King Elect, Jack, had joined them. He took to his duties admirably, but was only just coming out of his shell. It must be hard when every girl in the galaxy templated their face and hair to look like Jack's sister. May she rest in Eternity. It startled Bones whenever he went somewhere for a migration to see thousands of blue-eyed, black-haired, pale-skinned girls with similar noses and chins to Rayne. Nothing was ever quite perfect on them, but it continued to make Bones' skin crawl.

Iona Pax paid tribute to its dead.

But today was about life and coupling. Once Para and Bones finished with their own, he took himself drunk with love to the shower. It was too early to get ready, but the exhilaration was infectious.

A proper joining of Earth and Cinder, Generals Sagan and Korac represented everything right about the war they'd survived.

Plus, Bones couldn't wait for Korac to open Kyle's wedding gift. It would serve the Iona General right for turning down a bachelor party. It was enough to make Bones chuckle into the shower spray.

Fed and happy.

Sexed up and appreciated.

Never lonely. Never bored.

There wasn't much more Bones could ask for out of his idea of paradise. Without the constant threat of Imminent looming over them, the galaxy finally knew peace. And if something ever threatened that peace, may Elden show them mercy.

Because the Shadow sure wouldn't.

"Bones, Caedes is here!" Para called.

He grinned while drying his hair, saying, "I told you Korac grabbed Pehton already!"

His woman laughed. "You did. You did! What do I owe you?" There was a purr to Para's voice at the last.

"Don't worry, little Valkyrie. I'll think of something."

And it wouldn't be cheesecake and Cheetos. Although, those might be involved.

{ISHKUR | JOHN'S IONA}

Chris inspected his military dress, hanging in the closet. He'd located it on Earth for this special occasion. To think, General Korac had invited the entire Concerted Empire of Iona Pax to the wedding.

What a security nightmare.

As Jack's Chief Security Officer, this was a protocol disaster. Chris and Colton spent months preparing for all the elected kings to gather, but Xelan and Tameka's Primary team had assured them every precaution was taken. The ceremony was secure.

"Chris, are you in there?" Karter called before peering into the closet. "Hey, handsome. Are you ready to nab Echo from the groom?"

Chris smiled at her. She was glowing and didn't know it. Motherhood suited her, and Chris couldn't be more elated that Korac turned out to be her son. He glanced at the door to the King Elect's suites. "Yeah, Jack and Ross will be awake before too long. What do you think?" He gestured to the uniform.

Karter beamed. "I think you'll look very distinguished at the ceremony."

That's what Chris was going for—

A hint—a touch of the darkness tried to creep into his thoughts. A whisper of Celindria's voice in his ears, telling him what she thought of the uniform. But no. Practicing some meditation techniques he'd learned from the Yun, Chris pushed the trauma back. The monster wasn't welcome here.

Chris smiled, and Karter took his hand. He followed her to the shrine housing the special Shadow conduits, and they stepped through the one leading to Korac's chalet.

The tall Icarean General answered the door in silk jammies and a matching cap on his head.

In the background and out of sight, Pehton cried, "Oh, no. No! Not my feathers!"

Chris felt his eyes go wide.

Karter glanced at him and burst into hearty laughter.

Korac smirked. "Don't mind her. She's being a drama queen."

"I will *end* you!" Pehton sounded serious.

Korac chuckled, and it was a good sound Chris had noticed Korac was making more often lately.

Without ceremony, Karter reached up and pulled her son in for a hug. "I'm so happy the day is here."

The Iona General squeezed his mother, and Chris excused himself, taking a step down into the expansive living space. The low couches surrounding multiple fire features offered cozy perches for reading and snuggling. Like at Chris' place in John's Iona, the electronic media appeared on screens summoned anywhere within a nanite field, and it was adjustable to the desired size for viewing.

It blew Chris' mind to remember he'd started with picture tube TVs and antennae.

On Earth.

Korac gestured upstairs. "Echo's in her crib, if you want to get her."

Chris perked up as Karter glanced between the two men in the room. She took the hint and headed to the nursery off the master suite, while Korac descended into the space with Chris. When the half-Aegis moved, Chris could actually see Karter in him, comfortable in their long limbs and ready to fight at any given moment.

On his way over, Korac said, "I'm three millions years old."

Yeah. Every time someone reminded Chris of how bizarre their lives were, he did the big blink and shook his head. What could he say? He went for, "It's quite the lifespan."

"I would still appreciate some advice on my union day, if you have any to give."

Was... Was the Iona General reaching out to Chris as a paternal figure? How should he respond? He peered at the man who looked no older than twenty-five in Earth years and thought of the advice he'd want on his wedding day.

A few things came to mind. Chris said, "Do whatever she says. She's always right. Give her chocolate when she gets cranky. And trust her to know what she wants, except whatever you're having for dinner. Then you're shit out of luck."

A long pause followed, filling the living space with assessing consideration.

Eventually, Korac smirked, saying, "You'll do just fine."

It was a surprising thing for him to say, and Chris took it for the compliment it was.

Karter appeared then, holding the most precious bundle of whistling baby. With Echo in her arms, the Valkyrie was radiant.

The glow was catching, as Korac gave Echo his finger to grip. He said, "Thank you for watching her during the ceremony and the honeymoon."

Chris waved him off. "You couldn't give her enough excuses to babysit."

Karter beamed at him for speaking the absolute truth. Then she gave Korac an incredulous look. "Poor Pehton is upside down. What are subjecting her to in there?"

"Pure. Torture!" Again, Pehton's torment sounded authentic.

Chris chuckled when Korac winked at his mother. Baby Echo cooed and whistled, encouraging her father.

"Oh, there's my little girl. Don't forget she needs this." Korac handed over a bag and a jingling toy. "And take this, it's her favorite. And sing to her, but on pitch. She gets fussy if you're off key..."

This was what they'd fought for. The little moments of warmth and care.

This was Iona Pax, and they were its Shadow.

{ISHKUR | OLEEN'S IONA}

Bethany was hungry.

The Nice Man and Lucy had promised she could eat soon, but first they had to persuade Bethany's brother and sister to let her go on a hunting trip.

"After the wedding, we're heading to Pil. There's a smuggling ring and possibly some human trafficking. I'll convince them it's purely educational."

The Nice Man understood Bethany. He wanted nothing from her and offered her the abyss in his empty smiles. After spending weeks in a room full of faces waiting for Bethany to speak again or brush her hair, empty smiles with no expectations were a relief.

Like right now.

Ross was combing Bethany's wet curls, talking. The way Ross pronounced the syllables and the feel of the bristles pulling through Bethany's hair fed her heart. That was love.

Inflating memories of blisters until the skin of Bad Men boiled fed Bethany's soul. That was vitality.

The young girl needed the hurt to exist. Without it, Bethany was a collection of memories without reason. The pain held her together, and she starved for men who would hurt her. Men who would hurt Ross. To feed.

Ross said, "You look beautiful in your dress. Do you like it?"

Clothes.

Sheaths to prevent Bethany's nudity.

The union ceremony was themed. All guests must wear black, white, silver, or violet. The skater dress was lavender and brought out Bethany's honey-brown eyes. Korac would like it.

That mattered. A compliment from her half-Aegis, half-Icarean friend, was worth the humanity forced on Bethany's skin. She still met with him once a month. Their quiet walks were a platinum treasure in her brass world.

Aware of this, Ross was nice for dressing Bethany with thought and care. The youngest sister faced the eldest and wrapped her arms around her. This caused Bethany substantial suffering in her chest because Ross always pulled away with a shimmer of tears in her hazel eyes.

Love.

Bethany loved Kyle and Ross with all her heart. It hurt so much. They were bright as the light when the Nice Man removed the hood from her head. Blinding and well-missed, but not as accepting as Bethany remembered.

Ross kissed Bethany's forehead, and her sister's lips trembled. "Ready for some makeup?"

Fables painted on the skin.

"Korac will like it."

Bethany nodded.

They were in the bedroom off of the living space, allowing Bethany to eavesdrop on Jack's conversation with Chris. "That's downright spiffy, Batman." There was no mocking in the younger man's voice. Simply respect.

Pride warmed Chris' tone. "Well, Robin, I used to like dressing up occasionally before I met you on Invasion Day and became a galactic diplomat."

"Yeah. For funerals and weddings." Now Jack was mocking him.

Karter laughed, and Echo whistled with the sound.

Chris returned fire. "What about you? I doubt delinquents dressed like GQ models in high school. You look like a grown man. I couldn't be prouder, kid." It was a father's tone, and it suffused the entire suite with warmth.

Ross intruded on Bethany's thoughts. "Matt, Lucy, and Puk will be here soon. They're stopping by to get Twenty-One and Miy first."

Bethany wanted to ask if Yito was with them, but she kept the question to herself. She wasn't ready for casual conversation yet. Instead, she smiled while Ross applied lipstick.

Yito was old. So much older than any Icarus currently living. Even Karter. And he was another nice man. He let her play in his memory, full of plagues and famine. Because of this pastime, Bethany had learned she could inflict from anyone's memory she experienced—Not only her own. And the old Tritan asked for nothing in return. He was another person who simply accepted her.

As if hearing her little sister's thoughts, Ross smiled and said, "Yito is with them."

Bethany grinned.

Maybe... just maybe... her family was accepting her.

After all, family was why they'd fought in the Collective War. It was about time Bethany felt comfortable with her own.

Except Kyle.

When Korac finally opened *that* present, the next war would start.

On second thought, Bethany was fine with that.

{ISHKUR | JOHN'S IONA}

Lynn tangled her fingers in Pablo's tight curls as he listened to her ever-protruding, seven-month pregnant belly. His smile banished away all her stupid self-conscious thoughts about fitting in her bridesmaid dress.

Oh, and his beaming grin when the baby kicked.

Yes, Lynn loved fatherhood on her man.

"He's so strong." The wonder in Pablo's voice was worth the weight gain and overbearing cravings. He kissed her stomach, saying, "I can't wait to teach him the names of all the bones in his little hand."

Lynn, propped up on her pillows, beamed right back at him. "I hope he has your eyes."

Pablo dismissed her with a wave. "Nah, he'll be gorgeous like his mother." He lifted her hand and kissed her knuckles. "Like, look at this skin. So rich and beautiful. Soft."

They spent every morning like this, but it was especially potent today. Their friends were getting married, and love permeated Iona Pax. It was a splendid occasion to get mushy.

It was also a nice rest from work. The Concerted Emperors had promoted the couple to elevated positions within Ishkur. Lynn led the defense weapons division of military research, and Pablo headed a coalition of physicians, representing each species for shared medical procedures and instruction.

Busy didn't cover it.

But everyone was good to each other and allowed for regular days off, including an entire month of vacation since the positions began six months ago. So it wasn't all bad.

Especially when the days started and ended with Lynn in bed with her husband, cooing about the baby growing inside her.

"We'll have play dates. I mean, Pax is a little older, but I'm sure he'll still want to play with his cousins." Pablo's dreams warmed Lynn to her toes. "Echo can teach him to sing. Heck, she can teach me to sing while she's at it."

Lynn giggled at him, ruffling his hair.

They both sighed in content.

She said, "Not long now, and we'll need to get ready."

Pablo snorted. "I don't know who plans to follow this act, but good luck. The entire galaxy?" He scoffed, but it was good-natured. "They deserve it, though."

Yes. They did.

Lynn changed the subject. "I forgot to ask last night. How is Aya doing with the latest round of testing?"

Pablo hopped up with excitement. "Excellent responses. I think this might finally be it. No more faulty nacre. We'll see. I'd hate to give her false hope."

This was why Pablo was so important in Iona Pax. The passion and compassion. The man she loved cared deeply about all peoples. Lynn smoothed a hand over her belly. She couldn't wait for more little Pablos running around. Taking a moment to glance outside, she doubly appreciated the view.

It was of a treehouse with their vows carved into the door.

"Did you think you wouldn't make it?"

Lynn's question rang in the air between them as she stared out the window, reliving their already full lives.

Pablo followed her gaze and answered after a quiet stretch. "I know we both broke our vows a few times. How could we abandon people because of a promise we made to each other? But... I knew in doing those things, I was being the man you wanted to marry. Because that line of thinking brought us together in the first place. Two people willing to stay behind and help others. Lynn, it's who've always been. And it's who I want us to be going forward. Who I want our children to be."

Lynn smiled. "Can you imagine telling them the story? Once upon a time, on a planet faraway before super cool space technology, there was a school. Mommy and daddy were students there. Your uncle Korac and his best friend, who we aren't sure if we should forgive yet or not, invaded and burned the school to the ground. Mommy and daddy stayed to help people and suffered from smoke inhalation before they had nacres—That's right, kids. We didn't start off with nacres—"

Pablo laughed, rich and pure. "It's too ridiculous. But do you want to know something more ridiculous than that? They'll learn the entire story in school, anyway. Our Verses are required reading."

Right.

How could Lynn forget?

Pablo sat up, cupped her nape, and kissed Lynn with enough heat to make her want to try for twins. When he separated them by inches, he licked the taste of her from his lips. Those soft supple lips that started so much trouble.

Lynn beamed. She couldn't help it. "I'd marry you all over again."

"Ditto, Mrs. Renee-Suarez. Now c'mon. Let's go watch our friends get married. Then we can come home and finish what we started."

Enticing, but...

"I've got a better idea. Let's finish it now."

It wouldn't get them out of bed, but it sure was a beautiful way to start their day.

{ISHKUR | MERIT'S IONA}

This was the Probability to happiness, and Silence had finally found it.

The foremother dressed in front of a mirror with a small, knowing smile. Kyle's reflection smoldered as she slipped into the bikini after a morning of proper exercise. The first fighter to pin the other won.

Sometimes Silence let him win, and he rewarded her with hours of delicious pleasure. Watching her dress was simply a bonus. So she exaggerated stepping her long legs into the short dress, clinging to every curve in sheer black. She'd asked Sagan if she could go without the underclothes. The poor girl's eyes had drifted off, and she'd forgotten how to speak until seconds later she suggested the bikini might prove less distracting.

Silence beamed.

More so as Kyle entered, knelt at her feet, and helped her into matching heels. He mused, "As if you need more height," and kissed each knee.

"It's more about having a weapon strapped to my feet for your defense when Korac opens your gift."

"Hah!" Smith was always eavesdropping.

Neither he nor Lucas felt right about leaving her alone for the first one hundred years in case the nullifying hull failed or one of Dr. Suarez's tests went badly. Silence had only just convinced Lucas to go back to his prized zeppelin. Surely he missed his closet.

But Smith conveyed. The Shadow reinstated them both shortly after. Smith resided with Kyle and Silence. She enjoyed their humors and relished in their friction. This was her immediate family.

Silence returned her thoughts to the gift. "Must you?"

Kyle beamed, self-satisfied and anticipatory. "Oh, I must." He stood and kissed her nacre before booping her nose. "My turn. I don't think Sagan will let me into the wedding if my clothes aren't matching."

With a glance at his lime green Hawaiian shirt and blue basketball shorts, Silence threw her head back and laughed. "No. That won't do."

Every day was like this.

Easy. Simple. And right.

Even when Silence worked. Yes, her grandson had given his foremother an occupation. She, Smith, Lucas, and Andrew monitored the Probability Matrix. Since Rayne's destruction of Enki, the threads were boundless. Silence's team analyzed it closely; although Xelan never read the reports. Supposedly, other leaders requested the surveillance, so she reported to Tumu.

Silence divided her time between that task and the experiments with Dr. Suarez and Xelan. They talked at length with her about Xhi and Lon's nacres, and they gently but thoroughly interrogated Silence about her time as the Mother.

"How did you escape Quet's lab in the first place?"

"I never learned how. On that day, I awakened after the last birth with my cement bonds freed. I fled without a single backward glance."

Kyle smiled at her, changing into a button down. She gazed at him, appreciating how he never pried—Never asked about her eon-long life. There were other unanswered questions. Ones Silence couldn't answer with any honesty, and she despised withholding anything from her lover and her grandson.

"They've asked me repeatedly about the barrier, Lucas. They wish me to reproduce its effects."

"A little while longer, Mother. Keep your faith. It'll all come together with perfect clarity, and then everything will be right."

Silence trusted Lucas implicitly, so she evaded Tumu and Lynn's questions. The two researchers asked about the barrier less frequently to Silence's good fortune—

Kyle was staring into nothing, his forest green eyes locked onto nowhere in the closet. His messy brown curls were long enough to obstruct his vision, yet he paid them no mind. Simply lost in his thoughts. This was also happening less frequently, but when it did, only one person was on his mind.

Silence's approach required a delicate touch. With a gentle brushing of fingers, she took his hand.

Kyle startled, but calmed when he realized it was her. He cleared his throat before saying, "Sorry."

Silence traced her fingers down his jaw, saying, "Never apologize. Your mourning is mine."

Kyle's sigh rattled, and his hand shook. "I was thinking about how she'd be a bridesmaid. You know?"

Silence nodded for him to continue.

"There'd be dancing, and we would all get on the floor for a line dance or something. Like at the skating rink. She'd tease me for being off beat." His bruised laughter was heartbreaking. "Jack would tell some inspiring story about his big sister. Or an embarrassing one. You never know with those two—"

Kyle's voice broke, and Silence pulled him into her arms. She held him while he wept quiet tears. Smith popped his head in, and she gave him a sad smile. He nodded his understanding and left them alone.

With all the consolations Silence could offer, only one would suffice. "On your death, a world ends with you. Know the stars will fall still and weep for you."

"How do you manage?" Kyle asked against her neck. "With Elden gone, I mean."

A tall figure smelling of clover came to mind at the mention of his name. Two-toned hair. A burning sun reflected in his eyes, and gilded tattoos decorated his charcoal skin.

Elden.

Silence would be honest with Kyle. "Not a day passes that I don't think of him. The ache is hard to describe, but I believe you experience a similar hurt. Nothing will ever let you forget Rayne, and unfortunately, we both live in a world where our lost ones are quite celebrated. We encounter reminders of them every day. I have accepted the good in this. Because of Elden, my child and grandchildren fought for our people. Because of Rayne, the Shadow united the galaxy into Iona Pax. I find peace in knowing so much right was done in Elden's name. Can you do the same?"

Kyle separated them and met her eyes with a sad smile. "Yeah. I think that's exactly what I needed to hear." He cupped her chin and kissed her sweetly.

Silence let him return to dressing and considered what Remorse had said about Elden. Her mate went to the ends of the galaxy to find her while she slept in a mountain only kilometers away. But what a journey it had set Elden and the rest of Cinder on.

Savis.

Nox.

Xelan.

Eventually Rayne.

So much sacrifice, but so much good.

Elden smiled down on Iona Pax, knowing it was all worth it in the end.

{ISHKUR | NIKKI'S IONA}

Today was the six-month anniversary of Iona Pax, the perfect day for Sagan and Korac's wedding.

Except Korac had been calling non-stop since seven in the morning.

When the phone rang the first time, Andrew was upside-down and halfway to happy town. Lucas was vocal and oral about his guilt, and who was Andrew to deny his penance? Absolution felt divine between the sheets, in the bath, on the kitchen counter—Really everywhere.

And Andrew was drowning in it until Lucas' comms went off. The damned Icarus maintained eye contact while licking the taste of Andrew from his lips before answering, "Steel Peppermint?"

"Elden dammit. Sagan called me that once in your presence, and now you're under the impression you can call me by that name anytime you'd like?"

Quiet and lying back on the bed, Andrew quirked a brow.

Lucas kissed the inside of his lover's thigh, still maintaining gilded eye contact. He said to Korac, "No, not anytime. Just anytime before eight in the morning."

There was a long pause before Korac surrendered. "Fine. Pehton's here—"

"Subjected to torture, no doubt." Vicious in his temptation, Lucas licked Andrew in one long stroke of his warm, wet tongue.

Andrew's eyes rolled far enough back to meet Eternity, and the bed buckled when he gripped it.

"—I'd appreciate if you'd come over in an hour like we talked about. She'll need help with her straps before we start with me."

"I'll come before then." A mischievous wink punctuated Lucas' double entendres.

There was a heavy sigh on Korac's end of the phone before he deadpanned, "I called during sex, didn't I?"

Lucas' laughter was rich and answered the question, but for good measure, the Icarus gripped Andrew's throbbing skin so that he cried out, loud enough for Korac to hear. Lucas said, "Lazy morning sex, at that."

Korac sounded like he was pinching the bridge of his nose as he said, "Pass on my regrets to Andrew. Head over whenever you're ready." He promptly disconnected the call.

The moment it ended, Lucas put his mouth back to work. Andrew tried to protest, albeit weakly. "Shouldn't you... Oh, god... Shouldn't you go help?"

Availing himself of the task, Lucas looked at Andrew with glittering eyes. His smile suggested he knew the answer to the question before he asked it. "Would you like me to stop?"

Andrew swallowed hard enough to hear it. "No. But—" He stopped Lucas from immediately persisting. "Five more minutes."

"Challenge accepted."

An hour and a half later, Lucas pilfered through his closet for last-minute touches. The rosewood paneled room occupied half the zeppelin anchored to Nikki's Iona. The day Sagan opened a conduit big enough to fly it into Ishkur had felt like a momentous occasion, marking the return of Lucas and Smith to the Shadow. Andrew didn't move in immediately. In fact, he and Lucas took it slowly, going on dates for the first three months. But one night four months ago changed all that.

Andrew had fallen asleep in the Probability Matrix observation lab. Celindria's face came to him. Beautiful and demented. Deep violet skin and inviting curves wrapped in a golden gown. She'd woven gold thread in her braids and wrapped her locs in white ribbon. Painted gold and white patterns decorated her arms, chest, eyelids and lips.

The First Progeny stared her bright blue eyes at a view Andrew couldn't see, but it was a hungry stare. Whatever she craved was in danger. Then he realized he could see what she coveted in the reflection of Celindria's eyes.

What Andrew saw there was the end of everything.

He'd awakened with a deep drink of air, and his heart pounded like someone had defibrillated him. And all Andrew wanted—*needed*—in that moment was Lucas.

When he turned up at the Icarus' zeppelin, it took no convincing to let him inside. More double entendres. Because if the end was coming—again—Andrew didn't want to waste another second on taking things slow.

Like the air when he woke from his dream, Andrew drank deep of Lucas. Day after day. Night after night.

Sometimes the Icarus looked at the Progeny as if he knew, but never asked.

And how could Andrew answer? *Hey, I think Celindria's alive, and she's plotting her revenge in the Probability Matrix while looking fabulous.* It sounded ridiculous.

So Andrew gathered evidence, whispers, and rumors. Nothing had turned up so far, but vigilance was key. One day, he'd either confirm or disprove his dream.

Until then... Wedding day.

"Now, I'm ready for Korac." Lucas emerged from the closet with a warm smile, two garment bags, and three boxes of shoes. Polish included. "Are you certain my services aren't needed here?"

At Lucas' bouncing brows, Andrew laughed. "No. Andrius and Devis are on their way. We'll put something together for everyone. Do you think T.A.O. will actually turn up for Korac's union ceremony?"

When he reached the door, Lucas paused to shrug. "Hard to say. She needs more solitude and space than any other being I've encountered. And after spending thousands of years as Celindria's prisoner, who can blame the poor girl?"

Andrew shuddered and changed the subject. "Will you stop by the Palatial Grounds and help Tameka and Sagan?"

Lucas laughed and melted away Andrew's anxieties before saying, "I wouldn't abandon them in their hour of need. Both the bride and the groom will receive my services today."

Imperial Stylist.

What a title.

Lucas blew Andrew a kiss. "I'm off. Save a dance for me." He left with a sexy wink.

They'd fought so hard for these moments of peace, but Andrew knew in his bones...

Iona Pax was temporary.

But then again, what wasn't?

SIXTEEN
UNTIL ETERNITY TAKES ME

{ISHKUR | CHALET}

KORAC HAD NEVER FELT MORE SURE AND MORE RIGHT ABOUT ANYTHING IN HIS LONG LIFE.

Sagan.

Her name was synonymous with trust, acceptance, sex, and love for him.

So why was Korac fretting so much with his ensemble and constantly checking his hair? Straightening his matte black cufflinks for the thousandth time.

When he asked for Chris' advice earlier, it was in absence of another paternity figure. But that wasn't exactly true. Since commandeering Ishkur, Korac had upcycled Zero three times to ask for help with its operation. All three times, the Exalted proudly and gladly assisted the Shadow, especially with terraforming for the different species. 'Eager' was the right word. But in all three instances, Korac had tried to ask his father about Razor and the Aegis' treatment of him. 'Remote' didn't cover it. Zero's answers were clinical and alien.

"Three Two Four was an experiment of our reproduction outside the Seam. He was born with small bones and the Inanis affliction. We considered him a deficit to our race."

Inside his mind, Korac stared hard at the tall Aegis with hollow rings for pupils. He reasoned, "But his small bones were nature. How he employed Inanis was nurture. It resulted from your unkindness."

Zero cocked his head to the side in an avian gesture Korac had trademarked. The Exalted asked, "Are you suggesting we're responsible for Inanis?"

This required a deep breath to maintain patience before Korac answered, "The incident with Ishkur was an accident, but it was the direct consequence of you and his—our—brothers neglecting Razor."

The silence between them grew uncomfortable after such a great length of time. Then Zero abruptly requested, "Please, cycle me down."

Korac hadn't upcycled him for a month, but perhaps this occasion called for it. Standing in front of the mirror, he summoned Zero forth. When the Aegis leader answered, Korac sighed in unexpected relief. Nerves were a bitch. He stared into foreign eyes in the mirror and asked, "Do you know what today is?"

The Exalted lifted Korac's lips into a proper beam. "How could I not? It resonates in your consciousness and ours. Your matrimony elates us."

Again, a wave of relief washed over Korac. "Thank you."

"The Atheneum and the Seamswalker. Quite the match."

Korac smiled at his father, but the nerves returned. He asked, "Why am I anxious?"

A warm smile crossed the Exalted's face. "A lifetime commitment is significant with lifespans as long as ours. That and..."

When his father didn't finish his sentence, Korac pressed, "Yes?"

"You paid a high price for this bliss. Perhaps you're primed to expect further disaster."

That felt right. Damn, it felt exactly right.

Korac nodded, unable to speak. Something loomed. Or was it survivor's guilt? It took so much to get here. How could he not feel anxious about something ruining it? Or how could he take his mind off the people they'd lost?

"Korac."

Inside his mind, Zero stood within reach of Korac, who asked, "Yes?" Father.

The man's smile was kind and unexpected, given his effect was normally so alien. Zero said, "Let yourself be happy today with your love. Nox would want this for you. Rayne would *demand* it, if only for Sagan's sake. Besides... " He reached up and dusted Korac's shoulder, looking into the mirror. "Once you lay eyes on her, these anxieties will vanish. I speak from experience."

Zero was absolutely right, of course. The vision of Sagan's violet eyes glowing from across the aisle...

Yes.

"Thank you... father."

The Exalted beamed and gave a bow of his head. Internally, he stepped back and waited for the down cycle. "Until the next time."

When Korac opened his eyes, they were normal. Well, normal for him, and the nerves were somewhat tamed compared to earlier. He called to the other bedroom, "Lucas, have you finished with our General Warden?"

Pehton answered, "Yes. And I hate you."

Korac chuckled. Her torture was a sweet distraction from the big day jitters. "If you hate me, it's only because I was right and you look spectacular."

Lucas came to the doorway, beaming. "I'd have to say I agree with you, Korac." He'd changed into a silver brocade three-piece with a black necktie. His sandy blond hair was smoothed into a styled ponytail, letting his eyes shine without obstruction. He said, "Good choice. Although the bondage fetish is more your and Sagan's trademark, is it not?"

Korac smirked. The straps weren't that bad. "Let me see."

Pehton stepped out with more confidence than Korac was sure she'd intended, because how could one not feel confident when they looked like a goddess? The stylists had dipped each of her feathers in liquid silver leaf and braided them down her back, shining and contrasting beautifully with her pitch-black skin. Lucas painted one stripe of silver down the center of her lips and one down each of her eyelids. Korac had commissioned the tux tailored to her petite figure. Black, of course—They left the jacket open to expose her breasts strapped in thin silver bands, revealing enough to tantalize the imagination. Thick black straps hugged her ass and legs, flattering her height. Accented with silver piping, they complimented the silver six-inch stilettos lacing up her exposed ankles.

Oh, and they couldn't forget the collar. A simple silver band circled her throat.

Despite her ire, Pehton enjoyed it. Korac could see it on her face. With a reluctant huff, she said, "I'll admit. I look good."

Lucas laughed. "Just 'good?' Darling, you look like a wet dream."

Korac and Pehton turned simultaneously to gawk at the Imperial Stylist, who shrugged.

She gave an incredulous laugh. "But how will I get this off? It took four people to get me in it."

With a click of his tongue, Korac folded his arms, considering.

She pushed, "What?"

He said, "Well, I thought you'd have more confidence in Caedes' abilities six months into the relationship. Perhaps I overestimated him—"

Flying pillows. Evasive maneuvers.

"Now, now. Let's not destroy my masterpiece," Lucas argued reasonably. "Besides, it's time for you two to leave for the venue, and for me to visit the bride." He took a step into Korac's personal space and adjusted his tie before walking to the door with a backward shot, "Break a wing."

Korac called, "Take care of my girl."

"I think what I look forward to most during the ceremony is when you two see each other." With a wave, Lucas departed for the Palatial Grounds.

Pehton gazed at Korac, mouth a little open. It was her first time seeing him all finished. Now that she was done, did the Best Man upstage the groom? Lucas had tailored Korac's silk black slacks to emphasize the length of his legs and accentuate the definition of his quads. The tails of his black tuxedo jacket brushed the backs of his knees, framing him with the purple piped lapels. The vest matched the purple tie over his black silk button down. Matte black buttons finished the look.

Pehton's ensemble didn't outshine Korac's tux, but her feathers certainly surpassed his hair. Lucas had woven three separate braids along Korac's scalp on either side and one full braid across the top, which was finished in a full ponytail. Black and violet ribbon were threaded throughout each braid. The Imperial Stylist finished the effect with black diamonds and deep amethysts, fixed here and there. Pretty, but how did one compete with hand-dipped silver feathers?

The General Warden beamed at Korac. "Damn. Let me see." She crossed the room with a strut, feeling herself and making Korac smirk, to take his hand. With an incredulous laugh, Pehton said, "I knew you wouldn't skip even this detail."

Matte black nail polish with amethysts set in the center of each nail. Korac shook his head, equally incredulous. "You know me so well."

Pehton's garnet eyes were a little glassy as she said, "We've been through so much together. I'll see you through this and everything beyond it. You're my best friend, Korac."

He kept his face serious as he cupped her chin and leaned all the way down until he was an inch from her lips. Pehton's eyes crossed and widened slightly this close to him. Korac saw her pulse flutter in her neck. Cruel. He was so cruel because, while he flirted often, he never meant to follow through. "Don't ruin your mascara, General Warden."

Pehton fumed—As in Siren's Gale fumed.

Korac kissed her vermeil feathers with a teasing laugh. "I love you, too. C'mon. Let's go to the springs. Xelan's probably there already, pacing a rut in the dirt." He left Pehton in his chalet, glaring at him, and took a moment on his cleared walkway outside to appreciate the snowy glade surrounded by pines and cedars. Only stars were missing from the view, a velvet night sprinkled with diamond dust. He made a note to suggest a cosmos projection or something to Xelan.

Pehton finally exited the chalet. "Why springs anyway?" she asked, as they went through the first conduit.

In the special shrine meant for Shadow only, Korac explained, "I know it's hard to imagine, but once, long ago, mine and Sagan's relationship hinged on a decision for both of us. In Sagan's case, it was to trust me—An enemy General who had witnessed his King commit terrible atrocities. And in my case, I needed to decide who I wanted to serve more—A woman full of optimism and hope that I fell in love with, or..."

A shadow form with mirror eyes mouthing words.

Nacre. What?

Would Korac ever figure it out—

"You loved Nox so much." Pehton stated the painful but obvious. "I know Sagan, so I don't have to ask if she was really that special. Still, I know it wasn't a straightforward decision. But why the springs?"

Korac laughed. "Oh, right. It's where we made our decisions and had sex for the first time. Great, mind-blowing, foundation-shattering sex." He left her behind again, as he stepped through the final conduit into the venue. He got way too much satisfaction out of leaving that Lyrik with her jaw on the floor. Korac chuckled—

"What's so amusing?"

The Iona General turned to find Xelan dressed in a classic *James Bond* tuxedo. All 'shaken, not stirred' against the black maples and pines backdrop. Korac stated the truth. "Nice suit."

The Co-Emperor ran a hand through his utterly unadorned hair. "Thanks. You look..."

The expression accompanying that pause swelled Korac's chest with pride and confidence. And a bit of conceit. "Don't strain yourself. I already had to resuscitate Pehton."

"Oh, you wish." She stepped through the conduit with acute timing. The Lyrik walked right up to Xelan and dabbed a black handkerchief against his mouth. "There. Every now and again I wish someone would do that much for me around him, but alas..."

Korac barked out a laugh echoed by Xelan's chuckle.

Pax tore through the clearing. "Uncle Korac!" He jumped up.

Of course, Korac caught him. "Hey, nephew mine, are you ready to party?"

"I brought a straw." Pax held it out, all proud.

Xelan chuckled and held his arms out for his son. "C'mon. You don't want to ruin Uncle Korac's tux before he can marry Auntie Sagan. Do you?"

The boy in his matching tux ignored his father because he was gaping at Pehton.

An orange blush crept on her cheeks. "Am I not appropriate for public?"

"You look beautiful," Xelan said as he set Pax on his feet. "He'll get used to the feathers."

Korac clapped his hands together, delighting the kid, saying, "Our party is all together. What about everyone else?"

Xelan grinned. "I cannot wait for you to see Sagan."

Korac knew his grin was goofy because Pehton melted at it. But how could the Iona General help himself? Thoughts of Sagan were the only thing which calmed his nerves, and the thought of her dressed for this occasion...

This was Korac's happy place.

Outside of this spring, the Concerted Empire was gathered for their ceremony. Overseers would televise it across Ishkur. But inside this clearing, it was only the Shadow. Family, Korac supposed.

The reception was more public, held at the Palatial Grounds. Sagan would Seamswalk them straight into it, and they were expected to give an address.

No wonder Korac was nervous.

Xelan patted him on the back, interrupting his thoughts. "They're gathering. Are you ready?"

Tameka came to fetch them and her son. Matron of Honor.

God.

Damn.

Was she *trying* to upstage Korac?

Her black gown plunged to where it belted at her hips and gaped open to her feet from there. Open bell sleeves draped to the ground. Her dramatic heels gave her legs some length. She let her red coils speak for themselves, unadorned like her mate's hair. Her freckles stood out with silver glitter sprinkled across them like fairy dust.

Korac had to say something. "Fury."

She and Pax lingered at the edge of the clearing, waiting for Korac to continue.

Xelan smiled, as if he knew exactly how fantastic his woman looked.

Korac said, "Be honest. Were you determined to steal my thunder?"

What a smile. Peace looked good on Tameka. "Wait until you see your bride." With that, she went to join the rest of the wedding party.

Pehton nudged him. "You ready—"

The Afflicted One Seamswalked into the clearing, wearing a pale purple shift dress. She blinked those wild, Atramentous eyes at him, and Korac wrapped his arms around her. Fuck decorum and composure. "I'm so glad you came."

T.A.O. patted his side, unable to reach around him for her tiny stature. "The stars whisper of your names, bade me come. I stand at your side. Always."

"You will, yes. We made a position for you there."

Xelan reached out, and T.A.O. took his hand. She said, "Father."

"T.A.O."

Pehton gave a happy sigh. "This is good. *Now*, are you ready?"

Korac headed for the wedding. "Yes. I am."

They followed Tameka and Pax's trail into the springs. Korac's anxiety spiked when he took in all the faces of their loved ones, sitting in rented chairs, waiting. They gasped, and some clapped as the groomsmen entered.

Someone whistled—

It was Bones.

His cat calling helped with the nerves.

Iuo waited patiently at the arbor decorated in purple and black flowers. Their axes were mounted to its pinnacle. The King Elect had teared up when Korac and Sagan asked him to officiate. The Lamia was tearing up now as they filed in line on the right side.

Korac.

Pehton.

Xelan.

T.A.O.

And a black marble placeholder.

It was controversial, but both Sagan and Korac demanded placeholders. One for Rayne and one for Nox. Xelan and Tameka were *not* happy, but both caved with little protest. Understanding, thy name is Shadow.

On Sagan's side, the bridesmaids stood waiting.

Tameka.

Matt, also in a simple tux.

Lynn, with her pregnancy glow in a lavender dress.

And a purple marble placeholder.

The anxiety mounted as the pre-event staging dragged on, waiting for something to go wrong. There weren't bride and groom sides to the seats. Everyone sat with their nuclear groupings, which they'd naturally flocked to after Iona Day. The only person Korac needed to see—

There. In the front row, Karter sat up from playing with Echo in her bassinet to wave. Para and Chris followed suit. Korac gave them a composed nod.

Yup. Totally holding it together here.

Xelan leaned forward and started whispering to Korac, who knew the Co-Emperor was trying to soothe him.

Damn it. It was both comforting and unnerving that Xelan knew his General so well. "Given the grandeur I'm used to seeing from you, I'm surprised you didn't get married somewhere with more drama."

Korac humphed to himself. It seemed everyone had an opinion about the venue.

Pehton agreed. "Right? Somewhere super exclusive and exotic."

The string quartet started playing an Icarean Verse, and the audience of their loved ones stood. Pax grinned as he made his way up the aisle, dropping petals for the bride.

Contributing to the ongoing conversation, T.A.O. whispered, "Elden's Nacre Chamber."

Sagan Seamswalked to the beginning of the aisle—

And everything melted away.

No people.

No sound.

Just her and that smile. Korac changed the fate of Cinder for that smile.

It was shy and beaming all at once. The pale pink natural blush complimented her tan complexion and accentuated the dusting of freckles on her nose. Heavy liner accented the violet of her eyes. The rest of the makeup was understated. Lucas or Tameka had twisted her hair back from her face and tucked it behind and under. Little curled strands framed her cheekbones.

But that's not what made the blood in Korac's veins flow backward.

Sagan's dress was black and elegant. The silky material plunged between her breasts to her navel, where the skirt draped from her hips like an understated mermaid cut.

But that wasn't it either.

The dress was sheer. Through it, Korac could see all the individual Icarean union ribbons wrapped around her body, legs, and arms, like gloves.

"The more lacings you tie, the more faith you place in me to achieve this synchronized chorus."

Mercy for his mind. Sagan's faith in Korac banished all of his anxieties. He was ready for their wedding night.

Now.

Right at this moment.

So overwhelmed was he by the impulse to take her, it took Korac a minute to realize someone was with her. Sagan looped her arm through Andrew's offered elbow, who was 'giving her away' according to Earth custom. In a tux, which Lucas clearly didn't pick out, the young man smiled. But there was something 'half' about it. Half-sincere. Half-preoccupied. Or half-alive. The wattage of it increased once he and Sagan started walking toward Korac.

Only then did T.A.O.'s words sink in.

Nacre.

Chamber.

That's what Nox was trying to say.

{ISHKUR | SAVIS FOREST SPRINGS}

Sagan was sure and steady, almost serene. This was a moment worth fighting for, and although she could never forget the ones they'd lost, Sagan was content in knowing their fallen would be happy for her. Right here with her, in fact. She spared a glance for the marker where Rayne should be standing opposite to Nox and knew this was right.

This union was deserved.

So Sagan couldn't help but notice the flicker in her groom's eyes. Korac looked momentarily lost, but came back to her with his signature smirk. He let his eyes rake across her bindings, and when he met hers again, the snow of them smoldered.

Meanwhile, the closer Sagan came to him, the more she could see of his tux and hair.

Wow.

While staring, she mis-stepped, and Andrew saved it from looking obvious.

With his smirk even more crooked, Korac mouthed words which melted Sagan to the spot.

"I. Love. The. Way. You. Look. At. Me."

Her cheeks burned. Why was she blushing so much?! Jeez. Everything about Korac's eyes on Sagan burned her skin into a flustered frenzy. Maybe because everyone in this clearing knew what they'd get up to later tonight and for days after—

Weeks were more like it.

The rest of the crowd came into focus, and everyone—especially Pehton—looked amazing. The entire clearing glowed from the Shadow's elation. There were smiles and happy tears. Lamassau dispensed tissues throughout, dabbing his own voids.

Only Kyle looked... What was the expression on his face? Smug? Self-satisfaction?

It was so out of place it nearly made Sagan laugh.

With a small wave to Karter and Echo as they passed, Sagan and Andrew approached the ceremonial cushions. One for the bride and one for the groom, set between their parties. Over Korac's shoulder, Xelan met Sagan's eyes. No throbbing, stressed-out vein. No clenched jaw.

Wingmaster grinned at her with glistening eyes as he glanced at Rayne's marker. It wrenched the tears out of Sagan's heart, and she swallowed hard to keep them from ruining her makeup. Rayne would understand. She hated runny eyeliner as much as the next girl—

Screw it.

Sagan left the cushion to run into Xelan's arms. Her mentor and best friend clutched her close and kissed her twisted hair. He gave the best hugs. Elden, Sagan had considered asking him to give her away, but it seemed odd given the circumstances. This unexpected hug was perfect. Instead, he separated them and kissed her knuckles, straightened her hair, and walked her back to the cushions.

There, Korac waited with perfect patience and understanding. When Xelan took his hand, Korac's composure tweaked a bit, but he relaxed once the Co-Emperor joined the bride and groom's hands together.

Xelan gave a significant nod of approval—which meant so much—before returning to his place with the other groomsmen. Pehton tiptoed to whisper something to him, making his grin blossom again, and everything was back on track.

Iuo, already two tissues in, gestured for them to kneel. As was Icarean tradition, Sagan knelt on her cushion, staring into Korac's eyes, as he knelt on his. Both on their knees, their gazes were nearly level, with Korac only a fraction higher. So close it was intimate, and Sagan appreciated the custom.

"All of Iona Pax knows why we gather today," Iuo started, his black and blue reptilian eyes flicking across the crowd. "Welcome to the union of General Sagan Sterling and General Korac of Cinder."

Sagan smiled, happy Korac had finally adopted the world which had so readily accepted him. He smirked back, and her breath left her.

"In a beautiful blending of two races with a tempestuous history, this couple honors their unioned traditions to celebrate the establishment of our unified galaxy. The strife may not completely end with this ceremony, but hope will convey beyond it. It will act as a beacon we'll trust to follow on our journey to Eternity. So, no pressure, you two."

Sagan giggled, and Korac chuckled while the crowd joined them in the snickers—

"No pressure?! I got twenty thousand credits on you two lasting forever. Don't disappoint me!"

At Bone's cry, Twenty-One shouted, "Hah! I got thirty."

While Lamassau and the others went at it, Iuo discretely leaned in and whispered, "Fifty."

Sagan laughed, but let Korac see exactly what she thought on her face.

Staring into her eyes, he put them to shame. Korac said, "One million credits."

There wasn't a sound other than the breeze rustling through the trees and water pouring into the lower springs.

Iuo swallowed hard enough for the bride and groom to glance at him. His expression was so hard to describe. Awe. Joy. Pure faith. And love. When Sagan beamed back at him, the Lamian King Elect startled, as if he realized he'd been staring. "Ahem. Yes. In front of those who stand witness, exchange your vows of union. From these words forth, you are wedded and belong to each other."

This was the part of the ceremony Korac had glossed over when explaining it to Sagan. So she left it entirely to him to fill in the gaps.

Her groom held out his hands between them. She placed hers in his and searched his eyes for the next cue.

Korac smirked. "Sagan Sterling, state your terms."

The smile that spread across her lips was bright and unstoppable. Of all things... Their bedroom negotiations. Sagan considered for a moment. How much of her did she want Korac to have for Eternity? What was the right answer? Surrounded by springs similar to the clearing where they first made love, Sagan knew what to say. "All of it to you."

Korac didn't beam in his smiles often, but when he did...

Sagan almost had to ask Iuo to restart her heart. She cast him a glance, and the Lamia winked as if he got it. All of it. Her eyes went straight back to her man, gazing at her with that smile.

Staring into her eyes, Korac said, "Take from me what you need."

Oh, shit. Tears. They were coming back. Sagan's voice trembled as she said, "Give to me what you want."

Together, they finished as they would many times tonight and many times after. "Until Eternity takes me, I'm yours."

Korac leaned forward, Sagan thought at first to kiss her, but he smirked as he went lower than her General collar and kissed her nacre. A sacred act—a commitment among Icari to live and die together as one. It wasn't the first time Korac had kissed Sagan's nacre, but it was momentous to do it in front of so many witnesses.

Sagan let him straighten before returning the gesture. He looked as surprised as she'd felt. She kissed the tie which matched her bonds to symbolize kissing over his nacre. When she straightened, he captured her face in his hands and seared his lips to hers. She parted for him. Around them people cheered and threw rice. But they'd lost her. With that kiss, Korac opened her up and slipped inside—

"C'mon, you two. It's party time." Pehton's reproach made Iuo laugh, full and hearty. The best woman continued, "The entire Concerted Empire is waiting, and thanks to the groom, I haven't eaten all day."

Korac broke the kiss to laugh and say, "Yeah, but you can't deny it was worth it. What do you say, wife?"

Sagan liked the sound of that. "You look gorgeous, Pehton, but..." The next question, she asked louder, "What do you think, Caedes?"

The entire wedding turned and looked at the bald Icarus with his deep eyes. Known for his economy of words, Caedes simply said, "I'll set up that drawer tonight."

Tameka laughed. "Finally."

"Can I have a drawer, too?"

Pax's innocent request put the Shadow in a fit of giggles as Xelan and Tameka both knelt to explain this aspect of grownup relationships to their son.

Amid the hilarity, Korac kept his eyes on Sagan as he lifted her ribboned knuckles to his lips. He kissed them one at a time. Her fingertips next.

The intensity of his eyes stole Sagan's breath away, especially as his gaze drifted down her dress again. Tonight. They'd unwrap her with each shared experience.

Heart thundering, Sagan leaned in and urged against his ear, "We have to do the reception. Then the after party. And *then* get started on our wedding night."

Korac turned enough for her to see his face. His smirk was practically devilish. Against her neck, he confessed, "I don't intend to wait until the party is over."

Yes. This is exactly what Sagan had asked for when she gave her everything to Korac.

{ISHKUR | PALATIAL GROUNDS}

With the Imperial Prince between them, Co-Emperors Xelan and Tameka followed Sagan and Korac through the conduit which the Seamswalker had opened to the Palatial Grounds. As the location for all imperial business, Xelan left it open, with vistas of medicinal and experimental plants and flowers stretching to the horizon. A crowded horizon at that. Legir, F8, X, Tempest, and 2Lip waited to greet them, representing the force of people seated at the tables behind them.

With a nod from Xelan, the Monarch 3 Queen approached the wedding party to say, "Sagan and Korac, your union marks the six-month anniversary of Iona Pax, the Concerted Empire. We are honored to share in your marriage. Please, won't you speak to your guests?"

Sagan glanced back at Xelan, uncertain, but he offered her an encouraging nod. After which, she took Korac's hand and the microphone from F8. Colton, Chris, Lamassau, Aria, and Torch flanked the party, on high alert. Both Gargantuan Lyriks looked ready to activate the Siren's Gale shield, but Xelan was certain it wouldn't be necessary.

It wasn't optimism; although, there was some of that. No. Xelan knew no one would dare attack. Not today. The retaliation would be swift and great.

Sagan said, "Hello, everyone!" The crowd cheered and settled down for her to continue. "Thank you for joining us for our union day, but we don't mean to be a symbol of unity and hope."

As a hush fell, Tameka glanced up at Xelan. He smiled because he trusted Sagan.

Taking Korac's hand, Sagan said, "We are the same as any couple in the Concerted Empire. We simply started on opposite sides of the conflict. Any relationship out there is as special as ours. So we ask that you sit with your families and friends, eat your fill, and dance until your feet hurt or until you're ready to go home. In this way, you'll celebrate with us. What do you say?"

Korac smirked down at his wife, and Xelan knew she'd spared him some public speaking the Iona General truly detested. Korac's speeches were for war. Well, he'd have to grow out of that and work on his diplomacy skills again. Until then, Xelan would let this slide.

The audience of Mon3 drones and Queens, Yun healers, Pil Dwarves, Lyriks, Reipon Lamias, Luk jellyfish-capped males and females, Caprents in togas, human beings, and wing-ed Icari—Their cheers shook the ground and thundered across the sky. Screens captured the moment, using cameras from the Overseers. Immortalized.

A symbol, whether Korac and Sagan wanted it or not.

The ferocity of it left some of the wedding party shuffling and uncomfortable. Xelan didn't blame them. He remembered the first time he'd addressed millions of his own people. It was intimidating, but it also came with the territory. To break the spell, Xelan asked, "Eating and dancing, right, Sagan?"

It startled her, and Korac immediately put a hand on her back for comfort. She shot Xelan a wary smile. "Right. Let's party."

The Shadow's table was sheltered in a special nanite bubble—invisible, but effective at stopping anything moving faster than five miles an hour. Any slower, and Pax couldn't run and play inside it.

The Shadow sat at one massive table in their respective clusters. They'd prepared the buffet meals themselves, all of them, earlier in the day. No servants, no waiters, and no danger. Risk mitigation wasn't the only reason. Xelan detested servitude. In fact, he'd replaced the working class with non-sentient androids. People only worked in areas they liked, as with Lucas and Pehton, and they were compensated fairly for their time. Mostly, everything and everyone was provided for. Just how Xelan wanted it.

So why wasn't he able to enjoy himself? There was no guilt and no risk. Well. That wasn't entirely true, was it?

Celindria.

Xelan set her free to pursue the soul she'd been born without. He knew beyond all her other motivations, *emotion* was all she sought. Sympathizing with her tragedy, Xelan had refused to kill her. Yet again.

Was Celindria out there in the crowd, waiting for her next chance to take revenge against the maker who'd left her unfinished? Would she come after Pax again—

"Dad!" Pax called to Xelan as if he'd tried before. "Mommy wants to dance."

Tameka laughed but didn't deny it.

Sagan, sitting in Korac's lap, giggled. "The bride and groom usually dance first, kiddo." She glanced at Korac before saying, "But we'll make an exception for the Concerted Emperors."

Xelan grinned down at his son and ruffled his hair. "Thanks, wing man." He stood and went to Tameka's chair, pulling it out for her. "Your imperial majesty, may I have the pleasure of this dance?"

Slow Icarean music overtook the upbeat Earth music. Xelan glanced over to find Iuo giving him a thumbs up from the DJ booth. The Shadow cheered and yelled as Tameka and Xelan took to the open patio. The couple waved to their family before he bowed to her and she curtsied to him. It occurred to him that although they'd survived a lifetime's worth of drama and trauma together; they hadn't danced since he first taught her all those months—years ago in the park.

Both opened their wings, and Xelan took Tameka's waist with one hand and her fingers in the other. Despite how much more time had passed between then and now for her, Tameka remembered the steps admirably. She flared her wings at the right moments without having them at the time Xelan had taught her.

"How?"

Tameka grinned with pride, and Xelan raised a brow at her. She said, "Lucas gave me a refresher."

Xelan glimpsed the Icarus giving a little wave in the crowd. They came to the part where they twirled and brushed wings before taking hands again. "You're doing beautifully, as you do with everything."

Again, Tameka's smile was more incredulous now. "You are so cheesy."

He brought her close and kissed her—Completely out of step with the dance. When he pulled back, Xelan grinned to find her a little drunk from the kiss. He said, "You know you love it." Amid all the cheers from the Shadow, he asked, "What do you say to letting them join us?"

Tameka, still unable to speak, nodded.

Xelan waved the Shadow over and called, "I hope you don't mind, Sagan."

Balanced on Korac's thighs, She beamed with a bite of roast Pil duck on her fork. "Go for it. We'll steal the spotlight in a minute."

Korac said something that made her blush.

It was all enough to push Celindria from Xelan's mind. Something told him to enjoy this.

"So I feel like I haven't seen you all day while everyone prepared for this. How was the hangar?" Tameka pulled them closer together, placed her cheek and hands on his chest, and swayed them gently to the beat.

Xelan loved operating a Dyson's Sphere. Work kept his mind off—Well, everything. And Tameka was really understanding of this. He kissed the top of her head to show his appreciation. "We found two very different space craft parked in the bays."

Tameka turned her face to look up at him. "Really?! That's so exciting!"

It really was. Xelan didn't want to go on too much during the event, but he said, "We'll consult with Zero. Tumu suggested we run a special program to vet astronaut candidates. It's coming together."

With a kiss on his chest, Tameka's affection for him glittered in her eyes. "I want in."

"I got you..." Xelan's catch phrase trailed at the end because he'd spotted Matt and Lucy, sitting alone at one side of the table.

Kyle and Silence bumped into Xelan and Tameka on the dance floor. Namely, the young man wedged himself right in the middle of the imperial couple to say, "Every function. We can already smell them."

Tameka looked confused at first until she followed their line of sight and then she burst out in laughter. "Oh, my god. We had a buddy system in place for this."

Korac and Sagan made their way to the group, ready to dance, but paused when they saw their expressions. It took Sagan one glance at her male bridesmaid before looking straight ahead. "Why are they like this? At least Pax is dancing with Bethany by Ross and Jack. No one wants him to see this."

Shrugging out of his tuxedo jacket, Korac said, "I don't know why they're like this, but if anyone's engaging in bed sport at my wedding, it'll be me and the bride. Excuse me." He handed the jacket to Xelan before marching over to the not-so-subtle couple.

Lemonade and sandalwood.

Matt and Lucy hopped out of the seat as soon as they noticed Korac crossing the lawns to them. It was too far away to hear what he said, but the look on Lucy's face suggested it was either hilarious or tasty. Hard to say which.

Silence mused, "We can't fault them. Love is hard to restrain. Especially when young."

Kyle conceded the point with a nod, but added, "Yeah, but at *every* public function?"

Xelan appreciated the sympathy in Sagan's voice as she said, "A kink is a kink. It's nothing to shame them for."

Tameka shook her head. "Maybe. But not with my son around, they don't."

As Korac returned, the errant couple most efficient at murder laughed into their Yun wine, embarrassed but still in a good humor. The groom said, "They are two of the most interesting characters I've ever met."

"Cheers to that," Lamassau toasted from Tumu's arm.

Korac and Sagan took to the center of the dance floor while they celebrated their union. Tameka clung to Xelan's arm and let out a contented sigh. Everything had gone right today. Now, he needed to invite the entire Shadow to the stronghold for the after party.

After which, Xelan could search for Rayne the only way he knew how. Nothing could make him give up on her. Not even the total decimation of Enki.

{ISHKUR | PALATIAL GROUNDS}

The dancing went on forever. Tameka thought it was especially cute when T.A.O. took a turn with Korac, Seamswalking them all over the place. Pax danced with Sagan, finally getting over his shyness around her.

Tameka wanted more kids. A little girl with Xelan's hair. Then maybe he'd let Rayne rest.

Fury was sure Xelan wasn't aware she knew of his plans to find the fallen girl, and Tameka would never break Xelan's heart by trying to convince him she was dead. Just... no.

But how was this false hope any less cruel?

Half of the women in the galactic crowd were templated after Rayne, a monument to the fallen. They'd erected statues of her. She was required reading in all the schools. Iuo approached them about legitimate franchise rights.

"I would like to take the responsibility of providing an accurate and sensitive account, because if I don't, someone else less responsible will create Elden knows what."

Tameka was concerned, but Xelan, always seeing the logic first before his emotions, granted Iuo approval.

Movies and a series about them—What a weird world they lived in.

No weirder than Matt and Lucy joining the fun on the dance floor after Korac had to pry them apart only minutes earlier. Tameka was nosy, so she'd asked the Iona General, "What did you say to them?"

Sagan had laughed before she stopped herself with a hand to her mouth, as if Korac had already told her.

That piqued Tameka's interest more, and she raised a brow at the stoic warrior.

Korac caved with an indulgent look. "I told them no fucking on my wedding day unless they wanted me to join them."

Xelan, obviously eavesdropping, burst out into laughter, causing Sagan to lose control once again.

Tameka couldn't laugh because her mouth was gaping open. Wow. Well, that explained the look on Lucy's face. Tameka glanced at them in the crowd. They were moving their way toward Jack and Ross. Nosy, and not apologetic about it, Tameka took Xelan's hand and pulled him toward the action.

There, Tameka overheard Lucy finish an explanation. "...And so we're heading out to Pil. We were wondering if Bethany could come?"

Behind her, Yito was giving two thumbs up. Puk was pointing at the Tritan.

Bethany, who was still partying with Pax, stopped to give her older sister the same face Tameka had given her parents when she wanted to sleepover at Sagan or Rayne's. Big eyes and a slightly pouty lip.

Kyle overheard and gave Silence a violent spin in their direction, which she executed perfectly on her heels. Bethany's brother asked, "Can you repeat that?"

A little back and forth took place before Matt finished with, "I think it would be educational for her to come along."

Korac, Tameka knew, was every bit as nosy as her, squeezed his way through the group to give his two cents. "I think Bethany would be happy on the field trip. Would you like to go?" He looked down at the teenage girl, who absolutely beamed at him with pure adoration.

"Yes! Can I go, please?!"

Anytime Bethany spoke, her family stopped breathing, and Tameka swore their hearts stopped beating.

But while the others stared at Bethany in shock, Korac stepped into Matt's personal space and muttered barely loud enough for Tameka to hear, "If anything happens to her while she's with you, I will remove your ability to reproduce. And I know I don't need to tell you to keep your paws off each other around her, right?"

"Yes, sir." Matt didn't sound scared at all, and his eyes... At Korac's threat, whatever warmed the redhead's blood stopped and left him cold. "We'd do nothing to traumatize her further, and I appreciate you vouching for the trip."

"Damn right you do."

So... In the past, Tameka had appreciated why Sagan and Xelan were attracted to Korac's looks and confidence, but that display—

"Are you all right? You're flushed." Xelan sounded so concerned, and Tameka only turned redder—

Korac caught her stare, and the bastard winked.

Xelan sniffed and looked between Tameka and Korac. Rather than get upset, Xelan rolled his eyes and muttered, "Now he's claimed another victim."

Amid Tameka's personal crisis, Ross said, "I think it's okay if she goes. What do you think, Kyle?"

Kyle looked into his baby sister's beaming face and sighed. "All right."

The young girl jumped up into his arms and swung. "Thank you. Thank you. Thank you."

Tameka wondered if it hurt Kyle more that his sister hardly spoke at all or that when she did, it was to thank him for letting her go.

"Okay everyone," Sagan called.

Korac finished, "Gather around. We want to immortalize the moment."

Xelan took Tameka's hand, then Pax's, and lead them to the center of the Shadow. Kyle and Silence stood on her right. Andrew and Lucas stood on Xelan's left. Pablo and Lynn branched from there to Pehton and Caedes. Tumu and Lamassau completed the first row. Matt and Lucy were behind Silence with Bethany, Jack, and Ross. Chris, Karter, Para, and Bones collected behind Pehton, completing that row. Iuo, Twenty-One, Miy, Devis, T.A.O. on Andrius' shoulders, Smith, Colton, and Cypher completed the third row.

Shadow, new and old.

Shadow through and through.

They held still while Sagan and Korac sat at two easels; him sketching and her painting.

Twenty-One, grinning, muttered through his teeth without turning to anyone, "How long must we pose like this?"

Miy shrugged. "I don't know. I didn't bother smiling."

Pablo laughed—

"Be still just a few more minutes," Sagan called.

Kyle said, "She was talking to you, Pablo, in case you didn't know."

The tallest in the bunch on her brother's shoulders, T.A.O. said, "Without this we vanish. It's always best to obey Korac."

Everyone turned their heads and looked at her. Tameka nearly burst out into laughter when she saw Korac peek over the canvas with wide eyes.

Xelan chuckled.

Into the awkward scene, Sagan announced, "All done."

Korac echoed her. "You can relax now."

Tameka put a hand on her hip. "Well, do we get to see it?"

"Mommy!" Pax sounded so exasperated that it made Tameka smiled.

"Here we all are."

They turned their canvases simultaneously.

The Shadow.

Sagan and Korac had included themselves in the images at the very front.

Andrew called first, "I want a print!"

Silence said, "As do I!"

They all shouted requests including, Tameka and Xelan. Eventually, everyone sat back at the table, chatting about the day.

Beside Korac, Pehton blurted in her conversation with Tumu, "Ohhh... The Twelve Worlds. The Tritans counted Ishkur all that time."

Kyle and Silence passed Tameka's chair to interrupt Sagan's and Korac's kissing. A dangerous move to anyone with concern for self-preservation. Luckily, Kyle didn't have any, which made this all the more humorous.

"Ahem."

They stopped kissing to glare up at Kyle, who held out a fairly large box. It was wrapped funny, with holes in it.

No.

Not a box.

That was a kennel.

Tameka turned all the way in her seat to watch, and Xelan spared her an amused and curious grin.

"What's this?" Korac asked.

Kyle answered, "Your wedding gift."

Sagan laughed, incredulous. "Opening the gifts at the wedding isn't a thing, Kyle—"

The kennel barked, and Korac went completely devoid of color. His eyes widened to saucers.

Sagan recoiled at his reaction, and she growled at Kyle. "What the fuck is in the box?"

Kyle grinned as he handed it to Sagan, because Korac refused to touch it.

Tameka scooted to the edge of her seat, waiting. What kind of dog would do that to a grown Icarus—

Peeling back the paper revealed a black Chihuahua with a purple ribbon for a collar. The poor thing shivered, demonic and ugly as it was.

Tameka became acutely aware of the people pressing around the moment, suspended, watching with bated breath. Oh, Kyle had planned this for a while now. He looked so proud of himself. Sagan glanced between the dog and Korac, who looked ready to claw his way to freedom.

When the Chihuahua's lips peeled back from it's teeth with a snarl, Korac grabbed the nearest steak knife and—

Xelan grabbed him. "Whoa, whoa, animal rights' activist."

Lamassau said, "Pay. Up."

Bones groaned.

Iuo asked, "What about a stay at my villa? I don't have a thousand credits on me."

Twenty-One said, "Well, I think my bet stands since he technically tried to kill it."

Sagan held off her man and glared at Kyle, but it was half-hearted. Tameka could tell it was more of a sister's irritation with a brother. The bride groaned, "When, exactly, did you invade his memory for this information?"

Xelan took the knife from the General and walked him a few paces away to cool off.

Kyle looked less smug and a little apologetic. "I thought it would be more fun than this. I didn't think he was actually phobic."

"Well, he is. Apologize to my husband, then give the poor puppy to a family who will love it."

Tameka shook her head. She loved Kyle, but sometimes it seemed like his decision-making skills had never properly matured. He went over to Korac, who was regaining some color. When the groom didn't immediately kill the Progeny, Tameka supposed the apology went over well. She admitted to Sagan, "If I were Kyle, I'd fear retaliation."

"Oh, Korac won't have to retaliate. I will."

Behind them, Karter laughed, walking up with Chris and Echo. "I thought my son could use some angel time."

At the baby's whistle, Korac manifested like the man could Seamswalk, himself. "How is she doing, mother?"

Xelan came back to sit beside Tameka with a cheeky touch on her thigh while Karter recited everything Echo had eaten and tried to say during the day.

Sagan was playing with Echo's toes as Karter held the infant in her arms, when someone brought up naming the next Iona sector.

Tameka turned to Xelan, who was smiling and talking to Pax. "What will we name the next one?"

As everyone looked at him, Xelan said, "There are plenty of fallen to choose from."

Sagan tucked a loose tendril behind her ear. A gesture Tameka knew was her way of easing into something uncomfortable. The Seamswalker asked, "Have you thought about 'Nox?'"

Korac stopped mid-bite to stare at his bride with the truest love in his eyes.

Tameka raised her brows initially, but the more she thought about it...

Nox fought the good fight wrong and became lost in the violence—a mistake any of them could make—especially under pressure from Remorse's machinations. Maybe it wasn't such a bad idea.

When she turned to say as much to Xelan, she found him looking off into the distance. There was so much conflict there. Meeting no one's eyes, he said, "I understand him better now than when we were children, teens—brothers. His motivations... I see them and agree with them until he invaded Earth the second time. Everything after that is unforgivable. He was cruel and arrogant in his madness, and billions of people suffered for it. Humans, Icari, and... " Xelan swallowed, unable to say Rayne's name. "No. We honor him enough by distributing his Verse, and only because she wants it so."

There Xelan went again, talking about Rayne as if she might appear at any moment. Tameka wanted to acclimate to it, but this coping mechanism hurt so badly.

Abruptly, Xelan stood and addressed the Shadow. "I apologize. This isn't a toast. This is an invitation." He turned to Sagan. "Perhaps it isn't the best time with it being your wedding night, but I want to steal you away." He met everyone else's eyes. "All of you. I'm ready to tell you everything. Join us at the stronghold, and I will continue this journey the way it began.

"Together."

EPILOGUE

{ISHKUR | PALATIAL GROUNDS}

SAGAN AND KORAC LOOKED BEAUTIFUL TOGETHER. Their love shone like a beacon across the grounds. The warmth of it radiated through the others. The Shadow.

Xelan and Tameka.

Andrew and Kyle.

They all looked so happy. Even as Xelan stood at the table and asked them to follow him to the stronghold, home of the imperial family. He'd fortified it, hadn't he? And disabled the desert entrance. It was only accessible by conduit now.

All those treasures.

"Why don't you go to them?"

Nox stepped up beside Rayne with a dramatic billow of his cloak as it caught the breeze.

Under her hood, she passed him a sideways glance. "It might be hard to explain you."

The enormous Icarus stood so far above Rayne, she couldn't see, but rather heard the smirk in his baritone. "Can you imagine the gift it would be?"

"I love you, Rayne. You're not alone. Please don't be afraid, because I'll see you soon. I'll find you—

"I won't ever let you go—"

Rayne winced, but shored herself up to say, "It's better this way. Look at them—Thriving. They don't even know their enemy is alive, let alone at this event."

Nox's hood moved as he looked down at her. "You believe Celindria is here?"

"I *know*." Rayne could *feel* it. "But it's far too public to attack and not really her style." Not to mention slightly hypocritical to knock her for slinking around the event when... Well...

All the women and girls had templated themselves with Rayne's likeness. It helped her hide, but if Korac were to see her standing beside a giant in a cloak—It might be a tad obvious who they were.

No.

This was as close as Rayne could get. The placeholders at the wedding... She glanced at Nox again, wondering what he'd thought of them. Now that they weren't inside her head, things felt different. Less intimate and somehow more.

The storm in Rayne continued to rage on, and lingering here cost them time. Still... "I've never known a couple so perfect for each other."

Agreeing, Nox said, "Quite."

In an instant, Rayne flashed through Razor's entire dossier, checking and rechecking their itinerary. "Are you ready to get back to work?"

There was a humorous and faux-dramatic tone in Nox's voice. "To defend the Concerted Empire anonymously against its greatest threat? Why, yes. I'm always ready."

"Let's go."

Would the constant barrage of enemies manipulating the Probability Matrix ever end? Would the nightmares of dying to save her people, only for Celindria to survive, ever stop?

Yes, to both.

Rayne and Nox would see to it together.

{Ishkur | Palatial Grounds}

Celindria.

Wasn't.

Jealous.

How could she be? She could barely feel. And Korac and Sagan were a waste of lamentations.

No.

For a moment, Celindria wondered what Kyle would be like in bed. He'd ignited the humor centers of her brain when he'd unveiled the rat beast in the cage. Never could she recall that kind of visceral fear in Korac.

Yes.

She'd have Kyle next.

Perhaps he's enough—

No.

No.

None of them were enough.

Remorse was right. No matter how hard Celindria tried, her soul was still fragmented into pieces. No one understood her. No one could love her, because who could love a creature unable to love back—

Nox.

Nox admitted he had loved Celindria in his Verse. And they were the Eternal Bind. Always drawn together, and the world created around them created more. Multiplied infinitely to their demise.

Such poetry.

No.

Rayne killed him, and someone—something Aegis and eternal—had switched his nacre with father's.

Yes.

It had all went wrong there.

At least the little King Rayne had perished, as predicted. Now the Probability Matrix teemed, boundless. So much waited for Celindria to one day feel.

The wedding party collected their things to retreat to father's stronghold. So clever to disable its entry outside conduit travel. Celindria's father was never short on brilliance. Just heart.

Rayne had changed that, and the little king hadn't even known of her virtue when she died.

Celindria swayed, letting her golden gown move to the music. The song in her head.

They don't know what's coming to them.

They don't know what's coming to them.

But they will.

And they'll know they deserved it.

Quiet for now.

Let them know a peace worth mourning.

Because soon—So very soon...

Celindria would strip it all away.

All thanks to her father's clandestine charity, so spectacularly homogeneous with his history of deceit.

And when that history was told...

Celindria would have nothing left to hide.

THE VAST COLLECTIVE CHRONOLOGY

7M BCE	Enki Terminates Li, Elden's Sacrifice, Umbra Seizes Control of Cinder, Nox is born
3M BCE	Xelan is born, Nox becomes a weapon
2M BCE	Gait's children disappear, Korac joins Cinder's royal family
1.7M BCE	Umbra invades Lacceirus Capra
1M BCE	Umbra invades Monarch 3
500K BCE	Valkyries & Lyriks Revolt
250K BCE	Savis & Umbra pass into eternity, Nox becomes King of Cinder
6K BCE	First Icarean invasion of Earth, Nox invades Thailea, Xelan creates the Progeny
5.5K BCE	Celindria's uprising, Disbursement of Progeny lines, Formation of The Brethren, The Vacating
100 CE	Celindria 'dies' in Thailea incident
400 CE	Razor introduces Nox to Cascading Light, Xelan is banished to Earth, Nox & Korac plan their next invasion of Earth
1987 JAN	Tameka Phillips is born, Xelan builds Iona-oo
1993 May	Xelan saves Rayne Callahan from a fateful car accident
2002 SEP:	Xelan trains the Progeny, Icari commence 'soft' invasion of Earth
2006 APR	Full-Scale Invasion Day
2006 AUG	Volcano Day Battle
2008 JUL	Gait's destruction

AUTHOR'S NOTE

"It starts with him and ends with her."

Enki is finished, but the story is not.

Keep reading for a sneak peek at Xelan's Verse, Book XII of the Vast Collective Series.

And sign up for news of future books. Scan below to move right along in the series.

XELAN'S VERSE

I AM PAX'S FATHER, TAMEKA'S HUSBAND, THE PRINCE OF CINDER, MENTOR TO THE SHADOW, AND A CONCERTED EMPEROR OF THE VAST COLLECTIVE. While you never thought of me as a monster, there was a time in my life when I was certain I was one.

"That's not how the story starts, Superman."

Rayne, are you giggling at me?

When you nod, this four-year-old memory of you grins big enough to show a missing baby tooth while perched precariously on my knee.

Well, then it's only fair if I—Tickle attack!

"No! Hehehe stop!" You kick out with your tiny sneakers and try to wiggle away, but I'd earned every one of those high-pitched squeals.

I am safer inside this old Divine Booth than I am anywhere else in Iona Pax. Here, I can hide from those I love most. In this custom memory experience, I can talk to you and share the story of my Verse with you. I don't know where you are, Rayne, but I haven't forgotten my promise. I'll never stop looking for you.

But the others...

Now that they've met the monster in me, I fear their judgment. Their hurt, confused expressions. But most of all, I fear their doubt. How could they continue following someone like me when they can't even stand to look in my direction?

"Because you kept too much from them for too long."

Your mother had her hands full with you at this age. At twelve-years-old, the other figment of you borders the ages where blunt honesty comes less from innocence and more from a sudden awareness of the fables told by the adults around you. It's a hard place to dwell.

While I stare at you from across the coffee table in my study, you sit on the floor and write in your notebook, refusing to make eye contact.

It was never my plan to withhold information. The timing was never right. I wanted you to be there.

"We're always here, Superman." Your tiny hand reaches for my face, and I lean down into it, feeling at once whole and lost. "You don't have to look for us anymore."

The older you assures me without an upward glance, "It's okay to be afraid to let go. Hell, I think it makes you normal." This iteration of you is dressed with entirely too much defiance, all black and spiked. Long before the days when I taught you how to take care of yourself, you were already confident in your abilities and your words.

I'm not ready to hear them because both versions of you are correct.

I'm not telling it right.

With a ruffle of your little headband, I bounce my knee once, to your delight, before continuing properly.

Once upon a time, there was a handsome Prince who threw a glamorous party for his friends.

"YOU'D BETTER HAVE A GOOD FUCKING REASON FOR HIJACKING MY UNION NIGHT, TRAITOR PRINCE."

Was that anyway to refer to an Emperor? Korac was naturally upset with my timing. I didn't blame him, but he usually held such high regard for decorum.

At least Sagan was taking my ill-timed announcement with grace. "If you're ready to tell, I'm ready to listen." She opened a conduit to the stronghold.

Tameka left my side to stand by it. "Who's coming with us?"

"Me!" Pax hopped out of his seat, remembering to bring his straw—Current favorite quirk. I adore it. He took up at his mother's side.

Kyle asked, "Will there be more food?"

I stepped into the conduit, turning back to say, "I organized it all. Rooms are arranged, too. I wanted everyone together when I told my Verse—"

"But why did you wait until my wedding night?!" Korac growled out while pinching the bridge of his nose. He really was a sight to see when flustered.

This was so much payback for every smirk he'd given me when Tameka asked a question I wasn't ready to answer. For every snide comment referencing my less than pristine past. Yes. This was deliberate.

"I wish I'd been there to see it." Preteen you is experiencing a mean streak. Your wicked

grin belies your pretense of being too cool and absorbed in your writing to listen.

Every time I see you, Rayne, I beam at you because you're so much like me.

We relocated the wedding party to my stronghold, where Tameka, Pax, and I lived under Aria and Torch's guardianship. The two Gargantuan Lyriks took up posts at the entrances to the room, prepared at all times to defend the Imperial family.

I ordered, "Progeny with me. Everyone else is welcome to join as they like. We'll be in my study."

I didn't wait to see if anyone followed, as I climbed the synchronized steps up the ravine filled with mementos under glass, a museum of my life.

When I entered the hexagonal room lined with my journals and furnished with black couches, I saw you sitting there. Young and full of purpose, the figment of my memories asked me to deliver you into enemy territory and endanger your life for one sample of my brother's blood. It was the first time you said to me, "I love you, Superman—"

"It always smells of leather in here," Sagan remarked as she followed me inside. Her smile matched the place, warm and haunted.

Did Sagan know? Have you told her? About the day I tried to convince you to hide from it all in here, safe, and how you refused?

Tameka knew. She smoothed one warm hand up my shoulder and kissed my cheek. The soft smile on her beautiful lips spoke volumes of her empathy. I love her for it. She said, "Let's all get comfortable."

Andrew and Lucas filed in, stealing one plush loveseat to themselves. Korac sat in an armchair, and Sagan draped herself in his lap. It was fair, given I'd ruined their wedding night. Kyle and Silence followed, with her peering around the room until her gunmetal eyes located the small fireplace filled with Cascading Light. They remained standing. Tumu and Lamassau were the last to file in, occupying the big couch with the Gargantuan compressed to seven feet of his height. Outside, I could hear the others quietly talk amongst themselves.

Bones said, "I got a caramel cheesecake and one hundred credits that says Xelan's Verse will be the best of the three."

"I'll take that bet," Iuo answered.

Twenty-One raised him, "Two caramel cheesecakes that the original will reign supreme."

Lam hissed on the couch, and Tumu chuckled at him.

When Pehton said, "Three on Korac's," Korac beamed at Sagan.

The General said, "Proceed."

Tameka nudged me.

I guess I'd avoided it enough. "Because I know Rayne and Iona Pax will eventually want to hear this, I'm recording the moment in a perfect hologram. This room and anyone in it will appear in my Verse to her. Come and go as you please. I only ask that you participate while in the room."

Outside, Miy muttered, "Participate?"

Someone shushed her.

Tameka hid a wince as she always did when I mentioned Rayne.

She and the others thought I was struggling to grieve you, unaware of all the ways you could return to us.

Korac glared at me with a raised brow. Interested and eager for me to proceed. As much as he abhorred the timing, my General was looking forward to this.

I lifted Tameka's hand and kissed it.

Pax, abashed, cried, "Dad!"

We all melted for a moment at him, hiding his reddened face, then I nodded at one wall of journals. "Tameka, reach for the first. Yes, the highest." I directed her as she followed my request by climbing the ladder and collecting the very first volume. "Read the first line for me."

Tameka smiled at the gathered people before opening it. Then she frowned and read, "Our father is not—*cannot* be—mine." She peered curiously at me.

I nodded, more solemn this time before saying, "As I was telling Sagan months ago when Korac's Verse first aired, these histories steal away whatever sense I've made of my life."

Kyle says, "I don't know. It sounds like you were making perfect sense before."

I held up a finger. "Ah. But there's the issue. I had no confirmation. I was raised under a man I was certain couldn't be my father, but with no evidence to support me or reason to dare doubt my mother. Nox's Verse rocked my foundation."

As I understand it now, it also rocked yours, Rayne.

"Hee." During the telling of my story, a strand of your hair escaped your headband. I tuck it back under for you, and your eyes sparkle with glee.

Back to the tale.

Tameka returned to my side while I stared at the black fire, saying, "Given how much was already explained in the other two Verses, I must deviate from how each of them began. We don't open with my conception. The Shadow and the rest of the empire already know that. Instead, I'll start with my earliest memory."

www.ingramcontent.com/pod-product-compliance
Lightning Source LLC
Chambersburg PA
CBHW020247030826
48979CB00030B/2651/J

* 9 7 9 8 9 8 6 8 2 2 0 4 4 *